At the Stroke of Nine O'Clock

JANE DAVIS

First Edition

Printed and bound in Great Britain by Clays Ltd, Elcograf S.p.A.

for Rossdale Print Productions.

This is a work of fiction. Names, characters, places and incidents are either the product of the author's imagination or are used fictitiously. Wherever possible, the opinions of public figures used in fictitious context have been based on research.

ISBN-13: 978-0-9932776-9-6

Cover design by Andrew Candy of Tentacle Design
based on original artwork by Petrel, KathySG and
Alex Andrei @ Shutterstock and Shaunl @ iStock.

For my mother, Christine Frances Davis.

In an extraordinary oversight on my part,
she hasn't had a book dedication yet.

And there is always the possibility that
this one may be the last.

PRAISE FOR THE AUTHOR

'Davis is a phenomenal writer, whose ability to create well rounded characters that are easy to relate to feels effortless.'

Compulsion Reads

'Jane Davis is an extraordinary writer, whose deft blend of polished prose and imaginative intelligence makes you feel in the safest of hands.'

J.J. Marsh, author and founder of Triskele Books

PROLOGUE

It is just after nine o'clock in the evening. A woman stands on a pavement in Hampstead outside the Magdala pub, where Easter revellers who raise their glasses are oblivious to what is taking place just a few yards away. Between the pub and a parked motor-car, face down on the footway, lies a man – David is his name. Darkness has fallen, but the combination of street lighting and the yellow glow from the Magdala's windows allow the woman to see the grey worsted wool of his suit, on which bloody circles are expanding. She trains the gun in her trembling hand on his back. The man makes an attempt to prop himself up on one elbow, but any prospect of escape is ebbing away.

The parked motor-car is a grey-green Standard Vanguard. His – although, as the woman told the policemen who attended a disturbance in the early hours of Easter Sunday, it's as good as hers. After all, hasn't she lived with David these past two years? And it can't be vandalism if it's your own property. Why did she push in the windows? Because he didn't pick her up as he'd promised, that's why (one more broken promise in a trail of broken promises). She remembers the waiting. How at first she worried – he'd been drinking before he drove off, and this is a man who thinks nothing of speed. Speed is his business. It's in his blood. But worry turned to anger, and anger to hatred.

What she doesn't remember – not quite – is what brought them both to this place. Today. Everything has happened in a cold cold frenzy.

They are not alone, she sees. Here is David's friend Clive. She always rather liked Clive. Sensed he liked her too. And here, standing beside Hanshaw's news-stand, are two boys. Men, she supposes. Fighting age, but no more than eighteen. They look down at David, sprawled at their feet, one arm outstretched towards them, beseeching. Then, slack-jawed, they turn their faces towards her, as if she's a mirage: blonde, petite, horn-rimmed spectacles, a grey two-piece, stilettos. The last person they'd expect to be brandishing a firearm.

Clive doesn't know where to put himself. "Look what you've done, Ruth."

How can she reply when there is so much blood? She had no idea there would be so much; that it would seep between the slabs of the pavement and drip from the kerb into the gutter, and David is gasping for air that will not come.

And then, no more gasping. It's over. They are looking at her, the boys and Clive. Waiting to see what she will do. Ruth raises her arm, presses the barrel of the gun to her temple. This, she realises, was always her intention. She feels ready to die. Wants an end to it. Her finger squeezes the trigger, but some internal force pulls her hand away and the shot ricochets off the pub wall. Now there is no escape. Even if there were somewhere to run to, it wouldn't be an option she'd take. Ruth has never run away from problems. No, she always ran straight towards them. "Go and call the police," she says quietly.

PART ONE
AUGUST 1949

CHAPTER ONE

CAROLINE

What the hell does she think she's playing at? Seventeen, alone in a strange city and accepting an invitation from a man she's only just met. Finbar Weir. Well-dressed and judging by the size of the order he placed at the bar, with cash to burn. Right now, that's what Caroline's looking for. The term Sugar Daddy suggests something sickly sweet, an expectation. She prefers Ration Book. Stamps not just for meat and cooking oil, but for introductions. A means to earn enough to put a roof over her head and have money left over to send home. *Take a good look at this place. That's what you're here for.* A flat is too fancy a description for the living room, kitchenette and bedroom she can sense behind the door to her right. It's all so shabby, a clutter of things that make no attempt to match each other. *You'll need to tone down your expectations, girl.* Unlike at home (home in Suffolk, that is), there's a tower of shillings to feed the gas meter, teetering, as if someone's just brushed past. There's a gramophone player with a stack of 78s. A decanter on a tray, held aloft by a statue of a young Negro. Did it come with the rooms, or is it the kind of thing a man like Finbar Weir finds amusing?

Caught frowning at his Negro, Caroline colours from the neck upwards. *Quick, say something.* "It's ten to nine. Can you warm up the wireless?"

"Warm up the wireless? Will you listen to yourself?" All the same, he goes to switch on the radio set.

"It's something my da used to say." Though she's betrayed her age, something liberating strikes Caroline. Here, it's possible to mention her father. In her new London life she can parrot his favourite expressions without worrying that one of the younger ones will demand, 'When's Da coming home?' Without fear that her ma's eyes will glaze over. She forces a tense smile, says, "At 'ome, everything always stopped at ten to nine."

"At 'ome?"

His mockery ramps up her nerves. This must be what it feels like to be a boy whose voice is breaking; one moment BBC news reporter, the next lapsing into the language of childhood. Determined not to let on, Caroline raises a baton-like finger. "Haym. At ire hice," she enunciates in the King's English.

"That's more like it. We'll make a Londoner of you yet."

"We'd warm up the radio set in time for the news." *Slow down, you're blabbering.* Caroline crosses one leg over the other. She's in the early stages of turning herself into someone new, someone sophisticated. Not by choice – not exactly. Da's disappearance has forced her hand.

Caroline thought Ma was being kind, sending her on her way when she did. That she'd sensed what went on that evening when the bailiffs arrived and Ma pushed her towards the back door, hissing, "Fetch your Uncle Anthony." When Caroline did as she was told, her uncle cornered her, asking what she would do for him, and he was breath and hands and mouth. But sending her on her way was no kindness. When Ma gave her a last packed lunch, she held her close and said,

"We're all counting on yer." This, from the same woman who used to ruffle Caroline's hair and call her 'my little worryguts'. *We're all counting on yer.* With those words, her skin prickled, and she sensed that Ma *had* known. The war might be over but sacrifices weren't just expected. They were demanded.

This thought lurks behind every decision Caroline must make. Why she's here, in the rooms of a man she's only just met. A ridiculous situation to have put herself in, 'specially when you think what the newspaper hawkers have been hollering; after everything she's read. *A gallstone, the size of a grape, led to the discovery of human bone, dentures, a lipstick container.* Not everything, it turns out, dissolves in sulphuric acid.

She doesn't hold her newly acquired responsibility against the younger ones. Plenty of times she's benefited from being the oldest child. Besides, London was always Caroline's dream. She arrived, eyes gleaming, expecting to *find* herself, as if she'd pictured a second self who'd been playing hide-and-seek. It's not as if she'd believed in all that 'streets paved with gold' nonsense. She wasn't that daft. Even so, the reality hit her the way it hits you when you discover you're the punchline of a joke. There was no welcome committee as she stepped down from the bus outside Park Lane. Doors didn't open for her. Here, Caroline is no one. Here, she's on her own.

"Lord knows why anyone would think you'd need ten minutes to warm up the valves," Finbar is saying. "Ten seconds is long enough."

"I don't know the first thing about valves. This was musical chairs without the music."

He laughs, his forehead creasing into a frown.

She'd put him at thirty. Now she thinks, *Maybe thirty-five.* "We'd all scrum for a place on the sofa. Then, at the sound of the first bong…" Caroline uncrosses her legs, sits up straight, stares ahead, and mouths the words: *'The Silent Minute.'* It was the prime minister's idea: the entire nation bowing their heads during Big Ben's chimes to pray for the men on the battlefields.

Finbar is up on his feet. "Hey! Where d'you think you're off to?" Her hand reaches after him. Why, she has no idea – she's spent the past quarter of an hour fretting about what to do if he catches hold of her waist and pulls her towards him.

"All the way to my coat pocket, to fetch my cigarettes. *If* that's alright with you."

Grudgingly, she watches him go. *He has you pegged as some country bumpkin.* As he turns, she flashes the smile that is expected.

Finbar bends from the waist, an impression of a bow, and opens his pack of Craven A. The cigarettes form a line of skyscrapers. "Will you have one?"

No point worrying whether nice girls smoke. Caroline forfeited that label the moment she stepped through the door. "How long until the news?"

He appears amused by her hesitation. "Seven minutes."

Seven minutes. "Go on then."

A single shake of the pack and Finbar shunts two cigarettes upwards. He presses his lips around the ends of these and, head to one side, flicks the wheel of his lighter.

Caroline's nerves leap as high as the flame. "Mind out," she warns. "You'll have your eyebrows off."

"You're a funny girl." As he attends to each cigarette in turn, Caroline puts out a hand, two fingers forming Churchill's famous victory sign in reverse. She and her school friends perfected this pose using sweet cigarettes. But Finbar places a Craven A between her lips. She feels the casual graze of his fingertips – *Vampire Horror, Modern Day Dracula.* John Haigh thought he'd invented the perfect murder. Believed he couldn't be convicted unless the bodies were found. Can this man, this man with Brylcreemed hair who takes a seat next to her, be trusted?

But Finbar does not pounce. “What's so important about tonight's news?” he asks. “I thought you'd be keen to go out.”

Out would be good. The streets, a pub, anywhere but here. Caroline shrugs, hoping a display of nonchalance will disguise her panic. This man could be anyone. She shouldn't have come.

“Don't tell me you're another one.” His knee nudges hers.

She blows a steady plume of smoke. (She has remembered not to inhale. *'It will make you dizzy.')* “Another what?”

“You've been following the exploits of the Acid Bath Murderer. You know Pierrepoint hanged him two days ago!”

“Not soon enough,” Caroline blurts. There, she's said it. She's glad Haigh is dead, glad there's one less killer walking the streets of London.

Again, Finbar gives her that bemused half-smile of his. “What more do you want?”

“Six murders he was guilty of. Six stories he spun, all of them believable.” *'Gone into hiding to avoid military service.' 'Didn't he tell you? He bought a one-way ticket to America.' 'Come quickly. Your husband's been taken ill.'*

From the back of Finbar's throat comes the sound of grudging agreement. “Truc. But you can only hang a man once.”

Caroline looks at Finbar, really looks, trying to see through his polished exterior, thinking all the while of what have become familiar photographs of Haigh. There's one where he looks like Hitler. A candid shot taken as he was bustled up the steps of the Old Bailey. With narrowed eyes and his mouth slightly open, Haigh has the shifty look of a second-hand car salesman. Caroline is confident she would have known that man was trouble. But there's a third photograph, where Haigh's index finger is resting to the right of his mouth. The film star shot. It's the thought of how easily she might have been taken in by this version of Haigh that has frayed Caroline's nerves.

Why her stomach seizes when she hears footsteps behind her as she hurries from the bus stop to the YWCA, bracing herself for an attack. She knows hardly anyone in London. Who would report *her* missing? And when news eventually got back to Suffolk, would Ma fall for a story that Caroline has set sail to America to start a new life?

She puts it to Finbar: "Haigh said there were nine victims. Don't you want to know if he made a last-minute confession?"

Finbar sucks smoke through his teeth; shakes his head. "He's the type to leave everyone guessing. That way, he wins."

Something stubborn in Caroline can't accept this. Three mothers, three fathers, three wives, all of them permanently in the dark.

Finbar, who has been keeping one eye on his wristwatch, announces, "Nine o'clock!" But where Big Ben's first chime should ring out in E, there is silence.

She turns to him. "Where are the bongs?"

"The announcer must have been early." They both inhale, cigarette paper and tobacco crackling. "No," he says gravely. "No bongs."

Caroline thinks out loud: "Is the King dead?"

"There would be radio silence. Perhaps the prime minister –"

Not even the Luftwaffe managed to silence Big Ben. A chill crawls up the skin of Caroline's arms. "Perhaps we're at war."

"We can't be. There would have been an announcement."

"But if the prime minister's dead –"

"Shut up and listen!"

It's so like one of Da's outbursts that Caroline obeys (head down, stay well out of the way). The thud from her veins punctuates the silence before the news reporter's voice slices through the tension. *'My apologies to you all for the unusual start to tonight's programme. Big Ben is running four minutes slow. Swarms of starlings are sitting on the minute hand, holding it back.'*

One of Caroline's hands flies to her chest.

"Would you believe it?" Finbar's tone suggests he's heard everything now. As Caroline jumps to her feet, he says, "What's this? Lost interest in the news?"

"If the world isn't ending, I think I'd like to go out. If you don't mind." *Out, up the basement steps, into the street.*

"In that case," Finbar sits his fedora squarely on his head, "We mustn't keep the lady waiting!"

A reprieve. She feels peculiarly grateful to him for that.

CHAPTER TWO

URSULA

Standing in the wings, dressed as a parlour maid. It's more important than ever that Ursula doesn't slip out of character. Most actors prefer to stay in their dressing rooms until the last possible moment, but that would mean charging onstage when her entrance demands the kind of subtlety that can only come from stillness. Shadowed in one of the dark spaces between the wings, surrounded by pulleys and ropes, breathing in sawdust, Ursula should be making her final preparations. Instead she's distracted.

Tonight – opening night in her home country, on the very stage where her training began. The top balcony, remember that? It was up there that, as a student, Ursula would bribe ushers to unlock the door so she could sneak into rehearsals. If an usher appeared to be having second thoughts, she'd claim she had *no idea* it wasn't allowed; she would *never* ask him to risk his job, but seeing as she was there, could she please just use the Ladies room? Then, the moment the coast was clear, she would pull a hairpin from her chignon and pick the lock. Shortly after her second box-office success, in which she'd played the part of a nun, Ed Sullivan asked Ursula what she would have done if she hadn't made it as an actress. "I'd have been an excellent thief," she replied. The studio audience had been in uproar. As if someone who'd played a nun could be anything less than perfect! "No really," she insisted, "I'm an expert lock-picker."

In her student days, Ursula loved everything this theatre had to offer. Every undulation of the closed velvet curtain, the sight of scurrying feet. She learned from the best. Diction. The anatomy of a theatre set. How to translate directions. The ballet of moving across a stage. How an understated approach compares with melodrama. But also how to behave. How to react to a director's criticism (when to look haughty, when to appear humble). How to introduce subtle changes into unpromising dialogue. How to take a curtsey and react to an encore.

Theatre was her first love, but she thought she could have it all.

"You're telling me that you want to abandon a promising career to work in moving pictures?"

With Ursula's initial three-film contract came private lessons. Dancing, movement, voice production. *"I'm not abandoning anything. I'll hone my skills, hopefully earn a reputation, then I'll come back to the stage."*

"That shows how little you understand. It's one or the other!"

"Perhaps that's how it was. *It's not how it has to be."*

How did she ever have the nerve? Screen acting, she discovered, was a distant cousin of stage acting. *Do I* really *look like that?* She forced herself to watch her own performances. "Can you rewind? There!" Correcting every fault she found with her posture, every flawed inflection. Ursula taught herself how to breathe all over again. How to let her face become a reflection of her co-star's dialogue; how to speak *beyond* the camera with her eyes.

Who would she have become if she'd stuck with theatre? War would have put a hold on any ambitions for the West

End or Broadway. Hers would have been a life spent touring provincial venues, criss-crossing the country by train; a night here, a night there. Ursula's hand strays to her stomach. *There might have been compensations. Privacy, perhaps.* But without Hollywood, she reminds herself, she would never have met Mack. Mack, who has come to mean everything.

It's been a long time, but return she has. It feels right to be back where it all started, though there are plenty of good reasons for nerves. Last month, Ursula's agent suggested she audition for the role of a Broadway star who had just turned forty. A gift of a part, but the fact that her agent sees her as middle-aged came as a shock. Hollywood beauties aren't allowed to grow old – not even gracefully – so she must move towards character roles. This role, the role of Gladys Aylward, is as far removed from Hollywood glamour as it is possible to be. The only make-up Ursula has to rely on is a little light powder, pale lipstick. Her costumes are as basic as they come. And success is far from guaranteed. Last year, the response to Gertrude Lawrence's return to the stage was less than rapturous, and rumour has it that Tallulah Bankhead has decided to reinvent herself as a chat show hostess.

There is something else. After a seventeen-year absence, Gladys Aylward herself is back in Britain. Clement Meade (whose name is so often preceded by the words 'renowned director' that they might as well be part of it), has sent Miss Aylward a personal invitation, but who knows if she'll make an appearance? She's never sought publicity.

Ursula can hear rustling, the occasional mutterings from high in the rafters, where two men balancing on a wooden platform make final adjustments to spotlights. She learned to tune out the rumble and clatter of scenery long ago, but these suppressed whispers are something else. Most likely they're about technical details. All the same, Ursula can't help it. She imagines she's the subject of gossip.

Actresses survive scandals, Ursula reminds herself. Take Mae West. After she was convicted of corrupting the morals of youth, given the option of a fine or a prison sentence, she *chose* prison. Mae West behind bars would be a story and a half and she knew it. "They gave me eight days off for *good behaviour.* I couldn't have been more insulted!" Be the best of bad examples, live long enough, and you may even be hailed as a national treasure.

But Mae West doesn't have children to consider.

And with that thought, Ursula feels a fluttering response. She marvels, smiling at what for the time being remains a secret. Hers and Mack's. They have decided that, for as long as possible, it will be The Thing the Press Does Not Know About, and for that time it will be all the more precious. From this moment forwards, Ursula's thoughts take on a new dimension. They become a private conversation.

There'll be comparisons between Ursula Delancy and Gladys Aylward, we have to expect that. It doesn't matter how kind and flattering the critics are, the public's response will be, 'How could they have cast that harlot as a Christian missionary? After everything she's done!' But it hasn't stopped them from turning up. Look, the theatre's packed! We may be a curiosity, a freak show, *but we'll show them.*

Curtain fall. Applause. Whistles. The audience are on their feet, stamping. Ursula has done what she set out to do. She was the thirty-year-old wearing a bright orange jacket, setting off for China from Liverpool Street Station with just two suitcases and a bedroll. She was the foot inspector who told strange and wonderful Bible stories to the women she tended. She was a spy for the Chinese army, her foreign appearance an advantage when smuggling food across battle lines to trapped villagers. With a price on her head, she led more than a hundred orphans over the mountains and across the Yellow

River to safety. She was Ai-weh-deh, the Virtuous One, just one woman, and a small one at that. "I wasn't God's first choice," she said. Ursula, as Ursula, curtseys deeply, steeples her hands and nods in the direction of the royal box, then the upper balcony. Like Gladys, she has given her all.

Clement Meade is in the wings, bouncing on the balls of his feet. "That was *extraordinary*."

"Thank you."

"No, honestly." The renowned director holds one hand over his heart and takes an exaggerated sigh. "Even I didn't expect. But I said. I *said* I would only take this on if you played the lead. I stuck to my guns and by God I was right. You go to the lines without seeming to think."

Oh Lord, he's going to ask her out to toast their success. It won't just be the two of them, it will be the whole theatre crowd and she'll be expected to stay up all night. "Let's not get too excited," Ursula cautions. "It's bad luck to celebrate until we hear what the critics have to say. Does anyone know if Miss Aylward came?"

"Would anyone have recognised her if she had?"

Surely Clement must know whether the seat he reserved for her had been occupied. Ursula would hate to be lauded while the subject of the play is overlooked, but what she knows of Miss Aylward makes the actress reflect. "That's probably the way she'd want it."

She begins to navigate her way down the draughty backstage corridor, but Clement isn't alone in wanting to congratulate her. A trickle of stagehands tags along, each waiting their turn.

"The audience is still in their seats. They're refusing to budge. People will say it was you who stopped Big Ben!"

Ursula stops and turns. "Big Ben stopped?"

"For four minutes, apparently. Tonight's Nine O'Clock News began with radio silence." It was just as you started your monologue. The bets were that Queen Mary had popped her clogs. I was terrified the whispers would put you off."

Men everywhere would have removed their hats, the women reaching for handkerchiefs. *I have with great regret to announce...* "And was it Queen Mary?"

"False alarm. Something went wrong with one of the clock hands."

"Four minutes, you said?"

"I know." Clement is on his toes now, ecstatic. "The *exact* length of your monologue!" Stagehands confirm this with enthusiastic nods.

"They'll say I'm a witch." Although Ursula hadn't intended to make a joke, there's a polite outbreak of laughter. "I've been called many things" – harlot, whore, and home breaker spring to mind – "but never a witch. It will make a nice change, I suppose."

They don't know what to make of her. They blink nervously, waiting for her to give them a cue.

When she laughs, there is a collective sigh of relief before they join in. They are still laughing when Ursula slumps against the inside of her dressing-room door.

CHAPTER THREE

PATRICE

"Is that you?" Three words, and her husband's voice betrays him. It's not even possible to describe him as worse for wear. He's drunk. Of course he is. At this hour, anything else would be a miracle.

"Yes, Charles." Patrice looks in on him, seated in his usual armchair, facing the fire. "As you see, I've returned."

With the study's leather armchairs and mahogany panelling, Charles has succeeded in replicating a gentleman's club in miniature. A place of rationality and calm, where women are unwelcome. He calls over his shoulder. "Where have you been?"

Finger by finger, Patrice pulls off a soft butter-coloured buckskin glove. Must she put up with his supercilious Under-secretary of State for Home Affairs voice? "I hope I'm not expected to account for my every move."

"Why so defensive?" Her husband's head appears around the wing of the armchair. "All I wanted to know is if you caught tonight's news."

"I missed it." She unpins her hat, stabs the felt band. "If you must know, I took a box at the theatre."

"Then you won't have heard the rumpus. Rumours went

flying. World War Three, the King." Charles makes a double-clicking noise, more 'giddy-up' than the indication of a slit throat she presumes is his intention. But at least he isn't morose. Already, he's said more than he's said to her for the past week.

Curious, Patrice pauses in the doorway. "Why on earth –?"

"Big Ben ground to a halt. A flock of starlings, would you believe? Have a drink with me." Without waiting for her reply, he unstops the crystal decanter that sits within convenient reach, on the side table next to his chair. "Come on, live a little!"

The implication that she doesn't know how to let her hair down grates. "You know I don't indulge," she says, anticipating a sarcastic retort. *"That's right. Just your friends. It's so difficult to remember when the bills from your club keep arriving."*

In this imaginary conversation, she bites back. *"You may settle the bills, but I fund everything, Charles, as you know full well."* Patrice allows herself this private indulgence. Hawtree-Davenport Investments wasn't Charles's only failed business venture, but it was the one that brought them closest to ruin, and not just financially.

Displays of raw emotion always appalled Patrice's parents. They had no idea what to do in the face of them, except send her to her room, suggesting she needed a lie-down. Restraint was what she was taught and, for the most part, it is a lesson that has stood Patrice in good stead. But that isn't to say it has always come easily. The moment Charles made his confession is one Patrice will never forget.

"Let me get this straight." She was shaking, shaking so hard he must have been able to see it. "You entered into a business venture with this *man*, this Davenport character, you approached *our* friends and asked them to invest their money – without checking his credentials."

"I was introduced to him at the club."

Her hands seemed to lift of their own accord. "Of course you were!"

"You have to understand. No one is accepted by White's without a vigorous assessment."

"No. I'm well aware." Perhaps, she tried to convince herself, Charles was panicking unduly. (How wrong she was about that!) "We'll have Kenyon Senior take a look at the paperwork and see if he can find a way out."

Downcast eyes. Silence.

"Charles." Although the answer to the question she had not voiced was written on his face, Patrice approached the subject warily. "*Please* tell me that this *arrangement* wasn't set up on the strength of a handshake."

More helpless than she'd ever seen her husband; his voice pleading: "People invested because it was *me*."

Unable to contain her incredulity, Patrice clasped one cold hand over her mouth while the magnitude of their predicament sank in.

"I have to make it right. Don't you see?"

Yes, she saw. Charles had allowed himself to be seduced by words and promises, and now neither of them would be able to hold up their heads in public. She moved decisively towards the door.

"Patrice!" He was up on his feet. "Where are you going?"

She raised her voice then. Could not help herself. "Where do you think I'm going? To sort out your mess, of course!" It only struck Patrice later that Charles might have thought she had decided to leave him.

"How?"

"First, I shall do whatever I have to do to make sure this doesn't appear on tomorrow's front pages. Then I'll make an appointment with my solicitors. Thank God! Thank *God* Whitlocke is in my name, otherwise we'd both be bankrupt."

After that, she'd put her foot down. No more grand ideas and no more backing of other people's grand ideas.

Oblivious to the direction her thoughts have taken, topping up his own glass with a healthy measure (she can't help noticing the way his hand shakes), Charles is not offended. All he says is, "It needn't be whisky. There's no shortage of soda. Ice?"

Patrice had intended to retire for the night, keen to commit today's diary entry to ink while the details are fresh. But the peace the Hawtrees maintain is fragile. A thaw in relations, however brief, might make a welcome diversion. She enters the room, crossing the no-man's land that separates their lives, and takes a seat in the chair nearest his. "Thank you."

Charles uses the siphon and returns the tongs to their bucket. He presents her with a heavy tumbler, not letting go of his own. He cannot be without his glass. It would throw him off-balance, he jokes with Dr Fisher, who, in turn, insists to Patrice that he has done what he can to discourage Charles. Unfortunately this effort doesn't involve refusing the offer of a nightcap after he has taken Charles's blood pressure. Advice to cut back on the bottle might be more palatable coming from someone who shows slightly more restraint himself.

"Your good health, your grace," Charles says.

She clinks his glass. "You may call me ma'am."

"Wouldn't that be a little forward?" He lets out a small groan of discomfort as he sinks into his armchair, then feigns a sulk: "You didn't think to invite your husband to the theatre?"

"You never show the slightest interest in anything I want to see. On top of which you have an infuriating habit of double-booking yourself or changing your mind at the last moment."

"Still, I like to be asked. It's the courtesy above anything else."

Patrice sits forwards. "Have I got this right? You'd like me to *invite* you to the theatre, so that you can turn me down or, worse still, accept and then leave halfway through the performance?"

Not in the least put out, Charles looks rather pleased with himself. "Once I've guessed the ending, I really can't see any point in staying."

Evenly matched, there were several years when they'd been more than good sparring partners. Two halves of England's ancient dynasties representing tradition and duty, values many of Patrice's current acquaintances would struggle to understand.

His drink-sodden eyes sparkle. "Any good, was it? The thing you saw?"

"Very. Ursula Delancy played the lead."

"Delancy? I thought she'd sworn never to darken our shores again."

"She was tempted back by the role she was born to play. At least, that's the official line."

This raises a smile. "And what was the role?"

"Gladys Aylward." The name had meant nothing to Patrice, but she now says with authority, "British housemaid turned Chinese missionary."

"Hah! Nun turned whore turned missionary. Full circle."

"I rather think you're mistaking the actress for her characters." As soon as these words are out, Patrice dislikes herself for having uttered them.

"Doesn't sound like much of a plot."

"Well, that's where you're wrong. Paramount haven't wasted any time in snapping up the film rights."

"And Miss Delancy, in the flesh?" Her husband's grin crosses the border between wit and poor taste.

"Must you?" She glowers at him. "But since you ask, she was sublime." Prior to tonight, Patrice had understood acting to be a matter of pretending. Now she understands it's about *becoming*. In some scenes, Ursula seemed to do next to nothing, but when she moved, even the slightest motion made one breathless. "I believed every word she said." Patrice surprises herself by laughing. "I even began to believe in God!"

Charles widens his eyes. "You're not serious?"

"I wouldn't concern yourself." She shrugs his suggestion aside. "I'm sure it's only temporary." All the same, a sudden sense of emptiness has Patrice racking her brain, trying to locate the last time she did anything useful. Something that meant something. Probably not since the war (the first one, that is), when doing one's bit was one's duty. But, briefly, while the audience sat in darkness, Ursula Delancy had performed a small miracle. Nerves Patrice thought dead were coaxed back to life.

"Which one of the Marx brothers did you go with this time?"

"Do you *have* to be so rude about my friends?"

"Is it my fault that they all look the same?"

"If that's what you think, then your reference is quite wrong. The Marx brothers look nothing like one another." As a young man, Zeppo was actually quite handsome. "If you must know, it was Brian Waltham."

"Chap in my class at school called Whitey Waltham. Big teeth." Charles taps on an incisor with a fingernail. "Not him I suppose?"

"I doubt Brian was even born when you were at school."

"Brian, you say? Could be one of Whitey's sons."

What's the use? Charles thinks his influence is such that he'll always find a connection if he digs deep enough. There was a time when Patrice found this quirk amusing. In the days when her husband sought her opinion, he would rehearse his speeches for her in front of this very fire. Once, he used the phrase *general malaise* to describe the state of the nation, and Patrice couldn't help herself: "Oh, you've spoken about him before," she said. "Don't tell me. Didn't you serve together in France?" Now she sets her tumbler down and says wryly, "He could well be." Then she uncrosses her legs and stands.

"You still haven't asked how it went."

Patrice hesitates, wondering what she could have forgotten. No. Nothing springs to mind.

"I thought you'd be pleased to know it's safe to walk the streets again."

One step ahead, her mouth falls open. *John Haigh's execution.* Charles had mentioned that his presence at Wandsworth prison had been requested, but unlike Haigh, Charles was granted a stay of grace. The request had been put to him prematurely: the necessary permission had not been obtained. "You were *there?*" The fact of this is shocking. She sits down heavily.

For as long as Patrice has known Charles, he has petitioned against the death penalty. Resolute in his stance, Charles has railed against members of the legal profession. Hardly men of the world, what right do they have to pass judgement on those whose lives they can't begin to comprehend? People who, in dire circumstances – times of unrest, lacking security, or coming from broken homes – are driven to do desperate things. But Haigh was no victim of circumstance. Any bad luck he had was of his own making, formed out of greed and a disproportionate sense of his worth. Few people will mourn one monstrous individual who valued his own life so highly that he didn't spare a thought for his victims.

"I told you that I wouldn't look for a way out of doing my duty," Charles says.

The thing now is not to overreact. Patrice must pick her way carefully. This is not the first death Charles has witnessed at close quarters. He was a serving officer during the Great War. To place too great a significance on Haigh's execution would be to belittle those other deaths, men who were far more deserving of life.

But how could she not have known?

Patrice is no longer sure that she saw Charles on Wednesday. Certainly, he made no mention of Haigh last night – and she would never have pestered him. As vital as the cause is to him, it affects his moods terribly. This difficult man becomes nigh on impossible. The black dog last descended after the Lords rejected Silverman's bill which would have suspended the death penalty for five years. Time enough to talk the public round. Charles failed to rally when the King consented to a Royal Commission, tasked with *considering* if liability to suffer capital punishment for murder should be limited or modified. 'Consider' wasn't a strong enough word for Charles's liking. Patrice's suggestion was that, if he was concerned the job wouldn't be done properly, he should put himself forward, which he did, only to have Sir Ernest reject him – most likely because of Hawtree-Davenport, but, of course, his rejection had been *her* fault. No matter that she herself harbours strong feelings on the subject, Patrice hasn't been inclined to stick her oar in again save for asking her newspaper contacts to do all they can to keep the subject in the public eye.

But now it makes sense – why Charles wanted company. Now it seems only too clear what lies behind the weight of his eyes. "I suppose you are expected to produce a report."

Her husband shakes his head, a 'where to begin!' "The people who stood outside the prison, blocking our way. I looked at them and thought, Are you here to make sure justice is done, or are you just here on a jolly?"

She waits, knowing better than to interrupt.

"John Haigh," he continues sourly. "He showed no sign of remorse. Not a bit. He asked for a dress rehearsal, so they tell me. Wanted to be sure everything would go off without a hitch." Charles sighs, deeply. "Apparently when they offered him a brandy, Haigh joked, 'Make it a large one, old boy.'"

With one hand covering her mouth, she gives a helpless

shake of her head. What's normal under the circumstances? Not that there was anything remotely normal about Haigh. Uninvited questions crowd Patrice's mind. How far from the scaffold was Charles? Did he sit, like an audience member? She asks only this: "Has being there altered your view in any way?"

Charles sits forward, and as his passion surfaces Patrice is reminded what first attracted her to him. "What bothers me, what *really* bothers me, is that Haigh and his ilk are the reason capital punishment still exists."

"And the reason you have such a hard task ahead of you."

"Surely people must see that for men like Haigh, capital punishment is no deterrent. When he walked into the room, there was none of the heaviness you'd expect. He looked me straight in the eye, but I felt no human connection. None whatsoever." The look Charles gives Patrice is agonised and she feels bereft. To find his own sense of compassion scarred by such a monster!

Any comfort she can offer comes too late. "Haigh has made it very difficult for anyone to feel anything approaching sympathy for him," she says.

"Impossible!" her husband barks. "You know that Madame Tussaud's requested a fitting for a death mask?"

Patrice shivers as her blood recoils. "That's obscene."

"Oh, he was happy to oblige. More than happy."

Left with no practical way to help her husband, Patrice feels she must offer something. "Perhaps you might like to come with me to the house." Between husband and wife, the only definitions they use are 'the townhouse' when at Whitlocke and referring to their London address and 'the house' when in London and referring to her family's ancient foothold. "We could make a weekend of it."

"Must we?" Charles's tone flattens.

His refusal should come as no surprise. He never expresses

the slightest interest in Whitlocke. His natural habitat is a narrow terrain made up of the townhouse, White's Club, and the terraces of Portland stone that sit in between. "It was only a suggestion. If you'd rather not, then all you need do is say so."

"I'm not sure I can stomach a weekend of estate work."

Patrice bridles: "The estate is my responsibility, not yours." Besides, an overseer far more capable than her manages the house and land, and there are accountants and solicitors to handle the money side of things. "But I understand. It was the wrong moment to ask."

Still. Herself and Whitlocke: the only two things Patrice has to offer. She cannot decide which rejection wounds her more.

CHAPTER FOUR

CAROLINE

Caroline's tour of the YWCA concluded with the bathroom, a damp-smelling narrow space with a stained enamel bathtub opposite a cracked sink, all surrounded by chipped white tiles. Above the bath a high window offered a view not of sky, but of brickwork. But it was a room with a lock on the door!

"Here we are," said Esther, her tour-guide, still dressed in factory overalls. (Caroline suspects she rather likes wearing them.) "Luxury. And, as a bonus, you get to put your name on the rota for a weekly bath."

Not even the news that Caroline would have to share with eleven other young women dimmed her enthusiasm. At home, she was used to second-hand water in a tin bath in front of the fire. And if the fire was lit, someone would always want to toast bread over the embers, until Ma chased them away.

"Out! Give Caroline a bit of privacy!"

"It's only Betty, Ma. I don't mind Betty."

"Well you should, a young woman your age!"

"You don't mind, do you, Caroline?"

"We share a bed, don't we?"

"I've seen you wee in the pot."

"Oi, blabbermouth! Keep that tater trap shut!"

"Rule number one," Esther said, pocketing the worn bar of soap she found resting on the side of the bath. "Anything you leave lying around is fair game." Not even that put Caroline off, but the reality is this: your allocated slot for an evening bath never seems to coincide with the availability of hot water, so you sit clutching your knees, shivering in a couple of inches of tepid water. And sometimes, as it does today, washing your smalls takes priority.

As Caroline swims her nylons like eels in the sink, her mind wanders where it will. London doors still show no sign of opening. It turns out that for an unqualified, unskilled girl there are few options to choose from.

"Hey, Esther." She glances over her shoulder. "I don't suppose you know anything about Pitman courses?" Esther has already wrung out her smalls, and is stretching up to hang them on the line over the bathtub. "I read about one for shorthand and typing, but it costs an arm and a leg, and I doubt my English is nearly good enough." Heat rises to Caroline's neck. Even with Esther, the friendliest girl in her dorm by far, she frets that she's making a fool of herself. Coming from a corner of the country where watermen and farm labourers roll their eyes at the first sign of high and mighty ways, she's all too aware of how provincial she seems. Yesterday brought a fresh reminder. As she brewed tea in the kitchen, Caroline had asked one of the other girls where she was from. The answer: somewhere just to the north of Paris. The French girl reciprocated, "And you?"

"Felixstowe," Caroline said, quickly adding, "on the east coast."

"Of where?"

"England, of course!"

"Oh!" The girl laughed, paused, and then laughed some

more. "That is an Engleesh accent? I thought you were… You know, I think I have better Engleesh than you."

It's not just the pegs in Esther's mouth; Caroline senses agreement in her muffled response. It's true, then. Her English isn't up to scratch. "I could do with something to tide me over. Something that doesn't interfere with looking for a day job. Waitress, usherette…"

Esther's arms pause mid-air. "Good luck to you. Half the girls here are after that sort of thing."

Esther's on the production line at Decca, the company responsible for the first marine radar. It sounds rather grand, though she's the first to admit she only has a vague idea how the part her team produces contributes to the finished article. Besides, it could all end tomorrow. Her boss's view is that now they're home, manufacturing jobs should go to the men. He constantly rubs her face in it. 'Don't you think, after all they've been through…?' When it's still tolerated (which is barely), women's work is ring-fenced, labelled 'unskilled'. "But what can I do? Complain about how much I'm being paid and they'll show me the door."

Esther clearly knows the ropes. If she doesn't think Caroline has much chance of getting waitressing work, just imagine her reaction if Caroline were to admit that, back in Suffolk, she was one of 'the gang' who talked about moving to London, meeting famous people and becoming 'fillum' stars. Being discovered was simply a case of being in the right place at the right time. When Ma announced it was time for her to go and do her bit 'for the family', Caroline's first thought was relief – she wouldn't have to explain why she couldn't go on any more errands to see Uncle Anthony. (Thinking of him now conjures up the yeasty smell of his breath, the graze of his stubble.) And, once settled on the bus, her second had been, *Finally, my life is beginning!*

But what a beginning. Cast adrift in a strange and frightening city, whose post-Blitz palette is the black and white of grainy newspaper photographs. Chimneys spew pewter clouds, adding to the ceiling of smoke. The unswept doorsteps of pockmarked buildings have sandbags and buckets left in position, as if they might be needed at a moment's notice. And the clothing of those who clog the puddled pavements. Brimmed hats of no particular description. Shapeless black overcoats squared off at the shoulders; the only ornamentation a scarf tucked in at the neckline, neat as hospital bed corners. It's a far cry from the fashion pages of Caroline's magazines.

She's uneducated, unskilled, female and alone. That's what it boils down to. "While we're on the subject of eternal optimism." Caroline tries to match her voice to her words. "I could really do with a job that comes with a room."

"You and me both," Esther scoffs. "Anything to get me out of this place!"

"How long have you been here?"

"Six – no wait." Esther deploys her last peg. "Seven months."

That's practically permanent. Imagine six more months of linoleum corridors where the brooms, buckets and mops are left out as reminders to 'pitch in'. "How long did you plan on staying?"

Esther shrugs. "Same as everyone else. A week. But you've seen how it is. When the rent looks affordable, there's usually a good reason for it."

"And if you've a mother who expects you to send her most of your take-home…" Caroline says. There was a time when her mother was the person she took her cries of 'It's not fair!' to. But even when provided with proof that Caroline had been wronged, Ma's reply was always the same: *Life isn't fair. Get used to it.* You won't get the thing you think you're entitled to because someone else has been judged more deserving. You won't be judged on merit, but by rules that are as old as the Ten Commandments. Unless you're prepared to tell tales on your school friend, you'll have to accept the punishment for something you didn't do. And now *You'll have to shoulder the responsibility because you're the oldest.*

"Find me one who doesn't want most of your take-home!" says Esther.

Caroline steals a look in the mirror, past her own face to Esther's reflection. Did *her* ma hold her close and whisper a good luck that sounded like a threat?

"Honestly," Esther says, "when I didn't land a job in the first couple of weeks, she was jumping down my throat. 'Have you thought about domestic work?' she said. That's how much ambition she had for me!"

Girls of their age rub up against constant reminders that boys younger than them died for their country. Told they should be grateful for the opportunity to help out. Do whatever it takes. Caroline can't admit to Esther that she passed up an opportunity at a poultry dealer's, telling herself something better would come along. Caroline's broken the necks of enough chickens in her time. She had no business being repulsed by the sight of birds, pimple-skinned and headless. Not that she would have had to get her hands dirty. All they wanted was someone to deal with the takings. What put her off was the thought of spending six days a week in a cell-like booth, complete with metal bars. "Mine thinks I should be a shop assistant," is all she says.

Indignant, Esther puts her hands on her hips. "Ten hours a day, six days a week and one week's paid holiday a year to look forward to."

Even this conversation feels like a delicious act of rebellion. Though it shouldn't. Surely Esther's proved herself as capable as a man? Who says that things have to be done a certain way, just because that's how they were done in the past? And so Caroline warms to the theme. "When I'd be expected to go home and 'help out.'" But her thoughts stop in their tracks. When she goes home, what will she find?

"Promise me, you'll stay away from Uncle Anthony, Betty."

"Why? I like Uncle Anthony."

"Promise me. It's important."

"I won't promise if you won't say why."

"They can shove 'respectability,'" Esther is saying. "It's slavery."

Was it really so bad? A misplaced kiss? A full-bodied hug? A clumsily-placed hand? Had Caroline overreacted? Cut off from her siblings, she'll be allowed no contact until she proves herself by providing. *How many elder children are sacrificed for the sake of the rest?* Caroline wonders. "Are you the oldest?"

Esther sniffs, just once. "I wasn't. Am now."

Forgetting her wet hands, Caroline turns and reaches for Esther's arm. "I'm such an idiot."

"Nothing to be done." Esther perches on the side of the bath and stares down at her feet. There is no invitation to ask whether it was the war or illness, perhaps even childbirth. She sniffs again, then lifts her chin. "Are you serious about getting out of here?"

This change of subject catches Caroline off-guard. "Soon as I can."

"Have you thought about squatting?"

"Hasn't the council taken over all the unoccupied flats?"

Esther lowers her voice, "Not quite *all.* They're ignoring anything that's earmarked for demolition."

Black and white footage runs through Caroline's mind. A cascade of falling bricks. Her hands as shields in front of her eyes. "They wouldn't be safe, would they?" she finds herself gasping.

Esther shrugs the suggestion away. "The damage is above ground. Most of the basements are sound."

Is it possible that lives are being led beneath the ruined terraces Caroline walks past every day? Most are surrounded by bomb sites, but occasionally a single house stands alone in a sea of wasteland, now a playground for bare-legged opportunists. Boys who look uncannily like her brothers rake through rubble in search of souvenirs to lend realism to their war games. Only the other day she approached a motley crew to see what it was they were pelting with broken bricks; relieved to find it wasn't a stray cat.

"It's a UXB."

An unexploded bomb.

"And exactly what are you hoping to do?"

Lanky, with a missing front tooth, he looked at her as if she'd just parachuted in from another country. "Make it explode, of course!"

A far cry from her own childhood. For Caroline, 'risky' would have been ignoring the *beware of the bull* sign to take a shortcut through the field.

Now she asks Esther, "This squatting, is it legal?"

Esther grins. "It isn't exactly criminal. Only if you encourage others."

"Then we shouldn't be having this conversation."

"What conversation?" She stands, and Caroline assumes this is the end of their chat. "But if you ever fancy becoming a vigilante, you know where to find me."

Shaking her head, Caroline continues to wring out her hand-washing. There must be some other stepping-stone she can hop across. Modelling, perhaps? She eyes her reflection. *Problem is, you're all of five foot two.*

If she tells Finbar she wants to act, he'll laugh in her face. But Finbar knows people. That's already clear. And what's the alternative? Seven months in this hell-hole, or squatting in a squalid basement, something that may or may not be legal and would almost certainly be dangerous. The next time Finbar asks, 'Have you given any more thought to what you'd like to do?' Caroline should just come out with it. Hands immersed in milky lukewarm water, she experiments: "I want to act."

In a case of almost perfect timing, the bathroom door crashes against the tiled wall. It's Barb, a senior who's been here so long she's second only to staff in the pecking order. "Don't let *us* stop you, Diana Dors, but for God's sake, get a move on. You're not the only one who wants to use the bathroom tonight."

CHAPTER FIVE

URSULA

Early morning. Ursula's eyes are heavy as she looks out from the window of her top-floor hotel suite. Yesterday's standing ovation has faded into insignificance. What kept her awake most of the night was her impatience to tell Mack how, standing in the wings, she felt the baby move. Morning sickness aside, she wouldn't have dared allow herself to believe. Finally, something feels like hope; compensation for all they went through at the start of their life as a couple.

"Norma! I'm sorry to telephone so late but can you get Mack on the line?" There is the kind of pause you expect on a long-distance call, while you imagine your words travelling down thousands of miles of cables.

"Oh, Miss Delancy, he's not home from the studio yet."

"Dammit!" Ursula checks her watch. Los Angeles lags eight hours behind London. Mack works his actors and crew as hard as any director she's known, but would he keep them past ten o'clock? "Are you expecting him?" Again the words travel under the Atlantic, and the world's oceans wash the reply back to her.

"He asked me to leave supper on a tray."

"Again?"

Norma's shrug is almost audible. "That's all he wanted."

It's hardly Norma's fault that Mack sees no reason to account for himself. "All I can say is I'm glad he's not directing me!" Ursula pulls shower-damp hair away from the nape of her neck and drapes it over the thick hotel dressing gown. *Wait.* When Ursula last caught up with Mack, he spent most of the conversation complaining how, rather than reshoot a scene, he was trying to dub the voice of an actress. *"The blasted thing's driving me nuts. I can't get the tape to sync."*

To Norma, she says, "I'm probably being unfair. I expect Mack's the last one there, locked away in his editing suite."

"I'm sure that's it. Is there a message I can pass on?"

Ursula wants so badly to tell Mack that she hasn't felt this happy since the time they sped down the highway in the back of a car, laughing and clinging helplessly to each other. They'd escaped an ambush of photographers by swapping cars with a friend of Mack's while filling up with gasoline. Crouched down on their haunches, they made a crab-like scuttle between the two vehicles, an idea stolen directly from one of Mack's movies. He thought the press might appreciate the irony.

"I wanted to tell him how opening night went, that's all."

"I didn't like to ask. You always say it's bad luck to mention it before the critics have given their verdict."

Ursula closes her eyes; pinches the top of her nose. "You're right. And I haven't seen the papers yet," Ursula says, then adds, "You will tell Mack I called?"

"The moment I see him."

"Well, I'm keeping you up. I'll say goodnight."

Ursula keeps the receiver at her ear and taps the cradle. *"I'm sure that's it."* Ursula replays Norma's words, giving them her professional scrutiny. There was something placatory in the housekeeper's tone.

Don't do this to yourself.

Besides, you haven't even checked to see if Mack's left a message.

Ursula dials reception, announces brightly, "Room 47," the code she agreed with the hotel staff. "Are there any messages for me?"

"I'll just check. No. None this morning."

Not even so much as a cablegram to wish her luck! Admittedly, Mack indulges in a little paranoia. Ever since a reporter took a job as a hotel manager to get a scoop on one of his leading men, he insists *all* hotel managers are in cahoots with the press.

Ursula asks to be connected to Mack's studio. Whatever the hour, Joe is always on reception. She enquires after his wife and children by name.

"They're fine, fine, thanks for asking." But when it comes to Mack's whereabouts, Joe says, "Oh, no, Miss Delancy. He left hours ago."

"Would you mind just checking he's not in the editing suite?" She balances the receiver on her shoulder, while adjusting the belt of her robe. "But if you could make it quick. I'm calling long-distance."

"No need, Miss Delancy. Mr Flood said goodnight and I watched him drive off."

Perhaps she's forgotten some important function or other. "I don't suppose he mentioned where he was going?"

"He didn't. Sorry."

Ursula is on the verge of tears. When you're in the habit of speaking a couple of times a day, when you're keeping a secret and you're a long way from home… "Would you tell him I was trying to reach him?" *Mack's not avoiding you,* she scolds herself. *He's trying to be considerate. He knows you need your sleep.* "Tell him I don't mind what time he calls."

"I'll be sure to do that."

By the third day, Ursula is too embarrassed to say, 'It's me again.' She pretends to Norma that she's already spoken to Mack. To his secretary, she repeats the lie, prompting the response: "Aww, it's so sweet that you speak every day. Especially when you're on the other side of the world."

The novelty of the fluttering in her belly has worn off. The opposite is now true. If Ursula doesn't feel the baby move, her anxiety goes through the roof. Perhaps she should save her worry for Mack. But she knows Mack isn't lying in a ditch somewhere. He's been seen going about his normal business.

There is one number Ursula hasn't tried. Mack gave it to her for emergencies. "Honestly, you won't want to use it unless you have to." He's never spoken about Lindsay in favourable terms. The kindest reference he makes to her is 'the mother of my three boys'.

Soon to be Ursula's stepchildren.

She thinks of them, arriving chauffeur driven for weekends, hair neatly parted and slicked down, dressed in impractical white shorts. If the message Lindsay intends is that Mack shouldn't mess them up, she needs to be less subtle. The first thing he does is ruffle their hair, then he engages them in the kind of rough and tumble that always ends with grass stains. Mack loves those boys. Might he not use her absence as an opportunity to visit them in their own home? He's probably decided it would be good to talk things through with their mother, face to face.

The thought takes root.

How silly that Mack feels the need to keep this from her! If only she'd agreed to meet her ex-husband and talk things through. Not in the home she shared with Robin and still part-owns – that would have been too complicated. Somewhere neutral. A hotel overlooking the sea. Brighton, perhaps. Hasn't Ursula often told Mack that she wished she didn't need to write to her own daughter care of a solicitor? Of all people, an actress knows how easily inflections read into words on a page can alter their meaning.

Ursula can't avoid Lindsay forever. When she becomes Mack's wife, Lindsay will have to accept her role in the boys' lives. It's better that they learn to rub along sooner rather than later.

A decision, then.

She dials reception and asks to be connected. There is a wait. Ursula touches cold fingertips to her lips. Thinking and doing are very different things. This is stage fright, pure and simple.

"Miss Delancy, how wonderful to hear from you." A far cry from the cold sarcasm Ursula expected. "I wasn't aware that you were part of Donald's current project. In fact, I'm sure I remember reading someplace that you're busy treading the boards of the London stage."

"That's right, I am. I just wondered if you've heard from him recently."

"Oh, you Brits and your sense of humour. What a funny thing to say! We're just having breakfast with the children. We have so little time together, it's become something of a family ritual. But listen to me, lecturing the world's first leading lady about studio hours! Would you like me to disturb him?"

An actress is supposed to suppress her own personality, embody her character's motivation, reflect her director's vision. Sometimes, by the end of a movie, Ursula has done her job so thoroughly it takes a few days to find herself again.

"Miss Delancy, are you still there?"

"I'm still here. No, please don't disturb Mack." Ursula winces. However bright she meant to sound, by using her nickname for Donald, she's slipped up. "Let him enjoy his time with the boys."

"Speaking of the children," Lindsay lowers her voice.

Here it comes, Ursula braces herself. The *'Don't ever think that you can replace me.'*

"We have the most exciting news. Quite unexpected." Inside the hotel dressing gown, Ursula feels herself shrink.

She goes to sit, putting one hand behind her to locate the edge of the bed. "But perhaps I should let Donald tell you. I don't like to speak out of turn. Although you and I are *such* old friends."

Before this moment, Ursula would have passed on the opportunity to hear 'news' that follows this kind of fanfare from anyone other than Mack. When people are as famous as they are, even rumours with little substance tend to stick. Once, not long after she and Mack got together, after making the mistake of giving an old friend a peck on the cheek, she'd been forced to phone him from a film set, warning that he could expect the dear folk from the papers to delight in telling him she was having a full-blown affair. "Honest to God, you're insatiable," he'd said. "Where do you find the energy?" Whatever *this* is, it will be the explanation for Lindsay's confidence. Better to know, rather than allow Mack to do-si-do with the truth.

"Lindsay," she clutches the receiver harder, "after a build-up like that, you can't leave me guessing!"

"Well, alright. So long as you *promise* not to let slip that *I* was the one who told you."

"Scout's honour!"

"There you go again!" Lindsay laughs, pauses, then says, "We're expecting."

Breath forces itself from Ursula's mouth. *How?* Her hand goes to her stomach, so that she might shield her unborn child from the force of the blast.

"I know, I know! I'm as surprised as you are. After all, I'm pushing forty, which, let's face it, is going to make me pretty old for a mother. But we're both thrilled. It just feels right."

Ursula has played this role in a movie. She knows her lines. It's just that she never imagined she would speak them in her own life. "And when will the happy event be?" Her delivery is not quite as she would have wished it.

"June, we think, but both of my boys arrived early. They come when they're good and ready, don't they?"

"Oh, they do." September, October, then. The trip when Mack went to break the news to Lindsay that Ursula was expecting his child. And her reaction was to seduce him. *One last waltz, for old time's sake.* After all that they've been through, *he's* the one who found the energy for an affair. With his ex-wife. "Well. My very best to you both."

"I'll be sure to pass that along. Goodbye, Miss Delancy."

CHAPTER SIX

PATRICE

Patrice makes her way up to her bedroom, pursued by images and sounds she had hoped to leave in Charles's mahogany study. Eyelets cut in the hangman's hood, the particular resonance of the lever that releases the trapdoor, the snap of a neck being broken. Not things Patrice wants in her mind after a memorable evening of theatre.

Despite paying an exorbitant price for the box, she'd steeled herself for disappointment. Even the greatest of film actresses can lose their sheen on the stage. She's witnessed it before. Better entertainment can often be found in the stalls. Patrice's escort will cough discreetly, asking, "Isn't that...?" nodding in the direction of an acquaintance, someone whose divorce has not quite gone through, with someone they're not quite ready to be seen with in public yet. And Patrice will raise her opera glasses and say, "So it is," while pretending to be enthralled by some element of the set design.

Not tonight.

Ursula Delancy cast a spell with her voice, her eyes. In the dark, in a red velvet chair, Patrice gave herself over entirely and was levitated to what believers might call a state of grace. She'd imagined the memory of the performance as something she'd treasure. Now, it is tainted by thoughts of crowds queuing to see Haigh's death mask. A man for whom there will be no requiems.

Patrice's diary must wait. She feels the need for a long bath; to scrub her skin until it's raw. The hour is late. Crossland stayed up to greet her when she arrived home - really, her personal maid is nothing less than a saint. She will not trouble her again. Besides, in Patrice's current frame of mind, being alone suits her. She runs her own bath.

Though she remains submerged until the water cools, Patrice has no desire to close her eyes. She fears that Haigh will be waiting, still hanging there, his feet kicking, his body twitching. Most likely, Patrice thinks, she will not sleep, not without something to help her.

Wrapped in the largest of the towels, she opens the bathroom cabinet, stares at the row of brown bottles. A sedative, just one, which she washes down with water. There will be time enough to work on her diary while it gets to work in her bloodstream.

Strange. Her diary isn't in the drawer of her bedside table. Just the pen she uses to write in it, the one that is usually stowed in a leather pocket inside the binding. *Where the blazes can it be?* She pulls the drawer out as far as it will safely go and shuffles the contents. Could it have fallen down behind the drawer? Patrice removes the drawer, lifting it carefully and laying it on the bed's quilted coverlet. She looks into and then feels around the walnut hollow. Nothing.

Would he? It's not as if it could be anyone else. Crossland would not go rooting around, of that she's sure.

But they have agreements. Understandings. At no point has Patrice crossed the lines they drew for each other. There has been nothing indiscreet and more importantly, nothing serious. Only recently, she cut one young man off when it came to her notice that he'd made a boast in relation to her.

But this, this is an intrusion. That Charles would *open* her diary, let alone read it, is a bombshell.

Here is another: he knew *exactly* where to find it.

She stands, paces, and finds herself gripping the horizontal of a high-backed chair. Patrice remembers her grandmother telling her how she would grip the back of a chair and breathe in as far as she could before her personal maid yanked the laces of her corset tight. To endure all that pain to give the outward appearance of being an ideal you are not, even if that ideal is unnatural.

"Charles," she hisses, "I don't know what you're playing at, but this is beneath you. *Beneath* you!" The blatancy of it. No attempt to cover his tracks. The thought, the very thought of marching downstairs and confronting him, after he's been drinking heavily, makes Patrice feel sick to her stomach. As for herself, adrenaline and a sedative are hardly the best recipe for persuasive argument. As infuriating as it is, there is no alternative. This will have to wait until the morning.

Patrice wakes just before nine, surprised at how thoroughly the tranquilliser did its job. No memory of getting into bed has survived the night; none of lying awake before falling asleep. The pill has left a dullness in its wake; a sense of being off kilter. As she sits up, Patrice feels as if she's still lying sideways. Automatically, she throws out a hand to right herself, catching two fingers on something sharp. She shakes the pain away, watches a thin red line appear and sucks on it, cursing herself for misjudging the distance. But then she sees. The corner of the drawer has been left slightly ajar. Remembering and yet not quite remembering, Patrice pulls open the drawer and there, right in front of her, is her diary. "I must need my eyes tested!" she says out loud, knowing full well that she has always enjoyed twenty-twenty vision.

She scans the room as if expecting some logical explanation

to present itself. Crossland has been and gone. Her clothes are laid out. (She approves of the choice, elegant and understated. You can't go wrong with Hardy Amies.) Her tea tray sits on the table by the window. The curtains are drawn back, not fully, letting the day in gradually just as she likes them. Crossland is not the explanation she is looking for. And yet.

"Will there be anything else, ma'am?"

Patrice looks at herself critically in the mirror of her dressing table, from the left and the right and then back again. The appearance of crêpe skin in the hollow of her neck depresses her. "Crossland, you see me every day."

"I do, ma'am."

"Do you think I'm becoming forgetful?"

"Never, ma'am. Not you."

This, at least, is something. "Have you noticed anything out of place?"

Crossland bristles. "Is there a problem, ma'am?"

"Not with anything *you've* done." Patrice tries to smile. Crossland may be more than twenty years her senior, but she is indispensable. Without any exchange of words, Crossland knows exactly what she wants, the way she wants it. At some point, Patrice supposes, her personal maid may wish to retire, but she would never dare suggest it for fear she might be met with agreement. "It's simply a question."

"What kind of thing, ma'am?"

"Here. In my bedroom."

"No, ma'am. You're always most particular."

Crossland will be thinking about Patrice's clothes, how she checks to see if they need laundering and, after laundering, how she returns them to individual plastic zipped covers. The index cards she keeps inside each cover to refer to the matching handbag, gloves, shoes and wrap. "But what would you do? If you were to notice something where it shouldn't be?"

"I'd put it back in its rightful place, of course."

"I don't suppose," Patrice shakes her head, even as she says it, "I don't suppose I left my diary out, and you put it back in the drawer."

"Ah, now I'd make an exception for your diary, ma'am. I wouldn't have touched it when you were a girl, and I certainly wouldn't presume now. That, I'd have left where I found it."

"Yes," says Patrice. "That's exactly what I thought you'd say." But how she wishes it were not.

CHAPTER SEVEN

PATRICE

The club. From her seat behind the pillar in the alcove Patrice has laid claim to, she watches the drama unfold. The mirrors she had Terrence install, supposedly to improve the lighting, are set in panels, angled so that her reflection does not impede the view. There are blind spots, but they are few. An acceptable compromise. One step removed from the action, Patrice has already seen a reflected Margot trudge up and down the stairs from the club's main floor to the flat that the hostesses occupy. Now, stooping to leave a battered suitcase at the door to the main bar, the red-eyed girl approaches Terrence Blagdon. There is a certain inevitability about her movements. She knows what this is – an ending. Hugging the bar, the club's substantial owner seems prepared. He takes from his jacket pocket a brown envelope. The type he uses for the girls' wages and tips. He puts it on the bar, flattens one hand on top. Patrice knows that hand. Knows it is large and square; knows the oval of his gold signet ring. Margot looks down, waiting for the moment it is withdrawn. She nods several times, never once raising her eyes to meet Terrence's. The hostess understands she has broken the rules; that what is happening now (the suitcase, the day clothes she is wearing, her immediate dismissal) is the natural consequence. Margot would cut short this encounter if she could, but she cannot walk away, not yet. What is in that envelope is owed to her. Logic tells Patrice that Terrence has devised this particular form of torture. He wants the club's members – the tight knots of afternoon drinkers, armed with beers and cigarettes – to be absolutely clear. When one of them breaks the rules, his girls suffer. Look at the wise monkeys, how studiously they pretend not to be able to see or hear. How silent they remain. Is there one of them with a conscience? At last, Terrence lifts his hand. Shakes his head; looks away. Margot snatches the envelope, turns on her heel, stoops to pick up her belongings. Where will she go? Patrice looks to the men for a reaction, for a sign of sympathy, for anything. Not one of them breaks rank.

"Are you expecting anyone, ma'am?"

Patrice shifts her gaze; finds Vincent Stewart looking down at her. He has approached from her blind side. "Not imminently, no."

"Mind if I join you?" The newspaper journalist swings into a seat at the octagonal table which also faces the mirrored alcove, barely giving her a second glance.

Sigh as she may, although Patrice is not yet bored, the truth is that she soon will be. Normally she brings an amusing young person or two, volunteers willing to take the places of those who used to surround her. In certain circles, reputation is unimportant. In certain circles, notoriety is the thing. But today she has come alone. Many of the club's members are wary of her. Why would someone of Patrice's gender and from her background choose to while away her afternoons here? There must be places where women like her – socialites, wives of members of parliament and captains of industry – can go, where they lunch on oysters and trade *soupçons* of gossip. But suspicion isn't the only reason people keep their distance. Not everyone finds Patrice approachable. She isn't sure Vincent does, but they have been useful to each other. They have history. "I take it there's someone you want to keep an eye on."

"That *is* the chief advantage of your corner." He is scowling at something or someone beyond his own reflection.

"Charmed," Patrice says. From behind her pillar, she can watch without the majority being aware they are being watched. Vincent will have to be more careful.

"Cigarette?" His eyes trained on the glass, the journalist fumbles clumsily for his pack, succeeding in pushing it a little way in her direction.

"If it's all the same with you, I'll stick with my own." Patrice is not used to not being looked at. Not used to someone who doesn't care how she holds herself as she lifts her cigarette holder to her lips. What's more, with Vincent there, she no longer feels that she can be so blatant about watching others.

"A drink, then?"

"There is only so much soda water a person can stomach, but top up my glass if you must." Patrice nods to the ice bucket. Vincent tears his attention away from the mirror long enough to slosh an inch of water into the glass. "Thank you. So kind." She arches an eyebrow at the trail of small splashes he has left on the varnished wood of the table. Makes a point of unwrapping the linen napkin from the neck of the bottle, unfolding it and laying it over the spillage. Dark shadows appear on the white of the linen, spreading until they overlap.

With fewer distractions, the insipid watery music Terrence's new pianist is playing becomes harder to ignore. Almost an apology for itself. If this carries on, Patrice will be forced to have a word.

"So, what's new?" Vincent asks, his gaze suggesting that whatever she says will go over his head.

"Oh, just an average afternoon. A game of poker upstairs,

Margot's got herself into a spot of bother, poor girl, and if I'm not mistaken, our friend Sandy's day is heading in the same direction." Patrice decides to risk looking at what has Vincent gripped.

"Don't," he cautions urgently.

"Who or what shouldn't I be looking at?"

Down to his last inch of cigarette, Vincent takes one long pull, then grinds it into the ashtray. "Approaching Terry. Don't be taken in by appearances."

"How can I? I'm under strict instructions not to look." Patrice locates the club's owner who is shaking hands with someone she does not recognise. Suit a little too flashy, dark hair slicked back from his face, average height, slightly overweight but no match for Terrence's girth.

"Ever heard the name Maurice Conley?" Patrice feels her forehead furrow. "King of the Black Market," Vincent continues. "Known to his friends as Morrie. Owns a string of West End clubs, but has quite a track record, including a few spells on the inside."

She places the name. His repeated appearances at the Old Bailey have made headlines. A man who has a reputation for hearing of others' misfortunes and immediately wondering how he can turn them into a gold mine. "Fraud," she says with distaste.

"Not just fraud. Living off immoral earnings."

There is nothing threatening in the man's body language. But then she supposes Maurice Conley would be too clever for that. Patrice turns her attention to Terrence's youngest hostess, Valerie. She watches her greet Rory Chambers, one of the regulars (vague about his background, his business either shady or so dull as to be unworthy of comment) with a kiss on the cheek and then fuss about wiping off the imprint of her lipstick. Patrice remembers a time when she herself was someone who was worth watching. When she would put on quite a show. "Why would a man like Conley be interested in our little establishment?" she asks Vincent. "I can hardly imagine Terrence is a threat." Unless he's been branching out.

"Perhaps Conley's looking to buy, or expand his supply chain."

Patrice's eyebrows dance. Terrence is a man who knows how to get hold of things. Back in the day, he was her own black-market contact. Although Patrice always considered *her* needs entirely legitimate.

"Come along, Annie! Play us something that won't send us all to sleep. How about some swing?" Valerie's shout is met with murmurs of approval.

"Thank the Lord," says Patrice. Though she doesn't recognise the tune that the pianist strikes up, at least it has some life to it.

"Whatever the purpose of his visit *was*, I'd say Conley's interested in one thing and one thing only."

One glance is enough to tell Patrice that Valerie has captured his attention. With that instinct she seems to have for sensing whose eyes are fixed on her, Valerie looks over Rory's shoulder at the Black Market King, a quick combination of raised eyebrows and pressed-together lips that suggests she's sharing a private joke with him. "I take it he's not the sort you'd recommend as a boss to a sixteen-year-old girl," she says.

"Conley has no trouble recruiting. The more vulnerable, the better. He's there, posing as affable Uncle Morrie, ready to turn their desperation to his advantage. Wait, he's drinking up. Now they're shaking hands."

Patrice turns and looks directly. Sees only a back. She glances to the right, where Valerie is still fawning over Rory, but somehow the girl manages to catch Patrice's gaze and winks, and Patrice has that flustered feeling of having been caught out, yet wanting that eye contact, that wink. "Aren't you going to follow Conley?" she half-jokes, a cover for her discomfort.

"I'm more of a paper-trail sleuth. Besides, if there's a story, someone who isn't connected with the club will have to write it."

As Patrice suspected. "So you're not averse to leaking a little information to your colleagues at the news desk."

Vincent sips his ale, then turns his full attention to her. "Tell me, is the duke still fighting the good fight?"

This is what they do. Share titbits that the other might find useful. Patrice draws on the end of her cigarette holder. "A certain mass murderer has hardly helped the cause." Though she does not say it, the press has not helped either. A media circus had surrounded Haigh's case – little wonder when *The News of the World* paid for the man's defence. War has renewed the public's appetite for vengeance. Having fixated on the story of the Acid Bath Murderer for so long, they were baying for blood. No matter how much Patrice is tempted – and right now, seething as she is, she's sorely tempted – she won't steal Charles's thunder by telling Vincent that he saw the deed done. Not until her husband has delivered his report.

"No. I didn't see too many people jumping to Haigh's defence. What's your answer?"

Patrice has been thinking through an argument. There may be no better opportunity to try it out. "Reclassifying murder into different categories. I realise I may be oversimplifying matters but there must be a way of saying *this* man is a danger to the public and *this* man is not."

"But you'd retain the death penalty?"

"For the type there's no hope of rehabilitating, yes, but only as an interim measure."

"What does the duke have to say about that?"

"Charles is..." Patrice hesitates, a pause that fills with Valerie's laughter. It will not cause any damage if she continues. "He isn't open to compromise."

"Whereas you've set your sights on the endgame." This seems to be approval.

"We have to think of what the public will find palatable. You and I have lived through two wars in which a great number of good men lost their lives. I can understand those who might think that their husband or father or brother or son deserved to live, especially when compared with the man standing in the dock." It is impossible not to think of Haigh, laughing as his sentence was pronounced.

"Interesting."

"What?" Patrice's hands go to the hollow of her neck and find her string of pearls.

"You haven't once mentioned women; just men, fathers and brothers."

She mulls over what she has said (Vincent's right, of course) and defends herself. "Men are nine times more likely than women to commit murder. And as victims they are three times more likely than women to be killed by a stranger. Where we women come out on top is that we're at significantly higher risk of being murdered by our spouses." She gives Vincent a quick sarcastic smile. Although she says 'we', Patrice is well aware how unlikely it is that she will become a statistic. She may have come through humbling times, but this – this club, this finding herself alone, old friends refusing her invitations – is the worst of it.

"Men lack self-control, is that it?" Vincent sits back in his chair, smiling, challenging.

From a distance of several decades, it comes back to her. The moment she snapped. It was Easter, her cousin Laurie had come to stay and rain had them confined to the nursery wing. Laurie made use of his time by teasing her. Hours and hours of prodding, pulling pigtails, boasting, and all the while Patrice had repeated to herself, *sticks and stones,* holding it inside until, without any warning, her hand took charge.

The first she knew was the sharp sound of a slap and Laurie holding his cheek and bawling like a baby. And even though it was straight to bed with no dinner for Patrice, she had done something she would never have thought herself capable of. It set her apart from other girls. Marked her. Or that is how it seemed. "We women have subtler ways of settling our differences." And, with the diary incident on her mind, Patrice broods about what those ways might be.

Vincent salutes her with his pint glass. "Sometimes, ma'am, I wonder if it's worth trying to catch you out. You're obviously strongly in favour of abolition. Have you given any thought to becoming more actively involved?"

Patrice sets down her glass and says curtly. "It's Charles's cause. I've already told you where our views diverge."

"But yours is the better argument. I really think an interim measure might be the way to secure the long-term goal."

Vincent leans forward, and is so uncharacteristically animated, so encouraging, that for a moment Patrice thinks, *This could be my opportunity to be of use.* "You're not married, are you?" she asks.

"I think you already know the answer to that."

"I'd be pitting myself against my husband." And as Patrice says it, she imagines. In a public arena, in support of a cause, beating Charles in a debate.

"Pity." The journalist sits back. Gives her a shrug of a smile, and she feels disappointed. Disappointed that he should drop the subject, rather than say, *But this wouldn't be personal.* "One thing's certain. Abolition's an emotive subject. A Royal Commission isn't going to solve it."

"On that, Charles would be the first to agree. But if not that, then what?"

"Something beyond our control. A miscarriage of justice of such enormity that the majority agree it must never be allowed to happen again."

"A sacrificial lamb," Patrice muses, pursing her lips.

CHAPTER EIGHT

CAROLINE

Not that kind of model, you say? No, I'm not disappointed, why should I be? A private photography club? *The* centre of photographic excellence, is it? Oh, and *gentlemen,* are they? Just because I'm fresh out of Felixstowe doesn't mean I can't guess what goes on in those sorts of places. Well, I'm relieved they don't let just *anyone* in. Each photographer hires his own room and a model. You see, to me that says there isn't even safety in numbers! Well, why didn't you say you're a member? Gosh, now I feel awful. You'd be happy for a daughter of yours to model there, would you? Not that you have a daughter. I know. You mentioned that.

It's just that I, I thought that if I could get a little help with the way I speak, if I could lose my accent, I might apply to be a dance hostess. I'm not a professional dancer, no. *Although I fooled that American serviceman who took me to a dance club. And I'm a quick learner.* I went to take a look at the Café de Paris. Princess Margaret and the Duchess of Kent had been in the night before. The doorman gave me a tour. They've spent a fortune repairing the hole Hitler blew in the roof. Oh, you've been! You'd really take me? And you might know someone who'd help me with my elocution? Yes,

I'll give the Camera Club some serious thought. But I've no experience in modelling, and that's what you always come up against. No, I suppose a serious photographer wouldn't want his photographs to look like fashion adverts. Would I have to –? A guinea an hour. Yes, it might lead to something else. Absolutely no harm looking into it, as you say. Manchester Square? I pass it on my walk from Bond Street Tube.

Caroline removes the pipe cleaners from her hair; carefully makes up her face. Panstick, rouge and lipstick, all bought out of a suitcase on one of Brixton's back-street pavements.

"Genuine Max Factor. Ask no questions, I'll tell no lies." An expression of defiance teamed with turned-up trousers. Small-scale black-market racket. What's the harm? The man has a family to feed, and knock-down prices are all Caroline can afford. Besides, life in London is one long racket.

There's no full-length mirror at the YWCA. Just as well. Caroline might be tempted to try out some 'artistic poses'. On the walk from the tube, it takes every last measure of her resolve not to bolt. A public telephone box provides sanctuary for a few breathless moments. *There's nothing personal about it. It's like a trip to the doctor's. You're told to cough, and you cough.*

She pretends to be digging in her coat pockets for a coin, but there is no one she can call; no telephone at home. When Caroline needs to speak to her mother, she writes and arranges a time for Ma to make her way to the post office, although Ma lets Caroline know exactly how much of an inconvenience this is. In her mother's opinion, few things can't be dealt with on two sheets of writing paper. But not the thing that haunts her most. *Don't go to Uncle Anthony for money.* I'll *send you the money. But if you really can't wait, don't send Betty. Please don't send Betty.*

"If it's a hostessing job you're after, I belong to a club. The owner might be looking for someone." The photographer emerges from behind his tripod. "Chin just a little higher. And if you could perhaps move your hands along the back of the chair a little, so that they cover –. Oh, perfect. Perfect."

A body is just a body. Except that this is *her* body and Caroline is in a situation she's never before needed to imagine herself in. *Don't be such a baby. Actresses have to change costumes in front of cameramen. Pretend you're auditioning for a part.* She raises her chin and tries to look at home in her wood-panelled surroundings. "This club you belong to." Conversation is punctuated by small clicks of the shutter.

"I'm sorry?" The nameless man who's paid two guineas for her time looms behind the camera.

With no wish to ruin his shot, Caroline times her moment to speak. "There's dancing, is there?" It feels strange to be making conversation – any sort of conversation. But somehow Caroline thinks it would feel stranger still not to speak. Just to be looked at.

The man makes minute adjustments to the controls of his camera. "Not so much. It's the sort of place you go to get warmed up before going on to a nightclub."

One by one, her hopes deflate. Down goes Caroline's idea of a big band, a dance floor lit by crystal chandeliers.

"But we do have music. There's a pianist."

Down goes the image Caroline had of herself descending the staircase, indistinguishable in her finery from the socialites, and David Niven watching her, so dazzled that he can only stare blankly. "I see."

"Not what you had in mind?"

She'd known it wouldn't all be glamour. Not every dance hostess finds herself partnered by captains of industry, still less by film stars. But Caroline would make her dance partners feel good about themselves, and there would be tips. "I've rather set my sights on the Café de Paris."

"You and a hundred other girls!" He stands back from his camera, holds a hand over one eye, and with the other hand, signals that Caroline should move a fraction to her right.

She can see where he wants her. Half in and half out of the shadow, and it suits her. She'll be less recognisable. "Here?" she asks.

His only answer is to clear his throat. Older than her father, younger than her grandfather. Not unattractive, well-groomed with an RAF-style moustache, well-dressed. The type who might indulge in expensive shows of appreciation. And she needs to have someone else lined up in case things with Finbar don't work out. "The Café de Paris *is* the best," she ventures. "I expect it to be competitive."

"Aim high. I applaud you for that. With a face like yours, you'll have as good a chance as anyone – even if you have to hold out for the opportunity." He straightens his back once more, observes her and frowns. "If you could just perhaps put your left hand on your right shoulder. Oh, yes, that works very well. Hold still."

Caroline can't afford to 'hold out' for anything, not with her mother's constant reminders that they're counting on her – as if she could forget! She must find a stopgap. Occasional modelling work won't do. Not even at the rate this man is paying.

"Why don't you relax for a moment? Sometimes it's best to break the pose and come back to it." He repositions the tripod, moves a cable. "Ask away, I can tell you're dying to."

"Your club? If there's no dancing, how do hostesses earn their money?"

"From what I gather, it's a commission type of arrangement."

"Commission?"

"That's right. They sit, chat and encourage members to drink more than they might otherwise. Ready to try again?

Could you, er..." He draws his shoulders back, and Caroline mirrors his movement. "Whenever you offer one of the hostesses a drink, the answer's always, 'How sweet of you. I'd love a glass of champagne.' And champagne only comes by the bottle. My understanding is that when I buy a bottle, I'm paying the girl's wages."

Being paid to talk and drink doesn't sound too bad, not when you consider what she's doing right at this moment. And right at this moment Caroline has no hope of making ends meet.

"You like champagne, do you?"

The lens she's been viewing her dilemma through begins to shift. Caroline, who's never in her life tasted wine, let alone champagne, replies, "Show me a girl who doesn't."

"Quite."

"Perhaps I *should* explore my options."

"Never does any harm, in my opinion. I doubt whether a job at the Café de Paris comes with accommodation."

"Accommodation?" Her attempt at sounding casual fails.

"There's a flat above the club, quite nice. It's put aside for the hostesses. I imagine you'd be expected to share."

"Anything that gets me out of the YWCA." Too late, Caroline realises she's blabbed. Nothing shouts 'green' quite as loudly as giving the YWCA as your address. "It's my fifth week there and already it feels like months!" she admits.

"I could take you to meet the owner after we're finished here. Drinks are on me. Unless you have plans?"

Finbar will be waiting at the Argyll Arms, but the thing about Finbar knowing so many people is that Caroline needn't feel guilty about jilting him. If she doesn't show, he'll just tag along elsewhere. "No. No plans," she says.

"I'll tell you what. Why don't we call it a day? I'll pack away my kit and you go and get dressed."

Panic rises within her. "But we agreed on two hours."

"I'm not counting. Besides, I'm happy with the shots I've got."

Grateful, Caroline slips into the robe she was handed on arrival. "Give me five minutes." She makes her way along the narrow carpeted corridor to the small room where she left her clothes in a neat pile. Here, she checks that the seams of her stockings are straight, sighs at her reflection. Hardly the sort of thing to wear for an evening out, or a job interview for that matter, but it would be rude to back out.

He stands, tips his hat. "Alexander Scott."

It seems ridiculous to feel shy now that she's dressed, but Caroline does. She hadn't intended to go for a drink with a man who's seen her naked. It feels dangerous. "Caroline. Caroline Wilby."

"Actually, no one calls me Alexander. Call me Sandy."

"Then Sandy it is," she says.

The cab pulls up outside a parade of shops that occupy the ground floors of Dutch-style five-storey buildings. *You're exploring your options, that's all.* But Caroline's fears aren't founded. There's nothing seedy about these surroundings. This world of chauffeur-driven automobiles and green and gold Harrods livery is no place for a basement dive. Rather than leading her down a set of concrete steps, with jazz teasing from an unlit doorway as she'd anticipated, her friend from the Camera Club knocks at a discreet black door between a fashionable ladies' hairdressing salon and a shop that sells expensive-looking leather luggage.

They are greeted by a uniformed doorman. "Good to see you, Mr Scott."

"Likewise, George."

"And your lady friend, of course. Won't you come in, Miss?"

Sandy bends over the desk to sign a bottle green leather-bound book. "George here guards the membership book with his life. Isn't that right?"

"Quite so, sir."

Caroline doesn't steal a glance at the names that need guarding to this extent. Instead, looking at everything through her mother's eyes, she takes in her surroundings. The walls are duck-egg blue with cornicing picked out in white with traces of gold. If Ma were ever to pay a flying visit, her first impression would be one of respectability.

The doorman discreetly checks the name Sandy has written in the membership book before asking, "May I take your coat, Miss Wilby? Am I right in thinking it's your first visit with us?"

"It is, yes." Caroline turns as she slips her arms out of the sleeves of the raincoat she inherited when her mother was done with it. "Thank you." She pretends to be someone who always has her coat taken by doormen, trying not think about the tear in the lining.

"Have a pleasant evening, sir." George tips his hat. "And I hope you enjoy your time with us, Miss Wilby."

"Thank you."

"After you." Sandy indicates the streamlined curve of a Regency staircase that stretches up towards the light.

Caroline cannot help it. She takes an instant dislike to the man Sandy introduces her to. Terrence Blagdon. One of those men whose defining feature is his girth. He's surrounded by a dense haze of cigar smoke.

"Mr Blagdon." Caroline finds herself stifling a cough. She extends a hand, at the same time taking in his vein-threaded nose.

"Call me Terry. So you're looking for work, are you?"

"That's right."

He's shameless about the way he sizes her up, and as his eyes rake her body, down and then up again, Caroline feels it as a physical thing. As if his hands are on her. She might as well be standing here stark naked. "Are you single?" Terry asks.

"Yes." How can she object when she'd have been judged by the same criteria at the Café de Paris (though, there, Caroline imagined that she might be asked to demonstrate her foxtrot)? Here, it's his blatancy. To the club's owner, she's no more than teeth, tits and tail.

"I'll order some drinks, shall I?" As Sandy makes himself scarce, Caroline's heart skips. An introduction really did mean an introduction. She's very much on her own.

"I expect you'd like the grand tour?" Terry presses a large paw to the small of her back, lower than she's comfortable with, steering her in front of him. Caroline weaves her way, avoiding collisions with the twos and the threes, those who continue their tall stories in hoarse, loud tones, but turn their heads to scan her head to foot. She wonders if Terry is taking note, if this is part of her interview. He greets visitors by name, indulging in hearty handshakes and back slaps, leaving no one in doubt about his strength; shouting out to the barmaid, "Elise, Mr Summers is running dry!" and, raising an empty glass, "Another gin for Hugo and be sharp about it!"

All that parading and posturing. Pointing out the main bar, the separate dining area and, to the rear, the kitchens and cloakrooms. *How does a man like him make his money?* She doubts he's an ex-barrow boy who just happened to strike lucky. Newcomer though she may be, something tells Caroline that Terrence Blagdon hasn't stopped at doing what needs to be done to put a roof over his family's heads.

As they arrive in the hallway, a young woman shimmies past. Her figure has a sculpted look. Her swing dress strains tight around the bodice, every taut stitch on display. "Alright if I pop upstairs for a while?"

Terry consults his wristwatch. "Be back by nine fifteen."

The woman flashes him a smile. "Quarter of an hour should

do it." Perhaps it's the fact that Terry's cigar never strays far from his mouth that accounts for the way his eyes narrow, but Caroline can't help noticing the intimate sarcasm that passes between them. The lack of distance. They do not touch – not quite. They have a code. A shorthand. When Terry turns back to Caroline, he says, "One of my girls."

A man hurries past carrying an ice bucket, in it a bottle and two upturned cocktail glasses. Caroline turns her head to watch him take the stairs two at a time, just as the hostess, hand trailing, nails filed to points, turns towards a second flight. She's tempted to ask if the club has another floor above this one, but Mr Blagdon says, "Another devotee of the high life," cigar smoke in every word. Caroline's eyes smart in protest.

He shepherds her back towards the bar. "I pay my girls three pounds for every bottle of champagne they sell and ten per cent commission on any other food or drink they persuade customers to buy. The potential's there to earn double what you would in a factory or a shop, and compared to the alternatives the hours are more than sociable." He lays out his terms like a grand spread on a picnic blanket: everything too good to turn down. There must be a wasp in the jam. Caroline looks about for the flash of yellow and black, listens for the tell-tale buzz. She stands at the narrow bar, and takes in the impressive line-up of spirits, each bottle backlit in its own ornate alcove. Well-stocked *despite* rationing. For blind eyes to be turned, Terrence Blagdon must have his share of influential customers.

"Do you smoke?" he asks.

Working in a place like this, with the concentrated fug in the room, there would be no argument against it. Caroline thinks back to the way Finbar passed the cigarette from his mouth to hers, suggesting an intimacy had been established. Even if all she were to do was to lean closer… "If you pay commission on cigarettes, I do."

"Smart girl."

She looks around her to corner tables where tales are being spun, and to snug window seats where hostesses tease and fawn. "Apart from sales, what would I have to do, exactly?"

Terry shakes his head, dismissing her question as unnecessary. "Sit, chat, make our visitors feel at home. What we provide is a home from home. Sometimes a sanctuary *from* home. You know how it is. My number one rule is that nothing you hear, nothing you see, goes outside the doors of this club. When I say we provide sanctuary, I mean sanctuary. Do I make myself clear?"

She wants to say that she's good at keeping things close to her chest. That she's capable of locking secrets up and throwing away the key.

"You're not to tell a soul that your father's left us."

"Not even the boys and Betty?"

"Especially not them!"

"I'll have to say something."

"People disappear in wartime. It's not unusual."

"Am I to say he's doing his bit for the war effort?"

Her mother scoffed. *"They'll give him too much credit."* But she had no better suggestion, so that became the line they repeated.

All Caroline says to Terry is, "Completely."

"Good."

There is still something that hasn't been said. Caroline doesn't have the luxury of only thinking of herself. Too much is at stake. But neither can she afford to walk into a situation blinkered. "And for sitting and talking, you'll pay me three pounds?"

"*Provided* the customer buys a bottle of champagne."

"Do I still get ten per cent if they don't?"

"Champagne's your way in, then the ten per cent."

She lets this sink in. To earn enough to send money home,

Caroline will have to encourage men to spend money that should end up on their own tables. Didn't her father once hand their rent money over the bar of the Hound and Hares, knowing that Ma would give him hell?

"Plus, you keep your own tips, I supply your evening wear and as long as everything works out, we can discuss the option of a flat." He points his cigar at the ceiling. "Not a bad address, by all accounts." This is the clincher, and Terry knows it. He holds Caroline in his gaze; lowers his voice. Here comes the sting. "Anything above and beyond the conversation and the flattery is up to you. But I take my cut. Do we understand each other?"

We're counting on you. The constant whisper. Her mother, her conscience.

No. Caroline will not blush. "I think we do."

"You think we do, or we do?"

His directness makes her think beyond his ambitions to her own situation. "You asked if I'm single. What if I were to meet someone I liked?"

He shakes his head. "I expect my girls to treat all club members equally. No rivalry, no reasons for rivalry, that's my rule."

She smiles ruefully. "Why buy another man's girlfriend a bottle of champagne?"

"I knew you'd understand. Well. The offer's there. Mull it over." He squeezes her shoulder before moving on to the next person.

A job offer. Somehow, despite the way Caroline is dressed and a number of awkward gaffes, she's passed muster. What strikes her next is the absence of a high-pressure sell. Clever, when you think about it. She has the facts. The decision is entirely down to her.

"There you are!" Her friend from the Camera Club presents her with a shallow cocktail glass. "I believe you mentioned that you like champagne."

How would a girl who drinks champagne respond? "Lovely." Caroline grasps the slender stem as she would a pencil, her hand just underneath the bowl of the glass. Tiny bubbles stream upwards and burst on the surface. She should savour this moment. She's never had a glass so fine between her lips. Through it the room is concave, straw-coloured, blurred. Her first taste is bitter-sweet.

"Tell me," Sandy demands. "How did it go with Terry?"

Caroline tries to think of a response tactful enough to match her careful movement as she lowers her glass, trying not to spill a drop. "He's blunt, I'll give him that."

"I'll say! Of course," he plants his elbows on the high-polish of the mahogany and leans towards her, "he's also a crook."

She finds herself gaping.

"Surely you worked *that* out for yourself. But what's a little small-scale racketeering in the grand scheme of things?"

"But you brought me here! Are you on…?"

His raises his eyebrows unapologetically, inviting: *Do your worst.*

Caroline lowers her tone. "You don't have some kind of *arrangement* with Terry, do you?"

"Am I a procurer of callow young women?" A smooth shake of his head says that Sandy is quite unflappable. "What a first impression I seem to have made!"

"Then what?"

"It's really quite simple. I thought you deserved to know what your options were."

Caroline can't help herself. "You think I'm desperate." Outrage surfaces. "You're throwing me a crust!"

"Calm down. I think you're attractive, articulate, healthily cynical and not as easily impressed by money as other new-comers I've met. Which is just as well, because no shortage of it changes hands here. And you've just proved you're no walkover. I expect you can spot a bore or a bully from a mile off. Sadly," he scratches the side of his nose, "we all of us are beholden to someone. For many, it's parents or spouses, but Terrence Blagdon pays better and demands less, in the long run."

"So, I'm supposed to believe that you're just another man who comes here to meet girls?"

"Oh, my dear." Sandy shakes his head, a wistful smile playing on his lips. "You've got me all wrong." He pauses very slightly, long enough to place a hand on her forearm. "I'm a congenital bachelor." She looks at him blankly. "Girls don't interest me. At least not in the way you suggest."

His admission involves quite a risk. Back at home, after Mr Nicholls was arrested, their neighbour, Mrs Dickinson, took great pride in telling Caroline's mother it was she who'd informed on him. She considered it her Christian duty. Ma waited until Mrs Dickinson was out of the way to say, "Don't expect me to disapprove. I'm not in favour of all this modern broadmindedness." But this is London. Perhaps people here are more forward-thinking. Still, Caroline backpedals, perplexed. "But the Camera Club..."

"I appreciate the female form as much as the next person. Don't you?"

Her brow twitches. "I'm not sure I've ever thought about it." *Listen to yourself. You sound like a prude.*

"Think about it now. Over there." He nods towards a cross between the sort of soft, silky, well-groomed woman described on the pages of *Everywoman* and a blonde bombshell from the silver screen. She's squeezing through a gap between two drinkers, a gap that's obviously inches too narrow for her, and exaggerating an apology under the pretence of making sure that drinks haven't been spilt.

"Shall I tell you what I see when I look at Valerie?"

"Go on." Caroline lifts her glass to her lips, experiences again the tingle of champagne on the tip of her tongue.

"I admire the way she's wearing that dress."

It's a garment straight out of *How to Dress to Please Men*. Assuming, that is, the man isn't looking for someone to take home to meet his mother. "It certainly is a good dress." An indication of the trappings that being a hostess could bring.

"It's more than good!" Sandy counters, then zooms in. "She's in control of exactly how much she reveals. See how she rests her hand on the neckline? The way the fabric pulls tight across her buttocks when she leans forwards?" Never before has Caroline had a conversation with someone who uses the word 'buttocks' as casually as she would 'arm' or 'leg'. And the girl! To be so spirited, so uninhibited; to know how to turn every head in her direction. As Sandy continues, Caroline is drawn deeper into the performance. "Everything else about her says that she's helpless, incapable of lighting her own cigarette, too frail to go to the bar, even the way she twirls her glass."

Just think of the things you could learn from her. This girl knows how to navigate London's noisy streets; knows which buses go where; doesn't hesitate before stepping onto a moving staircase. When she summons a lift in a department store, she knows exactly which floor she needs, and when she leaves the lift she knows her way straight to the correct counter. She goes to the cinema regularly; probably eats tinned peaches. The few things she doesn't know, she knows how to get.

"It's so calculated." Sandy's voice is full of admiration. "Men's clothes don't offer the same opportunities."

Caroline looks at his well-cut suit, teamed with a pale blue silk tie; nothing but face, neck and hands on display. "I don't suppose they do." Her limbs feel liquid and her focus softens a shade. "So how do you…?"

"Show I'm interested? It's all in the look." He draws on his cigarette, sucking in his cheekbones in a way she suspects is calculated, identifies a target and drops his gaze to the man's crotch.

Caroline's eyes widen. A demonstration was the last thing she expected. In her glass bubbles burst, like water boatmen alighting on the surface of a pond. From above, her hand is a bird, her index finger a beak, the stem of the glass, its eye. "What if he..."

"Takes umbrage? I shall say, 'My good man, I don't know what you're talking about. You simply walked into my line of vision.'"

Caroline blinks. "Should I leave you to it?"

"Absolutely not! Have another drink. I insist."

It would have been disappointing had this signalled the end of their evening. The prospect of returning to her drab dorm at the YWCA is looking less and less attractive.

"Far less obvious for two men to strike up a conversation in the presence of an attractive young lady."

"Well?" Caroline asks. "Anything?"

"The gods don't seem to be smiling today." With admiring eyes, he watches the man walk the width of the room. "Pity."

There's a fearlessness about Sandy. To him, failure is water off a duck's back. Caroline thinks of the knock-backs, the bruised pride, the mistakes that made her wary of trying things a second time. She too must become an opportunist. More than that, she must learn to *invent* opportunities.

"Aren't there only so many, what I mean is, don't you already know who's likely to...?"

Sandy tops up her glass, and as bubbles cluster on the surface what comes to mind as inappropriately as laughter at a funeral is last spring's frogspawn; helping her brother decant his catch from the village pond into an empty jam jar.

"You can never be sure, just because someone's wearing a wedding ring. They wouldn't *be* here if they were happily married, now, would they?"

"You make it sound like rather a sad place."

"Our Kensington outpost?" Sandy feigns offence. "It's a game, this life. Didn't you realise that?"

"Of course I did," Caroline protests, but she doesn't know this set of rules. Someone could cheat and she would have no way of knowing.

"Have a good look. And by that, I mean a *really* good look beneath the tinsel. If you decide to take Terry up on his offer, your whole life will revolve around the club. You need to be sure that you're prepared for all that entails. Now here comes a breath of fresh air."

She notes the change in Sandy's tone and follows his gaze. Realisation that the girl in the killer dress is making her way towards their table makes Caroline giddy. The tips of her ears burn fiercely.

"Darling Sandy!" The girl swoops. "Rescue me from that crashing bore."

He returns the girl's embrace. "Didn't I warn you?"

"I suppose you did." She pouts. "But honestly. I've just had to endure a lecture on how we'll be at war again in three years' time. Apparently the Russians are up to their eyeballs in atomic bombs and won't stop until the whole of Europe is Communistic. I didn't dare question whether Communistic is actually in the dictionary. That would have triggered a whole new debate. What are you two talking about? Vital affairs of state?"

Caroline finds that the question is aimed at her.

"Our Kensington outpost, of course." Sandy dredges the champagne bottle from the ice bucket and tops up Valerie's glass. "Caroline here is considering whether she should take Mr Blagdon up on the offer of a job."

"Oh, but you must!" Valerie leans her head close to Caroline's. "Margot's just left us in the lurch. It's the perfect time to cash in on her tips."

"You like it here, do you?" Caroline ventures.

"Gosh, there's a question." Her laugh gives the impression of indecision. "Do I like it here, Sandy?"

"*I* like it, and I have to pay for the pleasure."

"When you think of it like that, it's free membership to a club I'd never be able to afford otherwise. Plus, collecting people is my hobby, and this is as good a place as any for that."

"Collecting people?" For the first time since arriving in London, Caroline is on the verge of losing the sense that she will at any moment be cast out of the Garden of Eden. She feels included.

"I have a copy of *Who's Who* – it's only a couple of years out of date –"

Behind a cupped hand, Sandy interjects, "Pre-war."

"And then there's the society columns. When I think I recognise a name, I look them up to see if they're a someone."

"Valerie's your person if you want to know who's who, who's courting who, and who's cheating on who."

She pushes at Sandy's arm. "You make it sound so trivial! This is essential research. A tip's a tip, but I prefer tips that are enjoyable to earn. And, besides, you can hardly expect me to pass up on the opportunity to hear someone confirm some of those rumours."

Caroline is aghast. "You *ask?*"

"Not straight out. But if we hit it off," a shrug, "I might just say that 'a little bird told me' and watch the reaction. You can always tell when they're not telling the truth."

"And do you get many someones?"

Valerie holds her glass so casually it looks as if she might drop it. "Everyone from minor royals and high court judges to gangsters. In between are socialites and the odd actor." Caroline holds her breath. What she wants to hear are the words *casting agents, acclaimed directors.* "MPs, diplomats, and the lowest of the low, the journalists." Valerie leans close enough for Caroline to feel her breath. "They're the ones who always look as if they're listening to what's going on behind them." As unlikely as this sounds, Valerie turns her back and proves that she's not only a shrewd observer but quite a comedienne.

"Only the ones Terry has vetted," Sandy says, with a raise of his eyebrows, "and that means those with secrets of their own to hide."

Sudden laughter draws Caroline's attention to the far reaches of the room. An older woman, handsome rather than beautiful, enviably dressed, though not in what Caroline thinks of as evening wear. "She isn't a hostess."

"Ah," agrees Sandy. "The corner cabaret! Well observed." He hunkers down to her height, a co-conspirator. "Tell me what else you see."

"Oh yes, do!" Valerie insists. "Can I squeeze in between you?" She takes her place on the window seat without waiting for an answer.

The moment is there for the taking. Caroline purses her lips as she zooms in on body language and what little dialogue drifts their way. "She's entertaining rather than being entertained. She's no guest."

A single nod from the Camera Club. "Again, correct."

Caroline lifts an index finger in disagreement. "'Entertaining' is the wrong word." She says this just as the three men in the woman's company throw back their heads and laugh, making no attempt to outdo her with anecdotes of their own.

Sandy raises his eyebrows. "Oh, she's quite the raconteur."

"What I mean is she's holding court."

"One of our few lady members. Something of an enigma."

"What sort of woman joins a club like this?"

Valerie crosses one leg over the other as if to say, *I'll take this one.* "There are several qualifying criteria. First you have to be moneyed."

"More so than the men," adds Sandy, topping up their champagne.

"And unhappily married."

Sandy leans across Valerie to clink Caroline's glass. "Divorce being more unthinkable than adultery."

"Social standing high enough to be above criticism." Valerie defers to Sandy.

"But in need of a safe place to let down your hair."

Caroline protests: "She doesn't look like someone who ever lets her hair down."

He winces. "You're only half correct. She doesn't drink."

"Then why join this type of club? Unless..." Caroline nods. She has answered her own question. "She *also* needs somewhere beyond the gaze of journalists."

"Actually," Valerie says confidentially, "the duchess is very practised at working our journalists. She feeds them scraps and in return she knows who to go to when she wants something published."

Sandy raises his eyebrows. "Or more importantly, not published."

"Anyway." Valerie raises one hand and ripples her fingers in the direction of someone she recognises. "She always has the corner table."

"Really?" says Caroline. "I had her down as someone who likes to be the centre of attention."

"It has the most flattering light." Valerie cups her face and leans backwards so that Caroline finds herself looking down at her fluttering eyelashes.

Sandy pooh-poohs the suggestion. "It's not because she knows which angle she looks best from. It's so she can keep watch."

"She likes women." Valerie's exaggerated whisper lifts the ends of Caroline's hair.

Again, Sandy is unconvinced. "I wouldn't be so sure!"

"Think what you like." Valerie sits up straight and shrugs. "I'm forever catching her eyeing me up."

Caroline isn't surprised. "But she's surrounded by men," she says. Right now an eager young escort is tripping over himself to earn a place at her right hand.

"Who invariably go home with Sandy." Valerie squeezes his knee and Sandy shrugs and spreads his hands. "Personally, I can't imagine anyone ever smudging that lipstick or putting a hair out of place. They're only there to give the duchess an excuse for looking."

Who's to say if Valerie expects to be taken seriously? All Caroline can do is play along. "What do you do when you catch her watching you?"

Valerie jumps to her feet, bends her knees and shimmies. "I give her a little wiggle."

"*Valerie! Mr Egheart is asking for you.*" Terry's voice cuts through the smoke.

"Dear Mr Egheart. Gave me the sweetest mink stole. Well, duty calls. You will say yes, won't you Caroline? We'll have such fun." Valerie blows a kiss then goes to attend to a man who might have been a sergeant major in a former life.

Caroline has lost count of how much champagne she's had. The beginnings of a headache are throbbing at her temples, but she can still think for herself. "How did you know I've been offered a job?" she asks.

"The same way I know this is your first bottle of champagne." Sandy refills her glass and lodges the empty bottle neck-down in the ice. "Shall we order another?"

CHAPTER NINE

URSULA

Once the hotel room comes back into focus, Ursula's first thought is to check that the curtains are drawn; that no photographers have captured the moment she flung herself down on the bed. Overnight, so it seemed, scaffolding sprang up on the building opposite. This morning's scene resembled those famous photographs of New York construction workers taking a break at the top of the Empire State building. Ursula doesn't want her tears to be misinterpreted. At the same time, it would be dishonest to pretend she doesn't feel sorry for her predicament. Of course she does.

She's struggling to make it add up. The night before she left for London, they'd got a little tipsy, she and Mack. He pulled her close and said, "Call me 'the renowned director'. I demand to be called 'the renowned director'," and Ursula had put on her haughtiest voice and said, "Your credentials don't impress me, Mr Clement Meade, I am soon to be married to the renowned director Donald Flood," and Mack had picked her up and said, "Damn right you are."

Damn right you are.

Ursula had thought she was going to be another Rita Hayworth. Still married to Robin at the beginning of her courtship with Mack, she'd expected the public to boycott her films, but when she married Mack, all that damage would be repaired. Everyone would understand that theirs wasn't some shabby affair. Her mistake had been marrying Robin. No one had warned Ursula that longing alone could be so powerful that she'd credit it with undeserved qualities. A yearning to give herself to another person. Once that sacrifice was made, 'love' was the obvious justification. Things were different with Mack. They had a meeting not just of bodies but of minds.

Or so she'd thought.

Now Mack has destroyed the only future Ursula imagined. And the alternative? She'll forever be cast as the wanton actress who failed in her attempt to destroy the Floods' sure-footed union. "All marriages have their ups and downs," Lindsay will say, stoic, steadfast, indulgent of her husband's lapses. "Believe me, I *never* considered *the actress* to be a serious threat." And the irony is, the ending couldn't be any more Hollywood had Preston Sturges scripted it. 'Other Woman Gets Her Comeuppance.'

Self-pity won't do. Silvia must be Ursula's focus. How will her daughter react when she learns that the man Mummy left her for has left Mummy? Will she assume that with *that man* removed from the picture, Mummy will come home? How to explain to a child that *Marrying Daddy was a mistake but you – you were very much wanted.* Especially when she's become virtually a stranger. All the time that Ursula is based in the States, it's been impossible to insist on visitation rights – she is, after all, that perversion of nature: a mother who left her child. But if Silvia were to discover that Ursula is in London, separated from her by no more than a dozen miles, and hasn't done everything in her power to try and see her – her own child – how would Silvia ever forgive her? Over there, in the bottom of the wardrobe, a pink cotton dress brought from America lies folded in layers of tissue paper. Ursula wanted to give it to her daughter in person (this is what she told Robin), to see her eyes light up, hear her say, 'I love it! Thank you, Mummy!'

"Silvia has dresses. She doesn't need any more dresses," he replied, and when Ursula pressed her ex-husband: "Look, Ursula, this really isn't a good time." He always had that way about him. When he used her name, Ursula felt that he was the adult, and she the child. This was his way of trying to exert authority over her.

"Another time, then," she'd said so breezily you'd never know another internal seam was being ripped apart. "Just let me know when. I'm here for the whole season."

There was a pause after that. She remembers the pause. Knew what was coming. "It isn't going to happen, Ursula. I have my reasons."

"Well, perhaps we should talk about them."

"I'll address them in court," Robin said. "If and when the time comes."

And that was his stance *before*. Lord knows what he'll say when he learns that Silvia will soon have a half-brother or sister, a child born out of wedlock, something Ursula must tell Silvia, first-hand, and soon. And, to make that possible, she'll have to get down on her knees and beg.

Robin is going to lap this up!

She catches sight of her red-rimmed eyes in the mirror; despairs at how puffy they are. Caught in the cogs of the twentieth century publicity machine, there's no point complaining about lack of privacy, the constant feeling that she's on trial. Outside Ursula's hotel and using trickery and disguises to gain access to the lobby, lurk the world's press photographers (like Robin, they have no inkling of the scoop that awaits them). Cameras are trained on doors and windows in the hope of snapping anything remotely usable: a picture of a goddess or a shot of Ursula looking slightly off-colour, so that they can speculate on the cause of her imperfections. Possible illness or – heaven forbid! – that she's let herself go. Never thinking that she might leave for the theatre without make-up; that the role of a missionary doesn't call for rouge. Ursula's own thoughts shift sideways, homewards: *I must warn Norma.*

"Norma! It's me. Listen, I was thinking. Seeing as I'm not there and Mack isn't either, you should take some time off."

"But Miss –"

"Let's not beat around the bush. I know Mack isn't coming back. And, no, I don't blame you one bit for not telling me. Your loyalties were torn." Ursula sees the framed photograph on her bedside table. Her and Mack. The shot was taken at a little shack-like place with gingham tablecloths and two options of wine: red or white. No one paid them the slightest attention. They were just two people in love, the sort that makes everything else irrelevant – or so Ursula had thought. A reminder of her self-deception. She slams the frame glass-side down. Mack was not her Prince Aly Khan.

What has she done?

"I've felt just awful, Miss Delancy. You have every right to be angry."

"Not with you! Mr Flood put you in a dreadful position. But now that I know, I think it would be a good idea for you to close up the house."

"Are you firing me?" The housekeeper's voice wobbles.

"Fire you, Norma? What would I do *without* you? Do you remember the time you spat at that photographer's lens when he was trying to harass me?"

"Oh, Miss, he had it coming. He was an awful man."

"Once the press get wind that Mack has left, there will be scores of awful men, and they'll descend in packs. I don't want *you* to have to deal with that, not on your own. Besides, you're due a vacation. Why don't you visit family? Or just go somewhere you've always wanted to visit. Take a month. And don't worry about the cost. I'll wire you some money."

"I don't know what to say."

"There's no need to say anything. But I would like you to take care of a couple of things before you go. The locks will need to be changed."

"But Mr Flood..."

"I doubt we'll be seeing him again." The words are out before Ursula realises the truth in them. Two years they have lived together, and what did it mean? "Although perhaps..." Her reaction will be everything, commented on by Hedda Hopper, Cholly Knickerbocker and every other damned Stateside columnist who'll soon be gleefully booking flights to London 'to do their jobs.' She needs to be seen behaving graciously. "Perhaps his things should be packaged and forwarded to him."

"Everything?"

"We don't need to go that far. Just a few of his best suits."

Hesitation. "He took those. I already checked."

"Did he?" This, to Ursula, is shocking. The narrative she convinced herself of is that Mack went to visit his ex-wife and Lindsay somehow snared him. Now, she's forced to confront the possibility that he planned this. All of it. He'd started making preparations the minute he dropped her off at the airport. Ursula imagines, for a moment, Norma standing in an empty hall in an empty house, the floorboards stripped of carpets, struggling with the telephone because even the Tiffany table it sat on and the Betty Joel chair are gone.

At that moment, a knock at the door.

She shields the mouthpiece and raises her voice. "Who is it?"

"Your flowers, Miss Delancy."

Ursula resists the urge to shout, *Take them away!* To Norma, she says, "Would you believe it? Flowers!"

"He's still sending them, huh?"

Every day, Mack has sent a bouquet. For the first few weeks, when they spoke each morning, he would be concerned: "Did they send rosebuds? I asked for rosebuds." She wonders if today's delivery will be white lilies.

"Hang on, would you? This I have to see for myself." Ursula sets down the receiver, checks her robe but can do nothing about the state of her eyes. Hotel workers must encounter worse, surely. She opens the door, just far enough to check this isn't a ruse. Ursula doesn't trust the military-styled jacket with its double row of brass buttons. She needs to see a face. But it's the usual lad, touchingly keen to impress, carrying a large vase overflowing with flowers. *Red rosebuds. Ha!* Ursula suspected that Mack had a repeat order. Here's her proof. However careful his plans had been, he overlooked this one thing. He forgot to have his secretary call the florist to cancel the order.

She would like to ask the boy to get rid of all of Mr Flood's flowers, but that would be one sure-fire way to tip off the press. "I'm so sorry, but I have so many cut flowers, I think I must be developing an allergy. Could you see to it that they're sent to a local hospital?"

"Of course, Miss Delancy. Is there anything I can get you?"

"Get me?"

"For your hay fever." He blushes. "I'm a sufferer myself."

"Oh, no! No, thank you. But you've been very thoughtful."

"If they're bothering you," he nods to another vase, "I could find out which ones cause the most irritation and remove them."

"Would you? That would be wonderful."

"I'll arrange it while you're at the theatre."

"Thank you so much." Ursula tips him generously, closes the door and returns to the phone. "Norma?"

"Still here, Miss Delancy."

"Ursula," she insists. "Did Mr Flood take anything else?"

"Just papers from his study, as far as I can tell."

She's checked, then. Good. Her heartbeat slows. Is it wise to let the house stand empty? "Once the locks have been changed, if you could make sure the place is shuttered, set the alarm – and while you're at it, change the code."

"I assume you'll want Frank to keep on top of the garden. I'll ask him to keep an eye out. He can handle himself."

"If you would." She imagines he'd take great pleasure in punching any photographer who dares trample on his rose beds.

"From now on. I just want to say that I know where my loyalties lie."

"That's good of you, Norma, but –" Ursula's hand is at her mouth. "I never doubted that."

"Are you? Are you *alright,* Ursula?" It is clearly an effort for Norma to break with years of decorum.

She clears her throat. "Thank you for your concern, but I'm fine. I'll let you get on."

Ursula isn't fine. How can she be when she has no explanation for why she – they – have been abandoned? (Although there is no explanation that would make it *acceptable.*) And she's terribly afraid. The public explosion will rival Krakatoa. Her heart goes out to Silvia, but she *cannot* let fear and sadness settle in her bones. It will harm the baby. And Ursula does, she realises, still want this baby. A second chance at motherhood. She presses cold fingertips to her swollen eyelids – the relief. How can she go on stage looking like this? Think. There's half an hour before she needs to leave for the theatre, then a half-hour car journey. She checks the silver teapot: two teabags.

She has no friend to ask the question, "Are you going to be able to perform tonight?" But if Ursula did, she knows exactly how she would reply: "It is the only way to stay sane."

To do the thing – the one thing – she's good at.

To walk onstage.

Inhabit another person's life. Completely. At this moment,

the thought of inhabiting her own is unthinkable. She needs to live someone else's for a few hours.

And she won't let down those who have queued all night for returns.

She will finish the job she came here to do.

Ursula squeezes the teabags against the inside of the pot, transports them to her bedside in a saucer. As straight as a convent girl, she lies herself down on the satin bedspread, closes her eyes and places a bag on each eyelid.

During her career she's played many outcasts – a condemned woman, a peasant, a disinherited rich girl, a battered housewife, a double agent – but none of them has prepared her for this. Ursula feels as if she's already been found out; that she's expected to slink out of the back door. But she promised herself, never again. She will walk down the marble staircase, heels clipping as she strides through the lobby. Dignity and decorum.

There might be another way.

Scarlet, Ursula thinks, as she removes the teabags and sets them down in the saucer. *I will wear scarlet.* In filmdom, a man who kills himself to avoid a jail sentence can go to Purgatory for sixteen years, then be given the opportunity to return to earth so he can redeem himself, but a scarlet woman – she goes straight to Hell. Ursula puts on her stockings and her silk slip and pads in bare feet to the wardrobe. Yes. She removes the deep red dress from its hanger; steps into it, zips herself up. Shoes (the highest heels she has with her). A headscarf. Today is not a day to forego sunglasses.

CHAPTER TEN

CAROLINE

"Come with me." Valerie leads the way, looking back over her shoulder. "Terry says you're to have one of Margot's dresses. Just until we get you fitted up."

"Margot won't mind, will she?"

"I thought I mentioned. Margot upped and left us. You should be about her size, but we might need a few strategic pins. Ta-da!" Valerie opens a door from the landing. "Home sweet home. Go on in."

Caroline finds herself in a neat sitting room. There is a two-seater sofa, two armchairs, a gate-leg table and dining chairs.

"Yvette's through that door – she has the room to herself – and I'm over here." Already Valerie is rummaging in a wardrobe.

Caroline scans the room; notes the two single beds, the top of the dressing table a clutter of creams, talcs and eau de cologne. "Would I share with you?" She feels herself colour. "If everything works out, I mean."

"Why wouldn't it work out? You'll have the bed closest to the dressing table. I'm up against the wall, that way I can be sure I don't get out of the wrong side. I'm a horror in the mornings. Don't say you haven't been warned." Valerie beckons impatiently. "Over here, in front of the mirror! What do you think?" She holds a dress up to Caroline.

It's like nothing she has ever worn before. Midnight blue rayon crepe with gilded leaves across the bodice. The neckline is a plunging V with the fabric ruched above and below the waist.

"It's a better-on-than-off dress," Valerie is saying. "The skirt is very full. You'll get a lot of movement when you walk. Strip off. You can pile your things on the chair over there."

As she undresses, Caroline is self-conscious, not of her figure but of her shameful once-white underwear.

"Oh, you're so lucky to have such a lovely flat stomach. Step in, I'll zip."

The material reeks of someone else's perfume, as if they've tried to compensate for the stale cigar smoke. But there's no point being precious. Soon Caroline will be able to smell smoke in her own hair; feel it in her pores.

Valerie fusses, adjusting shoulder pads, checking the drape of the fabric. "Do you know? I don't think you need pins at all. But we do need to do something about those shoes. What size are you?"

"Five."

More rummaging. "Margot was a four but they might have stretched. See if you can squeeze into these, Cinders."

Caroline sits on the side of the bed, bending to buckle the silver straps. "Just. Whether I can walk in them is another matter."

"Let me take a look at you. Oh, yes. That bra will have to come off. It's showing at the front."

Caroline looks in the mirror and hardly knows herself, but Valerie is frowning.

"Do you mind if I try something with your hair?"

Caroline has stepped further away from the Felixstowe girl, away from Ma, away from Betty. Valerie takes her hand, leading her down the stairs and into the club's main room. "Well?" she asks. "What do we think?"

Seated at the bar, Terrence Blagdon turns, cigar between his teeth. Forced into the spotlight, Caroline blushes. His eyes rake her, down then up again, but she holds her breath and realises that what she wants is approval. *His* approval. The frown clears from his face. "Nice work." The compliment is meant for Valerie, not her. "Of course, you'll show her the ropes."

"She'd learn so much quicker if she were living here."

Trepidation ripples through Caroline.

"Margot's bed *is* going spare."

Torn between embarrassment and wanting to hear a firm 'yes', Caroline holds her breath.

"That privilege has to be earned. Yvette had to earn it, you had to earn it. Why should she leapfrog the others?"

"They're happy where they are. Besides, it's easier to prove yourself when you don't have to worry about running off to catch the last bus."

Terrence bares his teeth, hissing smoke through them. "How did a sixteen-year-old get to be so damned manipulative?"

Valerie doesn't so much shrug as move one shoulder to the centre, move her chin towards that shoulder and pose. "Practice, I suppose."

Caroline can't take her eyes off her. Can Valerie *really* only be sixteen?

"Alright! Alright!" Terrence stands, makes for the door. He turns to point with his cigar. "But she'd better hit the ground running."

"Did you hear that?" Valerie turns to Caroline, wide-eyed and giggling with delight. "I didn't for one minute dream he'd say yes."

Caroline feels stunned. "Was he serious?"

"We'll move you in tomorrow. It'll be harder for Terry to change his mind once you're here. So." She turns on one heel. "First things first. Behind the bar we have Elise. Be nice to Elise. She keeps the tabs. *Very strict,*" she whispers.

Elise glowers. "I have to be."

"If ever you've had one too many, ask for a gin and Elise will give you water. They look exactly the same. Otherwise it's champagne, champagne, champagne."

"From three until eleven? I'll be sick."

Valerie looks startled. "Who said anything about eleven?"

"I thought that's when the club closes."

"Oh, darling, no one worries about that sort of thing around here. People drift in and out. You want to catch them on their way in, so their first order goes on your tab."

Elise scoffs and shakes her head. "And you wonder why I have to be strict!"

"Never carry a glass. You have to give them a reason to offer you a drink. Correction. An *empty* glass can be an excellent accessory. I approach everyone on the assumption that they're going to be pussycats. Men usually feel that they *should* offer a lady a drink. It's not just a question of etiquette but pride. They *love* unfolding their wads of banknotes."

"And if they don't have wads?"

"They wouldn't be here if they didn't, darling. Believe me, if they're not feeling generous they'll give themselves away in a couple of sentences, and you can make your excuses. But if they offer, make them feel good about it. That way they'll want to do it again. Don't look so horrified, it gets easier once you've got a few reliable regulars."

"And if I persuade someone to buy a bottle? Should I stay long enough to share it with them?"

"That depends." Valerie places a fresh cigarette between her lips and waves the carton under Caroline's nose.

"On what?" She helps herself. Perhaps smoking is a way to build female intimacies as well as male ones.

"Any number of things. Whether they're a someone, whether we're rushed off our feet, whether they really need to talk – some do, you know – or whether they're a bore. There's also the question of how generously they tip. My goodness, that mink stole I told you about? I suspect the gent bought it for a lady friend he's fallen out with and it was going spare, but it's a darling little thing. I shall make better use of it than she ever would."

"And if they get too personal?"

"Never part with the truth unless you absolutely have to." If Valerie understands what is behind Caroline's question, she dismisses it. "The minute someone asks where I'm from, I tell them they're looking in the wrong direction. They should be asking where I'm going. Gather information, don't give it away. Unless you plan to play the duchess's game."

"Which is what?"

"Feeding information to the journalists. And that's a dangerous road to tread. If you mention something about a visitor who then becomes a member, you'll find you've accidentally broken Terry's house rules."

The room begins to fill, slowly at first, and Valerie shimmies over to speak to each new arrival, addressing them by name. The level of suggestion she can cram into a simple 'Mis-ter *Car*-ter' is a revelation. Caroline hears herself introduced as a former model. "Newly escaped. We're very lucky to have her."

"I'll say!"

The change Caroline's new dress works is instantaneous. The cut and feel of the fabric make her move in an entirely new way. It's the difference, she imagines, between a rehearsal and a dress rehearsal. She decides she can be a former model if that's what the job requires.

"He likes you," Valerie whispers, and despite herself Caroline basks in this approval.

Then the arrivals begin to multiply. The room is abuzz.

"*...chap from Dulwich...*"

"*...caught the* SS Falaise *off St Malo, so they say...*"

"*...terribly bad form...*"

Valerie knows them all. "See that man who looks a bit like Ronald Colman? He's an award-winning war correspondent, newly-divorced – it was all a bit of a scandal. Oh, now here's the Colonel's table. He's a pussycat. I'll introduce you."

She does and Caroline cuts in: "Colonel, would you mind awfully if I sit down for a moment. My feet are absolutely killing me." Dressed as she is, it doesn't sound quite as ridiculous as she'd feared it might to talk this way.

Valerie looks tickled, as if her star pupil has dreamt up some clever ruse.

"Mind, my dear?" He stands and pulls out a chair for her. "I'd be delighted. Can I offer you a drink?"

"That's really terribly sweet of you." Already, Valerie has left. She's shimmying between two tables, bending down to deliver exaggerated greetings, as if each new arrival's choice of tie is worthy of comment. She is quicksilver. Her energy fills the bar room, setting off sparks. There's no point trying to be another Valerie. Caroline must be the moon to her sun.

"Champagne?"

You wanted to act. Now act. "Who can turn down the offer of champagne?"

And her first 'sale' really is as easy as that. Three pounds. Now, amid the rise and fall of voices, the clink of glasses, Caroline can settle into the conversation, absorb herself in whatever the Colonel has to say as if it's the most important thing in the world.

CHAPTER ELEVEN

RUTH

“Well, then.” It is clear that Joe has absolutely no idea how to take his leave. Goodbye – such a simple word – would weigh too heavily. He turns towards the door – the dimensions of the cell mean that there's no need for him to do anything other than turn, and there it is in front of him. A single step will take him out into the corridor.

The line comes to Ruth, the one she used to borrow from British Pathé. It might have been about Christmas turkeys, but it suited her mood during the Blitz. “A short life and a gay one.”

Joe turns back and, for a moment he's the young apprentice he was when they first met. “We had some good times, didn't we?” he asks, and for the first time he seems to want something from her.

“We had some fine times,” she agrees, holding her head high, her jaw steady.

A grimace of a smile, the iron door echoes shut, three walls become four, and Ruth's mouth gasps open. He came. *She bends her knees, feels for the edge of the narrow cot-like bed and lowers herself onto it.* He came. *The same day she was transferred from the hospital wing to a cell, too, when she wasn't expecting it.*

She had known Muttar would come, perhaps even her brother Granville, but not Joe Jakubait.

The wardress frowns. "We should have another think about visitors, if seeing them upsets you so much."

"I just need a lie down, that's all." Ruth makes a pillow of her steepled hands, lays down her head, draws up her knees and closes her eyes. It is like Ruth remembers it as a child: the urgency of wanting to be left alone.

"I'll leave you to it, then." The door clanks open and then echoes shut once more, a sound that vibrates deep in her marrow. The trouble with getting what you wish for is that often, you find it no more bearable than the alternative.

Behind her closed eyelids, the scene replays. She sees Joe's face. How he looked at her. He called her by her name – "Ruth" – and shook his head as if he could bear to look no more. That he should have seen her like this. Here, trapped in a hutch, under guard. Her brother-in-law. The father of the cousins Andy is so fond of. Andy. *No, she dare not allow herself to think of her son. Not until after the trial.*

Joe lived as part of the Neilson household, knows so many things about her – things she hasn't told her closest friends. But she doesn't think Joe knows everything there is to know. Muriel would not have told him everything.

He didn't ask. He didn't say, "How did it happen? Why did you do it?" He didn't need to. Everybody knows Ruth shot David. What's more, they know she meant to do it. It would be beneath her to make excuses, just as it would feel traitorous to involve others. It's no good, the solicitor can't persuade her to enter a plea of insanity. They've had her under observation round the clock, and the medical staff have found her fit to stand trial.

But even when someone is 'indifferent about her fate' – that's what they wrote in their notes, the doctors – it's hard to come face to face with the man who'll be left with the task of comforting your sister, explaining what has happened to your nephews and nieces – to your own ten-year-old son. To look that person in the eye.

"How's the old man?" Ruth would say to Muriel. "Miserable old so and so." But Joe was never miserable, not really. Spend a couple of weeks in Holloway and you'll understand what real misery is. Here, despair seeps from the drab stone walls, the grief of every soul who's passed through this place. Here, nets are strung from every landing, the kind you see in a Big Top, there to catch anyone who thinks of jumping.

No, Joe wasn't miserable. After working all hours, he simply had no energy to spare. Not for conversation and not for a game of cards. Five children; a family of seven to house and feed. There were weeks at a time when he was away from home, often grabbing a couple of hours' sleep in his workshop under the Rotherhithe arches. Joe was steady, the steady provider, that's all. How different Ruth's life would have been if she'd had someone like Joe.

It's why, only a few moments ago, Ruth asked: "You'll look after Andy? You'll keep him away from this?" The trial at the Old Bailey and everything that follows.

"It won't come to that," said Muttar, speaking with the Belgian accent she's never quite lost. An accent that people in Manchester mistook for German, the very people Muttar fled from, wearing only a nightdress until someone thought to offer her a blanket.

But Ruth wouldn't be put off. She knows how the script reads. An eye for an eye. A life for a life. "You'll look after him?" she pressed.

"Haven't we always?"

It's true. Muriel and Joe have always looked out for Andy. From the moment Ruth brought him home to London, wrapped in the shawl they sent for him. Under the clock at Waterloo, they met. "We've made up a room for you in the flat." She didn't have to ask. Over the years, Muriel has cared for Ruth's son while she's worked. In many ways – and it's hard to acknowledge this – her sister has been more of a mother to Andy than she ever was. After all, what kind of a mother forgets to collect a ten-year-old from boarding school at the end of term? What kind of a mother forgets to tell her son's school that she's moved to a new address? And what kind of a mother has her son come along for the ride when Uncle Desmond teaches her how to shoot a gun?

Ruth would have liked to reach for Joe's hand, but it wasn't allowed, not with the wardress acting as censor, there to report every breath the three of them took, every swallow. And so she nodded. Ruth nodded and Joe, all Joe could do was look at his shoes.

Andy will be better off – they will all *be better off without her.*

CHAPTER TWELVE

CAROLINE

Valerie pulls Caroline to one side to hiss, "Do you see who's here?" She points, mentions some name or other, then lists all the 'It Girls' he's been photographed with. "I'm just going to powder my nose. Don't let Yvette get her paws on him while I'm gone!"

"What about me?"

"Oh no you don't. I saw him first."

Left shaking her head and smiling, Caroline commences a circuit of the bar room, feeling the pull of the tighter-fitting fabric of her skirt. There seems to be a lull. Few people are on their own today and those drinking in groups are fully stoked.

"*...restrict the temptation for people to travel abroad...*"

"*...yet to see an XK 120...*"

"*...Alec Guinness is a genius!*"

"That's more like it. Something understated, classic and elegant." This, aimed at her.

It's strange to be complimented by the territorial woman at the corner table. Valerie has done her best to dress her like a Londoner, a transformation that has enabled Caroline to carry herself like a Londoner, possibly even begin to think like a Londoner. "Thank you," she says.

As if aware of the track Caroline's thoughts have taken, the duchess nods in Valerie's direction. "Your friend can get away with sackcloth and ashes, but women like us. We need good tailoring."

Women like us? What could she possibly have in common with the duchess? But here, in the soft indirect lighting, Caroline can't help indulging her curiosity. It's her first real opportunity to see 'the enigma' – as Sandy refers to the duchess – unguarded by her entourage. Caroline drinks in the soft grey chiffon of her dress, the stole around her shoulders, the lime green accessories. It's difficult to fathom what lies beneath the unlined porcelain skin (almost as if she's not only avoided strong sun, but smiling, too). The bright red lipstick set in a grim line. There are few hints – so far, at least – of what accounts for the volume of laughter that originates from this alcove. The duchess draws on her cigarette, held in its ebony holder, the tip of which (ivory perhaps) is stained a couple of shades lighter than her lipstick. "You're Terrence's latest recruit," she says. It is not a question.

"This is my second week."

"I make it two and a half." Apparently she's been taking notes. "And you know who I am, I imagine?"

Social standing high enough to be above criticism. That's what Sandy said. "I do."

"Of course you do. What it would be to start again where no one has read about you in the papers!"

A statement that is impossible to take seriously, given all that Caroline has heard about the duchess drip-feeding journalists quotes in the exact form she wants them published. "I've heard that you don't suffer fools," she says.

This comment produces a single, sharp *Ha!* "That snake Sandy told you that, did he? I must say it's one of the kinder things I've heard said about myself." The duchess turns her head and sips from her glass. Assuming their exchange is at an end, Caroline goes as if to move away.

"I don't normally take to women. Will you be the exception, I wonder?" Caroline's jaw drops just enough to part her lips. This doesn't go unnoticed by the duchess. "You don't want to be the exception. That's fine." The older woman crosses one elegant leg over its opposite. Her hair has the look of having been carefully arranged, not a strand out of place.

Wrong-footed, Caroline backtracks. "It isn't that –"

"If we're going to have this conversation, don't fawn. I detest fawning. Well. You know why I'm here." The look is direct, challenging.

The duchess is wrong. All Caroline has is guesswork, and her guess is this: the duchess may not be struggling to fit back into family life after firing at 'bandits' from the cockpit of a plane, she may not be delaying an inevitable return to a dreary hotel room, or forced to resort to flattery to close a business deal, but there's something in her present that she's trying to escape. Wary, Caroline says, "I hardly think that's any –"

"Business of yours?" Almost a sneer. "Don't insult me. I know what people say about me. What I don't know yet is why *you're* here."

Caroline feigns indifference. "The same as all the other girls, I imagine."

"Hoping to hook an eligible bachelor?"

You have no idea who I am. Caroline is doing what she has to. No more. No less. It is a strain to say, "I don't think that's very likely to happen, do you?"

"Oh, I don't know. I meet plenty of nice young men."

The fawning the duchess doesn't take objection to. "But *you* have something they want."

As the duchess's eyebrows arch, Caroline colours; wonders if in anger she's overstepped the mark, and what the consequences of doing so might be, but the enigma only says drily, "Asparagus and strawberries."

Caroline feels as if she's walked in on the punchline of a joke.

"So you're not in the market for a rich husband." Another calculating smile. (Perhaps it's deserved.) "What *did* bring you here?"

Valerie's warning to keep her personal business to herself rings loud in Caroline's ears, but what option is there? Refuse to answer and she'll be trapped in this cul-de-sac of a conversation. Reply and she can move on. "The need to earn enough so that I have money over to send home to my mother."

"Very noble. This mother of yours. Isn't she able to work?"

"She takes in work, but with three young children –" Caroline grits her teeth as she thinks of the latest letter to arrive from home. *I don't like to press you but when do you think we can expect…?*

"Does she know how you'll be earning this money?"

Her blood sings its resentment. This woman who has lived her entire life wrapped in cotton wool, who's probably never had to boil water, let alone an egg, *assumes.* And worse still, Caroline *will* have to, and soon, because what other way is there? Valerie says Caroline thinks too much. She'll get used to it. She might even enjoy it if she relaxes a little.

"I didn't think so. Well, sit down. I shall correct a few of the fictions you've heard. Accuracy has a mixed reputation, don't you find? If you want facts, you're better off with a train timetable than a newspaper."

"I'd question the accuracy of train timetables."

"My point precisely. There's no need to look so put out. I'll see to it that you don't miss out on your commission." Unaccustomed to being denied, the duchess raises one long-fingered hand. "Elise, a bottle, when you have a moment. And a glass for my friend here. What is it *now?*"

This last question, Caroline realises, is directed at her. She feels the rush of blood to her cheeks. "Mr Blagdon prefers us not to monopolise his female customers."

"*Mister* Blagdon!" The duchess rolls her emerald eyes.

A roll that, if she were the sort of woman who'd ever been employed as a nanny, would suggest she's about to trot out an embarrassing childhood anecdote about bath time, or how late Terry was to say his first word, and then the first thing to come out of his mouth was… "My custom has paid for Mr Blagdon's little club several times over."

Perhaps Valerie wasn't exaggerating when she said that the duchess's slate is ten times larger than any other member's. But this woman isn't only one of the club's biggest spenders, she comes with something more valuable. *Connections.* Dutifully, Caroline perches, mirroring the older woman's upright stature.

"Ah!" the duchess says as Elise delivers a champagne bottle. A crunch of ice, a few hastily wiped drips and a disapproving look for Caroline. "Help yourself, as you wish."

Why not? When every sentence is a fresh nick from a razor, anything that will dull the sting is welcome. "Thank you." Caroline picks up the bottle, extends her arm towards the duchess's glass.

"Not for me. I never touch the stuff." Her lip quivers. "It's why the duke dislikes settling my account. 'Would you have me serve my guests tonic water while you order port for yours?' I ask him." The quiver is replaced by a self-satisfied smile. "He would, actually."

This is the moment when Caroline imagines the duchess's male companions might laugh, but Caroline can't be sure that the duchess is joking. She fills her own glass. Streams of frog-spawn surface and cluster. Champagne on an empty stomach.

"My mother's family had the titles and the property, but the money was my father's. He was in oil. Before my arrival, they travelled wherever his work took him, but Mother insisted on returning to Britain to give birth to me. There was to be no doubt about my nationality. As soon as she felt it was decent, we sailed back to Egypt with an English nanny in tow. As far as I was concerned, Cairo was home. But although there was a perfectly good English-speaking school, I was uprooted again the minute the war was over – the Great War, as we call it now. We came home to the only place I've ever been truly happy. My mistake was thinking we would settle."

At least this makes a change from the usual well-worn tales of heroics. *A load of ole squit,* Da would have called them, and most of the time he wouldn't have been far wrong.

"The trouble with being the only child of a couple who married for love is never being allowed to forget what a terrible inconvenience you are." There's a precision to the duchess's speech that makes Caroline want to imitate it. She watches the lipstick-red mouth open and close, as if stresses and cadences are things that might be captured. "I didn't know it at the time, but the reason we came back was so that I could benefit from a proper English education. My grandfather had gone to a great deal of trouble to ensure that my mother could inherit his title. As you may know, dukedoms are normally inherited by male heirs."

"I didn't," Caroline says. "Not that it comes as any great surprise."

"Quite. The only heir my grandfather produced was a daughter, so he applied for a patent. The fact that there was a patent that allowed female heirs to inherit meant that if a brother didn't arrive, my mother's title and estate could pass to me. It was drummed into me how important it was that I worked hard to acquire the skills I would need to manage the estate. That was the reality of what my English education entailed – and it wasn't up to scratch. I doubt you're well educated, but you're perceptive, I can see that. I've watched how you measure people up."

Like Terry's remarks, this isn't delivered as a compliment, but as a commentary on the duchess's own finely-honed observational skills. Caroline muzzles her irritation and responds with a nod. "You mentioned a place where you were happy."

"I did. Whitlocke. The house and land have been in my family for generations. Later, I would be all for London, but in those days I was mad about the outdoors. I don't remember when I was told it would pass to me. Probably when my mother gave up all hope of trying to produce a son. It always seemed that Whitlocke belonged to me and I to it. Not that you ever really own a place like that. You're only ever a custodian for future generations."

"If you love it so much, why not live there?"

There's a pause. "My husband's work is here. We go when we can, but petrol rationing restricts us as it does everyone."

Caroline can see that her question has made the duchess uncomfortable. "Of course. So you were dragged off to school?"

"Kicking and screaming. And the moment my parents had me enrolled, they took off again. At the time, Egypt was *the* place to overwinter. As for me, I was abandoned with my galoshes and white tunics – that's what the school had us wear. If I'm honest, I rather disliked other children. Even before the question of inheritance arose, I never once demanded that my parents provide me with a brother or sister."

Imagine demanding anything! The idea is as foreign as the thought of *overwintering in Egypt.*

"Some girls thought sleeping in a dormitory was tremendous fun, but I found it impossible. All that creaking and pattering about in the middle of the night. From then until my coming out, my mother took no interest in me. At least that's how it felt. But my coming out had to be done properly, otherwise it would have reflected badly on her. A notice in *The Times*, and over four hundred guests." Just as the champagne spreads through Caroline's bloodstream, just as she begins to feel the blurring of the boundaries between them, there is something new. Some clear distinction. "Like all debutantes, I was expected to look like a bride minus a veil. But the idea of being paraded like a virginal sacrifice – it was demeaning. And so I arranged for my dress to have a little accident."

What Caroline would have given for a white dress and white shoes! "What kind of accident?"

"Port. Impossible to get out of white chiffon."

The sheer, unthinking waste of it. "What did you do?"

"I wore the dress I had planned to wear all along. Dark green silk." The duchess blinks at Caroline, as though it were possible to ignore the emerald of her shrewd and intelligent eyes. "My photograph appeared in all the papers. And then, after I was presented to Queen Mary, came my first London season. Three parties a night, and of course the invitation was always for mother and daughter. The understanding was that the mother would chaperone." The duchess shakes her head slowly. "They couldn't wait to marry us off. They would stalk any man with a title, it didn't even matter if he was of the wrong religion. I was engaged long before I had any right to be."

"How old were you?"

"The first time?"

"How many engagements *were* there?"

"Half a dozen, I should think." Caroline feels her eyebrows jump. "I expect that makes me sound rather giddy, but it wasn't that unusual. You couldn't be seen with a man in public until he'd expressed serious intent. Better to realise you'd made a mistake before that mistake became permanent. And you?"

"Have I been engaged?" The idea seems laughable. "Oh, no."

The way the duchess purrs suggests a lack of surprise. "I really did think I was in love with two of them, but the entire system was a cattle market. At the time of course, having been cooped up for years at boarding school, I thought it was heavenly. My first Derby, clubs where the men all wore white tie, weekends at country houses – Henley, Eton, Oxford, Bath. But perhaps you know some of them?"

"I don't."

"You will. All of the hostesses do. It's not like it was."

Underlying every comment is a suggestion that the order of things (cattle farming aside) was entirely correct. Caroline doesn't pause to ask; she helps herself to more champagne.

"I expect that, at some point, I shall find myself in need of your discretion."

Here's the crux of it. This is what their exchange (if it can be called that) is all about.

"Should our paths ever cross in the outside world we will both, I expect, need to turn a blind eye." The briefest and, Caroline feels, the least sincere of smiles. It's clear now. This conversation is necessary so that Caroline understands. Outside the club, they do not know each other. Outside the club, order – the proper order of things – will prevail.

CHAPTER THIRTEEN

URSULA

So much for making a quiet getaway. They are waiting outside the stage door. The press, the autograph hunters and, perhaps the most persistent of all, the would-be starlets. The adrenalin comedown has hit Ursula hard (her years away from the stage have made her forget how draining it can be). Combine it with first trimester fatigue and all she wants to do is sleep. Instead what awaits her at the hotel is the prospect of making one of the most difficult telephone calls she'll ever have to make. Much as she'd like to elbow through the crush and then duck inside the waiting car, such behaviour isn't acceptable. Publicity is an obligation, every appearance an advertisement for an upcoming film. This will be the fourth Act of the night. The role she should know best but feels the least comfortable in. Ursula Delancy, actress. And in it she must dazzle.

Ursula looks about, feigning surprise. "Have you all been waiting out here in the cold?"

She pretends to zone in on individual faces, to make eye contact, although she doesn't see them, not really. Faces blur and blend into one. She reaches blindly for pens, ticket stubs, programmes. Asks if there is a dedication. "Look at that! It's absolutely nothing like my signature." She holds the programme aloft so that a half dozen photographers can get a clear shot. "Shall I give it another try?"

"Could I have a dedication for my wife?" a man asks. "She should have been here tonight but she isn't feeling well." He turns his back, ducks down a little and leans forward.

"Nothing serious, I hope." Ursula rests the programme on his shoulder (his back seems too personal). The cameras love this. *So sorry you missed the show. Get well soon.* "Wish her all the best from me, won't you? And how about you?" She moves along the line.

"It's for me. I'm a Gladys too." Gladys needs no encouragement to lend her shoulder as a makeshift desk.

"From one Gladys to another!" Ursula says, genuinely delighted. "Will that do?"

"Why did you want to play Gladys?" someone asks. It could be a journalist. It could be an audience member.

"Her message. The idea that one person can make a difference, no matter how humble their beginnings, is so important. Don't you agree?"

Murmurs of approval.

The next item thrust into Ursula's hands is a copy of *Mirror Movie Magazine*, an American import. The photograph she's being asked to sign isn't one she's seen before. A candid shot and, judging by the dress she was wearing, taken at a private party. Ursula looks at the girl who's given her this thing as if confronting the photographer. "Goodness," she corrects her expression. "That must have been a powerful zoom!" She's heard about new prototypes. It seems her future is to be spied on from a distance.

"I think it's nice to see you looking so relaxed."

I was relaxed because I didn't know I was being watched. Ursula resolves not to upset herself by reading which of her friends has been quoted. She signs her name, the act purely mechanical, hands back the magazine and smiles.

"Actually," the girl says, "we wondered if you could answer a few questions."

"That all depends on what those questions are," Ursula replies in a way that raises laughter.

"Acting questions."

"Oh, so you're drama students!" Ursula sees it now. The girl is one of a well-groomed group. Collectively, they have the look of would-be starlets. Pretty, but not one of them with Bacall's arched eyebrows.

"No," another admits, glancing sideways at a friend, "but we'd like to be actresses. We wondered what we can do to improve our chances of being discovered."

It takes all of Ursula's acting skills to appear encouraging. Most would-be starlets get it into their heads that actresses are plucked from obscurity. Not that it's their fault. Movie magazines print what young girls want to read. That seemingly effortless performances are just that. Effortless. "Well, first things first. What groundwork have you done?"

Enthusiastically, they run through a list of diet and exercise, practising walking with books on their heads, the photographs they've had taken. "Professionally." They are most particular about this.

Ursula tries not to blink. "Anything else?"

They wave copies of *Mirror Movie Magazine* triumphantly, like flags. "We find out where people in the film industry go, and we show up." They think they've played their trump.

"What about auditions? Have any of you applied for roles?"

A couple of the girls exchange glances. *We're talking to the wrong person.* They don't want to hear about the years spent playing extras, promotion to understudy, the same lines to learn as the leads, but nowhere for those lines to go. And then, when it finally happens (hard to call it 'success' because, in this business, *nothing* is assured), the absence of support from people you think might be pleased for you. And from those who think you've landed the roles they themselves deserve, accusations that you must have dropped your knickers for casting directors. Humiliating occasions when you stooped that low and still didn't get the part.

Ursula has disappointed the girls, she can see that. And who is she to discourage? The truth is that talent and dedication aren't enough. Casting directors want a certain look, a particular body shape. Someone shorter, taller, someone different, someone with more experience, and then when you have experience to offer, they decide they're after a newcomer. Someone they can mould.

She reaches for another pen, another programme. "Really. Auditions. Get yourselves in front of casting directors!"

"That's enough, now," says the doorman, taking her elbow. "Let Miss Delancy through to her car."

"Thank you," she mouths.

Ursula unclips her right earring, safeguards it in her left fist and holds the telephone receiver to her right ear.

"Hello, Robin," she rehearses. "I'm sorry to call so late, but there's something I need to tell you. No, I'm afraid it can't wait." Try again. Take the 'I' out of it. "There's something you should know." She shakes her head. "Robin," she says to her reflection. "We need to talk about Silvia." But it isn't just Silvia they need to discuss. "Robin, we need to talk." Straight and to the point.

Ursula has further to fall in her ex-husband's estimation. Further still in the eyes of her daughter. It is as much as she can do to dial reception. She feels sick to her stomach as she asks the night manager to connect her, and the wait that follows is unendurable. It would be a relief if he were not in and yet –

"Five seven nine eight."

It is so familiar, his voice, the number that was once theirs, spoken from the hall of the house Ursula still part-owns. How was it that she could yearn for home when she was not there, and yet find it impossible to settle when she was? "Robin? Robin, I was just about to hang up."

"Ursula," he says. One word. No 'Hello.' No 'You got me out of bed.' With Robin, it was only ever a half-life, a half-home. Hard even to tell how he feels about hearing from her directly, without an intermediary.

"How are you?" she ventures, picturing the telephone table, where a framed copy of their wedding photo sat, so that Robin could look at her when she telephoned from a shoot. She has not been back to the house, but imagines that all of her photographs have been removed, as if he's tried to erase her.

"How do you expect me to respond?"

Ursula would like to hear something about Silvia, but has forfeited her right to ask. She loves her daughter – the daughter the press describes as 'motherless' – from a position of shame. "Can't we try to be civil?"

"You made your choice. We've said all that we can say to each other about that."

"Fine." She almost sighs the word. "I'm calling because I thought you should know. There are going to be headlines, and I'm afraid they're going to be ugly." Her heart is thumping.

"How ugly?"

"Donald has left me. He's gone back to his wife." Ursula allows her back to slide down the wall, feeling the contours of the velvet flock wallpaper through the silk of her dressing gown. She sits with her knees in her eyeline, waiting for the judgement that will surely come.

On the other end of the telephone line, breathing, and the breathing is that of a creature biding its time, preparing to pounce.

"Now's your moment." She offers him a cue. "Tell me that you told me so."

Robin's voice is wary rather than angry. "Has the studio asked for a family portrait, is that it? Have they asked you to convince me to pose as a shining example of how modern families operate after divorce?"

"The studio doesn't know about this yet. Robin, I really think it would be better if we could have a conversation face-to-face."

"Forgive me, Ursula, but I don't. You live your life as if you're on stage and, frankly, I've had it up to here with all your drama. So just tell me what you have to say."

She cannot say, 'If that's what you want.' She has used those words before only to have him respond, 'How dare you. None of this is what I want.' Instead, Ursula takes a deep breath. "Robin, there are three parts to what I have to tell you. Picking up the phone to you was one of the most difficult things I've ever had to do –"

"More difficult than leaving us?"

She pauses. It would be easier to lie, but she will not. "If I'm honest, yes."

He scoffs. "I can believe that."

"Oh, not in the way you think! When I left home that last time, it was to do a job of work." Robin always balked when she referred to acting as work and he balks now, but Ursula presses on. "I didn't know I wasn't coming back, so it was a goodbye like all of the other goodbyes."

"You left us *guessing*."

"Now that I know what it's like to be left with no explanation, I have more appreciation of what I did to you. It was cowardly of me not to have had that conversation in person." It is strange, how it is possible not to realise something until you say it. But now that it's said, she does. Ursula does.

"Flood did the same to you?"

"I had to work it out for myself." The suddenness, the finality and no means to respond. "And I'm still none the wiser."

"The –" Robin stifles whatever adjective comes to mind. "Even so, you have *no* appreciation of what it was like to explain to a child that her mother isn't coming home."

"That's why this time," Ursula winces at her clumsy choice of words, "I'd like to be the one to explain to Silvia." She adopts a humble tone, picking up from before Robin's interruption. "There are three things. Donald leaving was only the first. If you're going to hang up, please, wait until you've heard all three." Ursula's hand moves to her stomach. She cannot say, 'Silvia is going to have a little sister or a brother.' They remain a family, but not in any conventional sense. A judge presides over their little unit, reminding them how reasonable people should behave and what is best for their daughter. "I'm pregnant," she says. There. She's said it. Then it comes to Ursula: Robin thinks so badly of her, his understanding may be that she's given Mack good reason to leave. "There wasn't anyone else," she adds in a rush. "Donald can deny it all he likes but, I swear to you, Robin, it's his child."

The breathing on the end of the line is agitated.

Ursula presses on because she has come this far. "And this is the third part, Robin: Donald's wife is also pregnant."

The line goes dead, as Ursula had known it would. She is left with the burr of the dialling tone. "She's about six weeks behind me," she says into the mouthpiece, picturing Robin, one hand clamped over his mouth and, in the silence, an unholy tangle of questions and consequences.

CHAPTER FOURTEEN

CAROLINE

Dear Mother,

I am writing to you with my new address and some good news.

Caroline pauses. She imagines, for a moment, writing: *I am one of Terrence Blagdon's girls.*

Resentment still blooms, but guilt is hot on its tail. Now that she's made her decision, shouldn't she accept her lot gracefully? And what of the compensations? Unlike those who live in shabby bedsits, Caroline doesn't have to worry about folding down a couch every night. Her diet isn't restricted to tinned food that can be heated on a gas ring. Here at the club, meals come from the kitchen, prepared by a chef. Also high on the list of advantages comes no longer living out of a suitcase. Here, she wears evening dresses bought from a small, smart boutique.

The memory of how Valerie rejected the assistant's suggestions raises a smile. How the shop girl stalked Valerie as she chose alternatives from the rails, an efficient scrape of metal on metal as she brought them to Caroline in the changing room.

"I'd really prefer it if you didn't encourage your friend to try on things she can't afford." Hands wrung, neck craned.

Ashamed of her day wear, Caroline coloured, but Valerie didn't bat an eyelid. "Oh, but she can afford them. Mr Blagdon will be settling the account."

Which was all that needed to be said.

Here, in the sanctuary of the club, with members vetted and guests approved by George, Caroline is protected from the John Haighs of this world. Valerie told her how a photographer had once pointed his lens at her outside the club, and Terrence Blagdon had leapt from the back of a taxi cab and, beginning with a swift right hook, knocked two shades of purple out of the man, leaving him in the gutter with the smashed remains of his camera. Valerie had put one hand on Caroline's. "You see? We're safe here."

The idea wasn't as comforting as Valerie intended it to be. Protection comes at a price, and Caroline still isn't certain exactly what that price is. Already, it's apparent that the club is so much more than a safe haven. Often it's a smokescreen. A place for private meetings, illicit deals, illegal gambling and undercover operations. Only a fool would cross Terrence Blagdon. *She'd* be a fool to cross him.

Caroline scans the girlish clutter on the dressing table that doubles as her writing desk. The panstick, the rouge. Boxes of false eyelashes. *Writing home is just like applying make-up,* she tells herself. Some things she'll exaggerate, others she'll tone down.

I have a new job, and better still it comes with accommodation. I am now based in Knightsbridge, near the famous Harrods.

There! Nothing says respectable like a department store, and no London store is more upmarket.

I share with two other girls, who have done everything possible to make me feel at home.

The camaraderie is real. Together, the hostesses have identified themselves as girls who prefer a little glitz to the stench of the Oxo factory, at the same time insisting this existence is a stepping-stone. Perhaps the insistence isn't true for Yvette. Yvette is the oldest hostess (pushing thirty). She's dismissive of Valerie's attempts to speak as if she has a plum in her mouth. "She doesn't have dinner anymore, she has *lunch.* And she's not British, she's *English.*" Yvette isn't so much jaded as resigned. The frequent visits Terrence Blagdon pays to Yvette's room are impossible to ignore. As the girls drift off to sleep, unmistakable noises travel through the dividing wall. The first time it happened after Caroline's arrival, Valerie hissed, "Only earlier, I was reading that seventy-three per cent of women think that sex outside marriage is wrong."

"Very wrong." Caroline reached a hand over her head, ready to hammer on the wall.

"Don't!"

"Why ever not?"

"If Mr Blagdon wants to break his own rules, that's his business."

It was clear, in the dark, why Valerie had been so keen for Caroline to move in. The older hostess isn't a role model, she's the person Caroline risks becoming if she doesn't get out. If she truly becomes beholden.

From my bedroom window I look out over Hyde Park. I am glad to be living on-site. The job involves evening work so it is good to be able to just walk upstairs at the end of a long shift, without having to worry about how to get home.

So many details, she cannot share. Every toned-down sentence adds to the distance between Caroline and her mother.

The job itself is at a private members' club. I work as a –

As a what? Part of her still wants to protect her mother. The very person who burdened her with this unfair responsibility. Hasn't Ma forfeited the right to honesty? Caroline thinks of George, the doorman, white-haired and gentlemanly. The respectable face of the club.

A receptionist.

She is satisfied with this.

I sign people in, take their hats and coats, run around making sure everyone is happy and so on.

There's no point in writing unless Caroline offers a glimpse of what her mother wants: how much she'll get and when. Letters from Felixstowe contain no word of Betty. Caroline has been cast adrift, exiled until she fulfils her side of the bargain. At the same time, with her pay depending on men falling for her powers of persuasion, she needs to manage expectations.

The salary is not very high, but when you think that I am not forking out for rent or evening meals, I am almost certainly better off than I would have been working in a shop. My next pay packet is due at the end of the week. It has been an expensive time, but I have paid what I owe and will start to send –

Valerie bursts through the door of the bedroom. "Are you decent?"

"No more than halfway."

"Are you alone?" She pretends to look under the closest of the twin beds.

"Completely. Yvette's gone out."

"In that case," Valerie throws her new mink onto her own bed, and follows it in a dive, a child-like energy betraying her age. She stretches out luxuriously. "Would you be an absolute darling and make yourself scarce for a couple of hours. Oh." She turns her head, props herself up on one elbow. "Are you writing something terribly important? Can I see?"

Embarrassed by her thinly disguised lies, Caroline folds the sheet of writing paper. "Only a letter to my mother."

Valerie leaps up. Both hands on Caroline's shoulders, she leans forwards, cocks her head on one side. Her face reflected in the mirror registers concern, but she can't resist looking at herself and brushing aside a stray strand of hair.

"It's just to give her my new address."

"Mine has no idea where I am. I doubt she even cares." The little crease between Valerie's brows disappears. "So you don't mind popping out for a while?"

It's inconvenient, but how can Caroline object? She's only here because Valerie stuck her neck out for her. She slots her unfinished letter into the envelope she's already addressed, and hides it away in what is ostensibly 'her' drawer. "Mind? Why should I?"

"I hate to ask, but I've made rather an important new friend." Valerie giggles, suddenly coy. "In fact, I think I may be getting ideas above my station."

"Does that mean what I think it means?"

"Am I planning on breaking Terry's house rules?" Valerie's eyes flash wickedly.

"But look what happened to Margot."

"Margot got herself pregnant!"

"I –" A false start. At least there's clarity.

"You didn't realise? Perhaps I should have said. Anyway, if everything works out, I won't need Terry."

If Terry finds out that Valerie's seeing someone, there'll be hell to pay. And it won't just be Valerie who pays. "But why invite him here? It's not worth the risk."

She shrugs and stands up to her full height. "To give him an incentive to rescue me, I suppose."

Caroline wants to shake off her reservations. Valerie so clearly wants her to be happy for her. Can she do that? "Aren't you going to tell me who he is?"

"He has a title."

Caroline feigns nonchalance. "Titles," she says.

"And his family have the largest country pile."

"In that case!" Caroline pushes herself up, patting her hair and, checking her appearance, decides it will have to do. "But I'll need to get changed before opening time."

"Knock three times."

"Just in case," they chorus.

CHAPTER FIFTEEN

CAROLINE

Hyde Park; the place Caroline heads to when she itches for home. There is no endless horizon, no big sky, but what it offers is space enough to give the impression of freedom. There are no beaches where prize pebbles can be collected, but there is the Serpentine. No fields of wheat and sugar-beet, but freckles of yellow and white: daisies, dandelions, occasional buttercups. Deckchairs. Stick-wielding boys inching towards adolescence, running off the leash, baiting each other, or teasing girls of Betty's age. A life Caroline has supposedly outgrown. With a pang, she recalls her sister's simple pleasure at inheriting her old raincoat. Couldn't account for it until Betty showed her: a single sugared aniseed freed from the lining of the right-hand pocket. "Finders keepers," she'd said, popping it in her mouth without bothering to check for fluff.

At first, Caroline stuck to South Carriage Drive, finding the criss-cross lattice of paths confusing. On her third outing, convinced it was him – he was the right height, the right build, wearing that old coat of his – she detoured up what she now recognises as West Carriage Drive. There'd been no suggestion in the scribbled note propped up against the clock on the mantelpiece that he was headed for London, but where else do people end up when they need work and have exhausted all other options? Finally, Caroline would have the satisfaction of disowning *him*. Her elbows pumped. Yard by yard, she closed the distance between them, rehearsing what she'd say when she caught him up. *You've lost the right to call yourself our father* and *You're dead to us*. She could almost see his stricken expression; hear him beg for a second chance. Her fists had been clenched, ready to pummel his chest or, if he curled in on himself like a woodlouse, his arms and back. But he stepped off the path to light a cigarette behind the shield of a cupped hand, and the face in profile wasn't her father's.

She froze. Had it only been the fact that he was clean-shaven, Caroline still might have confronted him – shaving is the first thing a man does if he doesn't want to be recognised. But this man had a nose like a beak. How overwhelming it was to have been so convinced then proven so utterly wrong. Caroline about-turned, spitting, "Bastard! How could you have done it?" It was only then that she realised she was lost.

Late for her shift, Caroline was shame-faced.

"I put my faith in you, Valerie stuck out her neck for you, and this is how you repay us both."

"It won't happen again."

"It had better not."

Thanks to a guided tour from Sandy, a map has wormed its way inside Caroline's head. She now navigates by the features and landmarks he showed her.

"The trick is to think of London as a series of interconnecting villages. Forget the West End. Knightsbridge is your village. You'll get to know the faces soon enough. But before you can acclimatise, you must learn to appreciate the advantage of anonymity," he advised. "For the first time in your life, no one's reporting back to your mother about which reprobate they saw you with. There isn't a soul who knows your business unless *you* choose to tell them. Give it a couple of weeks. You'll be convinced that Felixstowe has been suffocating you all these years."

"Home wasn't all bad. We had a Butlin's, you know. With dodgems." Only when Caroline smiled did Sandy throw back his head and laugh.

He was certainly right about the faces. Here's the blind man, sitting at his makeshift stall, a shabby bowler on his head, his eyes shaded, legs covered with a threadbare blanket. His backdrop is a display of homemade signs. '13 years' service in India, Persia and Egypt.' 'Funds urgently needed for suet pudding.' His raggedy dog, who has a particular dislike of young boys, is insurance against the theft of his collection of gas masks and pith helmets. One of these days, Caroline will pluck up the courage to speak to him. A man like that must have quite a story.

On reaching the bronze statue of Achilles, she knows she's near Hyde Park Corner.

"All it took was melting down twenty-two French cannons seized in battle," Sandy had told her. "And there we have it. The best arse in London."

Caroline aimed an apologetic smile at an elderly couple before glancing up, only to find herself staring straight at the fig leaf. "Strategically placed," she said.

"A late addition."

"Oh?"

"We're expected to believe this was London's first nude statue. What they *mean* is that it was the first nude statue of a man. The good ladies of London found it all a bit much – although…" He sucked air through his teeth.

"What?"

"There was an attempt to chisel the fig leaf off."

She nudged him. "Not you, was it?"

"Miss Wilby, I'm *trying* to give you a history lesson. Perhaps you're not interested in self-improvement."

"I am." She broke into a trot to catch him up. "No, I am!"

These are her friends now, Sandy who jokes that he's a father figure, though he's unlike any father Caroline might have imagined, and Valerie, who lives entirely in the moment but isn't nearly as sophisticated when they're alone as the act she presents in the bar room suggests.

Caroline's return route brings her back via the Serpentine. Near the reeded point where she picks up the lakeside path is the place where the body of Shelley's estranged wife, Harriet, was found.

"She'd been missing for the best part of a month. I doubt very much that she looked like Ophelia," Sandy told her.

Caroline blinked, too embarrassed to admit that she had no idea who Shelley was, let alone Ophelia.

"Don't care for the Pre-Raphaelites? Not that I blame you. Too romantic to do justice to the lines:

Till that her garments, heavy with their drink,
Pull'd the poor wretch from her melodious lay
To muddy death."

It's the muddy death Caroline thinks of now. A bloated body, snagged in the reeds. Difficult to imagine a lonelier way to go. And all around, lovers courting and families at play.

"Not only that," Sandy had continued. "She was heavily pregnant."

Not one death, but two.

When Sandy told Caroline that Percy Shelley remarried only two weeks later, she assumed he was the villain of the tale.

"Things are rarely that simple. They'd lived apart for two years."

"In that case, whose child was Harriet carrying?"

Sandy shook his head dismissively. "Another man's?"

Forced to revise her opinion, Caroline asked, "How do people's lives get so complicated?" Conflicted, knowing what she knew by then, she focussed her attention on a man who had waded into the shallow waters in his Sunday best, intent on launching a four-foot model ship, complete with model lifeboats on its top deck. "Do you think he's wearing shoes?"

"What *are* you talking about?"

"Over there." She indicated. "The man with the model ship." He had his hat on, a handkerchief in his breast pocket. Tellingly, his trousers didn't seem to be rolled up.

Sandy gave a look of complete incomprehension. "The scale of that model is completely off," he said.

Since her move to Knightsbridge, with a growing appreciation of how complex lives can become, Caroline has made it her business to find out all she can about poor Harriet Shelley. Aware just how much she has to learn, she visits the public library, its atmosphere midway between schoolroom and cathedral, demanding best behaviour. Sandy was right in one respect: things are rarely simple. Two years before Harriet was found floating in the Serpentine, Percy Shelley – as large eyed and windswept as a poet should be – had left her. She'd been nineteen years old, with one daughter and another child on its way. Caroline stopped reading and sat with one hand over her mouth, taking in the extent of the tragedy. That made Harriet only sixteen when Percy married her and just twenty-one when she drowned herself!

It would get worse.

Her husband had become infatuated with a friend's sixteen-year-old daughter – the same young woman who would go on to write *Frankenstein*. A woman wrote *Frankenstein?* Abandoning her research, Caroline scanned the shelves to track down a copy. Embossed on leather binding was the name 'Shelley'. No hint of a Christian name. Back at her table, Caroline kept one hand on the novel's cover as if to keep the next Mrs Shelley at bay.

Deserted, finding herself 'neither wife nor widow', Harriet had returned to her parents' home, where she gave birth to Shelley's child, a boy named Charles. For two years, she lived quietly, subduing her desperation, deprived of the company of her children, who'd been sent to the country by her father. "For the sake of their health," he'd said, but the decision was taken out of Harriet's hands and it felt like a punishment. Then, in September 1816, pregnant once more, she closed the front door, leaving no word of where she was going. Initially, she took lodgings under the name of Smith and excused her husband's absence by saying he was abroad. After being tracked down and persuaded to return to her parents, Harriet disappeared a second time. This time, she covered her trail completely.

Following the discovery of her floating body, an inch-long column appeared in *The Times*. 'A respectable woman, far advanced in pregnancy' who was wearing a 'valuable ring'. She was buried at Bayswater Road Cemetery under the name Harriet Smith – the name she gave to her landlady. Shielded from scandal and miles away, Percy Shelley was able to marry Mary. (What kind of a woman would marry a man so soon after his first wife had drowned herself?) And as for Harriet's supposed lover, the man Sandy had spoken of with such conviction, there was no evidence of his existence. Instead, a suggestion that Shelley had met Harriet in London at about the time she became pregnant. Her suicide note addressed him: 'If you had never left me, I might have lived.' Perhaps she'd learned that Mary Godwin was also pregnant with Percy's child (not for the first time, but the third).

Now, passing in front of the tea pavilion, Caroline keeps her eyes on the reeds at the water's edge. All those unhappily married men at the club. Some of them must have fathered children with different women at about the same time. Terry assumes there's no rivalry between the club's members, but how can that be? Sex, when it happens, follows a courtship of sorts. First comes the champagne, then the dinners, theatre tickets, trips to the races, jewellery, mink coats. *Don't sell yourself cheap.* Of course the girls have their 'favourites'. The ones with the deepest pockets.

Again, Mary's child died.

So much misery, and for nothing.

It's a precarious game they're all playing.

CHAPTER SIXTEEN

CAROLINE

From the approach to the club, Caroline sees the slow crawl of Austins, Triumphs, Morris Minors. There must have been an accident, perhaps the discovery of another unexploded bomb – but the drivers aren't looking at the road. Something on the pavement has their attention. Now she sees. The club is under siege. A deluge of flashbulbs, men with clipboards scrambling for a better view, firing questions like bullets. A club member, perhaps a Fleet Street journalist, must have broken sacred house rules and spoken out of turn. Who'd be such a fool? It won't take Terry long to find out.

A glance at her wristwatch – a gift from the Colonel. It's quarter past two. Already she's late to begin to get ready. There's an impatience in Caroline's blood, a restlessness in her feet, but above all else is indecision. *Even if you can battle your way through, no one will thank you for opening the front door.* She'll have to make her way around the back. She quickens her pace.

Wait! What if the photographers' target is Terry? No doubt he has a past that's worth unearthing. For every friend, there must be two people who'd happily queue to see him get his comeuppance. Not just queuing – look, they're climbing!

One photographer is coiled around the upper branches of a London plane tree. And there's another, high on the parapet of the five-storey building opposite. This is bedlam.

What if it's Valerie's titled gentleman?

Think what that would mean.

There's nothing for it. Caroline marches purposefully across the road, between bumpers and sputtering exhausts, accosting the first newsman in her path. "What's going on? I need to get to my flat."

"Which one's yours?"

She nods her head. "The door between the hair salon and the leather goods shop."

"Five pounds if you'll take me inside."

"Forget it."

"Ten pounds!"

Already, she's elbowing forwards, the tone of each 'excuse me' less apologetic than the last, pushing against men in heavy overcoats, equally determined to hold their ground, but taller and stronger than she is. Then, unheralded, comes a sudden shift. Stepping into the free yard of space that opens up, Caroline finds herself face to face with a woman whose expression is so anguished, her only thought is to ask, "Are you alright?"

My heart alive!

The first lady of the silver screen. An actress who's been lauded in Hollywood, land of milk, honey and notoriety.

But Ursula Delancy's eyes do not smoulder. Instead they beg, *Get me out of here.* All Caroline can think of is the Suffolk hunt; a narrow path, little more than a tract of trampled earth; a fox, outnumbered, but still hoping to outrun its fate. Fast-approaching, baying hounds, bred for stamina and a keen sense of smell. "Do something!" Betty had implored. But hearing the thunder of horses, seeing the riders in their red jackets, Caroline felt powerless. She hauled Betty back into the nettles. Pelt and teeth and hooves flashed past in relentless pursuit. Betty had cried all the way home, but not because her legs were stung and snagged. Within earshot the shrill sounds of the kill were followed by the triumphant hunting horn. "We should have done something!" Betty lamented.

Caroline pulled up short, turning to demand, "What could we have done? We'd have been trampled to death."

"We should have tried!"

"Miss Delancy." Caroline takes the actress firmly by the arm; steers her towards the discreet black door. "I'm so sorry I'm late." Though her heart is pounding, Caroline finds she is perfectly capable of establishing fake credentials for the benefit of eavesdroppers. "I can't apologise enough, but I struggled to get through this dreadful crowd." This last sentence, she aims at the man who stands in her way. Accused, he sidesteps, far enough to let them pass. Caroline's door key has a habit of working its way to the bottom of her handbag. Not wanting to expose Ursula Delancy to the onslaught any longer than is absolutely necessary, she rings the bell. *Please George, be at your post.* The door opens instantly, wide enough to permit entry but no more; a suggestion that the doorman has been watching everything through the brass fisheye. Never has she felt so grateful.

He bolts the door, top and bottom. "That's better. The high street seems particularly congested today, Miss Wilby."

"And guest," Caroline says, certain from the way Miss Delancy has averted her eyes, from how vulnerable the nape of her neck looks, that as little must be made of her presence as possible. At the same time, to Caroline, the presence of an actress of this calibre is *everything*.

"Any guest of Miss Wilby's is most welcome. Would you like me to sign you in, perhaps?"

"Thank you." Miss Delancy reaches an unsteady hand to the nearest corner of the reception desk; finds an uncertain balance.

It's clear the actress is shell-shocked, but George doesn't flinch. "Am I right in thinking we have the pleasure of Miss Margaret Steele's company? With an 'e', if memory serves."

Caroline smiles what she hopes are further assurances. "George never forgets a name."

"Perhaps you'd like me to hang your coat, Miss Steele?"

Miss Delancy pulls the lapels of her collar inwards, over her chest. Her gaze appears to be fixed on the umbrella stand.

"Quite right. Now, you only need say the word if I can be of assistance. When you're ready to depart, we have access to a discreet taxi service. Or we have several parking spaces to the rear, should you wish to have your chauffeur call."

Miss Delancy seems to be in no fit state to respond, and so Caroline takes up the doorman's offer. "If you could reserve a parking space, I think, George. Has Mr Blagdon arrived yet?"

"Not yet, Miss Wilby. You'll have the bar room to yourselves for the next twenty minutes, I imagine."

"This way, Margaret." Caroline's heart gallops, though she tries not to think about whose arm she is taking. Miss Delancy allows herself to be led up the staircase. Gently does it. Once inside the club's main room, on finding it deserted, Caroline lifts the bar hatch. "Can I offer you a brandy?"

Miss Delancy gives the slightest of nods.

Caroline glances about the seating area as she presses the glass to the optic. The seat behind the pillar at the duchess's table offers the most privacy. Surely no one would object, just this once. "Shall we?" She leads the way.

They sit. For several moments, all Ursula Delancy does is cup the bowl of the glass, as if it's a hot drink and she's warming her frozen hands. It's as much as Caroline can do not to stare. In what her movie magazines now refer to as 'her heyday', Miss Delancy commanded the kind of adoration normally reserved for royalty.

"Why you waste your money on those things is beyond

me," Ma would say as she caught Caroline reading yet another American import. Caroline could hardly reply that here, in her hands, was living, breathing proof that hers was no impossible dream. But there was more. Her mother would rip the magazine from Caroline's grasp and flick violently through the pages until she came to what she was looking for. Not a peroxide blonde with painted lips – someone she knew how to label – but a fresh-faced beauty. "As if butter wouldn't melt. And all the time, she's been carrying on behind her husband's back." Caroline's mother wasn't alone in despising Ursula Delancy for not looking like a common tart. Anything Caroline might have said in Miss Delancy's defence would have made it sound as if she approved of adultery. The truth is that in Caroline's mind Ginger Rogers, Ursula Delancy and Ingrid Bergman are higher than mere mortals. Everyday rules don't apply to them.

It was because the film-going public had placed Ursula Delancy on a pedestal that her downfall seemed all the more scandalous. Looking at her now, with her guard lowered, Caroline feels only pity. "You'll feel better if you drink something," she says. "I'd be happy to make you a coffee if you'd prefer."

Prompted, Miss Delancy raises the brandy glass halfway to her lips, then hesitates. "I thought I would take a walk. A short walk. I've been trapped in my hotel room ever since I arrived. It isn't so very much to ask, is it?"

That voice. It gives the illusion that she's watching one of the world's most renowned actresses re-enact a famous scene. "No." Caroline shakes her head.

"But oh no! They were all outside, waiting to pounce. The high priests of British morality. And now they have me right where they want me."

After everything that's appeared in print, what *more* can they possibly have on Ursula Delancy?

"They think they own me, you see. All I am is fodder for their grubby little magazines."

Caroline's jaw slackens. She'd had an idea – at least she'd assumed – that actresses sanction the publication of their stories. She has been guilty of lapping up details of heartbreaks and divorces without a thought for the misery that lies behind them.

"I thought I was coming home. I thought that here, in my own country. But the British have always hated success. They pretend to raise you up, higher and higher, while all the time they're waiting, waiting for the moment you slip up. And when you fall from such a great height, people are there, queuing to crush you under the heels of their boots." Miss Delancy lapses into silence. Along with the art of small talk, Caroline has learned when not to speak. She waits. "What was I thinking, coming home after all these years?" For a moment, Caroline wonders if a reply is expected. "The thing is, I didn't *know* when I accepted the invitation. Plus," Ursula Delancy displays a sudden ferocity, as if something within her has come alive, "I've never left anyone in the lurch." She folds down the lapels of her coat, unties the belt. The bulge of her stomach is slight but undeniable.

Caroline takes stock. It was all over the press, how Ursula Delancy had left her husband and young daughter to take up with a Hollywood director. (Also married, but a married man having an affair is barely worthy of a headline.) First came the rumours. Although Miss Delancy brushed questions aside, it became all too apparent why denying the story was impossible. *"Ursula Delancy Baby Due in Three Months" "Report Ursula Delancy to have Baby Shocks Filmdom"* After a box-office flop *("The American people will not tolerate wanton behaviour")* came speculation that she'd be forced to step down from her role in the film she was shooting. Miss Delancy made a public statement. She intended to 'retire into private life'. She had sabotaged her marriage by absenting herself from it. She was determined to make a success of her new relationship, and if that meant sacrifices, so be it. There would be a swift divorce, a private but romantic marriage (in Venice, according to one gossip columnist). But instead, supported by a bishop of somewhere-or-other, her British husband responded with a public statement of his own, insisting that, before she took this drastic step, they 'sit down and talk'.

The next double-spread showed Miss Delancy standing flat-stomached at the prow of a yacht. No more mention of a baby, only a headline declaring Miss Delancy's relief for all concerned, her young daughter in particular, that she and her husband had agreed to an amicable separation. At long last, they could all move forwards. Some months later a discreet notice confirmed that her divorce had been finalised. A single comment from the English camp. "Perhaps, now, I'll no longer be referred to as Mr Delancy." He was right. If mentioned at all, he's referred to as 'Miss Delancy's ex-husband'. For the life of her, Caroline can't remember the man's name.

Why would a second pregnancy, now, be so shocking? Ursula Delancy hasn't yet married her Hollywood director, but second weddings tend to be simple. They can't take a lot of organisation. "I don't quite understand."

"I'm not sure *I* do, but what it boils down to is this." Miss Delancy's hand, on the tabletop, has a redundant look that makes it appear restless. She appears transfixed by the sight of it, unheld, ringless. "Mack's left me," she says. "He's gone back to his wife."

Caroline feels her brow tighten. "I thought she divorced him."

"She did, but they're both Catholic, so..." Ursula Delancy shrugs away her lover's decree absolute; something his church didn't recognise and will now happily overlook. "Also, she's pregnant."

Caroline blinks; she cannot help herself. "By him?"

"Who else?"

It's Percy Shelley all over again. And Miss Delancy is Harriet.

"Do you have a cigarette?" the actress asks.

'If you had never left me, I might have lived.'

Caroline rises, relieved to be offered this breather, even if all she does is walk as far as the bar. She returns with an open carton, a lighter. "Here, let me." She's become proficient in the use of both.

Ursula Delancy frowns as the flame takes and then inhales deeply. "Thank you. So here I am, in my home country. A woman who abandoned her first child, pregnant by a divorced man, who has now left *her.* And if that weren't enough, it's happening while I'm playing the role of a missionary in one of London's leading theatres."

The timing is cruel. How could you say what was real, what was true? "What will you do?"

"Do?"

Caroline colours. She cannot possibly voice her concern – that Ursula Delancy might take the same route as Harriet. "Will you go home?"

"Home?" The actress raises her eyes, lets her mouth fall open. "Now *there's* an interesting concept. No. I'll see the season out. This is one of those times when work means everything. God knows, nothing else makes sense right now."

Caroline glances towards the bay window. The photographer who scaled the building opposite has gone – for the time being. "How much do the newsmen know?"

"They'll soon get wind that Mack's gone back to his wife." A shake of Miss Delancy's head, then a look of intense suspicion. "It wouldn't surprise me if they've tapped the telephone in my hotel room." She alternates sips of brandy with impatient draws on her cigarette. "They might allow a week or so to pass. For discretion's sake. But Mack's wife – ex-wife – oh, what does it matter? She'll be keen to announce her pregnancy. It's not as if *she* has any reason to keep it a secret." She draws deeply on her cigarette.

"What about Mack?" It feels odd to refer to someone Caroline doesn't know by his nickname. "Does he know?"

"Oh, he knows." The actress gives a sharp laugh, one of her wronged-woman trademarks, and picks a stray strand of tobacco from her upper lip. "Mack knows *all* about the baby."

Caroline sees it. An ultimatum has been delivered. Donald Flood expects Ursula Delancy to do the 'decent thing'. Suffer a convenient miscarriage. Here, in London, these things are easily arranged, especially if you're not short of funds. (Yvette couldn't understand why Margot didn't take that route. No one need have known and she could have kept her job.) And if Ursula doesn't do as Mr Flood wishes? He'll deny being the child's father, of course. People will be only too willing to believe that a woman who abandoned her first child – an undeniably beautiful woman, rumoured to have had several liaisons with leading men – might have cheated on her lover. Her betrayal might have even driven him straight back into the arms of his ex-wife.

A glance at the clock: ten to three. There isn't much time. "Miss Delancy, this is a private members' club."

"Call me Ursula, I insist."

"Ursula," Caroline repeats, though the name feels unnatural on her lips. "You should know that we have a number of journalists among our members. You'll have our staff's discretion, but..." *Dammit, the duchess would know who to avoid. Where* is *she when she's needed?*

"I understand."

"I just thought you should be aware. Well –"

Grabbed by the forearm, Caroline meets Ursula's eyes. They are animated, a reminder of the photo from the cover of *Life Magazine*, the one where she's throwing herself at a soldier and pressing her lips to his during VE Day celebrations in the Champs-Élysées. Years before any hint of an affair. Later, Ursula Delancy dismissed it as a spur-of-the-moment thing. She'd been in Paris with her husband, who hadn't minded in the least! She'd simply followed the example of other young women who ran from the crowd to grab hold of the nearest serviceman.

"You think I should tell my side of the story before Mack tells his?"

Caroline had thought of nothing so strategic. But once the story hits the papers, how will Ursula be able to walk onto a West End stage? Definitely not to play the part of a missionary. "I wouldn't pretend to know how to advise you. You must have people who do that."

"People!" Ursula scoffs. "I made this trip alone. No secretary, no business manager, no public relations person. The studio wasn't too happy, but I didn't want to be accused of dragging my defences around with me. I meant to hold my head up high." Ignore the extraordinary situation Ursula Delancy finds herself in, and it's possible to see the actress as an ordinary woman. Close up, she has small lines at the corners of her eyes.

"What about family?"

"I have an ex-husband who's warned me to stay away from our daughter. Then there's my mother, who always sides with him. That's it, I'm afraid."

Discreetly, Caroline nods to Elise, who is lifting the hatch and taking her position behind the bar. She inhales deeply: no trace of fresh cigar smoke. Yet. "I'm sorry, but I need to go and get changed. I start work at three."

"Oh, of course. You mustn't let me get you into trouble. I'm most terribly grateful for what you've done."

"If you'd like to stay, I'll make sure you aren't disturbed. Or you could telephone your driver."

"The photographers? Are they still outside?"

Caroline walks over to the bay window and peers down at the street below. Several sentries still stand guard, smoking. "Some. Not nearly so many."

"One is enough. The others will have set up camp outside my hotel. I'll stay put – if you don't mind, that is."

"I promise I won't be long." Caroline feels embarrassed to ask, but she's no longer talking to a film star. "Would you mind standing me a drink? I know how awful that sounds, but I'm not allowed to sit and talk with customers unless…"

"Of course. Order whatever's appropriate."

"Thank you."

Ursula holds out her brandy glass. "And another one of these for me, if you don't mind." A look of mild panic. "But if you could be the one to bring it."

"You didn't knock!" Valerie is perched in front of the dressing-table mirror, applying lipstick. "Three times, remember?"

Already, Caroline is fumbling with the buttons on her blouse. "I lost track of time." What an admission! "How was your titled gentleman?" She peels off her sleeves at the same time as stepping out of her skirt.

"Gosh, I've only gone and got myself into another mess!"

"How so?"

"I've a horrible feeling I'm falling for him. He said I was exquisite." Valerie luxuriates, before twisting around in her seat. "That's good, isn't it?"

"I'll say so." Caroline opens the wardrobe and stares.

Valerie cocks her head. "You're distracted," she accuses.

"I'm late, is what I am." Her no-nonsense-self rattles hangers. "The silver or the aquamarine?"

"No contest. The aquamarine."

"Really?" Armed with a suggestion, Caroline feels almost reluctant to abandon the silver.

"Honestly. I've never seen you in such a flap. You've met someone!"

"Oh, what does it matter?" She takes the aquamarine off its hanger.

"Where?" Valerie sits up. "Was it in the park?"

"Did you and your gentleman friend stay here the whole time?"

"The whole time." Valerie looks at her dreamily.

"You didn't hear anything out of the ordinary?"

"We had the gramophone turned up. *Bali Ha'i.*"

"And your friend? Did he leave by the back door?"

"Why all the questions? What is this?"

"I've just fought my way through a crowd of press photographers."

"Photographers? You don't think they saw him?"

"Hopefully not. It was someone else they were after." Caroline turns her back on Valerie. "Do me up, will you?"

Valerie zips. "Who?"

"Ursula Delancy."

"You *met* her?"

Caroline turns and takes Valerie's hands. "She's downstairs. In the bar."

"Now?"

"I brought her here. I didn't know what else to do. What do you think Terry will say?"

"Depends what kind of mood he's in."

"All I could think of was getting her away from the photographers."

"Good thinking." Valerie nods rapidly, as if trying to convince the both of them. "He'll buy that."

"You think so?"

"Definitely. But let's get to him first."

"Let's get to who first?"

Heat rises to Caroline's face. For once, fresh cigar smoke didn't precede their boss's arrival. No time to exchange glances. Probably better that way; a glance could be interpreted. "Terry," Caroline says, turning. He's lolling against the doorframe, enough diagonal to let them know he hasn't arrived this minute but has stealthily taken up position.

He taps his wristwatch. "I was just coming to see where my girls were, but I seem to have stumbled in on something."

"It's nothing."

If Terry wore glasses, he would be peering over the top of them. "It's something."

"I was about to come and find you."

"And here I am."

Caroline pauses, then launches in. "We have a visitor."

"I gathered as much. Sitting at the duchess's table, no less."

"I didn't know where else to put her."

"Aw." Sarcasm. A frown. "Were no other tables spare?"

"It's Ursula Delancy," Caroline blurts.

Terry's eyebrows rise, his features flatten. Perhaps it's an effort to reconcile the woman in the headscarf and raincoat with more familiar images of the celluloid star. Then he gives what could almost be described as a smile.

"I didn't know it was her, not to begin with. She'd been cornered by photographers. I just wanted to get them away from the club before opening time."

"And who's entertaining Miss Delancy? Who's making sure she isn't harassed while the pair of you are idly gossiping?"

"Elise is keeping an eye on things. I just came upstairs to get changed."

"And now you're changed." One sweeping hand indicates her way to the door.

Caroline inclines her head and walks, but Terry intercepts her, grasping her shoulder. In that grip is an indication of the strength he could yield (as there is with every handshake, every clap on the back). *I could crush you.* His face close to hers, he says, "You did well."

And, as she walks down the stairs, Caroline feels it: a swell of pride. Until this moment, she hasn't realised how hard she's been trying to prove herself.

CHAPTER SEVENTEEN

PATRICE

Patrice pauses at the top of the stairs. With one hand on the balustrade, she frowns. A woman's back, a raincoat, a headscarf. Annoyingly, nothing can be seen in the mirror from this angle. A few steps further forward is the bar hatch. Not a place Patrice makes a habit of lingering, though some spend entire afternoons here by choice. "Elise, why is there someone at my table?"

Elise, who is busily slotting glasses into cubby holes above the bar, turns her head, her voice low. "I'd better leave it to Caroline to explain. She'll be down any minute."

Patrice looks around at her options. "Can't you just ask whoever it is to move?"

Elise puts down the glasses she's holding, comes closer. "I can't, ma'am."

"You can't?"

"No, ma'am, I can't."

Intrigued by the barmaid's lack of apology, Patrice cranes her neck to look in the direction of her alcove.

"*...The People's Republic of China, I ask you!*"

"*...Pronounced bay-jing. Don't ask me what was wrong with Peking...*"

"...Blame the Public Morality Council. They've created the demand. Call a play 'thoroughly indecent' and suddenly everyone wants to go..."

"She's not to be disturbed."

"Well, if *you* won't tell me who's upstaged me, I shall find someone who will." Patrice scans the room, trying to locate Vincent, but he isn't hugging the far end of the bar and doesn't seem to be at any of the tables. Blast! He must be out on the trail of a story. The entire city is fixated on unexplained disappearances – young women, which always creates more of a stir. Never mind. There's a potential here to enjoy herself.

Patrice strides across the carpeted room, calling out, "Who's been sitting in *my* chair?" Whoever it is doesn't turn, but other heads break away from wild boasts, commentary on world events, National Service this and Atlee that.

On reaching the table, Patrice begins, "Perhaps I could introduce myself," but gets no further. Her mouth would drop open if she'd let it.

There, in her seat, is the very woman she's been mentally composing a letter to, but confound it, she couldn't get the words right. Patrice's inept attempts made it sound as if she was asking someone to acknowledge her own struggle, her desire to be recognised for what she *is,* not for what they imagine she *has.* (Not nearly as much as it once was.) But the woman's eyes widen, and it is not with shock or annoyance.

"You're the Wyndham!" Ursula Delancy stands, as if Patrice and not the actress has just walked out of a celluloid frame, cigarette holder in hand. "I'm right, aren't I?"

"Nobody's used my maiden name for such a long time, certainly not in that context." In front of such incredible talent, she finds herself embarrassed to be recognised. Someone who was only ever famous for being an 'It Girl' and whose more recent press outings really *have* come under the heading of 'outings'. "It was all such a terribly long time ago."

"Not *that* long ago! I used to love reading *A Day in the Life of a Debutante.*"

For three years, not a day went by when Patrice's name didn't appear in the gossip columns, which had led to her being offered a column of her own. Just the other day, sitting where Ursula Delancy is sitting, she had boasted, "I developed a knack of projecting myself – like an actress. I had a flair for it, they said."

"I can't imagine that pleased your father," her companion had said.

"My dear, he was delighted. Every time my name appeared as 'daughter of oil baron', his company's share prices rocketed. And given that this was during what we now call 'the great depression', that was quite something."

Ursula Delancy smiles. "What should I call you?"

"Everyone calls me Patrice," she replies, though, in truth, few people do. Not these days.

"Patrice," Ursula Delancy takes her hand in the way that a woman takes another's hand, the lightest of squeezes. "Why, you and your friends were responsible for Norman Hartnell's success in the fashion world."

"I hardly think we can take the credit. No one understands women the way Norman does."

"But you wore his designs before anyone else."

"We didn't want to look like anyone else." Here she is, talking to Ursula Delancy about fashion, and so recently after seeing her in the role of a missionary. And yet, Patrice realises, she's doing exactly what she blames Charles for: confusing the actress with the roles she plays.

"No one could accuse you of that! Listen to me, where are my manners? I was just so… I've been sitting here eaves-dropping on a conversation about Vivienne Leigh. How she's too *well-bred* to show any real emotion." Patrice finds herself accepting that there may be something in that, but Ursula

Delancy laughs off the notion as ridiculous. Such a recognisable sound. Several heads turn, but the men mistakenly think they're looking for someone they know. Dressed as she is, the actress is hidden in plain sight. "I've been feeling that I should jump up and defend her."

"Everyone here has an opinion, I'm afraid."

"I think we know where they read them." They laugh, and Patrice is taken aback by how natural and easy it feels. Latterly, she has grown distrustful of women.

"Won't you have a seat?" Miss Delancy asks.

Surprised to find herself invited to sit at her own table, Patrice watches the actress pull the belt of her coat. Her waist isn't as tiny as Patrice assumed.

"Oh," Ursula looks up. "You're meeting someone. But of course you are. Don't let me keep you."

"Oh no. No." Patrice sits, rather inelegantly, she feels. "This is my club."

"Then I have you to thank!"

"I don't own it." Flustered (not something she's used to feeling), Patrice is keen to correct the misunderstanding. "I'm a member."

Again, that laugh. "There I go again. But how wonderful, to always have somewhere you can go."

"Surely there are similar clubs in the States?"

"Quite possibly. But I'm rarely in the same place for any length of time. Certainly not long enough to feel as if I might actually belong. Champagne?"

Patrice is about to decline, when she considers, perhaps for the first time, that she might be insulting her 'host'. "Please," she says.

Ursula doesn't summon a member of staff as Patrice would when there is no one she can ask to do the honours, but frees the bottle from its bed of ice and pours, then hands Patrice the glass.

Unwilling to let Ursula's signpost to her acting career pass without comment, Patrice blurts, "I saw you."

"Ah." Ursula dips her head, looking down.

Why so clumsy? She, with a reputation for 'cold precision'. "As Gladys. I was there for your opening night."

The actress raises her eyes to the ceiling, mouths the letter 'O', her face quite altered. "For a minute, I thought I was in for another lecture. I don't seem to be able to go anywhere without a whiff of scandal following me." Ursula looks at Patrice, and it is like an embrace. "You were there?" Her gratitude is touching.

Patrice tries to set aside her failed attempts to commit to ink all that Ursula's performance made her feel. "You were mesmerising. Really. Your voice." She nods, hoping that nodding will help to convey a little of her admiration.

"It means so much to hear *you* say that. It really does. The role, the central speech especially, is particularly important to me. I so admire Miss Aylward."

"I must admit, it certainly made me think."

"In what way?"

Patrice opens her mouth to reply, but something seems to catch in her throat. "I was trying to remember the last time I was of use. Genuinely of use. And I had to go all the way back to the Great War."

"I remember that famous photograph of you wearing pearls with a nurse's uniform."

Patrice raises her eyebrows. "I got a terrible dressing down for my trouble, I can tell you! Lord knows, the Red Cross didn't want me for my nursing skills. My contribution to the war effort was nothing so noble."

"Oh?"

"Originally, I applied to the Admiralty – something clerical – but they saw straight through me. 'Someone like you would be wasted,' they said. The gentlest of let-downs. Secretly, I was hugely relieved. To me, office work had as much appeal as a bowl of cold porridge."

"Oh, me too."

"But *unlike* you, I have few talents to boast of."

"I'm sure that's not true."

"I was capable of putting on as good a spread as could be had in wartime London, and that's about it. A chap from the officer's club approached me, so I became their go-getter. When they wanted asparagus or strawberries, I delivered. They were never without white linen, sliced lemon and curls of butter on my watch." Patrice winces, losing her taste for the subject. "That was the sum of it. Keeping the top brass supplied and amused."

"There's a lot to be said for boosting morale."

"Really, it was so little..."

"I know it felt that way. You probably read how I spent my war hiding away from the action. Yes, work took me to America, but I was constantly back and forth, and the studio sent us off to visit the troops. I wish I could say it was my choice, but that really *would* be taking too much credit. Then, in '44, I had my daughter. Our act of optimism, we called her. She kept me at home for a year. But according to some sources, I was *still* hiding as far away as I could from the action."

"The newspapers." Patrice shakes her head. "Even now, they can't let you have your moment without harking back." She worries she has said too much.

"Well, if I *will* provide them with so much ammunition!"

"No, I won't have that!" Not with champagne entering her bloodstream. "They wouldn't dare write the same thing about a man. I wired Max and Gomer and gave them short shrift. 'Look here,' I said, 'it's got to stop.'" Ursula shakes her head in incomprehension. "I'm sorry. I have a terrible habit of assuming that people I meet know the same people I do." Perhaps she and Charles are more alike than she cares to admit. "That's the *Daily Express* and the *Telegraph* to you."

"Newspaper men?"

"Magnates. They own the papers."

The actress laughs apologetically, then closes her eyes. "I don't know why I should be surprised that you have contacts in high places."

Terrence's new girl has put in an appearance. Late, and not for the first time. Standing in the doorway, she is deep in conversation with him – receiving a ticking off, no doubt – but she extracts herself and dons the self-possessed smile that made quite a first impression. Unlike the other girls who sashay, Caroline walks purposefully towards them. "Miss Delancy, ma'am, I hoped to be in time to introduce you, but I see you've already met."

"I've told you, no more of that nonsense. You must call me Patrice." A faint flicker of a 'V' forms between the girl's eyebrows.

"Patrice," Ursula Delancy puts one hand on her forearm, "this brave young woman rescued me from the press photographers. You must forgive me." She closes her eyes and presses her knuckles to her forehead, presenting a different version of herself. "In the chaos, I've completely forgotten your name."

"Caroline."

"Caroline! You'll join us for that glass of champagne?"

The girl looks restless. "If I'm not interrupting."

"Goodness, no. I don't know what I'd have done if you hadn't come along when you did. And I mustn't forget about your doorman."

"George." The girl doesn't pour her own drink, as staff tend to when invited, as she did when Patrice told her to help herself. Instead she perches. Her back is straight but an awkwardness remains. A former sloucher, perhaps.

"You'll thank him for me, won't you?"

The girl dips her head and gives a smile of gratitude as she accepts the champagne Ursula has poured. "He'd be embarrassed if I did."

"Whatever you think best. I'd hate to be the cause of any embarrassment."

The table falls silent. Caroline presses her lips together, keeping her eyes on Ursula, who seems to be disappearing into herself. Someone needs to take the lead. If it must be Patrice, so be it. "I was just telling Ursula that I saw her as Gladys Aylward."

Caroline's poise dissolves. "I'd *love* to see your play, but tickets are like gold dust. I hear that fights have broken out in the box office queue."

So this is how to impress the girl.

Ursula seems to bask. "Well, that's something small I can do to repay you. I'll put your name on my guest list and the next time you have an evening off, just come along to the theatre."

"That would be..." Caroline laughs and then breaks off, censoring herself. Patrice can see that she's keeping one eye on Terrence as he does his rounds, feeding on the kind of compliments men toss between one another when trying to stay on their good sides. The girl does it cleverly, in a way that would only be obvious to someone who's used to observing. Patrice sees the reason for her watchfulness. Terrence is circling closer and closer.

"George too – if you think he'd be interested."

Now that the offer has been made, you can make your excuses. Patrice looks pointedly at Caroline but the look she receives in return is unwavering.

"Patrice," Caroline says when Patrice makes it clear that a stalemate has been reached. "Might I have a private word with Miss Delancy?"

Am I being asked to leave my own table?

"No, it's fine," Ursula puts one hand on the girl's forearm

arm, a gesture born of confidences. "I think Patrice might be able to introduce me to one of her newspaper contacts."

The girl nods. "That's what I was about to suggest."

Ursula turns to Patrice, smiles a little crookedly. "I was wondering if you might know of a sympathetic journalist."

The girl cuts in. "Someone discreet." A certain possessiveness has crept into the girl's manner. Something has passed between her and the actress, something Patrice missed.

"A discreet journalist?" Patrice presses her lips together. "Is there such an animal? I'd have to think about that." Only Vincent springs to mind.

"There would be a story in it for them. Mine. It's going to break, no matter what, so I want to be the one who breaks it. The deal would be this. An exclusive. No speculation. And no approaching third parties for comments."

Patrice has been in this very same position. Knowing that even with all her resources and unquestionable credentials, the best she can hope for is a delay. Time to get to the people she must get to so that they wouldn't learn about their lost thousands – in one case hundreds of thousands – from the gutter press.

"Unless," Ursula flattens one hand on the table, "Your column? Did you write it yourself, Patrice?"

"The content came from my diary. Someone else turned it into a workable piece."

Ursula can clearly see potential. "Could we perhaps mock up a first draft, present it and see what they say?"

The girl addresses the actress. "*You* must know journalists."

Ursula shakes her head. "Publicity agents act for the studios. If we want a different kind of piece, we need a different kind of approach."

"Your story in your own words. Although..." The girl is hesitant.

"Go on."

She leans forward and, in a low urgent voice, says, "If you're going to do this, I think you need to act quickly. To stop someone else getting the story out first."

Ursula nods gravely.

Patrice volunteers: "I have time on my hands if you do. One moment."

"What is it?" Ursula's face is full of anticipation.

"Ladies!" It is Terrence. Come to say something crass, no doubt.

"Terrence." Patrice stands. The girl clearly has Ursula's trust. She, Patrice, must respect that. "I wondered if I might borrow Caroline."

His brow furrows with confusion. "Borrow her?"

"A couple of days should do it. You'll be amply compensated." She turns purposefully. "Caroline?"

The girl is wide eyed, waiting for Terrence's eruption, but Patrice knows that none will come. She is one of the few people Terrence Blagdon kowtows to.

"Can I suggest you go and pack a few things?" she directs.

Still, the girl looks to her employer as if expecting him to counter the instruction. He has no idea what's going on and clearly sees no way of asking. "Why are you still standing here, Caroline? The duchess asked you to go and pack your bag."

"The dress you were wearing the other day when we spoke would be ideal. And perhaps something for the evening." Patrice turns to Terrence. "I'm in your debt," she fawns, then lowers her voice. "I expect to hear that Caroline has been paid."

He recognises this as the dismissal it is intended to be. "Ma'am. Miss Delancy, we're so glad you chose to join us. It hardly needs to be said but you'd be most welcome at any time."

Patrice turns back to Ursula. "When do you finish at the theatre?"

"The play is over by half past ten. I'm usually free by eleven."

For once, Patrice dismisses concerns over her petrol ration. If necessary, she will call in a favour. "My driver will pick you up," she says. "The press won't know him. We'll go to Whitlocke. We won't be disturbed there."

PART TWO
DECEMBER 1952

CHAPTER EIGHTEEN

RUTH

A sense of unreality prevails, and yet at the same time, it is all too real. It comes as no surprise to Ruth that she's been found guilty and, guilty, she is stripped of the clothes she wore in court, her false nails and eyelashes. In their place, baggy prison-issue overalls. Flanked by two prison guards she is led down endless corridors with their smells of boiled food and disinfectant, their sounds of clanking pails and clinking keys, through the yellow glow of artificial light into CC wing, up a flight of stairs, a dip worn in the centre of each step by decades of tramping feet, her eyes hurrying over scratch marks etched on the walls.

The condemned cell. A wardress stands as Ruth enters, hands in front instead of behind her back, and Ruth understands that this woman will be with her night and day. She will not have to be alone, and for that she is peculiarly grateful.

"I'm Evelyn. Evelyn Galilee."

The wardress is clearly wary. She has become a person to be wary of. "Ruth. Ruth Ellis," she says. All that history in a name. Perhaps once she's got to know Evelyn she'll tell her that her father Arthur Nelson was born a Hornby. Ruth's sister Muriel has the name Hornby, her brother Granville too. But in 1926

Ruth's father changed his surname to Neilson, a variation on his middle name. Why was never explained and what her grandfather Walter made of it, Ruth doesn't know either. To women, names are lesser things, exchangeable, but men – men aren't used to having their family histories wiped out, their offspring disinherit them in that way. Although the whole family adopted their father's chosen name (even Julian, who wasn't a Hornby but had Muttar's family name, Cothals), Ruth was the first child to be christened a Neilson. Already, few remember Ruth Neilson. She's a fading photograph, a nine-year-old standing outside Worting County Junior School.

Ruth had thought she would become a McCallum. She'd accepted Clare's proposal. And in her naivety she'd rehearsed the name, practised the signature that would never be hers. Ruth McCallum.

Perhaps Ruth might have become a Blakely – who knows? On the last day of March David told her that no one was ever going to part them, but something inside Ruth had always told her that marriage wasn't their destiny. Someone – most likely David's mother – would have put a stop to it.

And so she will go to her grave as Ruth Ellis, though she was married to George so briefly. A year to the day between her wedding and the date he filed for divorce and custody of their daughter. What an anniversary that was!

Ruth looks about her. All her life, it seems, she's been on the move. She had only been at Egerton Gardens with David for two months, and at Goodwood Court with Desmond for the two before that. The room she stands in now isn't the small cell with iron window-bars that Ruth had feared. Larger than some of the living rooms she's known in her time, with its walls of pink and brown, this room will be her last home. To call it 'home' may sound like a joke, but it hits her, this realisation, and Ruth feels the need to square up to it.

"Home sweet home," she says, looking from the wardrobe to

the table and chairs before she goes to test the iron bed. "Springs could do with a drop of oil." And they could make more of an effort with the soft furnishings, she thinks, looking at the naked light bulb.

"Your bathroom's through there." The gesture the wardress makes towards the door is awkward and stilted.

"An en suite!" Ruth jumps up, taking in the wash basin, bath and lavatory. "I haven't had one of these since I stayed at the Hotel Bristol, and there they charged eleven guineas a week. I don't suppose there's room service?"

"Room service, including ten cigarettes a day."

"Ten!" The corners of Ruth's mouth are trembling, but she will not give in to tears. "Well, that is generous."

"And through that door is where you'll receive your visitors." Evelyn indicates a barrier with a small cell-like room on the other side.

"I'm allowed visitors?"

"They have to be approved but, other than that, as many as you want."

Not Joe. She couldn't bear for Joe to look at her like that again. *"And what's that?" Ruth asks of the green six-foot high screen that runs along the length of one wall. The type of screen that can easily be pushed aside.*

"Oh, I wouldn't worry about that," Evelyn says, but she's in too much of a hurry to say it. And from that single sentence, Ruth knows. One hand goes to her neck – her long neck. Remember how Father used to say, "All the better for hanging with"? At the time, they were living at the house in Dunsford Crescent, and there was a rope tied to the attic door. She shudders to think that those were the words he used. "All the better for hanging with."

This, then, is why they walked her so far away from the main prison, why she is hidden at the top of a winding staircase.

When the time comes, Ruth won't have far to go.

CHAPTER NINETEEN

URSULA

"Why not cast me as a femme fatale?" Ursula puts it to Aldo. The director has always had a reputation for being difficult. Expect the worst, and he rarely disappoints.

"Are you out of your mind? We came pretty darn close to suing you for breach of contract and you think I'm going to put you in a *lead?*"

If she lets him, he'll persist in throwing the morality clause back in her face. She's done her penance. In fact, since the moment she announced her second pregnancy, since she told the press that she intended to bring up her child alone, Ursula's done what feels like penance for every woman who's ever refused to live within the strict confines of predictability afforded to her generation, and dammit, she's taken it all on the chin. What's more, when Aldo's given her unpromising material, she's made the most of it, earning a Best Supporting Actress nomination for what was only supposed to have been a cameo. Publicly, Aldo was thrilled.

"Ten words, that's all we gave her. But look what she did with them!"

Behind closed doors he exploded. "I want awards, sure, but you –"

"I'm not supposed to be the one who wins them. Is that it?"

Denial wasn't his response. Instead, a low growl. Angry at being caught out, he was unrepentant nonetheless. Well, Ursula's had it. Aldo has two ex-wives and no journalist has ever camped outside his house to ask if any of his relationships overlapped. "You asked what kind of role I think I'm fit to play," she insists.

"I *asked* what kind of role the public will be persuaded to come and see you in."

"My answer's the same. I'm already seen as someone who refuses to stick to the rules. A judge called me promiscuous and amoral. Why not capitalise on that? Make me predatory, conniving, traitorous and monstrous. Let me spin a web of deceit. Throw in a love triangle. Make it look as if I'm getting away with it, then give the audience exactly what they want. Feed me to the lions."

"Actually, Aldo, sh-she might be on to something," Fredric begins nervously, but it's this very nervousness that makes him non-threatening. "They know Ursula's had her sh-showdown in real life, but they missed out on a ringside seat. Offer them that, and you'll have them qu-queuing round the block."

Aldo rubs his chin. "We cash in on negative publicity." It is not a no.

Fredric is warming to his theme. "S-something along the lines of *Blue Dahlia.* You could have the unfaithful wife *and* a seductive ex-wife of the wife's lover."

Ursula hadn't pictured anything quite so blatant, but it's too late to backtrack. And it doesn't seem to matter what role she takes, someone, somewhere will criticise her for it. *"I had fun with the role,"* she imagines telling an interviewer. *"Who wouldn't want to play someone dangerous?"*

"And you're prepared for the backlash?" Aldo points at Ursula. "Because, believe me, there will be a backlash. It might get ugly."

It might. Robin will hate it and God only knows what Mack will make of it. But she can't fall any lower in Robin's estimation, and as for Mack – he's lost his right to any opinion. This is a risk Ursula *has* to take. She can't just sit out the rest of her contract. She needs to be in the public eye and she needs hits. Without them, her career is as good as over. "I have a plane to catch. I'll be in London for a fortnight, but when I get back I want to work."

Aldo throws up his hands. "She wants to work! In that case, Fredric, you'd better get your team working on a script."

CHAPTER TWENTY

CAROLINE

Cliveden for the weekend. Opulence on a scale that, fresh out of Suffolk, Caroline would have found obscene. She's become used to free-flowing champagne, but here it is served on silver trays by waiters in black tie. A woman wearing what at a first glance appears to be a sequinned dress accepts a glass.

Caroline turns to Valerie: "I *love* that sequinned dress!"

"Those aren't sequins, darling." Valerie, who traipses into any room as if she owns it. "They're diamonds!"

"*I* want a diamond dress."

"Say no more, Cinderella. I'll have a word with Terry."

Proximity to privilege intoxicates. It makes you forget your misgivings and focus on advantages. And here there are no shortage of advantages.

In what to all intents and purposes is a ballroom, but is described modestly as 'the entrance hall', as Caroline and Valerie giggle and hold each other up, Patrice and her partner drift past leaving her signature perfume in their wake. Its effect is instantly sobering. Caroline separates from Valerie and holds herself upright. There is no question of the duchess doing anything other than avoiding eye contact but, over the shoulder of her male companion, Caroline admires how naturally she manages it, turning away to greet a huddle of young men.

Valerie doesn't want to be ignored. She moves into the duchess's eyeline, ready with her signature shimmy.

Caroline excuses herself and, her heels clicking across the marble, hurries to Valerie's side. "Not here," she says, ignoring Valerie's pout, taking a firm grip of her arm, and leading her back to the men.

"Ow, you're hurting me."

Caroline now understands what the duchess meant by discretion. This ability to turn a blind eye, that most British of attributes, isn't just a two-way exchange. Caroline has no good family name, no trust fund, no reputation to lose, but she desperately needs her job – a job that puts a roof over her head and supplements her mother's take-home. Simply by being here, Caroline has strayed into a grey area in terms of Terrence Blagdon's rules. The man she's with almost certainly knows the duke. This means that the duchess is safe, no matter who her young man might be. If Caroline's gentleman were to tell tales out of school, he might then be forced to admit he's taken a hostess off on a weekend jaunt while his wife is convalescing from one of those ailments middle and upper-class women go to the coast to convalesce from. And so it is easier, easier to pretend one has not seen the other, easier not to be seen talking to the other. That way, there will be fewer things to deny.

"There you are. Come and tell me what's new." The effort of speaking makes Sandy tail off in a hacking cough. He raises one hand to catch Elise's eye.

She slams a champagne bucket on the bar. "Be right with you!"

The noise Sandy makes, the way he gasps for air, is as

painful to watch as it is to listen to. Caroline waits for the fit to subside before asking, "Are you alright, Sandy? You don't look well." His skin has a waxy quality. Purple shadows below his eyes resemble bruises. A scarf hangs loose around his neck. Its soft silk may well have been white until a few days ago.

"It's this wonderful clean air of ours! Welcome to London, the most overpopulated and industrialised city in the world." Sandy thumps his chest with a clenched fist. "When I was a boy we used to say, 'It's a regular pea souper', but this stuff?" His voice thickens. "Pour me a drink, will you?" he manages to wheeze.

Caroline pours, saying, "I thought I was used to fog, but at least Suffolk dag knows its place. Strictly dawn and dusk." She hands Sandy a glass of champagne, which he downs as if it's lemonade. When did his cheekbones begin to look so finely sculpted? "Better?" she asks. For a moment the coughing ceases and she can hear cartwheeling piano notes.

"Another." Breathless and without letting go of the stem, Sandy presents his glass for a re-fill. "Last night," he continues, "walking home, I couldn't even see my feet. There were footsteps close behind. I turned to see who it was but, honestly, Sir David Maxwell Fyfe could have been on my tail and I wouldn't have had a clue. I only knew which building was mine because I recognised next-door's iron railings."

These stories we tell, skirting the real concern. In Sandy's cough, a dredging of silt is evidence of the filth Londoners suck down into their lungs. Only a fool would venture out without their nose and mouth covered. "Have you thought about getting a mask?"

He holds one hand to each side of his face and flutters his eyelashes. "And cover this up?"

"People are dying out there and you're concerned it might hamper your flirting!"

"How many London winters have you seen?"

"This is my third."

"When it's your fifty-ninth, *then* you can give me advice. The death tally's always higher in winter. That's a fact. Besides, gas masks were bad enough." Again, the bronchial rattle.

It's difficult to base a convincing argument on gut feeling alone. Like all smogs that have come before, this one will be burnt away by the sun or chased off by a stiff breeze. Londoners will get through it because they always do, trotting out, 'We survived the Blitz' as evidence of their resilience. Anyway, here *she* is, preparing a lecture as she blows smoke into the thick fug of the bar room, only hours after reading an article with the title *Cancer by the Carton*. If that isn't hypocritical, then what is? "It's a look." Caroline shrugs at her friend, breaking out a smile. "I thought it might have a certain appeal."

He throws her a sideways glance. "Miss Wilby, you're the most terrible influence." The coughing starts again, a roiling sound of thick smoke and coal dust.

"Everything I know I learned from you."

"To partners in crime." Sandy raises his glass, clinks hers and sips and, for a moment, it seems to help. "Your news..." he prompts, waving his cigarette in the air. "I'm waiting."

There *is* news, but the truth is that Caroline doesn't know what to make of it. She spent so long learning not to blink as men referred to her as 'crumpet' and spent more in a single afternoon than her father earned in a year. She's got to grips with the small talk, keeps pace with politics, horse-racing results, reviews for cinema and theatre. She's kept up with her library visits, no longer embarrassed by all the things she doesn't know but keen to add to the tally of what she does. She can give the appearance of hanging on a man's every word, even if it's the umpteenth time he's repeated the same story, having stopped asking herself if her laughter rings false, if they'll fall for it. The truth is they all *want* to fall for it.

"I knew it! There *is* something."

Found out, there's little point in holding back. "A letter."

"From whom?"

"Ursula Delancy." It is heavy in Caroline's pocket, but she doesn't unfold it, not here, not even for Sandy.

"Miss Delancy!" He's impressed by their ongoing correspondence. "What does she have to say for herself this time?"

"Actually, she's back in England and is thinking of settling here."

"Just after she's been restored as America's sweetheart?"

Not in the eyes of her daughter. Or her mother. The people who count. "You know what the press is like. Box-office success, an award, and suddenly they can't understand why, in this day and age, a child born out of wedlock is so shocking." Caroline shakes her head. The memory rankles.

Sandy nudges her. "She won't like the taxes."

"That's hardly her priority."

"Nobody thinks it is until they're asked to cough up. But you still haven't told me the reason she's telling you about her intentions."

"She's going to need a nanny."

"You?" He looks genuinely thrilled. "That's wonderful!"

The skin on Caroline's forehead tightens as her eyebrows rise.

"Why are you even hesitating?"

"I thought I'd done my share of looking after children. That's what I escaped when I came here." Caroline feels a pang of guilt. She has put off writing to Betty.

"They were family. *This* would be different. You'd be paid."

"I know." And she does.

"Plus, you'd have the opportunity to see how an actress lives. Don't tell me you haven't imagined it. The contacts who'll come to the house. You saying, 'Shall I get the telephone? I'm sorry, Sir Laurence, Miss Delancy isn't home right now.'"

Caroline looks down into her glass, smiles sadly. She can't begin to explain why the glimmer of possibility has lost its sheen. Perhaps she's embarrassed by the naïve seventeen-year-old she was. This, the here and now, is real life. And it could be one hell of a lot worse.

"Don't tell me you've had a *better* offer?" Sandy's use of the word *better* makes her flinch. "Not Miss Leigh!"

Caroline's offer comes from someone so far removed from Miss Leigh that she wants to shy away from his name. It feels dangerous to say it. "Maurice Conley."

"What of him?" Sandy says with all the revulsion she'd anticipated.

"He's looking for someone to manage his new club." She dips her head as if in confession. "My name cropped up in conversation." *"Think about it. You'd be the youngest manager at any West End club."* She'd felt flattered, of course she had. "Your name cropped up!" Valerie said excitedly. "Don't you see? You've arrived!"

Sandy's face is denial. Repudiation. "Oh, no. No."

"I knew you'd say that."

"Are you mad? Darling, I don't care how good he's made you feel about yourself, how much money he's offering." (More, so much more.) "Compared to Morrie Conley, Terry's a pussycat. Conley doesn't even bother with a veneer of respectability. Let him into your life, and it's a one-way ticket."

"I knew you'd say *that* as well."

"Then why do I get the impression that you're considering it?"

"I'd have the flat above the club to myself. I could bring my sister to live with me." Valerie, of course, thinks that the accommodation is as good as hers. And this idea of a continued double act makes things doubly difficult. Terry will see it as another betrayal.

"But you just *told* me: the chief advantage of being based in

London is that you're not lumbered with brothers and sisters."

"I wouldn't be *lumbered*. Betty's three years older than she was when I left." Old enough to be interesting to Uncle Anthony. "She'll be able to take care of herself."

Sandy sits back in his chair. His expression softens. "You can imagine her playing in Hyde Park. Feeding the ducks. Taking a boat out. Listening to the brass band."

She makes a half-hearted attempt at a smile. "Admiring the best arse in London."

"Oh, for sure! But you must realise that a flat above a club that's owned by Conley, with all that he'd expect, is hardly the ideal residence for an impressionable young girl."

Caroline has no answer to this. Ever since her father did what he did, her family have lived hand to mouth. Hand-me-downs, hand-outs, other people's leftovers, making do, scrimping, skimping, tightening their belts: the way so many people get by. But even with the money Caroline's been sending home, even with what Uncle Anthony can spare, her mother has run up debts. The family has moved to a couple of rented rooms. The boys top and tail. Her mother and Betty share a bed. Is *that* ideal?

Caroline can no longer afford to play the disgruntled daughter. There is no one else. She must do whatever it takes to shoulder her father's share of responsibility. And surely Maurice Conley would have to behave if Betty was living with her.

"How much is Miss Delancy offering?"

"She doesn't say."

"So, write back! Tell her you're interested but can't afford to be any worse off, and that you'd been hoping to apply for a job that might allow you to invite your sister to stay."

Caroline looks at Sandy, one of her few genuine friends. What place could he and Valerie possibly have in this new life of hers?

"Oh, no." Can she hide nothing from him? "I'm not part of your decision. I can't be and what's more I refuse to be," he says, with a ferocity she's rarely sensed in him before. "You're better than this club, and one hundred times better than Conley's, you marvellous, obstinate girl. Get out of here – and don't you dare look back."

CHAPTER TWENTY-ONE

PATRICE

"Aunt Patrice!"

The shout slices through the everyday sounds of the city. It's a summons from the past and it is not convenient. Her companion looks questioningly – *who's this?* – as she shrugs his hand away from her elbow.

"Aunt Patrice!"

It's unavoidable. They both turn to look at the young man who is approaching, one hand raised in greeting, slightly out of breath. "I *knew* it was you!" he calls from a short distance.

"Would you mind awfully if I refer to you as my secretary?" Patrice asks, a ridiculous request to make, and she knows it.

"I'd prefer to be your chauffeur than your secretary. I'll wait in the car." He peels away, taking the route around the back of his Jaguar. Berthram would never do that. Berthram would have touched the peak of his cap and nodded.

"Arnold," she says, taking in her godson's appearance. His gait might still be a young man's gait, but all trace of boyishness is gone. "I haven't seen you since –"

"Since I joined up."

Of course he is changed. "I'm relieved to see you looking so well." As a child, her godson was more Derek than Lucinda. Now Patrice sees more of Lucinda in his features.

Arnold's Adam's apple moves. "I'm at the Foreign Office now." He gives a smile that is not quite a smile.

"Following in the family tradition."

"Something like that," he says.

She will not drag him to a place he does not wish to go. One gets on with things the best one can. "Well, that's wonderful. Wonderful."

"Would you? What I mean to say is, could I persuade you to come for a drink?"

A tension in Patrice's shoulders makes itself known. "I'd be delighted to see you at any time, you know that."

"I thought now – if you're not doing anything, that is. You and I both know that if we go our separate ways it will never happen. And I think that would be an awful shame. Don't you?"

Part of her would like to say that she would love to, but there is somewhere else she must be. "Are you quite sure you're not embarrassed to be seen with me in public?" Easier to play the wicked aunt than to ask Arnold what he knows.

"Quite sure."

Patrice is not so sure. Not sure whether this meeting is accidental or carefully choreographed, but if she is to agree – if there is even the slimmest of chances that Arnold will report back to his parents – then whatever follows must be on her terms. She puts one hand on the top of the car and bends from the waist. She nods to her companion in the driver's seat. Then she tucks her hand behind Arnold's elbow. "We can walk to my club. It's not far." They leave behind them a screech of angry tyres.

By the time Patrice leads Arnold through the bar room, she has relaxed a little. Her hand remains tucked inside the crook of his elbow. People at the club may not see her as a tactile person, but Arnold makes it clear that he does.

"Ma'am," Elise says as they approach the mahogany of the bar. "Sir."

"This is my godson, Arnold." Patrice hopes he can hear the pride in her voice.

"Pleased to meet you. What will it be?"

"A pot of tea, and?" Patrice turns to Arnold.

"Gin and tonic, please."

Elise tongs ice into a tall glass, then turns her back to pour the drink and add the slice of lemon. "One gin and tonic. I'll bring your tea over, ma'am."

Arnold has his wallet out. Elise looks to Patrice as if asking for a decision. "Don't worry," she tells him in a lowered tone, "I have a slate."

"There's no point in arguing. I asked you."

Patrice tries to remember when someone last bought her a drink. She is not quite sure how to respond, but she feels lighter, somehow.

They are seated in her alcove when Arnold bridges her present and past: "Some of my favourite memories are of coming to Whitlocke as a child. Rolling down the grassy bank between the terrace and the lawn. My mother would try to stop me, but you would always say, 'Let him.'"

"I always worried you'd be bored."

"Not likely! I used to pretend the place was mine. I was the king of the castle." He lays one hand on hers, cold from the ice in his gin and tonic, and she thinks (it is a fleeting thought), *Perhaps. Perhaps I could leave Whitlocke to Arnold. He's almost family.* "I was so glad you didn't lose your family's home. Glad it didn't come to that."

He has found his way to the subject Patrice most wants to avoid. All other conversation in the bar is muted as she recalls a catalogue of painful decisions – we can't let the family portraits go, there's no point disposing of the Gainsborough because we'll be liable for inheritance tax. No. It has to be the holiday home – the packing crates housing treasures that were shipped to Sotheby's. And Patrice *knows* she should be thankful that she and Charles had things they could do without, but still she feels the echo of their humiliation. The smirks of those who attended the auctions, who raised hands to mouths, or touched the bridges of their noses, were only thinly disguised. But the full extent of their loss was not immediately apparent. Patrice's own ousting from social circles was subtly done. The wives – Lucinda (Arnold's mother) at their centre – engineered it perfectly. If ever they bumped into each other, the usual niceties were extended, but any invitation Patrice made was buffered by a well-rehearsed excuse. "Goodness, what a memory you have!" she allowed herself. "I can't remember where I'm supposed to be on Thursday, let alone at noon a month from now!"

Now, Arnold holds her hand. Holds it, as if he senses all she is thinking. "I'm well aware that there are two sides to any story. Particularly one that involves my mother."

"I appreciate your saying that." And she does. Patrice lost the illusion that her parents were perfect fairly early in her childhood. She has heard others tell of how a late discovery was a pivotal moment. Like her, she feels Arnold may have always known. "But I'm not sure it's my place to tell."

"You disappeared from my life. I'd like to understand why."

"I think you'll find it was the other way around." Patrice has been careful not to look in the mirrors, but she catches herself in the act of glancing at them, seeing a tableau with Valerie at its centre.

"So you do…" Arnold's seriousness draws her gaze. His eyes are clear and questioning. "You *do* feel that you were wronged."

"I think I'm entitled to feel a little hard done by." This feels like a small admission.

"If you're reluctant to begin, let me tell you what I was

told and you can correct me if it's wrong." He gives her no opportunity to disagree. "Uncle Charles lent his name to this Davenport character's money-making scheme and invited a few prominent friends to invest. My father didn't make the list. I remember how terribly put out he was. Why wasn't his money as good as anybody else's? And then he heard that other people had been added after approaching Uncle Charles, so that's what he did."

Patrice nods. "You had all come to Whitlocke for New Year's Eve. I remember Charles saying what a good night for business it had been." Patrice does not say that she remembers snapping, "Not the Linnets!" Not a premonition that things might go awry, but annoyance that her party was being hijacked.

"But Davenport didn't invest the money."

Suddenly the room is very hot. Patrice raises her teacup to her lips and sips. It is a moment before she recovers herself sufficiently to say, "He disappeared with the lot." Never to be seen again.

Arnold frowns. "And without waiting for any complaints, any actions, you took the decision to reimburse the investors."

"They were our friends. Not all as close to us as your parents were, but nonetheless." Friends she assumed would rally round. Friends she thought she could rely on.

"From what I understand no one was left out of pocket."

The Linnets had been gracious enough when accepting their offer, at least it had seemed that way. "I have no idea what more we could have done. Perhaps the investors expected to be recompensed for what they thought they'd make in profit." Patrice tries to be dispassionate about it, as much for her own sanity as Arnold's benefit.

"But returns are never guaranteed." Frustration alters her godson's voice. He wants something from her, something that is not in Patrice's power to give.

"I can only think people must have taken offence at how we went about it."

The pay-off itself was perfectly civil but for the setting – Messrs Pickering Kenyon's stifling boardroom, where Mr Kenyon Senior read the statement they had approved to one investor after another. Although the duke was in no way legally responsible for their losses, he wished to make restitution as a gesture of goodwill. By accepting the gesture, they were waiving their rights to further recourse or claims. Mr Kenyon then slid the declaration across the table.

"For his part," Patrice says to Arnold, "Charles was deeply, deeply embarrassed by the officialdom."

Perhaps embarrassed for him, Derek and Lucinda had been quick to add their signatures. She remembers distinctly how Derek said as he put down the pen, "We're glad to be able to draw a line under this episode." How grateful she was to hear those words. And what a fool she has been proven.

"It was me," Patrice says to Arnold, her fingers tightening around her cigarette holder. "I insisted on things being done the way they were done. In my mind, Charles landed himself in deep water because he relied on a gentleman's handshake." Not that Davenport was a gentleman. "Everything had to be watertight."

"So the investors accepted your offers and then shunned you?"

Patrice smiles unhappily. "That sums it up nicely." Charles, it must be said, fared slightly better than she did, because White's Club had never before cancelled a duke's membership and the committee was unsure if it would be proper.

Arnold has the decency to look perfectly bewildered. "But that's nothing less than hypocritical!"

"I spent an age trying to make sense of it." Exiled, Patrice wondered if revenge wasn't being enacted for some earlier offence, some jealousy, something that had not or could not be played out at the time. That creeping suspicion has remained, the feeling that she is the victim of a deep-seated grudge. "But I honestly don't know what we could have done differently."

"You should have let them take you to court. At least then you would have had the opportunity to stand up for yourselves."

"Can you imagine facing your friends across a courtroom?" She shakes her head. "At the time, all I wanted to do was keep it out of the papers." Patrice sits back and regards Arnold through the smoke from her cigarette. "It's rather gratifying to see you so riled on my account, but please don't say anything to your parents. It would do no good to rake this up."

"I shan't hide the fact that I've seen you and, if you don't mind, I shall say that I have every intention of seeing you again."

"I'd like that," Patrice says, with no small satisfaction, but she follows the trajectory of his gaze. For the time being at least, Arnold is lost in a vision, a pout, the curve of her hips, the arch of her back. "Her name is Valerie."

"Who?"

She smiles, knowingly. "The hostess you can't take your eyes off. Not that I blame you. Why don't I introduce you?" Patrice raises her hand and Valerie, keenly alert to any attention, brings one of her own to her chest, as if to ask, "Who? Me?"

CHAPTER TWENTY-TWO

URSULA

Ursula has her driver pull up outside the one venue in southern England that met with Robin's approval. An ordinary semi-detached house, mock-Tudor, belonging to a friend of her mother's. Someone she doesn't know, but Ursula feels certain will have heard all about her, not from newspapers or gossip magazines, but her mother's version – which would have been considerably less flattering.

Even as Ursula gets out of the car, a feeling of nausea rises upwards. She closes her eyes, summoning all of her inner reserve. Standing on the pavement side of the garden gate is worse than waiting in the wings on opening night, walking up the garden path worse than any entrance. Anxious and guilt-ridden though she is, Ursula wants this meeting with the daughter she hasn't seen for six years to be perfect. Six years! The last three with their own special brand of torture, knowing that her justification for leaving proved to be without foundation.

Deep breath. This day has been a long time coming. Robin did all that he could to delay it, at first suggesting that rather than come to England, Ursula should meet Silvia on neutral territory, then opposing her petitions to allow Silvia to fly to

Paris. No doubt he had second thoughts, imagining Ursula had dreamt up a plot to smuggle their daughter back to the States. (She's decided to wait until today is out of the way before breaking it to Robin that she plans to make England her permanent home.) Her ex-husband told the judge that he thought Mrs Sheard – he's the only person who refers to Ursula by her married name – showed an unnatural attitude towards their little girl. "Even now, when Mrs Sheard has troubled this court with a request to send our little daughter to Paris, she hasn't made the effort to appear in person. I have to ask myself, How much does she really want to make amends?"

Facts are easily manipulated if you have a mind to. The court had taken several months to schedule the hearing, by which time Ursula was on location shooting her next film. To attend in person would have meant breaching her contract. But Silvia stood up in court and told the judge in a clear, high voice that she didn't want to go to Paris, even though she understood it would only be for a visit. (She didn't see it as a holiday, but a duty she'd been asked to perform.) She had no intention of leaving her daddy. "He's already been left once. It wouldn't be fair on him."

Southern England was the judge's ruling.

And so Southern England it is.

Slowly, Ursula breathes out through her mouth. Rings the doorbell. Only then does she wonder if Robin is here, watching from the front seat of some parked motor-car. She is scanning car windows in the road for a familiar face when the front door opens inwards.

"Mrs Sheard?"

She turns, caught out by the arrival of this long-anticipated moment now that it's finally here. In one imagined version, Silvia opened the door, said, "Mummy!" and threw her arms around her. This is not to be that version. Instead, a woman who looks to be similar in age to Ursula's mother, regards her coldly. "If you'd step this way." There's a long-suffering, tight-lipped quality about her. "Mrs Sheard?"

"I'm so sorry." Ursula's grip tightens around the strap of her handbag. "It's been a long time since anyone's called me by that name."

"Is there something you'd prefer me to call you?"

At the prospect of seeing her mother, Ursula realises that a deeply-buried part of her was expecting to hear the name *Olive*. Few people know that Ursula isn't her given name. Not that it's unusual for actresses to take stage names. At her very first audition, after she was announced as Olive Delancy, the casting director said, "Well, that will have to go," backed up by the tutting of a woman with a clipboard. "Terribly old-fashioned." It was difficult to disagree, and so in response to the question, "What should I put you down as?" she chose Ursula, the she-bear. Olive hoped that in the same way that a medal had given the Cowardly Lion courage, the name might cure her of stage fright. Along with early failures, the name Olive was consigned to her distant past. It belongs, in particular, to her father, a smiling man she would meet at the end of the garden path when he returned from work at the same time every evening, and who would scoop her up and sit her on his broad shoulders. After he fell victim to a sniper while keeping watch in a trench, he was reduced to a photograph on the mantelpiece ("Don't touch, Olive!"). Olive made a vow not to refer to him, because doing so aroused such anger in her mother, she couldn't risk a repetition, but her mother allowed herself to refer to him frequently. "Your father would have agreed with me," "Olive, your father would have been ashamed of you," "All I can say, Olive, is that I'm glad your father isn't here to see this."

"No," Ursula says. "Mrs Sheard is fine."

Beyond the woman is the hall; a telephone table, a mirror,

a pot plant with glossy leaves. Three doors are visible, two of them ajar. Her daughter could be behind any one of them. Robin has sent photographs. He's allowed Ursula glimpses. She can guess where Silvia will come up to on her chest when they hug. But perhaps Silvia won't want to hug her. Ursula could hardly blame her if she clings to her grandmother. "I do hope I'm not late," she says. "We were held up in traffic."

"Not at all. Your mother and daughter haven't arrived yet."

What if they aren't coming? What if Robin has changed his mind?

The woman pushes open the first door on the left. "You can wait in here."

A living room. Upholstered chairs. A fringed lamp. A full coal bucket in front of the fireplace. All spotlessly clean. It is possible that the room is kept for best. It is also possible that the woman has gone to considerable trouble, but whether on her account or her mother's, Ursula won't hazard a guess. "What a lovely room," she says.

The woman smiles in such a way that suggests she's been briefed about Ursula's impeccable manners and understands she's not to be taken in by them. "Make yourself at home. Can I offer you some tea?"

"Tea would be wonderful, but please don't go to any trouble."

"It's no trouble. Your mother will want a cuppa the moment she sets foot."

They're expected, then.

Perhaps Silvia needed persuasion to get into the motorcar.

Perhaps, right at this moment, someone is trying to persuade her to get out.

Ursula sits. There is time enough to reflect on the courtroom transcript, delivered by the mailboy to her dressing-room trailer where she was sitting at her mirror, waiting for her call to set. Nothing but the large brown envelope it came in to suggest it was anything other than a manuscript.

Asked by the judge if she missed her mother, Silvia said, "I'm not sure I can remember my mother." For a comment designed to cut, Ursula can't think of a single playwright who could have done better.

"Do you feel that she doesn't care about you?"

"I don't know. She didn't seem to give me much thought before she left, or for a long time afterwards."

"But you had letters from her, surely?"

"She writes to me and I write back. But she only asked to see me again after she had another baby."

Not true, although that may have been Silvia's understanding. Before Marcus was born, Robin thought their daughter too young to have an opinion on what was right for her, and Ursula, knowing she'd been in the wrong, did as he demanded. She didn't fill her letters with requests, or say that she dreamed of the day. By the time Robin allowed her to mention the possibility – just the possibility – of a visit, Silvia's bias had been established and was very much in her daddy's favour.

Ursula didn't care that the judge found her proud and selfish. After all, a US Senator had launched a verbal attack on her, highlighting her blatant disregard for public morals. A woman holding a considerable position of influence who had assaulted the very institution of marriage by bringing two children into the world, one with no mother, and a second who is illegitimate.

She didn't agree with the judge who also thought Robin was at fault for doing precisely what the court had ordered and no more. Restrictions aside, she wouldn't have allowed a child so young to travel in the immediate aftermath of the war.

She cared not that the judge expressed the view that Silvia

has been used as currency in her parents' private battle. Ursula didn't keep count of the number of thousand-dollar telegrams she sent to the judge, although the press did. Ursula holds post office employees in the same contempt that Mack held hotel managers.

She didn't even care that the judge thought that Robin and she should see to it that there was a reconciliation between mother and daughter as soon as possible, not for Ursula's sake, but for the sake of the child's future welfare.

She cared that when the judge asked Silvia, "Do you love your mother?" her daughter responded, "I haven't seen enough of her to know if I do or I don't."

"But you sign your letters, 'Love from Silvia.'"

"That's how you're supposed to end letters."

That's how you're supposed to end letters.

It would be bad enough to read those words in a manuscript.

Voices. Voices in the hall. One high, the other a couple of octaves lower. Ursula is up on her feet. There is no mirror above the mantelpiece. As an afterthought, she swipes at her eyes. The living-room door doesn't fly open. Her daughter does not come running. Ursula takes a few paces. What to do? Should she wait and let Silvia come to her in her own time?

Who's she kidding? You think there will be a choice. You imagine you'll be in control, just as you imagined you'd have some vestige of control nine years ago when you gave birth. Do you think there's a right way and a wrong way to behave in front of your child? There is only the way you behave at this moment, as your hand reaches for the door handle. Only this moment when, after all the migraine-inducing build-up, Silvia is standing there with nine-year-old solemnity. So grown-up and yet still so small, so serious-looking. And though your own mother, a woman who believes all emotions should be stage-managed, would hold her back, there is something primal, instinctive. Something of kinship and belonging. You see it in her, the smallest possibility of an opening, and you fall to your knees. You both have your arms around each other and you are crying into her hair, a snivelling wreck, the furthest possible thing from a film star. "My baby, I am so, *so* sorry. I don't expect you to forgive me, not for a long time yet, but I want you to know how sorry I am."

And she says, "I'm not a baby, Mummy." (Yes, she calls you Mummy.)

"No, you're not a baby. You're my big, big girl."

And she says, muffled, "Did you used to cry this much?"

"No. No. I can't remember the last time I cried."

"I cried last week."

"Did you?"

And your mother uses the voice she reserves to let it be known that you have pushed her beyond any limit she can reasonably be expected to tolerate: "For goodness' sake, Olive, pull yourself together. When you're ready, we'll be waiting in the parlour."

Once she is out of earshot, Silvia puts a hand on each hip and says, "*When you're ready, we'll be waiting in the parlour.*"

It doesn't even strike you that for once you are without an audience – it is just you and Silvia, Silvia and you – because your daughter's impersonation of her grandmother is the most perfect piece of acting you have witnessed since Judith Anderson's Mrs Danvers or Richard Attenborough's Pinkie. And for one moment of pure bliss you allow yourself to imagine that everything is going to turn out for the best.

CHAPTER TWENTY-THREE

CAROLINE

Caroline, who has never been invited to Sandy's Kensington home, goes to the hospital alone. Valerie doesn't do hospitals.

"Just the smell of disinfectant sets me off. Besides, he'll be out soon enough."

It's pneumonia, the nurse explains. Caroline is not to tire him. Five minutes at the most. She nods her understanding, thinking she knows what to expect, but she is not prepared for what she encounters. Sandy seems to have collapsed inwards. He is breathing through an opaque mask. There will be no jokes today about covering up those razor sharp cheekbones. The lump in Caroline's throat prevents them. All she can offer is her hand, her intent to gently hold his, but Sandy's grip is startlingly fierce, and he slides aside his mask to wheeze, "Get out." A strange mewl follows this command, and the hawk-eyed nurse rushes forward to fuss over him.

Caroline steps back from the bed.

Sandy is dying. There can be no doubt about it. It's as if her father is leaving for a second time, burdening her with all that extra responsibility, and again she is wholly unprepared. The nurse eyes her accusingly. Did she hear the "Get out!"

and assume that Caroline had upset her patient? There is no goodbye. Neither of them says the words, but they look at each other and not saying them is somehow worse. Caroline knows this will be the last time. When she looks away, when she walks away, that will be it.

The hospital corridors are longer on the way out, the combination of Jeyes Fluid and carbolic suffocating. Desperately wanting to hold on to what she still has of Sandy, not knowing where to take her wealth of feeling, Caroline walks from the hospital to Church Street, barely noticing that the pavements are strewn with discarded bus tickets and muddied newspapers. She locates his building (the one with the iron railings next door), sees the glass outline of what he has always smilingly referred to as 'the penthouse'. Apparently, this prestigious Kensington address came surprisingly cheap. The landlord struggled to generate interest in the prospect of living somewhere that was so exposed to German bombs. *"But when I lay in bed, I had a first-rate view of the dogfights. Metal glinting, trails of black smoke and, occasionally, the sight of a drifting parachute. And I would will it,* Drift this way, parachute, this way."

"You've been gone for hours!" Valerie complains on Caroline's return. "How was he?"

Caroline slumps down on the end of her bed and again cannot find the words. The catch of Valerie's breath – her assumption – forces Caroline to say, "No. Not quite yet."

"But he's..." Valerie's eyes beg for denial, but Caroline can offer no such comfort.

The waiting, the inevitability, the helplessness. For two days Sandy clings on, breath by breath, mewl by mewl. After pilgrimages to the telephone booth, every glance that passes between the two girls is a question to which no answered shake of the head brings relief.

The end of January. They bury Sandy on a day of peculiar stillness, the kind cold weather heralds, as if time itself is frozen. Caroline has no black to wear. Would have made do with her ordinary coat but Valerie, with her flair for the dramatic, insists they pin squares of black veil to their hats. Too weak to resist, Caroline draws the line when she catches Valerie scrutinising other mourners and tugs her arm.

"Don't worry! I haven't brought my copy of *Who's Who*. Not that Sandy would have minded. All I'm trying to work out is who we should offer our condolences to."

Valerie's quite right. There is no obvious candidate. No woman of an age that she might be his mother.

One less homosexual for Sir David Maxwell Fyfe to obsess over. As she goes about the blank canvas of her daily existence, Caroline feels not only Sandy's loss, but lost. Though her exchanges with the duchess are usually limited to pleasantries, sometimes when Caroline looks across the bar room to the corner table, she catches the reflection of watchful eyes in the mirror. Although the thought of being watched is one of the few things that cheers her, Caroline isn't tempted to wiggle, as Valerie does. Valerie's essential joy isn't something that can be suppressed, even in a time of mourning.

When Caroline throws back her head and laughs, she recognises herself as just another person who's plugging a hole in her life with tall stories, alcohol and human contact. She drinks more. She laughs louder. She's tactile in a way she's never been before, needing the contact as much as the men do. They are all experiencing a kind of exile. Marriages, former lives, former homes. Valerie has volunteered little about her family. Up until this moment, mindful of the promise she made not to talk about her own background, Caroline hasn't pried. People are entitled to erase their pasts, even if they don't stray far from their roots. But tonight, lying in bed, it seems important to know.

"Where in London are you from?" she asks under the cover of darkness.

"Harrods," comes the reply. "The Ladies Department."

"But where were you born?"

"Arnold doesn't care, so why should you?"

At first, Caroline reserved judgement about the latest in a line-up of titled gentleman, wary of his connection with Patrice, afraid he might turn out to be just another privileged playboy, a type she's become all too familiar with. But Arnold seems genuine, delighting in all the ways that Valerie differs from the debs he's known.

"You won't mind if I make an honest woman of your friend?" he asked on an outing to an East End pub, after Valerie had taken his hand for balance and stepped up onto a tabletop where she danced, the varnish under her heels worn thin.

"You'd better mean it," Caroline had said.

"Oh, I mean it, alright." Unable to take his eyes off her friend, he tucked two fingers between his lips to whistle.

Now Caroline says to Valerie, "I don't *care.* Not in the way you're suggesting. It's just that I –" Her voice quakes. "I knew Sandy all that time and it's only now that I realise how little I knew about his life." She cannot bring herself to say, *How little I know of yours.*

There is no reply for such a long time that when it comes, the small voice that cuts through the dark is unexpected. "I asked my mother once. Where I was born."

"And?"

"She said she couldn't remember."

Caroline wants to reach a hand across the divide between the beds, but she has already forced this painful admission. Anything else would be a further intrusion. "I'm sorry," is all she can say. Sorry to have pried. Sorry that Valerie doesn't know the answer. Even if Caroline never returns to Felixstowe, she's still the same girl from Suffolk. Though she's left that life behind, she'll always have a foothold in both worlds. But the past can shift with the same ease as the present.

News from home is bad. Worse than bad. On the day that followed Sandy's funeral, Suffolk was inundated, its sea defences overwhelmed. The spring tide, such an innocuous phrase. The waters that wash the last of the frosts out to sea, the returning tide carrying the new season ashore, frothing it onto shingle beaches and inland. It washed inland alright. In the place of slow rollers came a great wall of water. Even those known for sky-watching, those who experience restlessness when a storm is on its way, failed to spot the signs. Warnings didn't trickle down the coast as might have been expected. To the north, telephone lines were felled like the tree trunks. In Felixstowe's West End, people were ambushed. The tide swept away the new wooden prefabs, and with them forty-one lives. Ma had been on the waiting list for one of those homes. It doesn't bear thinking about. Caroline battles with images. Desperate people spending the night straddling rooftops, lashing oilcans together, crafting crude rafts. The death toll in England is three hundred and seven, more if you include those that were lost in English and Irish waters. *You survive the war and for what? This?*

Reading the two sides of her mother's letter, it all comes back to her: their own humble preparations for the German invasion. She and her brothers and Betty pasted windows with strips of paper in the shape of a Union Jack. It seemed incredible that Hitler could be defeated by something so flimsy.

Her mother sees London as a flood-free haven. She doesn't understand that the city wasn't immune. The Royal docks, Silvertown and Canning Town all succumbed. Docklands, oil refineries, factories, cement works, gasworks and electricity generating stations were brought to a standstill. Over a thousand houses were inundated after the seawall collapsed, Thames water flowing through the streets of West Ham, and still the stench of overflowing sewers lingers. *We'd settle for a few overflowing sewers,* her mother writes. These are not the usual begging letters Caroline's come to expect.

She's distracted by her mother's words when Valerie leaves for her date with Arnold.

"Don't be upset with me," Valerie pouts.

"It's my bloody mother I'm upset with!" The suggestion that she was sent ahead to pave the way for the whole family. "Apparently it's up to *me* to find them a home in London." Caroline won't have it. She won't!

"My parents were constantly on the move." Valerie hangs on the doorframe. "It was the only way to stay ahead of their debts. Once they left in such a hurry, they forgot all about me."

Blind to everything but her mother's letter, Caroline misses Valerie's wounded expression as she says, "I'll be back tomorrow night." It's not just that Caroline has learnt to value her independence. She wants to know that her past is secure. That should she return, even if it can't be to the house she grew up in, Felixstowe remains as she pictures it in her mind – and that means her family must be there, waiting. And so Caroline treads water, waiting for the thing to happen that will finally make up her mind. Who is she? Hostess or nanny?

It bursts through the bedroom door without so much as a knock. (Wait till Valerie hears about this. The nerve!) Yvette takes a couple of steps towards the dressing table, then pivots. "Terry's downstairs asking for you."

Lapses into the language of Caroline's childhood still happen when she's thinking of home or simply plain irritated. Right now, she's both. "Tell him I'll be down dreckly," she says.

"I wouldn't keep him waiting if I were you." Uninvited, Yvette takes up position on the end of Valerie's bed, juts out her feet and stares down at her shoes.

"What kind of mood is he in?"

"He wants to be the one to tell you. That's all he'd say."

Caroline isn't so interested in what he *said* as what he *did.* Just as she used to interpret the mood of a cow or a horse, the girls interpret Terry's movements. Yvette should be better at it than any of them, but judging by her fixed gaze Caroline will get no more out of her.

Could news of Morrie Conley's job offer have filtered back to their boss? Will she be forced to make up her mind on the spot? Or should she deny it, saying it's a case of Russian Gossip? The small world of drinking clubs is incestuous, guests traipsing from one to another, carrying hearsay from door to door. Denial would be one way of whittling down her options.

Caroline holds the door wide open, inviting Yvette to leave, but Yvette shows no inclination to budge. She wouldn't put it past Terry to have asked her to search their room for evidence of rule breaking. *You look, I'll keep her occupied.*

Just once, on the staircase, Caroline's footsteps falter. *What if she denies Conley has approached her, then he gets to hear about it and accuses her of calling him a liar?* But she continues as she must, one hand on the bannister, preparing to run her full gamut of charm, everything from astonishment to bluster.

Unusually, Terry's back is to the door. He's sitting at the bar, shoulders hunched, his bulk overflowing the seat of an elegant long-legged stool. Something peculiar strikes Caroline: he isn't engulfed in the usual blue fog. She approaches. "You wanted to see me."

"Ah, there you are." His face is ashen. "Sit. Sit yourself down." He taps the stool next to his; shunts a glass of what can only be brandy along the bar, a drink he describes as 'Cognac's poor cousin'. Whatever Terry's about to say has nothing to do with Morrie Conley. It's something far worse. There was a time when Caroline would have refused spirits unless they'd been watered down. Now, anticipating the words to come, she sips. Her hand shaking, the rim of the glass clinks against her teeth.

"There's been an accident," Terry says, his face grave.

Not Betty. Oh, God, don't let it be Betty.

Without a cigar, Terry seems at a loss. One elbow on the bar, his free hand bunches the flesh around his mouth, moulding it like putty. When he removes the hand, his lips are quivering. He can barely bring himself to say it. "Valerie."

The relief of not hearing her sister's name.

The relief of it.

"I know how close the two of you were."

Caroline hasn't yet adjusted her thinking. The words catch up with her. You *were* close. "She's –?" *My God.*

Walls press inwards. *Valerie.*

"I'm afraid so."

Sandy gone and now – Caroline feels hollowed out. She tries to remember if she'd said goodbye. But all she can recall is her mother's letter. "How?" Her throat constricts painfully. More brandy.

"The motor-car she was travelling in. It overturned."

Caroline sees the motor-car ride the kerb and flip, thudding down onto its roof.

Terry's famous temper flares. "This is *exactly* why I try to discourage you girls. You *will* go racing off at the weekends."

Caroline is almost as stunned by the sight of her employer's tears as she is by the news. *Please, let it have been sudden!* She watches as he lets them roll unguarded down his cheeks and splash onto the bar. Caroline doesn't cry, not yet. Something inside her is blocked, and Caroline has no desire to unblock it until she can be alone. Valerie would have been safer if she hadn't taken risks, but she knew the danger and still she chose the risks. It wasn't death Valerie flirted with. It was life. "Was anyone else injured?" Caroline asks.

"No survivors. I don't have any details, except that her companion was a gentleman."

Not Arnold too!

Caroline thinks of the last time she was in the back seat of Arnold's car. When Valerie leaned out of the open window, just to feel the wind whip her hair. Valerie's joy wasn't something you wanted to dampen. When she turned to ask, "Isn't this wonderful?" her eyes bright jewels, it was impossible to disagree.

Terry blinks, winces, wipes a sleeve across his nose. "The police want to know everything you know. Take your time, finish your drink, then I'll take you to the station."

Caroline's throat hitches: "They're not suggesting anyone's committed a crime, are they?"

"As far as I know they're just going through the motions, although another motor-car was involved. I understand it happened on a narrow country lane." Caroline knows country lanes. She revises her vision. Their views blocked by hedgerows, the drivers round the bend only to be blinded by oncoming headlights. They slam their feet down on the brakes. Too late.

"The police wanted to know if Valerie had family. Not as far as I know, I told them."

Caroline thinks about the parents who moved house and left their daughter behind. She'd been so engrossed in her own world that she didn't even ask how old Valerie had been. How long it took for her parents to remember about her – if they remembered her at all.

Terry sighs. "They'll want something to tell the gentleman's next-of-kin, I expect."

Something consoling. Not that Arnold got down on bended knee to propose to a hostess. They'll want to erase

Valerie from their son's life or, if they'd been seen together in too many places, claim it was all just a bit of light-hearted fun.

"My worry's not the police." Terry's right hand is a fist. His thumb traces his knuckles. "It's the papers. I understand enough of their game to know that if anyone's going to be dragged through the mud, given Valerie's lack of family and connections, it will be her."

Caroline knows this to be true. It's a fact she rubs up against every day. Girls like them – girls who are slightly less than respectable – are dispensable. For them, life is never, ever going to be fair. "And nothing I can say will stop that," she says to Terrence, her voice ironed flat.

"I doubt it." A moment passes in silence, resignation rather than acceptance. "This gentleman of Valerie's. Was he connected to the club in any way?"

Terry can be as angry as he likes. It isn't Caroline's place to speak. Arnold isn't just any club member. An accident involving the godson of a duchess and a hostess could propel a story from a discreet column to the front pages.

Terry nods. "It's our members I worry about. You can't promise a safe haven only to have the place crawling with journalists. But I understand. You'll have to tell the police everything you know."

Caroline rallies. Temporarily, she rallies. "Not everything."

Terry looks at her as he's never looked before, his reddened eyes trained on her face and curious.

She thinks out loud. "The police already know that Valerie worked for you. I'll have to tell them we roomed together, but that needn't cause any embarrassment." Caroline's mind races. "If you could mislay the members' book. Have George make up another, just covering the last few weeks, but minus a few names."

"You're a good girl to put the club first. At a time like this."

"If anything leaks out, Patrice can take care of the press. She knows the right people."

"I didn't realise you were on first-name terms."

Heat rises to Caroline's neck. The truth, of course, is more complicated by far. Sometimes, alone, she and the duchess are on first-name terms. In front of others Patrice is 'ma'am', and away from the club they are strangers. And so Caroline makes light of Terry's remark. "Well, she *is* one of our best customers."

A moment passes, then Terry asks, "I read about Felixstowe. Any news from your mother?"

Caroline finds herself wincing. "She's had a devil of a time. They all have. You know what it's like. In a small place, everyone you know has lost someone."

He reaches one hand deep into a trouser pocket, extracts a roll of notes; offers her the entire thing, fatter than one of his cigars.

She stares hard at his hand. Now is not a moment Caroline wants to feel any further beholden. "I–I can't," she falters.

"It's not for you, it's for your family." His knuckles whiten. "Take it."

But she *is* beholden. How can she leave the club now, with Valerie gone? "Thank you," she says, trying to sound humble. It occurs to Caroline, though she's ashamed by the thought, that Valerie's death gives her a valid excuse. *I'm sorry, Ma. I can't find a way to bring you all to London just now, but here's some extra money to keep you going.*

"Be a good girl. Go and make sure Yvette's alright. Then I'll drive you to the police station."

Caroline gets as far as the landing before she turns. "It might be better if I go alone. The less we do to suggest a connection with the club, the better."

"You're right."

"Besides," she forces a half-smile. "Someone needs to be here to look after the guests."

CHAPTER TWENTY-FOUR

URSULA

The air in the cabin of the plane is thick with cigarette smoke, but her own carton is crushed, empty. The turbulence on the flight from London is the worst Ursula has ever known. In another brief interlude of calm, air stewardesses take to the aisles, spiriting away used sick bags and broken china, taking orders for food and drinks, maintaining the illusion of a party atmosphere that began what seems like a lifetime ago with group photos on the steps of the plane. Ursula had hoped, as she always hopes, to maintain a low profile, but the moment she presented herself at the boarding gate, she was escorted to the front of the queue and photographed with the pilot.

"Now what can I get for you, Miss Delancy?" Ursula feels an affinity with the stewardess in her sculpted uniform. Chosen for their looks, and with strict rules about how much they can weigh, stewardesses must be single – the appearance of availability being a requirement of the job – but, as with actresses, their contracts contain strict morality clauses. "Will you have the beef or the lobster?"

On the opposite side of the aisle, a couple watch as another stewardess carves pink slivers from a roast joint of meat. The woman – the wife, Ursula assumes – who does not know Ursula, catches her looking in their direction. There is recognition, then the woman's expression hardens. *You.*

All she's trying to do is to go about her day with a little dignity. Wounded as she is, Ursula tries to return the stewardess's smile. "It all looks wonderful but I'm not sure I can stomach any food."

"Perhaps just a glass of champagne?"

Everyone else is downing drink after drink. "What I'd really like is a pot of tea."

"Coming right up."

A man would lean across the aisle, say, 'Excuse me,' pleasantly enough and you'd have to reply because it might be an autograph he's after, but subjected to a tirade you'd be forced to hear him out. The whole plane would know about it because, like everyone else, he would raise his voice a notch or two to be heard above the engine noise. And he wouldn't hold back – oh, no – because he's read the papers and considers himself quite an authority on you. What's more, he saw that last film you made. It was so blatant, so *blatant*, the way you used things from your *own life,* and now you're here, actually showing your face in public.

A woman might not hold back, if it were just the two of them: *This isn't just what* I *think. It's what all right-minded women think.* But in front of her husband, afraid of the rage and venom she might release, afraid of appearing un-womanly and knowing she must either sit no more than a yard or two away for what remains of the flight or ask to be moved, this woman exerts her sly judgement, so that even Ursula's refusal of champagne is evidence of something unnatural. *I accepted my place in the world. What makes you think you're so different?*

"Here we are, Miss Delancy. Your tea."

She is aware now that the woman, who seems to think she cannot be seen, has turned to her husband, leaned close and whispered in his ear. The man turns his head – just far enough – to look. "Thank you. I don't suppose you have a weather forecast?"

"We can't rule out the possibility of another storm, I'm afraid." Endlessly cheerful, even when delivering bad news.

Ursula drinks the tea that has been poured, sits back and closes her eyes. She blocks out the woman and her husband. Tries to breathe calmly, slowly, bracing herself for the next onslaught of bumps and judders. Moments when it will be impossible to ignore the fact that they are skyborne and hurtling through the air and how little Ursula's understanding is of what keeps them there, suspended.

There is a bump, a collective moan. She grips the armrests. The teapot falls into the aisle. If they were in a car on the open road, Ursula would say that they have just run something over, something larger than a dog. Perhaps a deer.

Think of Marcus – the one positive to have come out of the mess she's created (just to think of him is to smile). He hasn't suffered in the way Silvia did. Not that Ursula can take any credit. It was only because the studio didn't call on her at the height of her post-Mack scandal that she was able to nurse her son.

Another deer in the road. Ursula is lifted out of her seat and set back down. She clenches her jaw shut to stop her teeth from rattling, so that she won't bite her tongue. All around her, the sound of breaking crockery.

And it was only being without demands from a man that she could have Marcus sleep in her room. When he woke crying, she could reach down into his bassinet, unfurl those tight little fists and kiss away his frown. And though for several months Ursula sleepwalked through days, when eventually she returned to the world, it was pushing Marcus in a pram.

The plane plunges violently, like a roller coaster's first drop, and there's no knowing if it will stop. The fear is palpable. Lockers burst open and things fall out. There can't be a single passenger who, gripping the armrest or the hand of a loved one, isn't thinking, *This is it, any minute now, let it be quick.*

Ursula spoke to Marcus constantly. *Look at the sky. What's that grumpy face for? Do you see the dog?* They will always have the bond of his early years. And knowing what Ursula now knows, the thought of all the things she didn't share with Silvia is a huge burden, the regret more than she can carry. (It dawns on her that her fate is inextricably linked with that of the woman across the aisle, though that woman would rather there was a wall between them.) Think, think yourself back to the hall of a mock-Tudor house, think yourself into your daughter's arms. The daughter you have seen twice this year. Twice. Ursula cannot be a mother, cannot demonstrate her commitment to Silvia, while living on a different continent. The judge was right. Children can't be expected to fit in with their parents' arrangements. She must do right by both of her children. And since Ursula could never risk putting Silvia through this hellish journey, it is she who must make changes. And she will. If only they survive the flight.

Ursula approaches Aldo's office with trepidation. After a fraught three years, what she has to say may well spell the end. *So be it.* His secretary June is at her post, don't-mess-with-me tortoiseshell glasses perched on the bridge of her nose, a cigarette burning in her ashtray, the click of fingernails dancing off typewriter keys.

"Is he in?"

She pauses to take a drag, narrowing her eyes. "He's not only in, he's expecting you."

Ursula's stomach dips, but she lifts her chin and one hand and knocks. Time to face the music.

"Come in!"

She pushes open the door to a long narrow rectangle of a room. Rather than make her walk the full length of it, Aldo has left his desk and is at the sofa and coffee table arrangement that occupies the central space. He pushes himself to his feet and opens his arms. "Ursula! A drink to calm those nerves of yours?"

A masterclass in how to put someone on the back foot. "Why not?" she says and perches on the seat that is opposite his.

He ambles over to a small drinks trolley and picks up the only decanter. "It's whisky and I'm all out of soda."

"Perfect."

He waits until the glass is almost at her mouth. "Donald always kept a good range of classic malts, didn't he?"

If he expects Ursula to choke, she disappoints him. She has long since accepted that her name will always be linked with Mack's. The press find any way they can to shoehorn it into the same sentence as hers. "Aldo, I do believe you're trying to rattle me," she says.

The look he gives is pure mischief. "Now why would I want to do that?"

"You tell me. I've been playing the publicity game just as you asked." Ursula no longer covers camera lenses with her hand, shields her own face, or uses a headscarf to cover Marcus's. She's not unwilling to be pictured with tousled hair, dressed in cropped trousers, looking less than polished. For three years now she's allowed herself to be captured carrying her son in a basket, pushing his pram, encouraging him to throw stale bread to disinterested ducks, holding out her arms and saying, "Walk to me", throwing a ball that bounces off his chest after he refuses to catch it. She hasn't needed to paint a picture of a mother who just happens to appear in the odd film. She's *been* that mother. And for allowing herself to be photographed with Marcus, the press has accused her of using him to try and curry favour. "I suppose if you want to bait me, you've no option but to delve into my past," she says.

Aldo crosses one leg and sits back, undeterred. "Out with it, then. Give me the little speech you've rehearsed."

Ursula lets her mouth drop open and emits an exasperated sigh. She is not some vain sorority girl. She will not fawn or flirt, and playing the diva has never been her thing, but these refusals remove several of her bargaining chips.

"Come on." He beckons. "From the top."

"Live on the moon for all I care," Aldo says, "just don't forget who pays your bills." He takes in her raised eyebrows. "Not the reaction you expected?"

"Frankly –"

"Selznick's shifted half his production to Europe. Who knows? We may well follow." He tosses a thick manuscript onto the table. *Into Exile.* He must have had it on the sofa, next to him. "Our very own sword-and-sandal Biblical epic."

It should come as no surprise. Every studio wants in on the success of *Quo Vadis.* 20th Century Fox already has *The Robe* in the can.

"It sounds expensive."

"I want you for the part of Rachel."

Ursula's Bible studies ended a long time ago, but she has an idea that Rachel was one of Jacob's wives. Something to do with the twelve tribes of Israel, then. "Where's the sand?" she asks.

"Arizona."

As she thought. Aldo's going to make her prove she'll still jump when he says jump, this time to a four-month stint on the outskirts of a desert. If domesticity is what Ursula wants, she'll have to buy her way out of her contract.

Is *that* his endgame?

"It's a smallish part but a critical one." Up on his feet, he begins to pace. "What's more, it's the right vehicle for you." Back and forth, back and forth, hands flying, fingers pointing. "Widescreen's the future. The only way for movies to compete with television. More than a hundred commercial stations, that's what we're up against."

"I agree with high-stake strategies, Aldo, but you don't need a production this lavish to challenge the majors' dominance. Comedy's the new thing. *The Father of the Bride* proved that."

His bark of contradiction is a full-stop. "Honey, much as I appreciate your advice, I don't know how to put this any more clearly. If you want your appearance in Hay's Doom Book to become a distant memory, we need you back in front of big family audiences." Ursula's cheeks burn with a cocktail of anger and humiliation. "I'm telling you this for nothing. Forget romantic comedies. You won't be playing my lead in a love story any time soon. Plus, I hardly need point out," Aldo stops his pacing to shrug, "we *can* insist."

She picks up the manuscript and thumbs blindly through it. Saying yes would mean moving Marcus to a new country and then absenting herself just as he's getting settled. She'd be on a different continent to *both* of her children.

Then it strikes her. "Is the funding in place?"

Aldo rubs his chin in a way that suggests he's offended she should ask such a question. "I'm working on it."

She sees it all now. Aldo needs her name, her Oscar-win, perhaps even her notoriety. Whichever third party he's asked to stump up a gargantuan loan has inserted a condition of their own. They've asked for her and won't take no for an answer. But even with funding secured, many a promising project falls by the wayside. All it takes is for an irresistible manuscript to land on a director's desk; something that leapfrogs everything in its path. It's impossible to predict which films will be ditched and which will go ahead. These decisions are made on the whims of domineering and abrasive autocrats. Ursula sighs. "Tell whoever you need to tell that I'll do it."

"You will?" He beams.

What's the point worrying about something that may never come about? Or if it does, may be several years away, by which time she'll be out of contract and the studio will have to pay hand over fist if they still want her. "Tell them I'm on board."

His smile falters, but they have an understanding. She can set the ball rolling. Start looking for a place to live, somewhere between Ealing and Shepperton. She'll write to Caroline and firm up the job offer. There's something so reassuring about the girl's presence, she's sure Marcus will feel it too. And once she has Caroline's agreement, then she'll tell Robin: "We can't put it off any longer. We *have* to sit down and talk about Silvia."

CHAPTER TWENTY-FIVE

PATRICE

Patrice sits to sign the members' book. She takes a fountain pen from her handbag. Not her best – she would be too nervous of losing it – but a perfectly acceptable Parker. Though Patrice has rarely suffered from a shortage of anything material in life, her enjoyment of something new has never lost its sheen. Rather like beginning a diary on the first day of the New Year. This book may have several pages of entries in it, but there's no doubt in her mind. It's new. She rounds off her signature with a trademark flourish. "George?" She raises her eyebrows.

"I was rather hoping no one would notice, ma'am."

"Oh?"

"I'm embarrassed to admit it, but I had a spillage. Butterfingers, that's what my mother used to call me."

"What was it?"

"A cup of coffee. I tried to dry it out but the ink, you see…"

"Well, it would. I remember once, I had an accident of my own. That time the culprit was port – on a white dress, would you believe! And not just any white dress, but the dress I was to wear for my coming-out party." As George frowns his sympathy, she leans closer. "Between the two of us, I maintain it was Lord Birkenhead's fault. He'd left his glass too close to the edge of the table. All *I* did was brush past."

"And what, might I ask, did you do, ma'am?"

I wore the dress I'd intended to wear all along. She steps back. "I had to make do. But it did feel like a punishment, being the only deb who wasn't in white."

"I wonder, could I ask for your discretion?"

"The book? Say no more, George."

"Are you expecting any guests this afternoon, ma'am?"

"I almost forgot." She takes a folded note from her handbag with three names written on it, which George slips into an inside pocket. "One or two, perhaps."

Something is definitely amiss. Terrence's hunched shoulders give the game away. There is no posturing today, no back slap for the man he greets. Quickly, Patrice scans the room for someone who can give her a discreet update. Strange. Not one of the live-in hostesses is on duty. Rather than make her way to her corner, she pauses by the bar where Vincent is resting his pint, no doubt as alert to the atmosphere as she is. "Vincent," she says, careful to keep her voice in a neutral gear.

"Your grace." His mood is teasing, but she sees that he has his notebook out, a pen tucked in its spiral.

"Any idea what's going on?"

"Terrence is doing the rounds, and he's leaving tables far more sombre than when he arrived at them."

Has the club gone under? If money were needed, he should have asked. "And he's missed you out?"

Vincent gives a wry smile. "All in good time."

"Well, I shan't wait. I'm going to find out what's what."

"Any chance of a word later on?"

"That rather depends what it's about."

"The proposal to suspend capital punishment. I assume the duke is backing the Bill."

She lets her chest rise and fall. So much is riding on this latest development. "I can't help thinking it's another case of terrible timing. Their last efforts were scuppered by the Acid Bath Murderer."

"And now we have women's bodies walled up in houses."

"Quite. And still no sign of our sacrificial lamb."

"Terrence." She greets the club owner affably as he bellies between two tables. His shirt front is creased, as if he's spent the morning with his arms tightly folded. A stony expression adds to the sombre impression. Patrice changes her tune. "Are you quite yourself? You look a little pale."

"Patrice." He sighs deeply, a release of something. "I admit today is taking its toll."

"Perhaps you should take a break. Join me for a drink."

Rather than make the excuses she'd anticipated, Terrence follows meekly and sits in the chair she directs him to. "Elise, when you have a moment, be a dear and send over my usual and one of whatever Mr Blagdon's having." It is not his usual, Patrice notices, but what appears to be brandy.

Elise gives a curt nod, but avoids eye contact. This, too, is out of the ordinary.

Patrice smiles at Terrence, employing the same expectant expression she's been assured is particularly effective at loosening tongues. It's remarkable how few people can abide silence.

"I wanted you to hear it from me," he begins, looking down at the dregs of his drink.

"Come on, Terrence. How long have we known each other?"

He makes a wistful sound that could almost be a laugh. "Oh, it's nothing like that." He looks up at her, self-deprecating. "I wish it were."

"So the club isn't in trouble?"

He gives her a look that says, *Is that what you heard?* His gaze drops once more. "It's Valerie."

A further prompt seems to be required. "Valerie, you say?"

"There was an accident. A motor-car."

Every muscle in Patrice's body clenches. "Oh good Lord." There is no doubt in Patrice's mind that Arnold was behind the wheel. He'll blame himself, poor boy. She must go to him, offer what comfort she can.

"I know." Terrence's hand moves from his glass to his mouth in agreement with something unspoken. "It's a terrible blow."

One last thing before she goes on her way. "The other girls? They weren't with Valerie, I hope?"

"No, no. Although they've taken the news very badly."

"Of course." It is in her still, the inclination to skirt around any mention of feelings.

"Yvette's having a lie-down." Someone else who is conditioned to take herself off and get it out of her system. "I don't know. It's not that I expected her to want to work today. God knows, she's no malingerer. But she's lying on Valerie's bed and won't move. When I suggested it might upset Caroline to see her there, she bit my head off."

"Then you can't be nearly as intimidating as you think you are." Patrice allows a moment to pass. "And Caroline?"

"The police wanted to speak to her. First Sandy and now..." Terrence shakes his head. "It's not as if they even care about Valerie. All they're after is something to comfort the gentleman's family."

"You don't mean –?" *The knock at the door. The telegram boy.*

"Both dead." There it is. The irrefutable black and white of it. "And the passengers in the other vehicle."

The Air Ministry regrets to inform. Letter to follow.

Terrence's face is ravaged. "I feel responsible," he says. "Poor girl."

Patrice's heart is pounding. The blood in her forearms seems to be flowing in the wrong direction. *Be a brave girl. We mustn't make a scene, must we?* "Tommyrot!" she manages, "You were her employer, you weren't acting in *loco parentis.*" As Arnold's godmother, that was *my* job. And I brought him here. *I* introduced him to Valerie. If anyone is responsible, it's me.

"It's her memory I feel responsible for. What the press are going to make her out to have been. And that has *everything* to do with me."

The room is stifling, the piano music jarring.

Arnold – my poor, poor Arnold. What Patrice wants – what she needs – is to get out of here.

"Admittedly, this wants careful handling," she hears herself say, but Elise has arrived.

"Ma'am." Elise slides a tray onto the table and it is impossible to leave. Patrice must wait; wait while the barmaid arranges the ice bucket with its bottle of mineral water, a chilled glass, and for Terrence, a tumbler containing a generous measure of amber spirit. Elise, still avoiding eye contact, pours water into the duchess's glass; Elise, who knew from the very first how she and Arnold were connected, says nothing more. Keeping Patrice's confidence, she walks back to the bar and closes the hatch on her own grief.

Terrence resumes the moment she's out of earshot. "And of course there's the responsibility I owe my members."

Your *members?* Irritation flickers at this reordering of priorities, but it is the excuse Patrice needs. "I should go to the police station."

"Right this minute?"

"I don't like to think of Caroline there on her own." Already, she is on her feet. "The poor girl might sabotage herself while trying to protect her friend."

Terrence's eyes widen. Clearly, he hadn't considered that

possibility. "How will you explain your connection with Valerie?"

Now she has said that she will do it, Patrice must carry the thing through. "I'm a prominent member of the club where she worked, one of the few women members, and obviously I'm shocked by the news. Valerie may not have had family, but it won't do any harm if I let the police know that she wasn't without friends."

A wan smile. "You're not nearly as intimidating as you like people to think you are."

But there is nothing intimidating about Patrice as she attempts to walk a steady line to the landing, nothing intimidating as she grips the handrail at the top of the staircase, grips hard, and feels every jerk as the laces are tightened, until her waist is twice the diameter of her throat and every last breath is forced from her lungs.

"Ma'am?" It is Elise, red-eyed, dignified. "Is there anything I can do for you?"

"No, I'm fine." She rights herself, surprised by the effort this takes. "I'm..."

"Will I see you down to your car?"

"Thank you," she concedes. "That would be a kindness."

CHAPTER TWENTY-SIX

URSULA

Dear Silvia,

By now, Daddy will have told you that I am selling my house in America and moving back to England. Hollywood has never really felt like home because it is so very far away from you. I understand that even though you came to visit me, it will take a long time before you can trust me again. It was a clever idea to make a list of your reasons and have Daddy send it to me. There is not one I can disagree with. I will not stop telling you how sorry I am about leaving you the way I did, even though this doesn't make it any better. I can only say that you were my first child and I hadn't had any practice at being a mother. As I watch Marcus take his first steps, I remember that I missed you taking yours, all because I was working. And to see you so very grown up and beautiful and smart and funny (I still laugh about your impression of Grandma) reminds me how very foolish I have been and how much of your life I have not been there for. If by some magic trick I could wind back the clock, I would do things very differently.

Daddy tells me that my work makes your life very difficult and that children at school ask you all sorts of awkward questions. I don't know if you realise, but the newspapers only ever print one side of a story. Sometimes they include an awful lot of guesswork. Rather than ask me what happened, they ask someone who heard the story from a friend. I used to jump up and down and make a big fuss whenever I read something about myself that wasn't true, but jumping up and down was turning into a full-time job. Because how I live is actually very dull, and because part of my job is to keep my name in the headlines, I let the journalists get away with it if they invent something, as long as it won't hurt you, Daddy or little Marcus. I don't know if you realise, but photographs are often 'inventions' too. When the newspapers can't get hold of a picture of me with the other person named in their story, they take another photograph of me, cut out my head and put it on someone else's body. Can you believe that? Sometimes I look at myself and think, 'That's a great dress, I wonder where I can get hold of it.' I want you to know that you can write to me with any questions you have (just ask Daddy to send me a list if you do not feel like writing me a letter). I will answer you truthfully.

I am sending you a photograph of Marcus. If you ask Daddy to show you your baby photos, you will see that he looks very like you at the same age. It must be very strange for you to have a half-brother with the same surname as you, when your mummy has a different surname. Although I became Ursula Sheard when I married Daddy, I will always be Ursula Delancy to the people who see my films. I talk to Marcus about you so that he knows who his sister Silvia is. Be as cross with me as you like but please don't blame him for my mistakes. More than anything, I would like you to get to know one another. If you would like to meet Marcus but decide that you do not want to see me, I promise to find a way to make that happen.

I mean to work very hard to earn your trust. I don't want you to feel you have to come and see me because a judge tells you that you must. I pray the day will eventually come when you ask Daddy if you can come and visit me. As I look for somewhere to live, I ask myself 'Will Silvia like it?' What I am looking for is a house with a bedroom and a garden and a view you will fall in love with. I don't say to myself, 'when you live here', not because I don't want that more than anything, but because I will never try to take you away from Daddy. I promise you that.

With all my love and kisses,

Mummy

CHAPTER TWENTY-SEVEN

PATRICE

Vincent is seated on a wooden chair in the police station's stark corridor. He isn't alone. A row of similarly aged, similarly dressed men have assembled. Either bad news travels fast or journalists spend their days here, waiting for something newsworthy to happen. The sight of them sickens Patrice. Terrence is right. There will be no arbiter and no appeal for a girl like Valerie. That is the way of the world. If the newsmen don't openly call her a prostitute, they will employ a word that suggests as much and, by implication and association, Arnold's memory will be sullied. Not that it's such an unusual thing for a young man to pay for sex, but Patrice would not have it appear in a report about his death, and it *will* not – not if she has anything to do with it. Ignoring Vincent (how can he allow himself to be party to this?) she clips her way to the front desk.

Epaulettes, polished silver buttons, blue shirt, black tie. Rather than wait for the police officer to look up from his ledger, Patrice launches straight in. "Good afternoon, officer. I understand you have a young lady by the name of Caroline Wilby with you."

"One minute please." Can he not see how agonising this is?

But the point must be made; members of the public cannot simply waltz up to the counter and interrupt him mid-sentence.

"She's here about the accident involving Mr Arnold Linnet and Miss Valerie Grant."

He presses the nib of his pen so hard that he risks spoiling the page. "And you are?" The officer's expression suggests scepticism until he raises his eyes. "Oh, your grace." He scrapes back his chair and pushes himself to his feet. Certainty turns to uncertainty. "It *is* your grace, isn't it?"

On another day, it might suit Patrice to have him on the back foot. Today, despite newfound determination, she feels fragile. "Please. Let's dispense with formalities. I came to see if I can be of assistance."

"You are aware, I take it...?"

Patrice bows her head. "I am." How she wishes, wishes that she were not.

"Terrible shame. So young. You knew Mr Linnet, did you?"

At the sound of someone else using his name, something inside Patrice – the part a religious person might call a soul – cries out. "Actually," she rallies, "I knew both of the young people. Arnold was my godson but Valerie was also very dear to me."

"We had no idea."

"Please," she reassures him. "There is no reason why you should have made a connection."

"Can I ask...?"

With no time to think this through, except that Valerie must be given some credentials, all Patrice can do is lend her name. "It was a great sadness that the duke and I couldn't have children of our own, but we always felt that there was support that we could and should give. And so when I meet a young person who inspires me..." She leaves the idea there, half-formed. It will take shape without her help.

"And Miss Wilby?"

"Another admirable young person. To be perfectly frank, I'm concerned that she should have been asked to attend so soon after learning about her friend's death."

"I assure you, your grace –"

"Please. Madam or ma'am will do."

"Ma'am." The officer looks uncomfortable, and so she nods to show her approval. "She came of her own free will. Like you, she was keen to assist in whatever way she could."

Patrice allows a moment to pass before replying. "As I say, an admirable soul, but she may not be aware that she's in shock. And shock makes people do and say very strange things." Here *she* is, doing and saying, praying her own judgement is not flawed.

The officer's expression suggests that he's suppressing the urge to run a finger around the collar of his shirt. "Of course, ma'am."

"If you have any questions about Miss Grant, I would be more than happy to answer them myself."

"We're very grateful, I'm sure. Miss Wilby's given us quite a detailed physical description. If you were able to verify, that would be most useful."

"Anything."

"It's being typed up. Actually no, I think this is it." He takes the top sheet from his 'in' tray. "Yes, here we are."

Patrice steadies herself. She allows her eyes to drift down the single sheet he has placed in front of her. Age, height, hair colour and cut (more might have been made of this, perhaps), appearance, stature, distinguishing features: so far quite impersonal. Then she finds it. A description of what Valerie was wearing when Caroline last saw her and what she might have been wearing at the time of the accident. Patrice's throat tightens. She remembers the dress, how it clung to Valerie's curves; the way that, with her back turned and her face in profile, she gave Patrice an exquisite little wiggle. "Very thorough." She slides the paper back across the desk. "I don't think I have anything useful to add."

"Miss Wilby also gave us these photographs."

Patrice had somehow thought that would be the end of her contribution.

"We understand they're recent, but would you say they're a good likeness?"

It takes a considerable effort but Patrice forces herself to look. *Arnold!* The photographs are of them both. "I would." Her voice is thick. "Miss Wilby will want them back, I'm sure."

"She said we could hang on to them."

"*I* would like her to have them back." Anger makes her businesslike. "I'm happy to pay for copies to be made if necessary. Just send the bill to the duke." She takes her Parker from her handbag and writes down the address of the townhouse. "Now, what can you tell me about the accident?"

"It was very sudden, as head-on collisions tend to be. But there were no witnesses – and sadly, no survivors."

"So I understand."

"When passengers are thrown from vehicles, there's always an element of doubt."

"Doubt? About what?"

"Well, to begin with, who was behind the wheel."

So this is how they intend to slander her. Patrice is certain that Arnold would not want Valerie's name to be slandered. If she doesn't defend Valerie, it will dishonour Arnold's memory. "In the case of our young couple, I can clear that up. Valerie didn't drive."

"We can't rule out the possibility that she took a turn."

Patrice can see it now. Derek saying, 'The car was his, certainly, but we have no way of knowing...' "You really think he'd have given his fiancée a driving lesson in the middle of the night? Besides, there would be fingerprints."

It is not the possibility of fingerprints that has his full attention. "They were to be married?"

"They were absolutely besotted with one another. You can see it." She nods to the photograph. "To have been so happy and then –"

The officer looks again and Patrice watches his expression. He no longer sees a model, a hostess, or any other description they might have used for Valerie. He sees a couple. "This is a little awkward." The officer clears his throat. "The Linnets seem to be completely unaware."

"I can't say I'm surprised. Arnold wanted my opinion about how I thought his parents would react to his engagement. 'Arnold,' I told him, 'you shouldn't underestimate them. They'll be overjoyed to know you've found the person you want to spend the rest of your life with.'" She realises what she has said, just how short a time that turned out to be. "And Valerie would have won them over. She was such a dear and wonderful person." True though this is, Patrice acknowledges that part of her – the part that is still smarting – would have liked to see how the Linnets fared when faced with a small-scale scandal of their own. But not this. Never this.

"There is perhaps *something* you can do."

"Anything."

"You might not be so keen when you hear what it is. We have no details for Miss Grant's next-of-kin. You know how it's been."

So many displaced Londoners. They moved for war work or were evacuated and, having put down new roots, chose to leave their memories intact. "I do," Patrice says, steeling herself for what comes next.

"It would save us from having to ask Miss Wilby."

She grips the straps of her handbag. "When would this be?"

"As soon as possible. Today, if you could manage it."

Patrice visits the Ladies room. A moment to breathe. "We must put on a brave face," her mother would say, then reach for lipstick and rouge. Beads of sweat have formed on her upper lip. *This is for Arnold,* she tells herself. *So that his life – the brief happiness he found – is not taken away from him.* Patrice unclasps her bag and fishes for her compact. When the familiar cold metal shape of it doesn't come to hand, she takes a closer look. Odd. She has a distinct recollection of putting it in her bag last night, and it couldn't have fallen out in the car. The clasp had been closed.

Patrice can hardly leave the police station without offering the Linnets her condolences. It would not be right. Lucinda's eyes are downturned, but she bites her lip and nods.

"You must excuse me, but I want to make sure Miss Wilby gets home safely and then, from there to the mortuary."

"Oh, but there's no need, we're his –" Derek flinches. His bewilderment clears. He understands. "You knew the young lady." It isn't a question.

Although Lucinda's face is wan and grey, her eyes red, she looks at Patrice directly, wanting an explanation.

Let them speculate. She feeds them only a scrap. "They were two wonderful young people, and what a future they would have had together. I shall miss them both. Terribly."

Seated next to Caroline in the back of the car, Patrice has the urge to reach out a gloved hand as if reaching out to her younger self. She recognises the need to choose words of sufficient weight. "It's horrific to think that they're both dead."

"Did you actually like them?" The girl turns on her. "You called Sandy a snake."

Caroline's priorities are different from hers. Patrice understands that. Didn't she say to the police officer only half an hour ago that shock makes you behave strangely? "I may be a little outspoken." Patrice corrects herself, "I *know* I can be outspoken, but I've always found much to admire in snakes."

The girl gives a sharp laugh, and Patrice envies her this freedom, but Caroline reins in her reflex, as if ashamed of it. "And Valerie? You told me that you don't like women."

"True." She nods. "But it was difficult not to admire Valerie. She had a certain *joie de vivre*. One watched her and hoped that just a little of it would rub off." Patrice hears the sound Caroline makes in the back of her throat. Remembrance and agreement. "Besides, I'm not sure what liking or not liking has to do with it. The club is like family."

"We're stuck with one another, you mean?"

Patrice reflects. Stuck is hardly the first word she would have chosen, just as Terrence's club would hardly have been her first choice. "She made my godson very happy and I'm not sure he had a lot of happiness. I'll always be grateful to her for that."

"I'm sorry."

Patrice glances at the girl whose eyes are downturned, tormented and glassy; whose hands are clasped in her lap. "No need to apologise."

"Yes there is. I wasn't thinking. I liked Arnold very much."

Patrice's smile is a reluctant grimace. She wants to say, 'Your first thoughts were for your friends, naturally,' but the words won't come. Instead, she finds herself nodding, not just once but as if her neck is attached to a spring. It is difficult not to think of the years she missed. Patrice remembers Arnold's christening, when she held a candle and made promises she has made little effort to keep. The spirited imp; the awkward teenager, gangly and remote. After that, just snapshots. His graduation. A soldier in uniform, paraded by his mother before Patrice. And then, the day when she called Valerie over to her table. The day she told Valerie that this was her godson, Arnold, and the girl sat straight down in Arnold's lap, making it quite clear that the display was for Patrice's benefit, and said, "Delighted, I'm sure."

They continue in silence, tyres slicing through surface water. Today, London is a city of slick pavements and black umbrellas. Patrice contemplates the club, where Arnold immediately seemed at home. She has always understood what it means to members who are ex-servicemen, who clung to an image of England. In their minds, they would return to the exact same views they left behind. That beech tree, the church steeple of St James's – the familiar landmarks people look out for when returning from a long journey. But the image changed. The beech tree succumbed to disease and the church steeple to a direct blast. What Terrence's club does so well is to provide an illusion that everything remains exactly as it was. Today, for this young woman beside her, that illusion has been shattered. Caroline now knows that anything can be taken away in an instant. "It might do you good to get away for a few days," Patrice ventures. "Go home, perhaps."

"Most of Felixstowe is still under water, but even if it weren't my mother didn't know about Sandy or Valerie. I could hardly tell her about them."

"I suppose not." It's a mother's place to disapprove of the company her daughter keeps, especially when that company consists of an aging homosexual and a young, hedonistic hostess. Now, when Caroline's grief is so apparent, she will find no comfort with her family. The girl's mother – fool that she is – created this divide.

"Miss Delancy wrote to me."

It is a distraction, but a welcome one. "Did she?"

"She's asked me to be nanny to her little boy."

They pull up to the kerb outside the club. Rainwater cascades from shop awnings, pooling in the small dip outside the glossed front door. "You'll be off to America then," Patrice says. The idea saddens her. It is one change too many.

"Actually, Miss Delancy is moving back to England." Caroline looks out of the car, up to the first-floor bay window, her expression one of intense concentration. "To be closer to her daughter."

The vehicle rocks as Berthram gets out from the driver's seat and gently closes the door.

"I didn't say yes before." Caroline's eyes plead with Patrice. "And now I'm not sure if I..."

"If you think you'll be letting the side down, you mustn't give it a second thought." Doused by all the British weather can throw at him, Berthram stands upright at the kerbside, his gaze seemingly averted, hands clasped in front of him ready to open the door as soon Patrice gives the nod.

"Mustn't I?" The question has the tone of an accusation.

"Of course not. There's no shortage of girls who'd bite off their right arm to have what Mr Blagdon can offer."

"Sandy said I was better than this. But I'm no better than Valerie was." The girl is clearly struggling to hold it together. "How can I be?"

It would feel disloyal to say you had any wish to be. "Today isn't a day for decisions. You need proper rest, and you won't get that here. Come home with me. Let me take care of you."

"No!"

Patrice winces at the sharp rebuttal.

Once again, Caroline reins in her reflex. "Like you said. The club is family."

Quite the worst thought to have planted in the girl's mind. All it will do is reinforce her false sense of loyalty. But Patrice knows enough about Caroline to understand that she won't be moved, not at this moment and not on this. "I understand."

"Thank you all the same." Caroline's hand comes to rest on top of Patrice's. The gesture quite takes her breath away. She can do no more than nod to Berthram, who opens the door. The vehicle rocks once again. Only with the slam of the driver's door is Patrice brought back to the moment. She breathes deeply. That peculiar smell of wet London pavements and damp wool from Berthram's uniform coat. And something else. "Is that *liquorice,* Berthram?"

"My apologies, ma'am. It's rather a strong scent."

"Oh, I don't mind. I haven't tasted liquorice in years!"

"Can I offer you some?" He turns, holding out a paper bag. "They were giving it away."

"In that case," she dips into the bag. "Do you mind if I ask you something?"

"Ask away, then I'll tell you if I mind."

"You were in combat during the war."

"I was, ma'am."

"I don't expect it's true what they say. That people are peaceful in death."

He hesitates. "No, ma'am. Though to some of the poor fellows I saw, I'd say it came as a relief." She can feel his eyes in the rear-view mirror. "They've asked you to identify the body, I take it."

Inside her coat, Patrice shudders. "It will mean another detour."

"I shall have to insist on coming in with you, ma'am."

"But you didn't know Valerie."

"They won't know that, now, will they?"

"No, they won't." Patrice settles back for what will be an hour-long drive, proven right in the choice she made to give Berthram a job when he was down on his luck. After a while, watching him in the rear-view mirror, she adds, "Do I pay you enough, Berthram?"

He looks as if he might choke. "Beg pardon, ma'am?"

"It's quite simple. I'm asking if I pay you enough."

"Enough that I can afford my own liquorice."

"But is it the going rate?"

"If you only paid me the going rate, then I really would be in trouble."

"We wouldn't want that." She must give him a raise. Crossland too.

CHAPTER TWENTY-EIGHT

CAROLINE

Though it feels cowardly, Caroline walks round the block and ducks inside what's called the tradesman's entrance. She can't stomach the thought of conversation, George's kindness especially. What she fears most is not someone wanting to talk about Valerie, but someone asking how she's feeling.

The usual noises suggest business as usual – a clatter of pans from the kitchen, the clink of glasses, a blur of conversation. Laughter, which, in Caroline's frame of mind, sounds unnaturally hearty. Music. Not the swing Valerie adored (Terry may have drawn the line at that) but a sedate waltz. On reaching the first-floor landing, Caroline sees Terry plant one hand on the bar to heave himself to his feet, but she holds up a hand, palm forwards, and quickens her pace. He makes no attempt to follow as she heads up to the second floor, and for this she's grateful.

There is still a little light in the day. No need to reach for the light switch, just close the door and lean against it. Here in the living room of the flat they shared, Valerie's absence is heightened by her pale blue cardigan that hangs on one of the high-backed dining chairs, as if draped over a set of shoulders. She might have just shrugged it off and stepped out of the room. Dammit, Patrice was right. How can she stay here? And why didn't she accept the duchess's offer?

Caroline remembers now, the reason for her refusal. Fear that Patrice might, in her own clipped curt way, be as capable of kindness as George. Already, sitting in the back of the Bentley, she'd felt tempted to say, *I'm here because my father left us. He left us, and my mother thought it so shameful she'd rather have my brothers and sister think he's –*. Now that Caroline knows grief, this pretence, this awful pretence, seems so much worse.

She will try, at least, to take some of Patrice's advice. Sleep. The door to Yvette's bedroom is shut, often an indication that she has company. The door to their bedroom – yes *their* bedroom, hers and Valerie's – is ajar, just as Caroline left it. She hesitates. *Breathe,* she tells herself. Her horror of Valerie's empty bed will be best combatted if Caroline sleeps on her left side with her back to it.

Yes, that will be best.

She pushes the door, lets it swing in an arc.

But Valerie's bed isn't empty. Caroline's fists clench. Curled in a foetal position on top of the comforter and facing the wall lies Yvette. An act of sacrilege has been committed, and if this much can be dared, if Yvette should move the blue cardigan from the chair, if she clears away the china cup and washes the lipstick from its rim, God help her, Caroline will not be responsible for her actions.

But Yvette senses none of this. The slow movement of her chest and the occasional twitch of her brow suggests a fitful and exhausted sleep. Her shoes lie on their sides, kicked off, an afterthought. Her legs are crossed at the ankles. Her feet rest one atop the other, as if keeping each other company.

Caroline sighs; unfurls her hands. Fingernails have gouged semi-circles in the crevice of her lifeline. Anger drains away, leaving a deep exhaustion in its wake. Yvette too had lived vicariously through Valerie, she realises. Neither had half her daring, half her light-hearted confidence. But in six months' time, an ever-diminishing number of people will ask, 'Whatever happened to that blonde hostess? What was her name?' And after they have their answer, they'll go back to their drinks, the stories told so many times Caroline knows them by heart, the hash the government is making of this or that, their latest conquests. And though some of the men had been on intimate terms with Valerie, she'll be replaced in their affections by the latest shimmying hostess, perhaps the one who's inherited Valerie's wardrobe. But first, before that, Valerie's bed will acquire a new occupant. Caroline can do nothing to stop the inevitable. Why not Yvette, whom she knows and who knew Valerie? As Patrice said, aren't they all family? Stuck with one another.

Caroline goes to the wardrobe, shakes out the spare blanket, reserved for what Valerie used to call 'two jersey days', and gently spreads it over Yvette who stirs just enough to say something that sounds like, 'Interfering old crone.'

Caroline didn't want to be alone tonight. Now she doesn't need to be.

CHAPTER TWENTY-NINE

PATRICE

They are led in silence to a room where, separated from them by a pane of glass, five sheet-covered corpses lie on gurneys, side-by-side. One of those…

"You understand that she has a little trauma around her head and face."

On hearing those words, Berthram puts one hand in the crook of Patrice's arm, a presumption they both know he would never normally take. Patrice is grateful because she understands she must prepare herself. She reaches for his hand (surprisingly warm), a presumption *she* would never normally take, and as the mortician goes to lift the white sheet, she holds her breath. Even with Berthram there to shore her up, she cannot help hoping that she will be able to say, 'No, I've never seen this girl before,' and, 'There must have been some mistake.'

But Patrice's heart clenches. The open mouth. The stitching around the eyes. She understands immediately that those who offer comfort to the bereaved dish up lies. Viewed through glass, the face is not calm, not serene. And really, what protection does glass offer? Patrice hears herself say, "Yes, it's her," and feels the touch of her own fingertips on her forehead, chest, right shoulder and left. It is over, but that doesn't diminish the part she has played. The fact that she was the one to condemn Valerie to death. And because this is Valerie, there can now be no denying that one of the other sheet-covered corpses – she looks at each in turn – is Arnold. She will miss him so dreadfully, this man she was just coming to know.

On returning home, Patrice goes straight upstairs. The hour is late, just how late she has no idea. Her tread is heavy, every step cumbersome, as if she's hauling herself to the top of a mountain rather than the second floor. How dare they put loved ones through that? There are those, she supposes, who would insist on seeing, who feel they must face the truth of what happened. But there must be others who would prefer not to. You cannot unsee what you have seen. Surely in this day and age, with everything scientists have at their disposal? During the war, identity tags did the job.

Patrice feels for the Linnets, she really does. For all the unfair treatment she's suffered at Lucinda's hands, for all they would willingly have put Valerie through, they've had to endure identifying their only son. Their heir. Thank goodness Derek and Lucinda had each other.

She assumes they had each other.

Imagine. Imagine one of you saying, "Yes, it's him," while the other doesn't want to believe. Would she herself have known it was Valerie if the suggestion hadn't been put to her? Without that devilish glint, the sway of her hips, it was not Valerie, not really. It was only the shell of her.

Heavy of heart, Patrice enters her bedroom, half expecting Crossland to be there to do the small comforting things she manages in her unobtrusive manner. Turning back the bed. Drawing the curtains. Instead, Patrice pulls up sharply. All other thoughts are shunted aside. Her husband is lying on her bed, propped up on her pillows. He is reading her *diary*.

Winded as thoroughly as if she'd taken a blow, Patrice stifles a gasp.

He is holding in his hands a post-mortem of her every day. In its pages she is both patient and surgeon, corpse and grave robber.

Patrice tightens the laces of her internal corsetry. *Stop and count to ten.* This is not something to blow up over until she has decided exactly what she thinks about it.

But look at him, just *look* at him, making no attempt to hide his betrayal.

Now there can be no room for doubt. He has stolen even that possibility from her.

Her outer semblance is calm. "Charles, would you be so good as to take your shoes off the furniture?" When he ignores her request, as she'd anticipated he would, Patrice walks briskly to the dressing table, where, heart pounding in her ears, she deposits her bag. "You needn't have waited up."

He lays the open diary pages down on his chest (she almost admires his brass) and folds his arms. "I've been waiting here since this afternoon."

"I didn't realise we had an arrangement. What brought you home so early?"

"Would it surprise you if I were to say it was a telephone call?"

"Then you've heard."

"Can you explain why you chose to embarrass me in this particular fashion?"

"I realise you may struggle with the notion, Charles, but embarrassing you wasn't uppermost in my mind."

"It never is. Not when you entertain men at my expense, and not when you become a gossip columnist for a day without thinking to consult me –"

Patrice's indignation emerges with a *Ha!* The gloves are raised, but they will dance around each other a little longer before any punches are thrown. "At *your* expense? I'm warning you, Charles, don't *ever* try that one with me." She does not give him the chance to get a word in, ploughing straight on. "As for that other matter, it's ancient history. I really can't see why you'd choose to drag it up now of all times. Neither can I see how Ursula Delancy's business was any concern of yours."

"No concern of –? You fired off hefty accusations at several highly influential people." Patrice is tempted to say that she had no idea Charles held film stars in such high esteem, but he is not finished. "And when you start questioning why people have been attacked for failing to uphold certain standards, it calls your own morals into question. Surely you see that?"

There is no need to match his vitriol, but neither will Patrice stand for a browbeating. "The article named no one."

"You didn't need to *name* Spencer Tracy when you provided so many clues!"

Blinkered to any opinion that contradicts his own, Charles prefers his opponents to take their time before replying. Immediately she says, "You thought it was Tracy? Interesting." The type who can ride out a publicity storm only to find himself honoured with an elevated level of notoriety his peers can only dream of. But to succeed in this, you have to not care what Joe Public thinks. And Ursula Delancy cares. She cares terribly. Sensitive people always suffer when they are cast into the spotlight.

"Among others."

"I simply pointed out the hypocrisy. When a man does the very same thing Ursula Delancy did, there's rarely a headline, let alone a Senator who considers it his *moral duty* to bring the matter before his President."

"And yet I *was* embarrassed."

"Instead of feeling sorry for yourself, you might have considered supporting the stance I was taking. Divorce as a private matter between husband and wife."

"Oh, so it was a serious point you were making!" Veins stand proud on his forehead, their appearance rarely a good sign.

"Charles, I've had a very tiring day. Say whatever it is you have to say and have done with it."

"Alright." He props himself up on an elbow. "What I want to know is this: what was it about this particular girl that made you plough on without stopping to consider whether your actions might backfire on your husband's political career? *If you don't mind my asking?*"

"Is it your career you're worried about, or your social standing?"

"I'm not sure I can separate the two."

No, she thinks, looking at him lying there. Perhaps being ostracised didn't bother Charles as much as it did her. He was never a particularly social animal. She takes a swipe at one of his brogues. "Your shoes, Charles, if you don't mind."

He grunts in an indignant manner; clasps her open diary to his chest, swings his legs around and sits, then moves the diary to his lap.

"The Linnets refused to acknowledge Arnold's relationship with Valerie because they thought her unsuitable. They made it quite clear that they thought his memory was more valuable than hers."

"Of course they did. He was their *son.* What concerns me is why you *lied!*"

Charles is riled, no doubt about it, but her own hackles are also at half-mast. "The Linnets hardly concerned themselves with the truth. They suggested to the police that Valerie was behind the wheel of their son's car." Patrice behaves as if hers is the last word, picking up the clean white towels that Crossland has left folded on the end of her bed.

"You didn't let the fact that it was the Linnets' son influence you when you decided which side to take."

"Good God, Charles, our godson and his fiancée are *dead!* I'd say that the fact that they were engaged to be married puts them very much on the same side, wouldn't you? All I did was what I thought Arnold would have wanted me to do."

"And you knew Arnold's mind, did you?"

"I believe I did, yes."

"But we've barely seen him –"

"I have seen him. Actually, I've seen quite a lot of him." For a moment, Patrice wonders if Charles will refer to her diary; demand, 'When?' "I evened out the odds by giving Valerie a few extra credentials. We all understood what was happening."

"Not everyone, apparently. I've been approached with a request that I verify a few facts."

She hugs the towels to her chest. "By whom?"

"The newspapers, of course! Linnet wouldn't have the stomach for a show-down at a time like this."

Patrice wouldn't have put it past the Linnets' inner circle to elect a spokesperson to voice collective disapproval. "As I say, everyone understood exactly what was going on." Patrice doesn't hesitate in her preparations for the bathroom. She sits at the dressing table to remove her necklace and lays it in its velvet-lined drawer.

"You *arranged* this?"

"That was my intention, certainly. How else could I hope to control what appears in the papers?" She unclasps her earrings, one at a time, placing them in a small porcelain bowl. "Unfortunately, by the time I arrived, a number of journalists were already at the police station. I suppose it's possible that they overheard me as I passed on our condolences."

"Our –?"

"Naturally. Arnold was your godson too." She looks beyond her own reflection and observes Charles; his hands, gripping the edges of her diary.

"Would you care to tell me what I'll need to agree to?"

"I'm glad you ask." She crosses one leg over the other and smooths her skirt. "As a childless couple, while we have not gone as far as to adopt, we have taken an interest, financially speaking, in the welfare of a couple of children. This has largely been my project. You haven't troubled yourself with the finer details, but you can verify that you have transferred funds to a Miss Valerie Grant –"

"You realise how this will be interpreted?"

"Really, Charles, it isn't so remarkable. The idea that a man of your standing had an affair and did his bit to support the child. Besides, it will stop tongues wagging."

"Wagging? About what?"

"Which of us was unable to conceive, of course." As penances go, this seems appropriate. To set a story in motion that becomes part of one's history, even though there's not a shred of truth in it.

"Another falsehood!"

It's touching to think this might be Charles's one sticking point. "Then you already know your remaining option."

"Tell the press that my wife, the duchess, is a *liar?*"

Patrice swivels round on the stool and looks at her husband directly. They both know that coming from him, a denial will be met with disbelief. "All I did was plant the seed of an idea. You must do as your conscience dictates." No need to say, 'You will do this one thing for me, Charles.' She says this in the knowledge of all the times she has covered for him; all the times she has stood by him. "I'm exhausted, Charles. If you don't mind, I'd like to have my bath now."

"How many people are dead?"

The blood drains from Patrice's face. She sees Valerie's face, really *sees* it. Not as she was, but as she is now. And that vision allows her to imagine how Arnold is. "Five, including the passengers in the other vehicle."

"And the Linnets wanted to pin four deaths on the girl?"

"It's too early to say if anyone was to blame. But on the basis that someone *might* be held responsible, they wanted to place Arnold in the passenger seat – a form of insurance, if you will. Do you still disapprove?"

"You could have waited for the police to finish their investigation."

"Yes, I could have waited. I could have waited until the press wrote whatever they liked about Valerie's profession, I could have stood by while the Linnets denied that their son was engaged to be married, until Valerie had been placed behind the wheel and condemned, and *then* made a public accusation that the Linnets had attempted a cover-up. Tell me, how would that have gone down at your club?"

Charles broods silently, unwilling to concede, but Patrice's anger with her husband ramps up a gear. Even if she could put a name to this particular cocktail of feelings, she will not risk reducing herself to the child whose parents accused her of having temper tantrums. Not today, and certainly not in front of Charles. At the same time, she can resist it no longer. "Incidentally," she inclines her head towards the diary, which is still lying upside down in his lap. "Did you find what you were looking for?"

CHAPTER THIRTY

RUTH

They remain wary of each other, she and Evelyn. Ruth decides to say it before the wardress has the chance. "You're not at all what I expected."

"What did you expect?"

"A frumpy matron, I suppose. Not someone my age."

"We're the exact same age." Evelyn's blink is an admission that she's read all about Ruth's court appearances. Well, who hasn't? "You're not what I expected either."

"Give me five minutes in make-up and she'll show up."

"You don't need make-up. Not with those eyes."

Though Ruth chose the frames of her spectacles to bring out their blue, she dismisses the compliment with a smile. "My daughter has my eyes. Forget-me-not blue. I almost died giving birth to her, you know." Even as she says it, Ruth is aware that she's broached two forbidden subjects. Death and her children. Anything, in fact, that might unsettle her. Calm is the thing. At the very least, a pretence of calm.

She has taken up sewing – she, Ruth Ellis, one-time manageress of the Little Club, and now London's most notorious murderer – is sewing. Can you imagine? Stuffed animals. And after she pooh-poohed the felt and kapok her mother brought in. "Keep you busy," Berta said, "Keep your hands busy." She hates that her mother is right. Hates the history that binds them. The secrets. Berta with her mustard baths, her Epsom salts, her generous doses of Parrish's pick-me-up tonic. Berta who often kept Andy for her, but in return demanded she handed over virtually every penny she earned, and even then thought nothing of calling Ruth at the club to demand more. Money for her precious cigs and Father's tuppenny Woodbines.

Ruth has no sewing pattern to work from, so she tries to recreate something from her childhood. A bear of a little-known pedigree. More of a cross-breed. The Woman's Sunday Mirror *want to know all about her childhood. What went into the making of a cold-blooded killer?* "Don't come straight home from school. Stay at Pearl's until Muttar's home from work." *That's not for them to know. Let the journalists write their fairy tales about her idyllic childhood, the games of happy families, from sunny Rhyl straight to London and first love.*

My God, the lives they have led, the cost of surviving! Now it is almost at an end, and there is a rightness about this. It wasn't a lie, the letter she wrote to David's mother. She truly believes her sentence is justice. Until then, Ruth is alert to every grain of time. Do you wish it away, these idle hours? Don't be in any rush, she tells herself. But at other times, she thinks, What's the point? I'd just prefer it all to be over.

CHAPTER THIRTY-ONE

URSULA

Ursula looks up from the headlines. Queen Mary is dead. Almost four years after Big Ben stopped and bets were placed on her demise being the reason.

Four years since Ursula's last success on the London stage, a success she must now work hard to exploit.

On the one hand, the blink of an eye. On the other, an eternity.

But here is Marcus, all the proof she needs of the passage of time. Marcus, who at this moment is sitting on the rug in their rented Thames-side home, playing a complicated game of his own invention that takes every ounce of his concentration. Ursula smiles, but she won't distract him. Not when he's so intent on working something out for himself.

She returns to the newspaper columns. *The last of a bygone era.* Oh, the old Queen was certainly that. Never a typical invalid, a recent Pathé newsreel captured her being wheeled about dressed in fur stoles and strings of pearls, with a white parasol ready to prod any commoner who dared step out of line. *In a world where nothing seemed sure, her standards remained unchanged and unchangeable.* Only in England is being consistently out of touch considered a virtue.

A photograph shows a single policeman discreetly looking away as orderly well-wishers file past the bulletin posted on a screen of corrugated iron, as if paying respects to a queen who lies in state. *While sleeping peacefully.*

Four years since Big Ben stopped, four years since Ursula last made headlines for all the wrong reasons. Work is the thing, of course. If she can do good work, not everything is wasted. And, of course, she has Marcus. She abandons her newspaper, stealthily creeps up on him, and stoops to scoop him up. "Gotcha!"

"Mommy!" Will he lose that American accent now that they are in England, or is it already part of who he is?

"You're getting so heavy, I could easily –" He squeals with delight as she pretends she's about to drop him.

Look at that face. How can Mack continue to deny he's Marcus's father? As photos appear in countless newspapers and magazines, Ursula can't help wondering if Lindsay has noticed that Marcus has Mack's eyes. Their exact shape and spacing. The Floods have managed to keep pictures of their three-year-old out of the papers (a director's family is allowed a private life in a way that an actress's family is not). But people from the closeted world of filmdom, the same people who attended those extravagant Hollywood parties Ursula shunned towards the end of her time in America, people who have seen photographs of both boys, can't resist telling Ursula how struck they are by the similarity, hoping for confirmation or denial.

As yet, it hasn't occurred to Marcus that anyone is missing from his life. There is Mommy, and when Mommy has to work there is Noo-noo, who worships and spoils him. But the day will come, Ursula worries, as she watches him clamber onto the seat of an armchair as if it's his personal climbing frame.

"Come down from there, Marcus. You'll fall." She goes to remove him as he stretches a chubby hand out over a divide.

"No floor, no!" he insists.

"So that's your game, is it?" Ursula damps down her nerves, even as he launches himself from armchair to sofa, from sofa to coffee table, allowing him to complete a full circuit of the furniture, before she hauls him up under the arms and spins him round. Even as he shrieks, she thinks, *When I tell you the truth, will you be as disapproving as my mother?* It won't matter that she says, *I wanted you so much that I was happy to put myself through all that criticism again.* At some point she'll have to find a way to explain that he has a half-brother. One who's the same age as him. *No, Marcus, not a twin. A brother.* Even the thought of how she'll find the words churns the contents of Ursula's stomach. She could insist that Mack takes a blood test, but that would involve a court case, and Lord knows, she's seen the inside of enough family courtrooms. Besides, a test might prove more than she intended. That Marcus's father is a liar. Even when presented with evidence, Ursula wouldn't put it past Mack to reject Marcus outright, or to blow hot and cold, treating him so differently from the son he considers to be 'legitimate' that it would amount to the same thing.

It's not just his father Marcus doesn't know. He has yet to meet his British grandmother. Ursula's mother has made her allegiances clear. She never made a secret of the fact that she'd always wanted a son, and when the time came to make a choice, she didn't blink before choosing Robin. Ursula likes to think that were he still alive, her father wouldn't have refused to meet his grandson on the grounds that he's illegitimate, although she may be wrong about this.

Like Silvia's friends, Marcus's will make cruel jibes, and he won't come crying to her, because she'll be their cause – in part at least. And so Ursula thinks that when Marcus gets to the age of eight it might be best to send him to boarding school, where he can be his own person. A lump clogs her throat, but she *must* look to the future, must prepare herself. So that there is less to associate a boy called Marcus Sheard with the person the newspapers and the studios created, a person she barely recognises: the actress, Ursula Delancy.

"The mail's here," announces Norma, entering the room carrying a stack of envelopes. Her face brightens as Marcus says, "Noo-noo!" None of the succession of nursery nurses have been as popular with Marcus as Noo-noo, because she was there first and he takes comfort in familiarity.

"Want me to take him off your hands?" The offer is made as if this would be a terrible imposition.

"I don't know if he'll let you. His latest game is to get round the room without using the floor."

Norma's hands move to her hips and she looks down at Marcus, with wary disapproval. "Is it now, young man?"

"No floor!" Marcus grins, undeterred.

"On the bright side," says Ursula, "the furniture's rented."

"You'd better show me how it's done while your mother answers her letters. But I'm not making any promises." Norma groans as she toes off her slip-on shoes.

"Not you, Noo-noo! Me!"

"Well, that's a relief. I think my climbing days are over, what with my hips being as they are."

Ursula mouths 'Thank you' and Norma shoos her from the room as if she's batting a fly. At this time of day the morning room has the best light and the space to spread out. Now that they're back in England, there's much to be done. Ursula needs a British agent. What she'll do, she thinks, is call Clement Meade *("Dammit. I demand to be called 'the renowned director'")*, just a friendly chat about the play he's working on and what's in the pipeline. She has earmarked a couple of promising manuscripts to show him, but that's not a request for the first call after a long absence. And Ursula has an idea that down the road in Bray, Hammer Film Productions could use an actress with a little notoriety. But first, the post. A stray knife left over from breakfast serves as a letter opener. Bills that have followed Ursula from the States. Details from estate agents – Good Lord! They seem to be under the impression that she has unlimited funds. Although that one in Egham makes it to her 'action' pile. What's this?

She scans the official-looking letter.

The studio is entitled, but she never actually thought... She'd reached an understanding with Aldo. He used her name, and it secured his funding. To sue now, over her refusal to play what's little more than a cameo, and when she has less than eighteen months to run on her seven-year contract. It doesn't even make good business sense!

"Norma!" she yells.

"Coming!" Norma appears, slightly breathless, holding onto the doorframe.

"Aldo says that if I don't get myself back over there, the studio will sue."

Norma's eyebrows quickly rise and fall, an expression devoid of surprise. "In that case, it's probably just as well we don't have our own furniture yet."

CHAPTER THIRTY-TWO

CAROLINE

It's only mid-afternoon and already Caroline feels loose-limbed.

"Gin please, Elise." She no longer asks for gin when she means water, although there have been occasions when Elise thought she was too drunk to notice the difference. "Real gin." She slams her glass on the bar, making the distinction clear.

"Whose tab?"

"Mine, I suppose."

Elise glares, but whisks the glass away and presses its rim to an optic. "You should eat something."

"I ate something."

Elise gives her a look of disbelief.

"I had a sandwich!" Caroline insists. When was that? Her life is increasingly structureless. She cannot separate one day from another. Sometimes she forgets she has a sister called Betty. Her old self fading, Caroline is insubstantial, temporary. Nothing she has done or will do matters terribly much.

A volley of names: Cliff, David, Mike. At least this latest group of arrivals have a bit of life in them.

Up on tiptoes, she leans forwards to hiss at Elise, "Any idea who they are?"

"The crowd from the Steering Wheel Club, sitting it out until opening time."

Caroline sees a narrow country lane, headlights on full beam, and Valerie, oblivious to the fate that lies just around the bend.

"I'd give them a wide berth if I were you." Elise glowers. "I've already had to confiscate a soda syphon. They were using it for a water fight."

Hard drinkers and plenty of horseplay. The type whose nice girlfriends and little wives put in an appearance at dinner dances and sporting fixtures, but are kept at a safe distance from boozy London exploits. It suits Caroline's urge to rip everything in her path to shreds. Ruin seems like a destination.

"I couldn't help overhearing," she cuts through the racket and the whorls of cigarette smoke. "You're a racing-car driver." She says it as if this were the cleverest thing in the world. "How exciting!"

"Not just me." The man wears his hair with a centre parting and has a surprisingly bushy moustache. "We all race."

"I don't," one of the revellers pipes up.

Caroline wastes no time in latching on to him. "And what do you do?"

"Design and build. I'm not daft enough to race."

"Exactly how daft would you have to be to race one of the cars you design and build?"

Laughter. Back-slapping. They approve, issuing warnings to one another: *Watch what you say. She's a sharp one.*

"See that daft-looking bugger?" Design and Build points to a dark-haired man, no Brylcreemed centre parting, no walrus moustache. Dressed in a dark grey worsted wool suit and a tie with diagonal stripes of navy, burgundy and gold, the kind intent on announcing that its wearer had an expensive education. Perhaps, Caroline calculates, a few years older than her.

She changes position and takes Daft-Looking Bugger by the arm. "Do you mean this one?"

"That's him. He's just taken Hunter's record for the fastest lap of Berkeley Square."

"Almost beaten by a taxi cab! I did better at the Royal Albert Hall. Sixty miles an hour with a police car on my tail."

Already she has him down. Raffish. Spoilt. The sort of man who won't pass it up. She smiles up at him. "Hello."

"Hello."

"I don't suppose you have a cigarette on you?"

He flips the lid of his carton and offers it to her.

Caroline's head feels too heavy for her neck. "Light it for me, will you?" she asks.

"You've very demanding. Has anyone ever told you that?"

"You have no idea how flammable hairspray is." There it is. The accidental brush of hands. The physical connection. Only one route leads from here. "What kind of motor-car do you drive?"

"An HRG."

"Would it surprise you to know that I have absolutely no idea what that is?" Is she slurring her words?

"It's lightweight and aerodynamic, built for long-distance racing."

"And that's what you do, is it? Long-distance racing."

"Anything up to twenty-four hours."

"You do know that twenty-four hours isn't a distance, I suppose?"

The man called Mike cuts in: "It's quite a distance, I can tell you."

Caroline blanks Mike. Her target is already in her sights. "Do you have a name?"

"David."

"Take me for a spin, *David?*" she asks. Valerie taught her well.

One of the other men whoops.

"Only one seat, I'm afraid, and that's mine."

"All the same, I'd like to *see* a racing-car."

He draws on his cigarette and frowns. "It's parked around the corner."

She has him now. "Well, I can't walk that far, not in these heels." Already, her hands are linked around his neck, her fingers woven. "You'll have to carry me."

"I'm glad that's over." Caroline leaves Yvette to close the door to the flat. It is only ostensibly theirs. They don't have the luxury of a lock. She kicks off her shoes, abandoning them where they topple, flat-footing it to the sideboard, feeling her weight redistribute itself from the balls of her feet to her heels. "What an evening!"

"Good for business." Yvette reaches inside her bra, extracts a number of notes and counts them.

Fearful of the moment when the alcohol buzz wears off, when she's left alone in the dark, Caroline pours a generous measure of gin, perhaps more than she'd intended. She offers the glass to Yvette. "Nightcap?"

"Not for me. I've put away so much Pernod, I reek of the stuff."

"Suit yourself." Caroline sits heavily in the armchair, stretches out her legs and lifts her feet to flex them. She slouches down into the cushions and cradles the glass. She would rather sleep here than face the room, the place where she and Valerie reclined, smoked and gossiped.

"What do you think of the name Bibi?"

"Who for?"

"For me, of course!"

"You already have a name."

"It's a bit dull, don't you think? And lots of people are known by their nicknames." Valerie giggles. "Bibi Linnet."

Where Valerie's hairbrush still sits on the dressing table, blonde strands woven into its bristles.

Yvette hesitates at the door to her bedroom and turns.

"Second thoughts?" Caroline asks.

"I've just realised, it's not me who reeks." Yvette disappears into their room – hers and Valerie's – and returns carrying an overflowing ashtray at arm's length, which she deposits outside the door on the landing.

"Since when did you develop such a delicate nose?"

"There's a difference between fresh tobacco and a days-old ashtray!" Yvette marches past. "Perhaps you should take it a little easier."

Caroline gives her a wooden smile. "I didn't realise you were keeping count."

"Do what you like. I don't have time to keep tabs on you."

"I shall," Caroline says to the bottom of her glass. She takes advice from no one.

They don't mention Valerie. To do so would stoke their grief. And yet she's everywhere. In the chipped teacup she drank from because she 'felt sorry for it'. The sash window she propped open while she shook out a few crumbs for the huddled pigeons on the narrow sill. How could you be so fond of those stupid birds? In London, you're hard pressed to find a bench or a statue where they haven't left their mark.

"By the way, did you hear? Morrie Conley's appointed a female manager at Carroll's."

"Has he?" Caroline's teeth crunch against the rim of her glass as she takes another swig. Another opportunity evaporated; options narrowed.

"Sassy. Peroxide blonde. Ruth Something-or-other. Give me a minute, it'll come to me."

"Do I need to know her name?"

"Mrs Ruth Ellis! That's it. 'She's married?' I asked, because that's no job for a married woman."

"And is she?"

"Divorced, apparently. Anyway, rumour is, Conley's paying her a fortune."

"I expect she has to earn it. I hear he's a lot more demanding than Terry."

"Huh." Yvette shrugs this off.

Because it can't be spoken of, Caroline has no idea if Terry makes demands of Yvette or if the arrangement suits her.

"She's turning the place around, so I'm told. The coffers are flowing. He's even letting her change its name to the Little Club."

"Good for her," Caroline says flatly. She's unsure how she feels, hearing about someone else making a success of something that could have been hers. Unsure if she feels anything any longer.

"And as for lover boy – the public schoolboy you took up with tonight?"

"Which one?"

"Clean-shaven. Dark-haired. Threw you over his shoulder and ran downstairs with you."

"Oh, him." *David,* she thinks.

"That's her boyfriend."

Caroline feels no guilt. It's not as if women who do what they do (what they *have* to do if they have families relying on their pay packets) are in any position to accuse a man of cheating. Her thought is *Good.* There's a symmetry to it. She's managed to claw back something for herself, if only a generous tip. "Funny. He didn't mention her."

"I just thought you should know." Yvette disguises her warning with a smile. "You'd better watch yourself, if she has Conley eating out of her hand."

Caroline dismisses this threat. "You think Conley would have employed her if he knew she had a regular boyfriend?" Now she knows she's slurring.

Yvette shrugs. "A boyfriend could have arrived on the scene afterwards."

"Then Mrs Ellis is taking quite a risk." Caroline pauses long enough to let this sink in. "Besides, the boyfriend would hardly make a point of mentioning me. And I doubt we'll see the Steering Wheel Crowd again."

"I don't know. I get the impression you gave them a good time."

Caroline closes her eyes to see if there is any satisfaction to be squeezed from this. Beyond the orange of her eyelids, the room cartwheels.

Chrome dials. En route to her weekend destination, hurtling down a country lane in an open-topped car, Caroline watches as the speedometer tops one hundred miles an hour. The engine's thrum counters the sound of the road; the rev limiter bounces off the red line. 6500 revs per minute: an arbitrary number on a scale of arbitrary numbers. David's grip on the steering wheel is light. "So that the car can self-correct," he tells her. Exhilarated and terrified in equal measure, Caroline leans back against the red leather headrest.

"Here," he says. A silver hip flask. She avoids the engraving. Doesn't doubt it's from another woman. Quite possibly the manageress (sassy, blonde, paid a fortune). She drinks deeply. As the liquor burns a trail to her stomach, clouds race overhead. Twice, she whoops at the sky. It is no longer Caroline's mother who whispers in her ear. In recent weeks, despite weekly reminders that people at home are relying on her, the constant nagging whisper has been silenced. Instead, Valerie is calling, calling, calling. And, today, this call, the one voice Caroline aches to hear, is a summons. She surrenders to the speed, to the Scotch, to the scudding clouds. *I'm coming.*

As David slams his foot on the brake, she feels a momentous pull, hears a terrible screeching, Caroline braces herself for what must be. A tree. A steep grass verge. A brick wall. Shunted forwards, her hands fly out. *I'm coming.* There is no imagined scenario in which her body does not follow. Her forehead bounces off the dashboard.

The car skids.

But tyres grip the road.

"Oops." His grin is boyish. "Overshot a little."

Caroline wrestles with what just happened, a triumph of engineering over physics. *Oops. Is that all you can say?* The engine roars its protest as he throws the car into reverse, one sharp elbow jutting over the back of his seat. There is a vicious spinning of wheels before the car lurches sharply to the right.

Between two towering pillars, they pull onto a potholed drive, some distant vast ivy-clad monstrosity up ahead, tennis courts off to the left, a stray peacock or two. She is not present in the moment. Not really. After all that, having given herself up to it, how can Caroline accept that this will just be another weekend when elegant society women look down their noses, as if she's some charwoman? Whose eyes move away quickly as if they've seen something they would prefer not to have seen.

"Shall we?" David cranks on the handbrake, then hesitates. "You could have asked me to slow down, you know."

Caroline must be a better actress than she thought. "Do I look a fright?" She turns to him, as if waiting for his all-important opinion, though she cares little how he sees her. After all, she took one look at him, saw all his weaknesses and decided she had a use for him.

"Look as windswept as you like." He leans across the hand-brake and presses his mouth to hers. She yields, to warmth, to life, but Caroline has no illusions. She is one of several women he might have telephoned at the last minute. He wants his country house hosts to know he has any number of them at his beck and call. Not just his peroxide blonde manageress, but the sensible girl he hasn't quite got round to breaking off his engagement with, dancers, waitresses, usherettes.

As they enter the place, she hangs off his arm, resolved to make the best of it. Now that chandeliers and gleaming brass work are familiar, details blend with so many other country houses.

"Catch!" See how casually David throws the key to his motor-car to the first liveried member of staff. Hear how he barks instructions for luggage to be brought inside; the vehicle to be parked. Allow yourself to enjoy being on the arm of a man whose instructions are carried out to the letter, but know this for what it is. A diversion. Caroline has seen the scratches that criss-cross his shoulders, his back, his buttocks; scratches he tries to pass off as occupational, but no one could mistake them for racing injuries. They were scored by manicured talons. Caroline has left coded messages of her own. Know who you're dealing with. Not a good man or a nice man, not a man with anything more than a fleeting interest in you.

She catches her reflection in a mirror and laughs. The red mark where her forehead hit the dashboard needs foundation. "Look at me! I'd better go and tidy myself up."

Another member of staff (there's no shortage of them) nods. "Second on the left, at the far end of the corridor."

She's powdering her forehead when she catches sight of a familiar reflection. No one can curdle a moment faster than Patrice. Logic tells Caroline that she's infiltrated the duchess's social circle, not the other way around, but honestly, must she be *everywhere?* Patrice has no shortage of spare time and all Caroline has is one day a week.

The duchess isn't looking at her own reflection. She's looking at Caroline's. Observing.

Caroline bristles as Patrice sidles up to her. Her mouth barely moves as she says in a low voice, "My dear, you need to be a little more discerning about the company you're keeping."

Caroline matches the duchess's tone. "What business is it of yours?"

"Rather handy with his fists, I hear."

And Caroline opens her mouth to answer back, *This* (she would have pointed to the mark on her forehead) *was an accident.* But the duchess is gone.

"You know what you smell of?" she says, nuzzling his neck.

"What?"

"Petrol and metal. No, wait. It's rust."

"You know what you smell of?" He is still smiling.

"What?" She bites his bottom lip.

Without warning, David's hands are around her neck; he has her up against the headboard. "Terrence Blagdon."

Caroline's heels scramble, her hands tear at the sheets, and she cannot understand. Cannot understand what she did to cause him to move so swiftly from giving pleasure to doling out punishment.

She's angry with the world, the world that has robbed her of so many things. Her anger feels justified, but there's nothing she can do with it. She needs someone to be angry with. Another afternoon, this time at the club, Caroline finds a target. Over there in her corner, Mother Superior is watching – watching with that imperious expression of hers – not directly, nothing as honest as that, but in the mirror. She sees red. "I've had about as much of this as I can take."

"Hey! Where are you off to? I thought we..."

But Caroline doesn't stick around to hear the end of her companion's sentence. She makes a beeline for the duchess's alcove. The room is tilting. The heel of one shoe gives way, folding under her, a shoe that has never given her any trouble in the past. Her right ankle makes contact with the floor. It takes a moment for the pain to bypass the gin and hit home. Clean, breath-taking, Caroline welcomes it as she would one of David's punches, as she navigates coils of blue smoke, snippets of conversation, bars of piano music. Aware of being off-kilter, she lifts her hands, using the tips of her fingers like whiskers, testing the air as a cat would.

"Let's hear it," she demands of the duchess. "What is it you're so desperate to say to me?" There's a fine ringing in her ears.

The duchess, who clearly saw her approach, doesn't look in the least put out. "Sit down, my dear."

Superior calm is not the response Caroline wants. "Thank you, I'll stand."

The duchess nods at a chair. "Do sit. You look a little off-balance."

Caroline goes to grip the edge of the table, but in doing so finds that she was already gripping it and is now grasping at thin air. "I'm fine."

A thin smile. "As you prefer. My concern seems to cause you offence. Why is that?"

"What *offends* me is you sitting here in judgement, day after day."

The duchess appears to take a moment to contemplate this. "Your behaviour is following a certain pattern. One that's all too familiar to me."

"If this is going to be one of your lectures, then at least have the guts to say what you mean." Hearing her own voice, Caroline hates it. "Is *promiscuity* the word you're trying to avoid?"

"Fine. If you prefer it, I can cut to the chase. Although that's *not* the word I would have chosen." Patrice cannot let her high-handedness slip. She has to lord it over everyone. "*Promiscuity*, as you call it, is a common way to fill a vacuum."

Caroline has no idea how she came to be seated the chair,

but in the chair she is. And, what's more, she's been found out.

"As is alcohol," the duchess continues. "The trouble is, neither offers a cure. And the kind of emptiness you're suffering from may not necessarily be temporary."

Something about the duchess's choice of word forces Caroline to listen. Grief is not behaving as she expected it to. She imagined it would be like the time she was chopping an onion and sliced her finger with a kitchen knife. That her skin would knit itself back together, even if it left an ugly scar. In many ways she would have welcomed a scar, something that singled her out as having been marked. But wanting to hear what the duchess has to say does nothing for Caroline's temper. "What right do you have to speak to me like this?"

"I dare to speak, Caroline, because I wish someone had stood up to me when I was busy sabotaging myself. You see, I have done things I regret terribly."

Caroline bridles. "You?" Somehow, she cannot imagine the duchess locked in a frenzied embrace in an alcove, not far from the eyes of diners had they cared to look up from their lamb chops. But an intuitive part of her knows that Patrice is at last revealing something that wasn't printed in the gossip columns. Something true.

"Why do think I don't drink? Oh, you know the British way. Turn a blind eye. Avoid a scene. Sandy, snake that he was, would *not* have turned a blind eye." Curiosity turns to indignance. How dare she, the duchess, invoke Sandy's name? "But he isn't here, and you have no one to take you to task, so I don't have the luxury of remaining silent. The whole of my life, that is to say my *adult* life, has been shaped by absence. If you've lost someone you love – and you've lost two good friends in quick succession – it is only when there is no possibility of making meaningful connections – none whatsoever – that you feel safe. It tends to start with married men, but that's not where it ends. It ends with bad men."

"Don't worry yourself about me. I'm not going to end up walled up in a house."

"Not deliberate killers, you foolish girl! I'm talking about rakes who make no pretence of being anything other than rakes. The ones who think honesty justifies behaving the way they do. And in your job, of course, you have no shortage of access to men like that."

This remark touches an exposed nerve. That Caroline's compass it is a little off at the moment, doesn't stop her from biting back. "Whereas you have to go out and look for yours!"

That sad, wry smile makes another appearance. The smile that says *I'm disappointed in you.* "No. They find me too. What I think is this. You've established a pattern. You may even have convinced yourself that what you're doing is no more than your job entails, and there isn't a soul here who doesn't know Terrence's rules. Bed the same customer twice and it's a relationship – and it's no secret how he feels about his girls having relationships. But even though there's a pattern, there is usually a point at which the sensible part of yourself asks the part that is suffering what the blazes it thinks it's up to. But the part of you that's in pain is more convincing." Caroline steels herself as the duchess continues. "'You need this,' it tells the sensible half. And temporarily this may be true. Who knows? Perhaps you feel that having set the whole thing in motion it would be bad form to back down. But whatever thoughts go through your mind, once the champagne and the gin has worn off, you feel very differently."

Caroline's cheeks burn. "Do I?" She will not cry. She will *not.*

"You know you do."

"Have you finished?"

"Not quite. How you choose to ease your pain is your business. But your choice of men has become a problem. The latest one, the one I saw you with. He's the type who will kill you slowly."

"I told you, David isn't violent."

"Oh he is, believe me. Perhaps his temper hasn't shown itself yet. Perhaps you're still trying to work out how to provoke it. But I don't accept that." The duchess adjusts her chin so that her gaze is even more direct. "I think you've convinced yourself that whatever he does, you deserve it. I expect you were brought up to have a very low opinion of yourself. I know I was."

Caroline is so staggered she forgets to object. This time, "You?" is a genuine question.

"You think that because I had advantages you didn't I wasn't brought up to be submissive and dutiful? You don't think that the moment I got above my station I was slapped back down?" The duchess shakes her head slowly. "This latest fellow of yours. I think you recognised his potential for violence the moment you saw him. Perhaps you experienced it at your father's hands. And you walked towards it."

Caroline pushes herself to standing. She's furious that the duchess thinks she has the right to talk about her life like this; furious that she's right. "I don't have to listen to this!"

"No. No you don't. But I shan't give up. You're alive, you can't help that. So you must find a way to stop punishing yourself for it." The duchess takes Caroline's hand but she pulls it away. "You may not think of me as a friend, but I'm here. When you decide that you need me, you know where to find me."

Caroline feels as if she's about to capsize. "Oh, I *always* know where to find you, *your grace*." She shoulders her way back to the stocky little bore who considers himself quite the charmer.

"There you are," he says. "I thought you'd abandoned me!"

He is someone whose advances she would reject on any other day. But this is not any other day. There is a point to be made. "Never. But when a duchess says jump, jump we must." Caroline swings into the window seat, landing more heavily than she'd intended. What is one more bruise? "Actually." She crosses her leg so that the toe of her shoe gently nudges his calf. "I wondered if you'd like to finish your drink upstairs."

"Upstairs?" No further prompting is needed. Already he's on his feet, a glass in each hand.

As she leads the way, Caroline makes a point of glancing at Patrice's reflected face. The duchess looks down into her glass of mineral water, and there is sadness there. If Caroline expected to notch up a point, the moment is lost. But it is too late. The thing has been set in motion. It would be bad form to back down.

Once dressed, Caroline applies foundation to any bruising that will show above the cut of her dress. Just another step added to her beauty routine. The result isn't perfect, but if others notice they do not say. The day after a battering is always worse than the battering itself. At first, she welcomed the physical pain as a distraction. She baited David: "Again. Go on, hit me again." Now she's grown wary. How can she trust herself? How did she allow it to happen at all, let alone go so far? She cannot make this stop on her own. Neither can Caroline afford to go under. If she can't think of her mother, she must think of Betty.

There is only one person she can turn to.

In her alcove, the duchess is keeping court. Her companions are not the black tie brigade, not today. In their plain white shirts and sports jackets, they look like journalists. Caroline waits, hanging stiffly from the doorframe. It won't be long before the duchess glances over. It can't be. Caroline feels like a child in a classroom, her hand held up to ask an urgent question. *Please. Look this way.* The ache in her arm.

Holding it in place with her opposite hand. When at last she catches sight of Patrice's raised eyebrow, the relief Caroline feels is overwhelming. She smiles weakly, eyes pleading.

In the same crisp and precise manner that she does everything, the duchess excuses herself and walks the width of the room, efficient but unhurried. Caroline steps out onto the landing. This is one conversation that she doesn't want overheard. It is so long since she has said anything that isn't an exaggeration or a lie.

"My dear," the duchess catches her up, "You look a little peaky. A couple of days in the country would do you the world of good. Lots of fresh air and rest. Pack a bag. I'll have Berthram drive you to Whitlocke."

Though Caroline's head pounds with the effort of trying, the apology she has rehearsed will not come.

"All you need do is nod."

She nods.

"Good girl. And don't worry. I'll deal with Terrence. Is there anything else you need? Any medical attention?"

"I –" Caroline answers with a shake of her head.

Patrice goes to make a telephone call. On her return she asks, "Can you be ready in half an hour?"

Caroline looks down at her feet, her voice small. "Won't you be coming with me?"

"Perhaps I'll join you in a few days' time. First, there is the small matter of the coronation. It would be rather bad form not to show up. Anything you need, just ask Mrs Hargreaves." The duchess leans towards her, takes her arm just above the elbow.

She opens her mouth to say something. *I'm so sorry. I didn't mean. I've behaved appallingly. I'm so ashamed.*

"No need. We're all family here." Forgiveness, unfussy, delivered briskly. And then Patrice is gone. Back to her corner, where she apologises charmingly for abandoning her company for so long. "Now where were we?"

Caroline leans against the wall, closes her eyes momentarily, then takes one long grateful look to the right, towards Patrice. *Family.* Unlike any family she has ever known. She makes her way upstairs.

CHAPTER THIRTY-THREE

PATRICE

"Apologies for the interruption, ma'am." It is Elise, not with a delivery of drinks, but wearing an anxious expression. "There's a visitor in reception asking for you."

"Have George send whoever it is up." Patrice returns her gaze to the attentive young man to her left. *What a pity he prefers men.*

"It isn't someone from your guest list."

"Can we dispense with the riddles? If they've made it through the front door, I'm sure there can't be too much of an issue."

Though the barmaid colours, she persists, "George has asked if you wouldn't mind coming down to sign her in."

Patrice pushes back her chair, having every intention of showing Elise just how much of an inconvenience she's being put to, but even as she does so her thoughts steer towards the *her.* Would Lucinda seek her out at the club? The townhouse would have offered more privacy. Unless, of course, she's after a public showdown.

"Apparently, she has a child with her."

Patrice smiles a wistful apology at her young man. "Excuse

me, gentlemen." She feels a hand graze her knee, thinks fleetingly, *Have I got him wrong?* "Elise, would you be so kind as to make sure everyone has whatever they need?"

In her delight, Patrice doesn't pause to consider how she should address the actress. "Ursula!" she calls out from halfway down the stairs.

Relief transforms Ursula's face. "So you *are* here! I asked for Caroline but apparently she's taken a couple of days' leave."

"She has."

"I couldn't go without at least trying to see you, but I wasn't sure if it would be acceptable to bring Marcus onto the premises. George has been very kind."

The doorman's expression is one of distant indulgence, if such a thing were possible. People do leave children unguarded on pavements, but not the children of famous actresses. "So this is the young man?" she asks.

"Marcus," Ursula addresses the child she holds on her hip, the pleasure she takes in him apparent. "This lady is a duchess. What do you have to say about that?"

The boy nestles coyly against his mother's shoulder. (Patrice is rather relieved. People tend to pass their children to you when they need a spare hand, with the expectation that you'll know what to do.) "What's a duchess?" His voice has the pronounced twang of child actors in American films. How strange to have a child who speaks differently from you; to know that you have not influenced it.

Ursula opens her mouth, then promptly closes it and turns to Patrice. "Do you know, I'm not sure I know the answer to that. What a terrible admission!"

"I'm not sure *I* know what it means any more. Technically, I believe I'm below a princess but a step above a marchioness."

"There you are." Ursula kisses the child's golden curls. "Someone very important."

"Is it above an actress?" he asks.

"Oh," she laughs that easy laugh of hers. "By quite a few steps, I'm afraid. Patrice, I don't suppose you know of somewhere private we can talk? If you're not too busy, that is."

"I'm never too busy for you." She scours her memory for an appropriate establishment, one where Ursula Delancy's presence won't cause a stir.

"If you don't mind a suggestion," George cuts in apologetically. "It's hardly the Ritz, but I doubt anyone is using the upstairs flat at this hour. It has quite a pleasant sitting room. I'm sure Yvette wouldn't object if she were asked, and Elise might be persuaded to make you tea."

Patrice defers to Ursula. "Shall we?"

"It sounds just the thing."

Patrice looks to George.

"I'm terribly sorry, ma'am, but I can't abandon my post."

She will have to be the one. "Do excuse me, Ursula. I won't be a moment."

The duchess returns to the bar and scans the room. Yvette is huddled next to a customer, her head bent close to his in a way that suggests intimate conversation, their knees touching. "Elise, would you mind asking Yvette if she could spare me a moment."

"Of course." Elise opens the hatch and backs out.

Yvette untangles herself and looks up, a little alarmed. News has not been happy of late, and Patrice knows full well that a request coming from her will seem unusual, to say the least. She smiles, and nods slightly, to convey (she hopes) that Yvette would be doing her a personal favour. When she sees the hostess make her apology and stand, Patrice turns to face the bar.

Yvette sidles up. "What can I do for you, *your grace?*"

Patrice doesn't rise to what may or may not be sarcasm. "I'm so sorry to drag you away, but I have something to ask."

The hostess raises her eyebrows. "Ask away."

"It's something of a delicate matter. You see, a friend has called on me – a lady friend. I'm afraid it wouldn't be appropriate to bring her up to the club room, and she isn't someone I can take to a public place without attracting attention." The look Yvette gives her says, *Embarrassed to be seen with her, are you?* "I was wondering – that is to say, George suggested – that we might borrow your living room."

The hostess does not go quite as far as folding her arms. "Oh, he did, did he?"

"Only if I'm not putting you out. It wouldn't be for very long."

Yvette sashays to the landing, bends her knees and peers down the staircase. The way she squints suggests short-sightedness, something Patrice has not suspected. Patrice decides not to intrude on the moment that Yvette reacts, but is unsurprised when she returns looking a little dazed. "I'll just go and make sure everything's in order." And she runs upstairs, holding the skirt of her dress, her heels a series of neat little kicks.

Patrice turns to Elise. "When you have a moment, would it be possible to send a tea tray upstairs? Yvette has kindly agreed to the loan of her sitting room."

"So you see, I have a difficult decision to make."

Patrice glances at Marcus, who is sitting in an armchair, legs jutting straight out in front of him, occupied by the task of making teeth marks in the peel of an orange, checking them carefully, then prising the peel away from the fruit. "Do you have any contact with the boy's father?"

"Oh, no," Ursula shakes her head. "There's no 'for old time's sake' between us. Even if I was open to the idea, Lindsay would find a way to make sure it didn't happen. And bearing in mind the resemblance between…" again she turns to look at Marcus, "I imagine she'd do anything to keep them apart."

From what Patrice has read, Donald Flood's judgement hasn't been too clever of late. "I hear Mr Flood has been having a bit of a dry spell. Film-wise."

With a flurry of wings, a pigeon alights on the outside windowsill. Distracted, the boy drops the orange and Ursula jumps up before it can do any damage to chair or carpet. Marcus looks horrified.

"No harm done." She blows on the fruit, crouches down and turns it around for him to inspect. "See?"

He regards the pigeon warily. "He might come indoors."

"No, darling. Look, he isn't the slightest bit interested in us."

"He might."

"How about I shut the window?" The actress pushes down the sash. "There. Now he can't get in even if he wants to." To Patrice, she says as she takes her seat, "Failure happens to the best of us." This shrugging aside seems generous. Ursula is obviously capable of separating the professional from the personal. "You think you know what the public wants, but you never really do. After everything the world's been through, who'd have guessed that Biblical epics would be the next craze?"

"You don't think cinema audiences have taken against him?"

She shakes her head. "Audiences, getting in a flap about a man having an affair? Besides, our little fling is old hat. Three years is a lifetime in Hollywood."

"Not for you."

"They've made an exception for me. I'm special."

"This part the studio wants you to play, is it a good one?"

"It's terrible!" Ursula throws up her hands and lets them drop. "No, that's unfair. Jacob's favourite wife is a critical part, but it's also a small one. I could make a good job of it, but so could any number of other actresses. It's not as if they need a British accent!"

Patrice lets a minute pass. "Caroline told me you wrote to her. Does the job offer still stand?"

"Actually, that's what brought me here. I know the poor girl's had a torrid time of it. How is she, by the way?"

"Putting on a brave face." Patrice frowns, unsure what to say, convinced as she is that the nanny job will be the best thing for Caroline. "I persuaded Mr Blagdon – you'll remember him?"

"The club's owner. Of course I remember."

"I persuaded him I needed her at Whitlocke. Just to give her a few days away from here."

Ursula nods approvingly. "This is going to sound terribly selfish, but I need an answer straight away. Maybe now isn't the time." Another glance at the boy, who still seems fascinated by the pigeon's throaty coo.

"Why not pay her a visit? Judge for yourself."

"The problem is that the details are still so up in the air." Ursula lowers her voice. "Caroline might have to come with us to America, or she might need to take responsibility for a child she barely knows. It would hardly be fair." She glances lovingly at her son, her expression saying, *Not to Marcus and not to her.*

"What about the housekeeper you mentioned?"

"I'd rather imagined that Norma would come with me."

"Where's Noo-Noo?" Marcus pipes up.

"At home, darling," his mother assures him. "How are you getting on with that orange?"

"*I'm* doing it," he says, his face set.

"You do it then."

"I dare say she'd follow you anywhere if you asked, but going back and forth may suit her rather less than you think it will. She's already made her decision. She chose England – and that can't have been easy."

Ursula closes her eyes and keeps them closed for several moments, then she nods. "Perhaps you're right. And if you are…" Again she looks to Marcus. Her distress at the prospect of being parted from him is only too apparent.

"If it makes things any easier, you'd be welcome to use Whitlocke as a base. The nursery wing hasn't been used for some time."

"Not since your children were young, I expect."

"Not since I was young." Patrice tries not to linger on the 'I'. Tries not to watch for Ursula's reaction. "But it won't take long to tidy up. That way, if Norma does want to go with you, Caroline would have the support of the staff."

"Oh, I couldn't –"

"I wouldn't make the offer if I didn't mean it. I hate to think of the place standing empty."

Ursula's eyes pool, in gratitude rather than pity, Patrice hopes. "Gosh, I don't know what to say," she manages.

"Say yes!"

For a moment, all Ursula can do is nod. Eventually she says "Yes?" A nervous question.

"That's settled, then." Patrice, too, finds herself quite overcome, especially when Ursula takes both of her hands in hers and holds them. And there they remain.

"So that leaves Silvia. I told her that I was moving back to England to be closer to her." Ursula is overtaken by a sigh.

"Perhaps," Patrice leans forwards, "you don't need to make the decision on your own."

"But I do. And, this time, I really can't afford to get it wrong."

"Silvia is how old?"

"Nine."

"By that age, I had a very clear sense of right and wrong."

Ursula looks wistful. "Things were so much simpler then."

"If your concern is what she'll think of you, there really is only one way to find out."

"I must ask her."

Patrice nods. "You must ask her."

CHAPTER THIRTY-FOUR

URSULA

Dearest Silvia,

Do you remember, darling, how a few weeks ago you suggested that I make a list when I needed to make a difficult decision? It was such good advice. Already, I find myself facing another tough choice. Unfortunately, I don't think this is a situation where a list will help. (I have tried, believe me!) There are just too many different things to think about. I wonder if you have any more advice for me.

I think you understand that I have signed something called a contract with an American film studio. They pay me an amount of money and, in return, I act in their films. You know when your school puts on a play at the end of term? Like you, we don't always get to choose the parts we play. The studio decides who is right for each role. They don't only think about who would be best, but who would be most popular with cinema audiences. There have been years when I had to work very hard, and there have been years when the studio has not given me very much work, and I have been able to say, 'If you don't want me for the next few months, would you mind if I act at the theatre?' Usually the answer is yes because if I make a good job of it, it reflects well on the studio.

When I told the studio that I planned to move back to England to be closer to you, I thought they might be very cross, but instead they said it would be an excellent idea, because so many films are made in Europe these days. If I had to be away from home, it wouldn't be for so long. I might even be able to get home at weekends. It would have been very wrong of me to promise you that I would never go away again, because the life of an actress always involves travel, but I honestly didn't expect to be called back to America so soon after arriving – and so soon after seeing you again, my darling. It was something I hoped we could make a regular thing. If I say no, the studio can take me to court for failing to keep my side of the bargain. This would cost a lot of money, although money is not the most important thing. I am more worried that my name would be in the newspapers again for a bad reason, and I know how much you and Daddy hate that.

If I decide I must go, I need to make up my mind whether to take your little brother with me. Because I had to leave you behind when you were his age, I know that I will miss him dreadfully, but that is not a good enough reason to take Marcus with me. If he were a little older, it might be quite an adventure. He so loved the big ship, but I honestly don't think it is fair to make him travel all that way again. If I do take him, he will probably still be asleep when I leave in the mornings and in bed by the time I get home, although there would be weekends, and there might be days when I could take him to the film set. We have arrived in England so recently he has not had time to make any friends, but here he would have Norma, who has been with me since before he was born. So my second question is, do you think it would be better for him to be with me some of the time, or with someone familiar all of the time?

Please write back as soon as you get this. What you think is terribly important to me.

With all my love and kisses,

Mummy

Dear Mummy,

It wouldn't be right if I said that I think you were wrong to break your promise to Daddy but that I want you to break your promise to the film studio. A promise is a promise, it does not matter what it is about. If you break your promise to the film people, how will other people know you are telling the truth when you promise them something? You have to go.

I do not know Marcus and I do not remember what it was like to be three. Daddy tells me that when I was little, you went away to make films and did not take me with you, but I still had him. I only remember the last time when you went away and I thought it would be like all of the other times and I told myself that you would come back but you did not come back. If you leave Marcus behind in England, I could go and see him and tell him that I know you are coming back. I think I would like to meet him.

Love, Silvia

CHAPTER THIRTY-FIVE

PATRICE

Patrice wakes with a blinding headache. She sits on the side of the bed, lets her toes explore the floor, reassuring herself that it will not give way, before making an attempt to stand. Fresh waves of pain break as she stumbles to the bathroom door, opens the cabinet above the sink and reaches for the aspirin. She bites off the lid (if they could see you now) and upends the bottle into her hand. Wrong colour. The tablets should be white. A tearing sound rips straight through her. The sound of curtains being drawn.

"Crossland? Crossland, is that you?"

"I've just brought your tea, ma'am."

Thank God. She is not alone. "Would you mind seeing if you can find my painkillers? They're not in their normal place and I can't seem to..." The sentence peters out. She shuffles backwards a few steps until her heels find the side of the bath, where she perches gingerly and puts the back of one hand to her forehead.

Crossland bustles in, familiar in shape and size, but otherwise blurred. "You do look pale, ma'am. Are you sure it's just your head?"

"Just my head," Patrice agrees weakly. Already, her hand has warmed against her forehead. The pain pulses.

"Had a little reorganise, have we?" There is a shuffling sound, what is perhaps the shake of a bottle, then running water. "Hold out your hand for me."

Something light drops into the centre of Patrice's palm. She brings her hand to her mouth. Her lips find two small, round tablets.

"Water, ma'am." The cold rim of a glass touches her lips and she tips her head back slightly, allowing the liquid to flow into her mouth. She swallows. "All gone?" Crossland asks.

Patrice nods. The effort has made her breathless.

"Why don't you go back to bed until the aspirin start working? And no arguments. You won't be going anywhere as you are." A hand circles her upper arm. "Up you get." Another hand, high on her back. Usually, Patrice can find her way in the dark, but she allows Crossland to be her rudder, lift her legs, tuck her in. It was always Crossland who did this, never her mother. Patrice feels the weight of a palm on her forehead, just below her hairline. She would clasp that hand and hold it in place if she could. "Do you ever wake up feeling like this, Crossland?"

"I'm lucky, ma'am. I have the constitution of an ox. An elderly ox, but an ox nonetheless."

Patrice feels a pull at the corners of her mouth.

The hand moves to the side of her neck, two kindly fingers searching out a pulse. (Crossland is the only person who would do this.) If she expects a verdict, none is forthcoming. "I'll draw those curtains again, shall I? You won't be needing your newspapers today."

Two sharp scrapes and the dawn is snuffed out. The insides of Patrice's eyelids fade from fiery orange to subdued grey, the volume of the pain dials down a notch.

"I'll look in on you in half an hour." And she is gone.

"Fresh tea, ma'am. We don't want you getting dehydrated."

Patrice props herself up on her pillows and watches Crossland in her stout shoes walk the width of the room and deposit the tray on the table by the window. "What time is it?"

"Seven thirty."

Only seven thirty. She hasn't missed anything.

"How's the head?" Crossland pours the milk and then the tea, stirs.

Patrice assesses the damage. The pain feels like someone pressing down on her skull. It spikes when she blinks, but is a shadow of what she woke to. "Manageable."

"We got to it in time." Crossland hands Patrice a cup and saucer. "At least that's something."

"You asked if I'd rearranged the bathroom cabinet."

"I did, ma'am," agrees her personal maid.

"The answer is no."

"I see." There is nothing accusatory about this seeing. It is purely perfunctory. Crossland is paid to see how things are and to accommodate them.

"Have any other things been rearranged recently? Things that you've put back?"

Crossland's expression is troubled. She is not the type to tell tales. "Keeping order's my job. I can't be mentioning every small –"

"Then there *have* been other things?"

"The top of your dressing table."

Patrice glances over at the perfumes and cosmetics. "Anything else?"

Crossland winces. "And your silks."

Patrice, who had been in the process of putting the cup and saucer on her bedside table, startles. "My silks?" *Has Charles been systematically going through my most private belongings?*

"Mixed in with the nylons," the maid blurts. "It did seem a little odd."

"But, such a small thing. In itself." Over the last few weeks, several small things have bothered Patrice, each in itself so trifling that to mention them would have been to make a fuss. She has not overreacted (in fact, her initial reaction was *Why?*). Together, small irritations add up, and the tally seems to be more than the sum of its parts. "Thank you, Crossland," she says, preoccupied.

"Will I run your bath, ma'am?"

"Please." Patrice has tried not rocking the boat, avoided speaking in haste, but this cannot continue. She determines to have it out with Charles – before she loses her nerve.

Seated at one end of the dining table, she bides her time. Patrice wishes they didn't have to sit fifteen feet apart, but it's the Done Thing, and one must always adhere to the Done Thing, no matter how ridiculous it seems. Newly married, she once brought a tennis racquet to breakfast, threw a bread roll into the air and gave it her best serve. A certain distance can be useful, she accepts this. Today, when there is something to say, it will not be. Finally! "Ah, there you are –"

"Did you hear?" Immediately, Charles commandeers the conversation. "There's a fresh proposal to suspend the death penalty. I really think we might do it this time." There is a lightness about the way he pulls out his chair, instead of waiting for it to be done for him.

"Do you?" she says, newly conscious of the throbbing at her temples. Intense as her irritation is, Patrice prays he's right, not just because it would be a huge step in the right direction. A success might distract Charles from whatever paranoia is causing this obsessive behaviour of his. Unfortunately, she struggles to match his optimism.

"It takes an outrage to force change. And now, with Timothy Evans, we may at last have one!"

Poor Evans. Twenty-five years old, a father with no father

of his own to speak of, and very little in the way of education. Why he confessed to what the press dubbed the Wash-house Murder when he did, so far from Notting Hill, is something Patrice can't fathom. Of course, that monster Christie may well have succeeded in convincing Evans that he had been an accessory. Poor Evans was so wracked with guilt that the difference between being an accessory and actually carrying out the deed may have seemed immaterial – until it was explained by his defence lawyer. And then to learn that the body of his thirteen-month-old daughter had also been found. But before Patrice can say to her husband, *'We'll only have an outrage if Evans is given a posthumous pardon,'* there is activity at the far end of the table. Coffee is poured and Charles says that he thinks he will have a poached egg. No, make that two. It feels like a two-egg kind of day.

"On toast?"

"Well, of course I shall need some toast!" Patrice captures a glimpse of the playful man she married. What a time for *him* to put in an appearance!

"Very good, sir."

She waits her turn to have her say, as she must. While she waits she muses, picturing Evans' rabbit-in-the-headlights expression. The idea that Christie was principal witness for the prosecution and, later, present at the Old Bailey when Evans was convicted of strangling his pregnant wife and his daughter is for her one of the most horrific aspects of the case. It was almost as if Christie grew in confidence. Imagine a man who would use a human thigh bone to prop up a fence in that small rubbish-strewn back garden.

"That? It's my last victim's thigh bone."

"Oh, Reg, your sense of humour will get you into trouble one of these days."

"Then I must be more careful about what I say."

For three years, Christie thought he'd got away with it.

His wife, Ethel, lent him warmth and respectability. Someone who would never think ill of another person, not least of her husband. Who had babysat for the Evanses. Such a nice baby.

Now that Charles's breakfast is served, he holds up his newspaper and rustles it. "You have an opinion. I know you do."

Patrice prods her kedgeree then sets her fork aside. It is unavoidable, she supposes. They cannot move on to the subject she wants to discuss until she's told Charles what she thinks. Already, a few of her belongings being moved is beginning to feel a little less urgent. "Christie is the reason the Royal Commission didn't recommend abolition. The public will always demand the death sentence for monsters like him. I hate to say it, but even if it is proven that Evans was wrongfully convicted –"

Charles wields his knife in a way that would have met with her mother's disapproval. "*If?*"

"Yes, *if.*" Patrice leans forward, a failed attempt to reduce the distance between them. "You *cannot* be blinkered about this, not if you want to make the most of this opportunity. The majority of people simply can't accept that there was smoke without fire."

"They're willing to believe that there were two murderers living in the same house, acting entirely independently?" Her husband's face reddens with incredulity. "Even after Christie was convicted of killing several women in exactly the same way?"

"We're not talking about what *I* believe! I'm telling you what I *hear.*"

"Which is?"

"That either Evans and Christie were in it together, or Evans murdered his wife after she arranged to have their child aborted." Such an unpleasant word. Even less suited to the breakfast table than hanging, but it would be a hindrance not to say what she means. If Patrice can be brisk and matter-of-fact on a topic of Charles's choosing, surely she can be brisk and matter-of-fact about her own subject?

Charles scoffs. "It's the newspapers. They've always been in favour of capital punishment."

Patrice allows herself a wry smile. "Newspapers have always been in favour of the newspapers. They print whatever sells. A good murder and the circulation goes through the roof. You have to admit, they did a fairly good job on the botch Scott Henderson made of his enquiry into Evans' conviction."

"He was handed a poisoned chalice. *Had* Henderson found in favour of Evans, his would have been the first declaration that the state had executed an innocent man."

And there they would have had him: their sacrificial lamb. Who would ever have thought that the killer and the lamb might be found living under the same roof? "Hobson's choice," Patrice says. "End your career by supporting the state and being publicly humiliated – as Henderson must have known he would be – or write your own letter of resignation by siding with the rabble rousers."

Charles feigns shock. "Am *I* a rabble rouser?"

She smiles, thinking back to her conversation with Vincent. She has always respected her husband's dedication to the cause, but is fast losing confidence that his approach can succeed. "I sincerely hope you are."

"And you?"

Patrice squares her place mat. "I do all I can to support you, you know that."

"Is there a new angle you can sell your contacts?"

Only a compromise that you'd be unwilling to accept. But perhaps this is an opportunity. She purses her lips and narrows her eyes. "Do you know what I'd really like to see?"

"What's that?"

"The newspapers holding an unofficial enquiry on themselves."

Charles hoots and shakes his head.

"I'm serious! They have the public baying for blood before a man even gets to court on a murder charge. Reporters do everything they can to encourage an unseemly fascination with killers. What did they do before and after the murder? Did they smoke a pipe or did they have a cup of tea?"

"You think censorship is the answer?"

"Good Lord, no. But the press could behave with a little more responsibility."

"Self-regulation?"

"That would be a start! There is only so much damage *Fabian of the Yard* can undo."

"What do you think of that rubbish?"

"Is that what you refer to in the House as a leading question?"

Charles smirks. "They did their darndest to make the baddie look like Christie. Bald head. Little round glasses."

"I saw!" Patrice shakes her head.

"And all that sensationalist language. They called him a psycho, for goodness' sake."

"It's what Joe Public wants to believe." She summonses Fabian's authority. *"Sane people do not go around killing people."*

Charles pats his jacket pockets, extracts his silver cigarette case. "Tempting though it is."

CHAPTER THIRTY-SIX

CAROLINE

"No need to go tearing about," says Mrs Hargreaves, who has made it her personal business to bring an early morning tea tray upstairs to Caroline's room. "You need your rest. Now, is there anything else I can do for you?" The housekeeper seems to think that she's her personal responsibility. Perhaps that's how Patrice put it to her.

"No thank you." She is being checked up on; a report will be made about her appearance and demeanour. Caroline's bruises may be hidden, but the thought of what the staff have been told about why she's convalescing at Whitlocke makes her bristle. "I have everything I need."

Left to her own devices, Caroline kicks her heels, ruching the cotton sheets. Rest, rest, rest. That's all she's heard since her arrival, a litany that goes against her nature. Drummed into her from an early age was the idea that she should be doing, doing, doing – and while doing, thinking ahead to the next thing, and the next. Life at the club was different, with its own challenges and irregular hours, but whether in Suffolk or in her London reincarnation, Caroline has never been treated as if she were fragile.

Besides, how can she relax in a place where rules govern everything? She'd thought it might seem more respectful not to ring the bell when she needed something, but oh no, cook has put her right on that. The kitchens with their flagstone floors, the dark passages, even the scrubbed-wood staircases, are all out of bounds. Not for her sake, it was explained. "The servants are entitled to their privacy."

Caroline's previous visit to Whitlocke had been no occasion for a guided tour. They'd confined themselves largely to the morning room, sounding out ideas and sharpening the sentences that would break Ursula's story. Caroline had been too much in awe of her surroundings *(do people actually live here?)* to comment on them. Her impression was one of oversized marble fireplaces; ceilings as high as you'd find in any cathedral and too many decorations, rather like a woman who wears so much jewellery that she ends up looking cheap. Ursula didn't feel similarly restricted. Or perhaps she was ready for distraction.

"That's you!" she said, looking up at an oil painting that hung above the main staircase.

Patrice gave the young woman with long Titian hair a critical look. "It's my Augustus John."

"It's marvellous!"

"Do you think so? I find it difficult to marry the way I see myself with the way someone else sees me."

Caroline looked closer. *But that's a challenge for all of us.*

Now she feels it again. Who do the staff think she is? She's so obviously not of the duchess's class, so obviously underdressed.

Upstairs, with the majority of rooms cold and sheeted, Whitlocke has an abandoned air. Molly (the maid closest to Caroline's age, who frees Caroline from the embarrassment of asking Mrs Hargreaves what seem like obvious questions) explained, "Even if the duke and duchess are at home, there's only so many rooms they can use." The minute Caroline goes exploring, someone appears, unlatching and folding back shutters, whipping dust covers off islands of furniture, lighting fires. And then, to make all of that furious activity worthwhile, Caroline feels obliged to remain somewhere she hadn't planned to linger. Whatever she does, it seems she's either intruding, putting someone out or causing extra work.

And there is no escape from her thoughts. No champagne, no gin, not even the need to put a smile on her face and make a sale.

She closes her eyes momentarily, rubbing at their corners. Time is passing her by. There is a day outside, happening. She throws back the bedsheets. As she brings herself to a sitting position, damaged body tissue makes itself known. Caroline denies it reign, trudging through pain to reach the window. Rain hurls itself at the glass, making a prisoner of her. Caroline knows exactly how ungrateful she is. Here, she is warm and dry while the world outside is in motion; the bare branches of the great oaks, the needles of the firs. A landscape that refuses to be tamed, though she's heard how successive generations of Wyndhams have tried, adding lakes, fountains, follies, box hedges that the head gardener checks with a spirit level, a sunken garden, a pet cemetery. But while reflecting – even acknowledging – how desperately she needed to get away from the club, Caroline remains unrepentant.

Outside, perhaps, it would be possible to wander without fear of disturbing anyone. Later, if it stops raining; if she can put to the back of her mind the thought that on her return she might muddy a rug that turns out to be an irreplaceable heirloom. But the rain doesn't stop. It pelts from a stealthy creep of pewter clouds, tinting the parkland with layers of grey.

It isn't until her third day of enforced confinement that Caroline takes the wrong door from the entrance hall and stumbles upon the library. Though the room is shuttered, it is possible to make out bookcases in fern green with gold detailing to match the gilt cornicing, and ceiling-height windows with deep, upholstered window seats. Imagine, this room has been here all along, waiting for her to discover it.

She has only taken her first exploratory steps, when Molly comes bustling in. "You should have said! Nobody's been in here for ages."

Caroline will never find standing by and watching someone work a comfortable experience, but as furnishings are revealed she walks the length of the room in wonder. It is the first room she has entered where, once she's admired what there is to be admired, her next thought isn't, *What a terrible waste.* Instead she marvels at how tidy the shelves are. All these books that have been read and re-read. She imagines reaching out a hand for a book only to have her mother slap it away. *'Don't touch!'*

But she wants to touch. She feels the books need it. *Considerations on Volcanos. The Life and Adventures of Martin Chuzzlewit. Death in the Clouds. Select Views in Mysore, The Country of Tippoo Sultan: From Drawings Taken on the Spot. Picturesque Representations of the Dress and Manner of the Russians.* Books that represent the pastimes and passions of generations of Wyndhams. The mother and father Patrice spoke about, the ones who 'over-wintered' like pot-plants.

"May I use the telephone?" she asks Molly.

"No need to ask." The maid is on her hands and knees in front of the fireplace. "We're under instructions that you're to treat everything as your own." She sits back on her heels. "You *are* coming back, Miss?"

"Straight back, yes."

Somehow it doesn't seem right not to ask. Caroline wouldn't like it if she invited someone into her home and they just helped themselves. Not that she's ever owned anything valuable, but even seemingly insignificant things – a green satin ribbon and a fake mother of pearl hair grip – are precious if they're all you have.

Caroline reaches the duchess at the club. "I'm sorry to disturb you."

"Is there a problem?"

"Everything's fine, thank you. I was just wondering. Would you mind if I looked at some of the books from the library?"

"You mustn't stand on ceremony. And if there's anything you can't find, the staff know their way around the shelves."

Permission, and the only instruction is to ask for help if she needs it! At last, here is a place where Caroline can busy her mind while giving the appearance of doing very little. Surely, not even Mrs Hargreaves can object to reading.

"Someone here to see you, Miss Caroline." Molly is down from her stepladder in the entrance hall.

Staff no longer knock before entering the library, but Caroline has failed in her bid to be called plain Caroline.

"Where would you like to receive her?"

"Here, I suppose." Is that the right thing to say? She goes to follow the maid – it seems natural to Caroline that she should greet her guest – but Molly turns.

"You stop here, Miss. That's how it works."

Like a dog commanded to 'stay', Caroline stands stock still, waiting for her next instruction. She is still waiting, not knowing where to put herself, when a small boy with a halo of curls comes running through the mahogany door without looking where he's going. "Whoa, there!" Instinctively, she throws up her hands as he collides with her thighs. The boy falls backwards. He stares up, wide-eyed, horrified, wanting confirmation that he's got away with it or warning that something's going to smart like billy-oh.

Caroline crouches down to his level. "You're alright. No

broken bones." When his large eyes look doubtful, she adds, "Don't believe me? Alright. Let's do a stocktake. Head." She puts both hands on her head. "One," she says.

He mirrors her actions. "One."

"Hands." She holds hers out, palms up. "Two."

He looks at his own. "Two," he agrees. *Tyew*. He has an accent. With so little to go on, Caroline can't pinpoint it. Is it Irish?

"So far so good. Now, let's see. Legs," she says. "One," she taps her left leg. (Watch out for that tender spot.) "Two," she grabs her right, and then goes for the boy's left, which has the chilled feel wet weather brings even if you haven't had a good soaking. "Three –"

"Hey, that one's mine!"

"I told you to stay put, young man!" A plainly dressed woman in late middle-age strides into the room, tutting loudly. American, no doubt about it. Something inside Caroline gives a joyful jolt. Following closely behind comes a younger woman, a white coat hanging from her shoulders like a cape, a pea green scarf tied around her neck, a square green handbag hooked over one arm.

"Ursula!"

"Now you've spoiled my best surprise, Marcus! This is the lady I was telling you about."

Caroline doubts it will ever feel ordinary to find herself breathing the same air as Ursula Delancy. Behind this single face are so many women, some intimidating, some brazen, others wronged. Though he's from across the ocean, the boy may be easier to fathom. "Pleased to meet you, Marcus," she says.

Ursula puts her hands on her hips and looks down at him. "Who is too old to be crawling around on the floor."

"I fell!"

"Did you now? Up you get, young man." The child grips

the edge of a rug, as if to protest that he's quite happy where he is, thank you very much. "And Caroline, I'd like you to meet Norma."

"Best supporting actress." No nonsense, dry, not a hint of vanity.

"Norma's been with me for... How long is it now, Norma?"

"Forever." A woman who clearly has no trouble distinguishing between Ursula Delancy and the characters she's played. "At least that's how it seems."

Intimidated, Caroline attempts a smile and nods a hello. Norma holds her ground.

"Norma isn't impressed with our weather."

"I am not!" She holds out a hand to Marcus. "You heard your mother, up you get! And don't start on the *whys?* or you'll get a *because I said so.*" Leading with his bottom, the boy spirals to his feet. "There we are. Brush down those knees, now, because my back isn't up to crouching down."

This leaves Caroline free to ask Ursula, "How did you know I was here?"

"Patrice suggested you might appreciate a visitor, although I can't pretend that I don't have an ulterior motive. But first – and don't feel you have to reply – I want to say how sorry I was to hear about your friend."

The library is no longer a sanctuary. Grief finds Caroline, threatening to unmask her. *Please don't ask me how I am.* "And Patrice's godson," she manages.

"Patrice's *godson?* I had no idea! Why wouldn't she have said?" Ursula clasps and unclasps her hands. "How awful for her."

Caroline is glad that Molly picks this moment to bustle in.

"Shall I put the tea tray on the table, Miss Caroline?" Perhaps rules do serve a purpose. They give the illusion of control, even when everything is crashing down around your ears. "There's orange squash for Master Marcus, and in case he doesn't like that, I've brought an extra-large jug of milk."

"Do you like orange squash, Marcus?" asks Caroline.

Marcus clings to Norma's legs.

"I'll say so." The maid ruffles his hair and replies on his behalf. "I think we've seen the last of that wretched rain for now. Let's take our drinks out onto the terrace. That way, there's no risk of spilling it on that nice-looking rug." Norma steers Marcus towards one of the ceiling-height windows and rattles its handle. (She's obviously seen a few French doors masquerading as windows in her time.)

"Don't go jumping in too many puddles," Ursula calls after her son.

And then there were two.

A short blast of cold air reaches them. Ursula shivers, pulls her coat around her and turns on the spot, taking in the top shelves, the hobbies of the house's previous occupants. "Imagine owning somewhere like this and leaving it shut up for most of the year."

"I suppose if you're used to London, Whitlocke must seem very quiet."

"Isn't that the attraction? An escape from all the madness." Ursula winces, as if she's bitten the tip of her tongue. "Speaking of which, I don't suppose you know who those men in the hall were?"

"Which men?"

"Two of them. Overcoats and suits. They were outside taking measurements when we arrived, but they followed us into the house."

Caroline walks to the door and peers out into the hall. "There's no one there now."

"I'm sure it's nothing."

Something tells Caroline it's never nothing. Not with Ursula. "All the same, I'll mention it to Mrs Hargreaves. Tea?"

"Please." While Caroline pours, Ursula laughs. "I have the distinct impression we're on our best behaviour."

"Is it being in a library?" Caroline asks, knowing full well that the room they're sitting in has nothing to do with it. She passes Ursula a cup and saucer. *Careful does it.*

"You mustn't be nervous, not of me."

"I'm not. At least, not exactly." There is still that peculiar mix of awe – being in the presence of someone famous – and familiarity. The face she knows so well from the big screen, even in close-up. "Actually I was just remembering."

"Oh, yes?" Ursula sits forward.

"One time, during the war, I'd gone to see you at the Regal. Halfway through the film, a message flashed up on the screen telling us that an air raid was in progress and anybody wishing to leave should do so." She smiles. "Not a soul moved."

Very gently, Ursula places her teacup back in its saucer, then she looks directly at Caroline. "I'm not her, the person on the screen, the one you read about." She pauses. "Do you know, when Cary Grant was asked who gives the best Cary Grant impression, he said, 'I do.' That's what it's like, pretending to be who they want you to be."

Without thinking, Caroline finds herself agreeing. "It's exhausting."

Ursula's eyes are searching "So you know."

"Nothing on your scale, of course." The thought of comparing her own situation to Ursula's! "But working at the club." This admission feels like a confession. At the club, the act almost became part of Caroline.

"You can so rarely be yourself. Sometimes even *I'm* not sure who I am. That's why Marcus has been so good for me. He grounds me."

"I'm sorry I didn't give you a definite answer." Caroline feels flustered. "About working for you, I mean."

"*I'm* sorry I wasn't in a position to make you a firm job offer!" Ursula's smile wavers. "Actually, that's what I wanted to talk to you about."

"Oh?"

"My studio is insisting I go back to the States."

Something inside Caroline sinks. *Then I won't be needed.* "Can they do that?"

"They *can.* I just didn't think they *would.* Not so soon at any rate." Again, that self-deprecating smile. "I'm not exactly box office gold these days."

Caroline backtracks. "It wouldn't be permanent, then?"

"Didn't I say? It's for a film shoot. Sixteen weeks is the estimate, but these things tend to overrun."

"And Marcus?"

Ursula looks up to the top bookshelves again, then leans back in her chair. It seems that some of the fight has gone out of her. "I've decided to leave him here."

"That will be hard on you."

"It's the least selfish option, but I can't expect Norma to keep up with a three-year-old. So I suppose what I'm saying, and I realise this isn't the best of timing, but I wondered if you would –"

"Yes." It surprises Caroline, how much she wants to distance herself from her London life.

Ursula laughs. "Before you agree, I'd prefer it if you were completely in the picture."

There's going to be a 'but'. Caroline can feel it.

"Firstly, I want to reassure you that salary won't be an issue. I'd hope we can make you a bit better off than you were at the club. But the thing is this. So far, I've been renting a house by the week. I've already outstayed my welcome, and because I have to leave almost immediately, there isn't time to find somewhere more permanent."

Don't screw this up. Caroline frowns and nods.

Ursula shakes her head as if she can hardly believe her luck. "Patrice has been an absolute sweetheart and offered us use of Whitlocke."

"Better still," Caroline tries to sound enthusiastic. She had thought, that's to say, she'd *assumed* she would be leaving Whitlocke's rules behind her. What she'd pictured was somewhere smaller, somewhere less intimidating.

"Looking after Marcus will be the easy part. My concern is that the press might get wind of who he is."

Perhaps things would be different if she were staff. If she had a purpose, Caroline would have the right to move from room to room. "Why would that be news?"

"People love to read about what a terrible mother I am. They'll say, 'Ursula Delancy simply refuses to put her children before her Hollywood career. She's had another child to replace the girl she abandoned, and now she's abandoned him too.'" Caroline's eyes drift to the window, where Marcus is using paving stones as a puddled hopscotch grid. It isn't difficult to imagine him on the front pages, his halo of curls, his questioning eyes, his pouting mouth. "And across the pond, I'll be photographed chatting to the cast and crew, and the newspapers – they'll crop every last person out of those photos, except for me and the leading man. No doubt they'll manage to make it look as if I'm staring straight into his eyes. And that's the photograph they'll print, right next to a shot of my son looking hard-done-by and miserable.

"Don't worry." Ursula reaches out a hand. "If Marcus ends up in the papers, he ends up in the papers. I won't blame you. But please, if you could limit the number of people who know you're here, working for me. As for having your sister to stay, I have to say no. At least not while I'm away." Her mouth twists in recognition of the months she'll miss, but she rallies. "I'm sorry if I sound a little paranoid, but believe me, the press stop at nothing. So? Is it still a yes?"

"It's still a yes."

Ursula grabs both of Caroline's hands. "I'm so glad, I can't tell you. You've set my mind at rest."

"Don't you want a reference?"

"I don't need one. I've seen you in action in a crisis and I saw the way you were with Marcus, without knowing who he was. I can tell when someone's good with children."

"*Who sent you?*" Outside, there is shouting. "*Who put you up to this?*"

The alarm on Ursula's face is the same cornered-fox expression that Caroline saw in Knightsbridge. The expression that says Ursula knows she's powerless in the face of larger forces.

Caroline puts one hand out and slightly behind her – *hold fire* – and hurries over to the French windows. Outside, Norma has accosted two men dressed in overcoats and dark suits. Still holding Marcus by the hand, she grabs a clipboard from one of them, who tries to wrestle it away. Released from Norma's grip, Marcus looks on in disbelief as a tug-of-war commences. Two adults squabbling over a clipboard? Caroline turns her head to ask Ursula, "Should I bring Marcus inside?"

But, before Ursula can reply, Mrs Hargreaves comes crunching across the gravel and up the steps onto the terrace. If she feels the cold through her cotton uniform, she gives no sign. "*I* shall take that, thank you," she addresses Norma, pressing the clipboard to her chest as if its contents are of no consequence. "And yours, if you don't mind!" She thrusts out a hand at the other suited man. When he holds his ground, she adds, "I hardly need remind you, this is private property and you are trespassing."

The man's ears redden. He will not give up what he has without voicing an objection. "We are acting under instruction."

His protest falls on flat ears. "Not from the owner of the property."

"We're here to do a job of work."

"And what exactly is that, might I ask?"

Stubborn silence.

"Then perhaps you can tell me who sent you."

Nothing.

"Are you from the police?"

"No!"

"Do you have anything to do with the taxman?"

"No."

"Well, are you from any other government agency?" Mrs Hargreaves looks at each man in turn. "No?" She grabs the second clipboard. "In that case, gentlemen, that is your way out." She points in the direction of the drive which leads to the distant gate. "Simmons?" she calls out to a gardener and beckons him over. "Would you please do the honours and escort these gentlemen off the premises?"

Norma and Mrs Hargreaves make two formidable figures, arms folded across their chests and chins raised. Barely the height of the terracotta urns, Marcus joins them in solidarity.

Caroline makes her way over. "Mrs Hargreaves, is there any security on the gates?"

"That's never been necessary, not even when we've had royalty to stay."

Caroline can see her point. The entrance to Whitlocke is in a quiet backwater, imposing to the point of being off-putting. Someone on horseback might take advantage of their elevated position, but the house can't be seen until you're almost upon it. Even from the oak-lined drive, the odd glimmer through the branches only hints at what's to come.

Unimpressed, Norma takes up the theme. "Well, we can't afford a repetition."

Mrs Hargreaves sighs deeply, clearly unhappy that the new additions to the household are going to cause her staff a logistical nightmare. "Before we jump to conclusions, let's see what we have here." She consults the papers that are attached to the clipboard with a bulldog clip.

Plans drawn on the type of squared paper that maths books are made of. "Ursula was right," Caroline says. "They were taking measurements."

Ursula is only a heartbeat behind her. "Yes, but for what?"

CHAPTER THIRTY-SEVEN

PATRICE

Patrice places the telephone handset back on its cradle and finds herself frowning at her own reflection. “How very odd,” she remarks to herself.

“What’s that you say?” Charles calls from his study.

She has no recollection of the door being ajar when she took the call. In fact, she is certain it was closed. Imagine Charles, actually getting up to answer the telephone. That would be a turn up for the books. “Something most peculiar.” Patrice opens the door a fraction more. A strip of daylight creates a runway on the parquet floor. “Mrs Hargreaves tells me she’s just apprehended two men in the grounds.”

“Doing what?”

“They claimed to be there on official business, but wouldn’t say what it was. Anyway, you know what a stickler Mrs Hargreaves is. She confiscated their clipboards and saw them off. Now she’s in a tizz about security.”

“What need do we have for security when we have Hargreaves?”

“Quite.” Patrice does not let on that from now on the stakes will be higher than usual. Already, Charles has accused her of being taken in by Ursula’s ‘sob story’.

"Did Hargreaves say what was on the clipboards?"

"Measurements." Patrice frowns, trying to work out what it is she's missing. "There isn't some new government survey you're aware of?"

"Some new kind of tax scheme, perhaps?" Her husband's smile is fuelled by scorn. "Perhaps it's someone planning a burglary."

Anxiety pricks. Not a burglary, but a kidnapping. Rare on British soil, but the child of a Hollywood actress might attract that sort of attention.

"Honestly, Patrice, your face! I was joking."

"Well, don't." Marcus's father is more likely to be the culprit. After everything she's heard (and read) about Flood, Patrice wouldn't put it past him to deny the boy is his, yet still want a close eye kept on him.

"You leave me with few options. You *refuse* to consider that the staff might be anything less than paragons of virtue."

"Staff are easy targets," she says curtly. No. Patrice cannot confide in Charles. A couple of single malts, and news that Ursula Delancy's son is staying at Whitlocke would be all over his club, and straight from White's to Fleet Street. She has given assurances that Marcus will have privacy, and it will be so.

"If you're so worried, ask Hargreaves to send you whatever it was she took from the men."

"I should take a look for myself," says Patrice. "I'll have Berthram drive me down."

"I really think you'd be wasting your time."

Charles's grudging response grates on Patrice's nerves. "I wasn't asking for *permission*. The house is my responsibility. Besides, it's high time I visited."

"Will you be gone for long?"

No offer to keep her company. That comes as no surprise. "I wouldn't have thought so."

"Well, when can I expect you?"

"Charles, if I get down there and find that something needs attending to, then I shall attend to it. You can manage without me for a day or two, can't you?"

"I should start to pine if it were more than two."

You cannot be trusted for more than two! "Then let us agree on two."

The end of March. By this time of year, country lanes would normally be starting to green, plants that would be labelled as weeds in the garden of the townhouse sprouting proudly from hedgerows. Winter was late to arrive, later than Patrice can recall. At one point it seemed that England would jump straight from autumn to spring. Few warnings arrived to suggest they should burrow in for the long haul. Now, Patrice yearns for daffodils.

But then, through the branches of the great oaks, the first sight of it.

The house.

Her childhood.

Whitlocke, exactly as she remembers it, an unburied time-capsule. That deep-rooted, deep-seated sense of belonging.

Despite everything she'd wanted to leave behind, seeing the place again is like stumbling upon a missing part of herself when with all the distractions London has to offer, she had failed to appreciate that anything was amiss. Until this moment.

She knows Whitlocke's secrets and it knows hers. Here, she must confront her failures. Her inability to conceive (how different things might have been if she and Charles had had children as common ground.) Something rarely discussed outside doctors' consulting rooms, and certainly never between her and Charles, but once raised with her mother. A conversation that shed an entirely different light on Patrice's childhood, the narrative she had told herself – still tells, on occasion.

"My gynaecologist asked if there is any family history." An excruciating way to begin a conversation for two people who avoided talking about anything remotely personal (and, as it turned out, the gynaecologist had been looking in the wrong direction entirely). The wait for a response was agonising, but it came. Eventually.

"You may tell this fellow of yours that I had no trouble conceiving, I conceived a good many times, but you are the only child I carried to term."

Stunned by this revelation, Patrice stammered, "But..." failing to frame a question.

"Trying almost killed me, so that was that." Pain was etched into every aspect of her mother's expression. It was clear that this was as much as she would or could say. Perhaps the indifference with which Patrice thought she was treated was actually deep-seated grief? What if Cairo had been her mother's only escape?

And yet despite regular and sometimes lengthy absences, her mother was a far better custodian to Whitlocke than Patrice has been. She was no greater builder or landscaper. She didn't plant an avenue of lime trees as her great-great-grandfather had, or have Capability Brown dam the river to create a series of lakes. She never got round to completing the Gothic stables. But neither was she idle. She oversaw the renovation of the kitchen gardens, adding the glass houses which produce tomatoes all year round, responsible for Whitlocke Chutney. Later, she saw to the restoration of the Marie Antoinette styled boudoir whose pastel-painted grotesques and arabesque motifs were all but destroyed when an undetected leak brought the domed ceiling crashing down. Patrice can remember how she helped rummage through the debris collecting fragments of cherubs from the roundels, said to have been the work of Louis-Andre Delabrière. Everyone who knew the room before the restoration declared that her mother had worked several small miracles.

The dukedom will end with Patrice's death, but her family's history can be conserved with Whitlocke.

There are things she has neglected.

Things that need attending to.

The tyres move from tarmac to gravel. "It looks as if all of the staff have come out to greet you, ma'am. I'm afraid I shall have to park here."

"Here will be fine, Berthram. It wouldn't do to run them over."

"Measurements of the square footage, ma'am," her estate manager, Mr Woodham, agrees.

"Don't we already know them?"

"Last taken at the turn of the century, and I doubt they've changed. I'm as curious as you are about who else would want that information."

Patrice's thoughts travel back to Christmas. Now that her social sphere is diminished, Whitlocke's guest book no longer reads like a roll-call of intellectuals and power-brokers. Wyndhams and stray Hawtrees are supplemented with local dignitaries: a junior MP, the new choirmaster, senior huntsmen. People who want to secure a venue for next year's fete, festival or county fair, or are simply curious to see for themselves if the rumours are true. This year, a guest – a man she barely knew – asked Patrice if she was thinking of turning Whitlocke into a hotel. To her face! "Things haven't come to that, not just yet," she had replied. At the time his question set her thoughts in motion. Who will she bequeath Whitlocke to? Not Charles (although she dreads the prospect of that conversation). It should be a Wyndham, but the Wyndhams are an endangered species. There is only Cousin Sophie in Australia, who couldn't have made her feelings about the place clearer, and Patrice would rather put Whitlocke to the torch than see it go to someone who does not love it. When Arnold renewed their acquaintance, Patrice had begun to think – quite seriously in fact – that *he* might be the answer. He may not have been a blood relative, but he gave her a taste of kinship, and how she had missed that.

Misses it. Her mouth twitches.

Added to which, Patrice has an inkling Arnold would have made rather a good custodian.

But then the question of his engagement cropped up and she decided not to act impulsively, but to wait. Though it pains her, the truth is that she herself was every bit as guilty of narrow-mindedness as the Linnets. Is it that same guilt that makes her so keen to see Caroline back on her feet? Not entirely – but it may be part of it.

Patrice had all but decided to take against the man who had spouted the hotel nonsense when he handed her a gift box, leaning in to add, "I'm afraid they were all out of eggs." It turned out to contain the Fabergé paperweight, a delightful thing, predominantly gold, with a phoenix rising from its dome. "But this is far too generous," she'd protested.

Now, he is her chief suspect. Frustrating, how little detail memory can conjure. Neither a name nor a face for the person most likely to have commissioned a survey of the house.

"Mr Woodham," Patrice asks, "have you heard any talk that Whitlocke is going to be turned into a hotel?"

"I heard just the other day that the National Trust are taking it over. People say all sorts of things, ma'am. Mind you, I wouldn't be the least bit surprised if you were approached with an offer."

The paperweight, the thing Patrice had hoped would jog her memory, is nowhere to be found. "Mrs Hargreaves, I don't suppose you've seen my Fabergé paperweight?"

"I'm afraid I haven't, ma'am. I rather assumed you'd taken it back to London."

Not an unreasonable assumption. While certain things belong at Whitlocke (things that, to an only child, were substitutes for playmates), smaller moveable pieces with no history or association with one house or the other, might be 'tried out', as if competing for a permanent home.

She puts the same question to Caroline. After all, only days ago, Patrice insisted that she treat everything as her own.

"What does it look like?"

Patrice describes the gold, the phoenix.

"No." Caroline shakes her head. "Though the dust sheets come off and go back on so quickly, I barely get a chance to see what's underneath."

Caroline's right. The paperweight *could* be hidden under a dust sheet. "No doubt it will show up the minute I stop worrying about it." Patrice is pleased, now she looks properly, to see that Caroline is looking much improved. Gone is the tightness around her mouth, as if she was only just managing to contain whatever bubbled below her surface. Whitlocke has done this. "And what about you? You've made good use of the library, I hear."

"I have, thank you. It's a beautiful room."

"I suppose it is. My feelings towards the library are rather mixed. I rather rebelled against the idea that I should sit quietly and take responsibility for 'improving myself'. I far preferred running wild to reading."

Caroline simply smiles. Patrice feels as if they are back at square one. If anything, the distance between them seems to have widened.

"Excuse me, ma'am." It is Molly. "The Master of the Hounds is here to see you."

"Show him to my morning room." To Caroline she says, "Dinner at seven thirty? No need to dress."

She has already turned when Caroline says, "I've accepted Ursula's job offer. But I expect she told you."

Patrice turns. "She did, yes."

"I'm going to buy a dog," Ursula had told Patrice over the telephone. "One small enough to take with me."

"Whatever for?" she'd replied.

"To make myself the story. Now the newsmen will be able to write that I chose to leave my son behind but took my dog. That should buy Marcus a few weeks' privacy."

What must it be to feel you have to make a trade-off like this? Not even news, but froth. There are those, no doubt, who will lap this up, use it to evaluate their own lives, and feel smug with their respective lots. The same people who would suggest it achieves nothing to lend Whitlocke to a woman who isn't short of many of the good things in life. Patrice doesn't see it like that. She has lent her house to the one person who reminds her that life can be meaningful, and so that Caroline has a purpose while she finds her footing. Whitlocke's future may not yet be secure, but she can make sure it serves some purpose in the present.

For now, Patrice longs to say something meaningful to the girl – helpful would do – but she is afraid of blundering. Social etiquette she has by the bucket full. The ability to mother she does not. "I've asked Mrs Hargreaves to give the nursery wing a good airing. It hasn't been used for some time, I'm afraid. I'll have her show it to you. You must tell me if there's anything you need." The girl appears to be on the cusp of saying something. "Anything," Patrice repeats.

"If you don't mind, at dinner perhaps, there's something I'd like your advice about." Caroline appears hesitant. Strange, when she has always seemed so worldly.

"Why not now?"

The girl looks in the direction of the morning room. "I thought you had someone waiting for you."

Patrice looks at the grandfather clock and says wickedly, "If the Master of the Hounds chooses to arrive early, that's his lookout."

"I've written to tell Mr Blagdon that I won't be going back to the club, but I don't know, shouldn't that sort of thing be done in person?"

Patrice can see it now. Terrence welcoming Caroline back into the fold. He might not intend to play on torn loyalties, but what do intentions matter if the end result is the same? Over her dead body will she see the girl back in the same turmoil she was in. "In normal circumstances, that would be entirely proper." She winces, hoping to suggest that delicate handling is required. "But Ursula leaves for the States as soon as she can get a crossing. My concern is that Mr Blagdon might feel within his rights to insist you work a notice period."

The girl's eyes drop. "In that case, I shan't go. He can't insist if I'm not there."

"The right decision, I think. And you might want to be a little economical with the truth."

Their eyes meet. "How economical?" asks the girl.

"No need to tell him you've taken another job. Suffice to say that you wouldn't be of much use to him at the moment and that you completely understand he will have to fill your position."

Caroline nods, apparently working it through. "The paperweight?" she asks. "Is it valuable?"

"To a collector, very much so."

"What about the intruders Mrs Hargreaves saw off?"

Patrice starts. "I thought they were apprehended *outside* the house?"

"They were, but Ursula said they followed her into the entrance hall."

"I wasn't aware of that."

"*She* thought they were on official business, and the staff thought she'd brought her own bodyguards."

Her chest rises and falls. "Thank you for letting me know."

Is it possible that security *is* an issue? Aware how sensitive the staff are, treating questions as accusations, Patrice adopts a neutral tone when she seeks out the housekeeper. "Mrs Hargreaves, is there anything else you assumed I'd taken with me to London?"

"When I said 'you', I included the duke, ma'am."

"Of course," she nods. Her next question presents itself, the reason for it as yet unclear. "And when you referred to the last time we were here, did you mean Christmas, or when the duke last visited?"

"The duke's last visit, ma'am."

The laces are tightened, tighter, tighter still, but this time Patrice has nothing solid to grip. "I do hope he gives you adequate notice."

"It's no trouble, ma'am. We can always cater for a couple more on the spur of the moment."

A couple. Patrice holds herself upright, as if she has a whalebone ribcage. It isn't the thought that Charles has a mistress, but that he deigns to bring her here when, to her – Patrice – he feigns complete disinterest in Whitlocke. Hoping to impress, no doubt, and now he has made a gift of something that belongs to Patrice while trying to make her doubt her staff! "I wonder if I'm being neglectful about the way I run the two households," she says.

Unlike the shuffled contents of her bathroom cabinet, this revelation feels like *something.* But what to do with the information? Confront Charles and see where the conversation leads? No, Patrice will add it to her store for a later time when it might come in useful. For now she takes comfort in small compensations. The next time Charles turns up unannounced, he'll find rather more than he bargained for. A small boy, his nanny and an elderly cantankerous maid who doesn't suffer fools. "I know apple sauce when I hear it," Norma says to the boy. "Drop the act, young man. *You're* not in the running for this year's Oscars." English as spoken by the English doesn't lend itself to directness. Patrice tries to imagine hearing her husband out, then saying, *I'm afraid, Charles, that your hogwash no longer washes with me.*

Her business at Whitlocke is done. With no great desire to go straight back to the townhouse, Patrice has Berthram drive her to the club. She will deliver Caroline's resignation letter safely into Terrence's hands.

"I had a mind to make her manager of this place," he says, folding the letter and putting it back in its envelope. "She was so clear-thinking. Even on the day of Valerie's –. You'll tell her, won't you? That I was minded to make her manager."

"Listen to me, Terrence." Patrice squeezes his forearm in commiseration. "The poor girl is heartbroken. She's made herself quite ill and I'm afraid that alcohol has played no small part in that." She waits for this to sink in. How can a hostess persuade club members to buy bottles of champagne unless she herself is drinking? And how can a hostess hope to earn enough to live on without talking customers into buying bottles of champagne? "What Caroline needs now is time."

"I'll make up her wage packet," Terrence concedes miserably, and sucks on his cigar. "You'll make sure she gets it?"

"I will." Patrice averts her eyes, avoiding the worst of the smoke.

"She's a good girl."

"Yes," Patrice smiles sadly. "Yes, she is."

CHAPTER THIRTY-EIGHT

CAROLINE

"Why can't I have a go on the horse?"

Caroline frees the tail from Marcus's grip. It's a fair question. Why should a child care that the rocking horse is an antique? It is there in Marcus's bedroom. Even if it is not 'his', logic tells him it must be for his use. Besides, that frame was made for climbing on.

"I want to!"

"I'm afraid you can't do everything just because you want to." Even to her own ears, it sounds ridiculous. Why blame a three-year-old if he finds Whitlocke's rules as confusing as she does?

Somewhere below them, the telephone starts ringing.

"Just a minute, I have to get this. It might be your mummy. Norma, would you mind taking over?" Caroline hates asking, especially in the middle of what might turn into a tantrum.

Norma sets down her knitting needles. "Well, I can hardly run for the phone. By the time I get there, whoever it is will have lost interest."

Caroline mouths a quick 'Thank you', then races the length of the landing and down two flights of stairs. She grabs the polished bannister to corner, down to the entrance hall where the floor covering changes from carpet to marble, then left into the corridor.

Molly is there before her, delivering the place name and the last four digits of the telephone number, an anglicised version of *Pennsylvania 6-5000.* She hands Caroline the receiver. "A young lady asking for Master Marcus Sheard." Now that they're both staff, it is quite obvious when she's taking the Mick, although it's always good-humoured.

"Hello," Caroline gasps, breathless.

"Please may I speak to Master Marcus Sheard?" It is the voice of a child, either one who's very comfortable using a telephone or has rehearsed what she wants to say.

"Who am I speaking to?"

"Silvia Sheard, his sister. I promised Mummy I would telephone to see how he is getting on, so that's what I'm doing."

Caroline cups the receiver, holds it to her chest. They have waited for this, hoping it would happen, hoping that curiosity about the brother she hasn't met (if nothing else) would make Silvia pick up the phone, but all that waiting and hoping mustn't make Caroline hasty. The call could be a ruse. Ursula warned that there are journalists who would think nothing of bribing a young child, possibly even their own, to impersonate her daughter. "Silvia, this is Caroline. Did your mummy write to you about me?"

"Yes, she did. She said you were very nice."

"And did she give you a password to give to me when you telephoned."

"Yes, she did."

"Can you tell me the password now?"

"Olive. Do you know what it means?"

"I don't, but I'd like to," Caroline says, her mind racing. How will Marcus react? Still too young to have any concept of time, when Ursula told him that he has a sister, his first question was 'Where was I when she was born?' He can't grasp that he's the one who hasn't always been here; that it hasn't always been him and Mommy and Noo-noo, just the way he likes it.

"You can't tell anyone. You must swear." Silvia, it seems, is as guarded as she is.

"I solemnly swear that I won't tell."

"It's her name." The girl's whisper gives way to sudden laughter. "Her real name is Olive Sheard."

"What do you think of the name Bibi?"

"Who for?"

"For me, of course!"

"Caroline? Are you still there?"

"I'm still here. It isn't that funny a name."

"It is, for an actress."

"I bet I can think of funnier ones."

"Like what?"

Bibi Linnet. "Dorothea Bedwetter."

The girl has a delicious giggle.

"Silvia, I'm going to fetch Marcus, but I have to go up two flights of stairs to get him. Don't hang up, will you?"

"I won't."

"Silvia?"

"Yes."

"I can't tell you how glad I am that you decided to call." Does she have any right to say this?

"I made a promise."

"Well, it isn't always easy to keep promises."

"That's what people keep telling me."

"And it's true. I'll go and get Marcus."

Caroline grabs the bannister and hauls herself upwards, swinging wildly between hope and apprehension. Perhaps, at last, brother and sister will have the opportunity to get to know each other. Perhaps between them it won't have to be complicated. Between them, they might even manage to show the warring adults a way forward.

PART THREE
1955

CHAPTER THIRTY-NINE

RUTH

"Keep me company?" asks Ruth, offering her pack of cigarettes.

"Oh, I can't take one of yours."

"You can if I say you can." She waves the carton under Evelyn's nose. "Go on, live dangerously."

Ruth waits for Evelyn to accept and then flicks the wheel of her lighter, creating sparks, but no flame. "I never could light a cigarette the first time, and now my talent seems to extend to helping others. Oh, wait. Success!"

Evelyn sucks and lets the flame do its work, then removes the cigarette and checks that the end is glowing. "I thought you worked in a club?"

"Oh, it's not for want of practice." Again, Ruth has several attempts with the lighter before she produces a flame. "See what I mean? I've always been hopeless."

Forget where you are for a moment and the thing that brought you here, forget the pink and brown walls, the sealed window, forget to glance in the direction of the green screen, forget that Evelyn is in her uniform and you are in your prison-issue smock, forget that Evelyn is paid to be here, to guard you (although it rarely feels like it), forget that you can't simply get up and leave when you have finished your coffees and cigarettes. Forget all that and there are moments when you might just be two women, not as young as you once were, with a little experience behind you. It is companionable, sitting at the table and smoking. It is possible to smile, on occasion to laugh. "Cards?" Ruth takes up the pack and shuffles.

"Not right now."

She didn't expect a rebuttal. "Some other urgent business to attend to?"

"I've had an idea."

"Oh?"

"Don't ask me what it is until I know if it will work."

For quarter of an hour, while Ruth plays a game of patience, the wardress works, concentrating on a piece of cardboard, experimenting with various conical shapes and methods of fixing them in place. There are no scissors here.

"I should probably tell you," Ruth tells her, "I'm not a hat person."

"This isn't for your head."

"No?"

"No," says Evelyn, more certain than Ruth has heard her before. In the end, she settles for a system of slots and seems satisfied with her handiwork. She takes the chair she was sitting on, positions it under the naked light bulb that remains lit twenty-four hours a day, and steps up.

"Oh, I see," says Ruth, genuinely delighted. Her only complaint – although it has been a constant one – has been that she can't sleep. She tried to move the bed away from the glare, but discovered that like the table, it is screwed to the floor.

"Ta-da!" The wardress steps back down. Evelyn has made her a light shade.

"You clever thing! I'd have never thought of that. And even if I had, I would have assumed it was against the rules."

"Oh, it is. Strictly against the rules. We'll have to put it up

last thing at night and take it down first thing, before the Governor sees it. Do you know, I actually think it's going to hold. Try it." Evelyn nods towards the bed.

Happy to oblige, Ruth lays herself down.

"Does it make a difference?" Evelyn asks before she has even closed her eyes.

The difference is slight but, in a place like this, the gesture is what matters. In this place, small kindnesses are everything.

Ruth props herself up on her elbows. There are tears in her eyes as she says, "Evelyn Galilee, that's the nicest light shade anyone has ever made me."

CHAPTER FORTY

PATRICE

Patrice finds Vincent at the bar, propping his chin in his hands. "I've been meaning to ask," she says, "are you employed these days, or do you freelance?"

"You know me." The journalist pulls himself up to his full height and straightens his tie. "I'm for sale to the highest bidder."

Patrice makes a noise at the back of her throat. *Just as I thought.* "And if no one is bidding, what then?"

"There's always someone." He gives her a sideways frown. "Not that I don't appreciate the attention, but why the sudden interest in my livelihood?"

"Just something Charles heard. Talk of a strike at the newspapers."

"Oh. That." Vincent knocks back the last of his drink.

"It sounds as if maintenance staff could shut down the whole of Fleet Street." Patrice manages to catch Elise's eye. "My usual and another whisky, when you have a minute." She turns to Vincent. "Is it true?"

He shrugs. "Too much rumour-mongering to ignore. Not all of it from the unions, I might add."

Drinks are poured and set before them. Vincent's thanks are brushed aside, glasses are clinked. "No?"

"Let's just say that certain parties might benefit from a strike."

Patrice sips her tonic water coolly. "You mean it might be possible to brush something under the carpet."

"It might."

I knew it! She smiles into her thoughts. "Is the thing that needs to be brushed under the carpet a retirement?"

He looks at her wickedly. "No comment."

Without her being aware, Patrice's strand of pearls has become an abacus. "Then the strike *will* happen."

Vincent raises his glass and keeps it an inch or so from his lips, parallel to his cigarette. "Oh, I'm sure of it. Just a question of someone giving the nod to someone else who's in the know."

"How they've kept a lid on it so far is nothing short of a miracle."

"You're not the only one with friends in high places."

Camrose, Beaverbrook and Bracken. Quite the trio. Only they could get their colleagues in Fleet Street to toe the line. "As a newsman, where do you stand on this sort of thing?"

"You? You're asking *me* how I feel about suppressing a story?" The journalist widens his eyes, and Patrice presses her lips together to acknowledge the substantial role Vincent has played in continuing to keep the Hawtree-Davenport scandal out of the papers.

"I was referring to this story in particular."

"Believe me," he says, "This is nothing compared to the stuff we buried during the war. And nothing compared to the stories the courts order us not to print. But," Vincent sucks cigarette smoke through his teeth, "Churchill can't put off retirement indefinitely. At his age, what's the shame in admitting you're ill?"

Patrice sighs. "The last of the great statesmen. Eden will seem like a colourless substitute." *If he pulls through.*

"What do you know?"

"You don't miss a trick, do you?"

"I should hope not."

What's the harm? "Something Charles had from someone at White's. Apparently, Eden's surgery was botched. The knife slipped. It's touch and go."

Vincent considers this. "Both the premier and his successor within a whisker of death. Where does that leave the country?"

"I take it that's a rhetorical question?"

"Anything else for me?" and, as something of an afterthought, "Ma'am."

"Such as?"

"Oh, I don't know. If there were anything about a certain actress, say."

"Oh, come on! Cheap journalism is hardly your style. You're not some by-line hungry hack."

"*You* haven't seen the photographs from the set of *To Scale a Volcano.*"

"I have, but I've also heard of photo cropping. Perhaps you're not familiar with the technique? Let me explain –"

"The son. Is he still camped out at your country pile?"

All of Patrice's defensive armoury slips into place. "Who told you?" Word might have leaked during the filming of *Into Exile*, but two years have passed without any interference.

"You said it. I don't miss a trick." Vincent raises his glass in a mock toast and then drains it.

Wait. Might Vincent be forced into that kind of journalism if the strike goes ahead? "There will be nothing – and I *do* mean nothing," her eyes meet his, "without Ursula's say-so."

"Pity. A piece like that would sell here *and* in the States. And it would make a change from writing about sheep being dug out of snowdrifts. A journalist can only make so many headlines about the weather sound interesting."

"I don't know. I hear that the RAF are locating sheep using equipment designed to track down enemy submarines."

He scoffs. "And you?"

"No one's had to rescue me from a snowdrift. Not yet, at any rate."

"I meant, how are you? I can't help noticing there have been rather a lot of dramatic sighs."

"Really?" Patrice feigns lightness. "It must have been the talk of snow. I was remembering how it snowed the evening we learned that Hitler was dead." Snow in May, settling on tulips and lilac blossom, setting forget-me-nots and pansies shivering. That sense of a new beginning. As if one expected life to move with the speed of a film towards some happy conclusion.

"If you say so." Vincent dismisses her diversion for what it is.

Patrice looks down at her ring finger and arrives at an unusual decision. She loosens her lacing, just a little. "Lately, I've been finding it very difficult to understand what Charles wants from me."

"Like me to try and find out?"

Because Vincent pitches his suggestion in the guise of a joke, Patrice can afford to ask: "Do you do a little spying on the side?"

"If there's a strike, I'll have to consider *all* my options."

"*If* there's a strike, I'll bear you in mind." This really is the time for Patrice to make her exit. A journalist acting as a private detective! The thought tickles her as Elise helps her into her furs. There's a conflict if ever she's heard of one! News is Vincent's profession. He finds something out, he goes to print. How could he possibly not?

CHAPTER FORTY-ONE

CAROLINE

"Hello Caroline, it's Silvia. Is it too late to speak to Marcus? I've only just finished my homework."

These telephone calls have become fortnightly occurrences. What may have started out as curiosity on the girl's part have become important to Marcus. "I haven't persuaded him to go to bed yet. In fact, if you could pretend it's almost your bedtime, you'd be doing me a favour." Caroline switches to her best voice of officialdom. "And what is today's password?"

"Cucumber sandwiches!"

She puts her hand over the receiver to yell, *"Marcus! It's Silvia for you!"* Caroline yells out of habit rather than need. The days of traipsing up and down two flights of stairs are consigned to the past. The nursery wing now has its own telephone, another sign that what was only supposed to have been a temporary arrangement is now more or less permanent. "Hold on, he's just untangling himself. You know, strictly speaking, I think cucumber sandwiches is two words."

Trouserless but wearing socks, Marcus hurtles down the hallway, holding his hand out for the receiver. Silvia is *his*. He doesn't like anyone else to speak to his big sister, let alone joke with her.

"Not so fast." Caroline lifts the handset out of reach, keeping a firm grasp. "Five minutes."

His face is less rounded than it was this time last year, but he's still capable of puffing out those cheeks of his. "That's not fair."

"If you have any sense, you won't waste it arguing. I'll be setting the egg timer." She relinquishes the receiver, makes a point of checking her watch a second time, and walks brusquely away.

"Hello, Silvia. Did you hear? She only gave me a lousy five minutes."

"Five-year-olds!" Caroline exclaims to Norma, who has taken up her knitting for the evening. It's too early to tell what this particular oblong of garter stitch will grow into. Norma uses patterns called 4 Designs for Boys and 'lets the thing decide' which of the four possibilities it wants to be. The boys pictured on the pattern sleeves either look like miniature versions of imagined fathers or older versions of themselves. As imagined fathers they play golf or sit behind the wheels of sports cars. As their older selves they leave houses unaccompanied, carrying great piles of books.

Norma glances up from her needles. "Teach them to speak and they answer you back."

Caroline sits down in the chair that is the pair to Norma's. "I'll let him have ten minutes."

"Pushover!"

"It's not every day that his sister calls." Norma can frown all she likes. In Caroline's place, she would have said, 'I'm wise to you, mister,' but would still have fallen victim to Master Marcus's negotiation technique – a combination of bravado, sob stories and complaints.

"If only Silvia would set a date to visit. Wouldn't that be something?"

Caroline crosses the first two fingers of both hands and

holds them up for Norma to see. They have discussed this. Their hope is that it isn't too late.

"What about that sister of yours?"

"Betty."

"That's right, Betty." The needles clack-clack. "Heard from her recently?"

Caroline tries to recall when the last envelope arrived. "I probably owe her a letter, but," she breaks mid-sentence to shrug, "it's hard."

"Pretending to have news?" Norma shunts her woollen creation along, stitch by stitch, mouthing numbers as she goes.

"That too. But this place." Caroline's eyes range the four corners of the room they call the lounge, while Mrs Hargreaves insists on 'the upper sitting-room'.

"I know what you mean. My sister writes me, *You still living in that palace of yours?*"

Caroline laughs her agreement, but it's impossible not to reflect. "Some things aren't ours to tell."

"You're not wrong there! Say, did you see the photo of our lady boss and her pooch?" Norma nods to the folded newspaper on the coffee table.

Caroline picks it up and looks at the photograph of Ursula coming down the steps of a swanky hotel, pretending to make the dog wave. *Today, the British actress was all smiles, but rumour has it that on-set tension runs so high, Delancy and her co-star do not speak except to say their lines.* "No hint of an affair, so *this* is what they come up with?"

"Do you see Marcus's name?"

"I don't."

"She's been playing this game a long time." There is pride in Norma's voice, but the game still feels foreign to Caroline.

"Do you miss home, Norma?"

"Where'd that come from?"

Caroline shrugs. Perhaps the mention of Betty, of letters, has made her homesick for the small intimacies that stem from sharing not just a bedroom, but a bed with a younger sister; for the sound of her brothers baiting each other while fencing with sticks in the back garden, for the taste of her mother's gravy. Sometimes, even now, she misses the smell of her father's pipe tobacco.

"When I'm living with the pair of you in a palace? Hah! Truth is, I've spent my entire adult life in service. My sister can complain about that husband and those kids all she likes, but at least she has people to call hers. And a home – even if it *is* a shack. You should maybe give that some thought. Who are you going to meet, stuck out here?"

Caroline's never met someone in the normal way; wouldn't know how to. "Oh, no." She finds herself blushing.

"What? You're not all that bad looking."

Norma doesn't know about Caroline's life as a hostess. She was a different person then, cast adrift. It took so long to piece herself together, fragment by fragment, but days still arrive when she feels like an interloper who's bluffed her way into a comfortable life.

"I don't have a daddy!"

The two women's eyes lock, a collision rather than a meeting. "I don't like the sound of that." Caroline pushes herself to standing.

"Not so fast!" Caroline feels her forearm being grabbed; an abandoned needle drops to the floor and rolls. "Let's see how it plays out."

"Won't Ursula want to be the one to tell Marcus about his father?"

"My money says that ship's sailed. Besides, a brother and a sister, trying to work out why they've never met? I'm surprised it hasn't come up before now."

"No I don't! I've never had a daddy."

Caroline fights the urge to run to Marcus's side. "Little Miss Blabbermouth," she says through clenched teeth.

"Don't go blaming Silvia. Poor mite's had to grow up fast. Whatever's been said won't have been in spite."

"Spite or not, it's one thing to find out you have a father and another to discover you have a brother who's your mirror image."

"We don't know it's gone *that* far."

"You're lying!"

"That's it. I only hope Marcus doesn't feel as if *we've* lied to him." Caroline picks up the egg timer, which she never intended to upend, and marches along the corridor. "Time's up," she announces.

"I'm five."

"Time for bed. Say goodnight to your sister, and give me the phone."

"I hate you!" he yells into the receiver.

"That's not very nice, Marcus. Tell Silvia you're sorry."

"I'm not sorry!" Marcus slams the receiver into Caroline's waiting hand and stamps off towards his room. Watching him go, Caroline holds the mouthpiece to her chest. She hears Norma's, "Whoa, there, mister!"

Slowly, she brings the receiver to her ear. What to say? "Marcus seems very upset. What happened, Silvia?"

"I didn't mean anything. It just came out." Silvia sounds cornered. It's easy to imagine that she's shrunk into herself.

"No one's accusing you of anything." Marcus is crying, Caroline can hear it, not just crying but wailing. "But it would really help if you could tell me what you said to your brother."

"I'd better phone Mummy." Silvia's voice is shaking.

"That's a good idea, but she's a long way from here, and I need to know how to help your brother. Can't you tell me what you told him?"

"I told him how Mummy left us for a man she was making

a film with, and that his name was Donald Flood. I told him that Donald Flood is his daddy."

It's obvious that Silvia feels awful. "Is that everything?" Caroline asks, as gently as she can.

"I told him that Mummy wrote to me and said she wanted me to meet Mr Flood, but I never actually met him. At least I don't think I did."

"I think you'd remember if you had."

"I haven't even met Marcus yet, and I was going to, I was going to, but now he hates me."

"Oh, no. Brothers and sisters argue all the time. *All* the time. He'll come round, trust me."

"Do you think so?" Silvia sniffs. "Oh, wait." The sound of muffled voices. "Daddy says he wants a word."

"Am I speaking to Miss Wilby?" The voice is blunt. No attempt to sound pleasant.

Unprepared, Caroline is wary. "Mr Sheard." It's hard to think of him as Ursula's ex-husband. They've lived apart for so long. "I'm –"

"You can tell my ex-wife that this is exactly why I was so concerned about Silvia being in contact with her brother. Frankly, I've never been happy that she's been exposed to the *situation.*" Caroline flinches as surely as if she's been speckled with spittle. "Silvia doesn't know what she's allowed to say to whom, and she cannot be expected to lie."

It strikes Caroline: without questioning his daughter, Silvia's father knows more about the conversation than she herself does. "Mr Sheard, did you listen to the children's conversation?"

"I was on the extension in my study."

Has he listened to *all* of their conversations? "Could you tell where it was going?"

"I had no way of knowing for sure –"

"But you could have headed it off. If you'd wanted to."

Another light bulb moment. "Oh, I *see*. You didn't want your daughter to know you were listening. You didn't want her to know that you don't trust her."

"I trust my daughter. I was *protecting* her."

Where Caroline finds the courage to bite back from she barely knows, but bite back she does. "Just as Miss Delancy has been protecting Marcus. Until she judges that he's old enough to know."

"Tell me if you will, because I honestly don't know. What age does a boy have to be before he hears about his mother's immoral lifestyle? Marcus should thank Silvia. At least this way, he won't be the last to know."

Caroline finds that she has slammed down the receiver. A moment ago, it was up by her ear, and it is now back in its cradle. She splays her fingers, takes in her fingernails, knuckles, veins. The palm side has a sheen of sweat.

Norma's voice rings out. "Everything alright out there?"

Less in control of herself than she'd like to be, Caroline makes her way back to the lounge. If a hand can slam down a phone, what else can it do? As she enters the room, the toe of her shoe displaces something light. A ball of wool that looks like the dog's been at it. Marcus is in Norma's lap, crying as if his sobs might choke him. She is rocking him as she would a much younger child, but the boy seems to want to be babied. Norma's knitting has been cast aside, needles akimbo. Caroline stoops to pick up the wool and winds it as she makes her way over.

"I was just telling Marcus that I've known him since the day after the day he was born." Norma addresses the boy, her voice soft and low. "I don't think I've ever told you that before, have I? Actually, you could say that I knew you even *before* you were born, because I felt you kick and I said to your mommy, 'This one's a boy, and what's more, he's going to be a handful.' So you gave us warning. Yes, you did. And, of course, I've known your mommy since the first week she arrived in the States."

Not part of this conversation, Caroline perches on the arm of her chair. What Norma is telling Marcus is this: *I have the answers. If you decide that you want to know, all you have to do is ask.*

"That would have been, oh, let me see now, was it '35? Well, it was round about that time. How are we doing there?" Marcus turns his head and buries it in Norma's bosom. Norma looks at Caroline and she nods. "Not quite done, huh? So, as I say, I've known your mom almost as long as Caroline here's been on this earth. Sometimes your mom says to me, 'You know me better than I know myself.' And as you know yourself, your Noo-noo is the elephant who never forgets."

CHAPTER FORTY-TWO

PATRICE

"I've done a little digging in relation to the subject we spoke about."

"Eden?"

"The duke."

Patrice's breath hitches. "You've done *what?*"

"I thought, perhaps, I might be able to prove how useful I could be to you."

"I'll tell you when you can be useful, not the other way around!" Anger flares, but briefly. Patrice has been standing on the edge of a precipice for so long. Instinct tells her this is the final step. Why be afraid of taking it? "You've found something," she says, though there is still part of her that would rather not know.

"Is there somewhere private we can talk? I need you to help me join a few dots."

So this is it. She scribbles an address on the pad of paper that Elise leaves on the bar for such emergencies, rips the sheet out, folds it and places it within Vincent's reach. "I keep a room there. I'll follow in fifteen minutes."

Alone, Patrice clamps one hand to her mouth. *Whatever this is, you can handle it.* She's buried many a scandal before. If there's one thing she knows, it's how to create a diversion.

"Anything I can get you, ma'am?" It is Elise. "Your usual?"

She rallies. "No. No thank you. In fact, I really must be going. I'm late for an appointment."

The hotel's upper corridor feels claustrophobic. Walls are closing in. Until now, no one other than Berthram knew of this address. Berthram, waiting downstairs in the Bentley, reading his newspaper, doing his best to ignore the plummeting temperature, knows more of Patrice's life than anyone, and even Berthram has no idea of the room number. Already, Vincent will have had time to make what he will of the hotel, its size, location, the discretion of the desk staff; guessed what purpose Patrice keeps the room for. Everything seems to be warning, *Be on your guard.*

Installed at the dressing table, Vincent doesn't move to stand when he hears her enter, denying Patrice the opportunity to tell him not to bother. Instead, he simply twists his head to check that she isn't some young man with a spare key, about to garble an unlikely excuse that he must have the wrong room, or a maid who backs out saying she'll come back later.

"You don't mind if I dispense with the 'ma'ams'?"

There is to be no preamble, no skirting around the issue. "I don't," she says curtly.

Vincent still has his overcoat on, suggesting that he wants to keep their exchange brief. This hasn't stopped him from helping himself to two miniature bottles of Scotch. Dutch courage perhaps. Patrice acknowledges the slight ache in her jaw, the one she gets when she has set her mouth in a grim line. She lifts her chin, smooths the thick pile of her sable coat and lowers herself onto a corner of the bed, very upright.

"Whitlocke's been in your family for hundreds of years, is that right?" An easy question to put her at her ease. What... what if Vincent has lured her here under some sort of false pretence? What if he also made his offer to Charles? *Like me to try and find out?*

"Since the seventeen hundreds." Patrice would like to adjust her sitting position, but comfort is not what this occasion calls for. She must be tight-laced. Alert.

"It didn't pass to Charles as a dowry?" The journalist doesn't look her in the eye. Patrice doesn't think he is *avoiding* her gaze, just intent on joining those dots of his.

Patrice looks longingly at Vincent's cigarette, burning unattended in the ashtray. "I inherited it *after* my marriage."

"Outright?"

She dispenses with her well-rehearsed line about being a custodian. Vincent knows full well that there are no future generations. "Whitlocke is in my sole name."

"As I thought. I'm sorry if this seems a little vulgar, but I do need to ask." He looks up from his notes, straight at Patrice. She sees that he wants to capture her reaction. "Are you in any financial difficulty?"

There is little point in not responding. Quite aside from talk at the club – and she knows that behind cupped hands, people do talk – Vincent is a serious journalist. He wouldn't dream of bothering her with this unless he'd done his homework. "Thankfully, there's been nothing since the Hawtree-Davenport fiasco."

Vincent narrows his eyes; takes another drag on his cigarette. He is waiting for more.

"Had it happened in my grandmother's day, I would have been saddled with Charles's debts and we might have lost everything. As it was, Whitlocke was protected."

He returns to his notebook, his pen scratching the page. "So there's been nothing recent?"

His persistence is unsettling. "No," Patrice insists. What is this? Has someone else come forward claiming that Charles owes them money? Or did those signatures they extracted from the investors stand for less than Kenyon had hoped? It is possible that the Linnets – perhaps even friends of the Linnets – have taken their revenge because Patrice would not stand by while poor Valerie's name was sullied?

"And you allow Charles to manage your finances?"

Indignant, Patrice lets out a small scoffing noise. "I allow him to give that appearance when it would hurt his standing to do otherwise. But it *is* just an appearance."

"I understand." Vincent chews his bottom lip for a moment before asking, "Would it come as a surprise if I were to tell you that a new mortgage has been taken out on Whitlocke?"

"A *mortgage?*" It's unthinkable. Any threat to Whitlocke is a direct threat to Patrice.

"It's been drawn up in your name, but –"

"*My* name? No. You've been fed a line, I'm afraid." Patrice allows herself to delve into her handbag for her cigarette holder, for her silver cigarette case. Vincent bends towards her with a lighter. "My own bank is perfectly aware."

Vincent's gaze is direct. "The contracts were drawn up in your name." His voice is slow, insistent. "With what appears to be your signature."

It dawns on Patrice: "You're serious."

He nods, just once. "I'm afraid so."

"*My* signature." The words echo inside her whalebone ribcage. She draws on her cigarette holder, holds the smoke inside her lungs, delaying what will be.

"What *appears* to be your signature." Vincent reaches for an envelope.

"Show me."

He holds the glass out and nods at it. Now Patrice sees: the Scotch wasn't for him. She takes it, shaking, and Vincent curves her fingers around its contours, making sure she has a firm grip. Even now, the whisky trembles. He shows her a series of photographs. Sales chits from auction houses, dating not from the time when the Hawtree-Davenport scam came to light, but from the last couple of years. Six paintings including Roman scenes by Clerisseau, a Zoffany painting, a harvest scene (something Patrice never cared for), a Swiss landscape. All things she assumed were covered by sheets to protect them from dust and sunlight. Air leaves her mouth in a rush as she reads *A Chippendale design kneehole desk.* "That price is an insult!"

"I'm afraid the real slap in the face has yet to come."

Documents.

Deeds.

What appears to be her signature. Look: there's her trade-mark flourish.

My God! Charles wasn't going through my things because he wanted to know who I was seeing. He wanted samples of my handwriting. Thoughts ambush Patrice, emerging as spoken words. "But that was years ago!" Years of marriage. Years of deception.

"Whatever this is – and this may not be all of it – has been going on for some time." Her thoughts are fed back to her. Confirmation. "He started off small. Stocks, mainly –"

"Gambling!" Something has Patrice's heart in a fierce, cold grip.

Vincent's shrug is not a denial. *The horses, then!* "But it seems he got himself in deeper and deeper."

Deeper and deeper or more and more sure of himself? He must have persuaded Kenyon Senior that he'd won back her trust. But how? "May I?" She thrusts one hand towards the photographs, making it understood that refusal will be unacceptable, exchanging them for the glass, which she passes back to Vincent, untouched. She holds the photographs by their very edges, forcing herself to look closer. Outwardly, Patrice is the girl who will not make a fuss, the young woman who holds so much inside that she comes across as cold.

Inside, she's seething. She is wrath. She is fury. "Thank you, Vincent, I'll take it from here."

"But I can –"

She wants him gone. What he does with what he's uncovered, she no longer cares. He can plaster posters the length of Fleet Street if he likes. "You've done quite enough."

He looks exasperated, but Patrice will not be argued with. He takes what little is left of his cigarette, his notebook and fedora and the black great-coated silhouette of him blurs through her tunnel vision.

There is absolute clarity of thought.

This time there will be no procrastination.

She must deliver her fury to its target.

She is on the move.

She must unleash it, undiluted.

"My keys."

"Good day to you, ma'am."

She must say, 'I know what you've done, Charles. Did you really think I wouldn't find out?'

She does not pause to consider that she may be ill-equipped; does not stop to ask, 'How does one go about this?' The icy wall of air that hits her cheeks as she emerges from the hotel lobby is nothing to her. She is brimstone, fire and whirlwind. She is untouchable.

"Where to, ma'am?"

"The duke's club."

"Ma'am."

She is unaware of Berthram closing the back door of the Bentley; unaware that his eyes search for hers in the rear-view mirror. She is speeding to a destination to fulfil a specific purpose. It doesn't seem to be a contradiction that inside her fury is a place of absolute calm. Her purpose is righteous. She can see an outcome: a clear unbroken line. All she has to do is hold onto everything she is feeling, everything she has ever felt, every provocation, every broken promise, every slight, every betrayal, every outlet that has been denied her, every put-down, every time she propped Charles up, took up his causes, entertained his tiresome colleagues.

White's. Portland stone columns adorning a Palladian facade. A club that takes the moral high ground, a club whose very existence now seems to offend. How Charles loved to quote Disraeli. "There are only two things an Englishman cannot command – being made a Knight of the Garter or a member of White's Club." He is about to discover that there is a third: an aggrieved wife.

"Mind yourself on the pavement, ma'am. The snow's been cleared, but there's black ice." Small crystals glitter on Berthram's lapels and epaulets. "Shall I come in with you, ma'am?"

"I can find my own way, thank you."

"I don't doubt that, but they might not let you past the front desk."

Each of Patrice's senses seems heightened. "Let them try to stop me."

She steps out of the midst of the fire, strides past the liveried staff. Raised voices are of no concern to her. No woman has ever set foot! Hah! "Do you suppose I believe that you have *men* polish the brass?" she roars, her voice a tumult, like the noise of an army.

No need for directions. Charles will be in the testosterone-fuelled den that is the lounge, and the lounge will be on the first floor. Up the main staircase, rising between two colossal stone columns. Look at the walls, the portraits of pampered narcissists striking poses; wigged, moustached and bearded. Believing they look so poised. And look how everything is done to deter non-members. Window bars, wrought iron railings, even the tops of the carriage lights are spiked. Not in the least discouraged, Patrice has four faces: the face of a woman, the face of a lioness, the face of a cow and the face of an eagle. She has four wings: two upstretched, tips touching; two covering her body like armour. Her outstretched arms force open a pair of double doors, ready to cast aside anyone who dares stand in her way.

Where is he?

Like burning coals, Patrice has the appearance of a torch as she goes back and forth among armchairs and card tables, drawing stares from men who wear dinner jackets as uniform, differing from each other only in colouring, build and hairlines. Eliminated as targets – wrong jawline, too paunchy – they rise to their feet, ostensibly to protest, but seem paralysed, even to warn Charles. *Ah, there he is!*

Her husband's drinking companion, a man Patrice doesn't recognise, kicks his heels, slowing his own escape. Charles turns his head; sees her. Something must tell him that his moment of reckoning has arrived. He grips the arms of his chair, his knuckles whitening. "I can explain," he begins, but the truth is writ across his face.

Patrice's hands are the only weapons at her disposal. They seem to know what their target should be. She is upon him, one knee on his thigh, his neck in her stranglehold. His fingers claw, trying to prise hers away, then his hands flail desperately, signalling for help. Onlookers, slow to realise her purpose, are forced into action. Where there was stillness, chaos ensues. They cannot pull Patrice off, no matter how red Charles's face becomes, no matter that his eyes are bulging, no matter that the chair tips onto its hind legs, balances for one perfectly choreographed moment and then crashes to the floor, leaving her towering above him, bearing down. Her wings protect her; Patrice has the power to shrug grown men aside.

"Ma'am," she hears. "Ma'am." A hand on her shoulder, not clawing or pulling, but gentle. It is Berthram, come to drive her home. He must have been glad of his greatcoat in the cold.

"Your handbag, ma'am. You left it in the car."

Compliant as a child, she lets go. "Thank you, Berthram. Always looking out for me."

As she stands, there is a moment when her bearings are not all they should be. She cannot place the room, the people. "Where is it you've brought me?" she asks Berthram.

"White's, ma'am."

She looks about her. The place is much as she imagined it. She feels unable to ask what they are doing here and so she quips, "And they let us in? Standards must be slipping."

He takes her elbow, as he did that day when they went together to identify Valerie's body, and leads her over to Vincent. Dressed for the outdoors, the newsman has his fedora in his hands, is holding it before him and breathing hard. Like the two of them, he is a fish out of water. "Three non-members," Patrice says, surprised that such attire is allowed in the lounge. But here she is, in her sable, and Vincent is looking at a point somewhere beyond her. The cogs turn, the journalist's words write themselves. Patrice turns to see what has his attention. A flurry of activity near an upturned chair. Signs of a recent brawl. White's is not so civilised after all.

People are keeping their distance. People with faces of stone. Faces like gargoyles. But Patrice is used to being a social pariah. In any event, she doesn't think that she likes White's. Once it might have been her type of place, but no longer. "I'm ready to go home now," she says to Berthram.

"I'm afraid we may have to take a short detour, ma'am."

"Whatever you think best." She turns back to Vincent; cannot understand why he would be here. "Did you come looking for me?" she asks.

"Ma'am, you have my word." Vincent's voice is low. "I will pull every string I can to keep this out of the papers. The strike has been a long time coming. This may be the moment."

A frown tugs at Patrice's forehead. That Churchill will go

is no surprise, but why would that bring Vincent to White's? Unless this is where his information comes from.

"Ma'am."

There is a man at her elbow, brisk-mannered. Like the majority, he wears a dress suit. Impossible to tell whether he's a dignitary, a politician or staff. "Excuse me one moment," she says to Vincent, glad of the distraction, but finding herself glancing back towards the newsman, furrowed.

"I'm Doctor Vaughan." A doctor then. "I've examined your husband."

"Charles? Has he been taken ill?"

"I'm afraid," the doctor clears his throat, appears hesitant, "I've had to call for an ambulance. His condition is critical."

CHAPTER FORTY-THREE

URSULA

"I don't know how much more of this I can take. Did you see? Aldo slapped my face – he actually *slapped* me." Dora de Whitt, Aldo's latest blonde lead, flounces about in her silk kimono, appealing to anyone who'll listen. "Apparently I didn't look *shocked* enough for his liking!"

On a shoot already plagued by delays, the cast and crew have been flat out. Six-day, seventy-hour weeks, in these temperatures, too. Everyone is exhausted, morale at an all-time low. Ursula, who has her own battles to fight, keeps her head down, sitting quietly in front of her mirror, photographs of her children tucked into the frame, applying cold cream to remove the day's make-up.

Silk billows as Dora strides across the room. Something inside Ursula sinks, as the starlet says, "You were there, Ursula. *You* saw how it was."

No one calls her by her first name. It is always Miss Delancy until the moment she says otherwise. Ursula carries on wiping cotton wool over a closed eyelid. "I saw how it was," she says. Some things are impossible to deny.

"I don't see how I can carry on working with the man!"

What point is there in telling Dora that, in six months'

time, she'll cut off her right arm for a part in Aldo's next film? "Then you have your answer."

"Exactly!" Dora says, satisfied that she's made her point, then her brow furrows; those full lips of hers part.

Ursula feels a pang of pity. It isn't Dora's fault that she was plucked from obscurity. That the girl has something is undeniable. What she lacks are discipline and training. And her ego has clearly never been bruised before. "Look," Ursula relents. "Do you actually want my opinion or do you just want a witness?"

"Your opinion." The starlet blinks, as if the question should be unnecessary. "Of course."

She swivels around in her chair. All smeared make-up, Ursula looks up into a face she would have good cause to envy. Just shy enough of perfection to be interesting. "Granted, Aldo's difficult. There are no lengths he won't go to when he believes that the performance he's after – the performance you're capable of – is only one take away. If he wants to shoot sixty takes of a scene in which you don't utter a single word, so be it. Without words to hide behind, the light in your eyes will be *everything*, but *you* can't see that light. Only he can." Ursula swivels back to her mirror, away from luminous skin and arched brows to a trail of black mascara and streaked foundation. "As for your slapped-face moment," she continues. "I'd put good money on it being *the* shot that earns you an Oscar nomination."

In the mirror, one of Dora's slender manicured hands finds her collar bone. "Me?"

"I can picture it now. You, humbly accepting compliments about the uncanny precision of your acting, when the moment critics will describe as 'a kick in the guts' was pure shock. In film-making, the end always justifies the means."

"But you think I might be nominated for an Oscar?" Her eyes are wide, child-like. She wants to hear Ursula repeat herself, but Ursula will not go that far.

"Not if you don't finish the film."

Now that her unscripted pep talk is over, Ursula expects to be left alone, but Dora cocks her head and studies Ursula's reflection with cool detachment. "Tell me, because I'm curious," the starlet asks. "Do you remember me?"

"Should I?"

"I thought you might. But I suppose so many girls waited outside stage doors to meet you."

Waited. Dora talks about her career in the past tense. "Where was this?"

"London. I was holidaying with friends when we saw your name on a theatre poster. We couldn't get tickets for the play, but I had a copy of *Mirror Movie Magazine.* I tried my British accent out on you." Her look verges on smugness. *Had you fooled, didn't I?*

The past comes into focus. "You got yourself in front of casting directors," Ursula says, wondering if she'll be forced to revise her opinion.

A knowing smile plays at the corner of Dora's mouth. "Not in the way that you suggested. Harris Clay approached me. In a nightclub." She tastes the words, words with the power to inspire. "He told me I had a face for the movies."

That old chestnut! Man enters club, sits at a table at the edge of the dance floor and makes a careful study of all the young women. Only one meets his gaze. While the rest turn away in discomfort, she alone basks in his attention. It helps that he's handsome, with high cheekbones and a neat moustache, but as yet he could be anyone. He doesn't have to mention the words *star potential* to get her to cross those exquisite legs of hers. That is how she'll be in front of the camera.

"He flew me out to California for a screen test," Dora positions herself prettily, "I signed a contract and *then* took lessons. Elocution, movement, scenes." *Weeks,* thinks Ursula, *not years.* "But the way *I* did it, the studio footed the bill."

As Dora makes a perfect exit, Ursula feels as if she's been played. But didn't she once have the audacity to look a middle-aged theatre director in the eye and tell him things were about to change? And hasn't she been part of that change, one of a new generation who flirted with both stage and film, and probably wouldn't say no to television if the script were right? Still, that does not – does *not* – give Dora the right to look at her as if she's a relic from the silent movie era.

June is guarding her post, don't-mess-with-me tortoiseshell glasses perched on the bridge of her nose, a cigarette burning in her ashtray, the slightest click of fingernails dancing off typewriter keys.

"Is he in?"

"You've just missed him."

"Damn!" Damn Aldo and damn Dora's dramatics.

"Anything urgent?"

Marcus, sobbing in the background when Caroline called. Silvia's distress, Robin's fury. "I'll see you back in court before I allow my daughter to be exposed to your poison again."

"Never mind." She forces a smile. "I'll try him tomorrow."

"Shall I pencil you in or would you prefer the element of surprise?"

In two minds, Ursula finds the small gap between her front teeth with a fingernail. "What do you recommend?"

On Ursula's approach, June's typewriter hands pause long enough for her to take a drag of her cigarette. She raises her ungroomed eyebrows. "Be my guest."

"Any chance he might be in a good mood?"

"Just peachy. You know Aldo."

Ursula raises a hand to knock but stops herself. The twenty-four-hour delay has played on her nerves. She runs through what she knows. All of the filming on location, the scenes that were dependent on weather and light conditions, are complete. Aldo won't be happy, but it's not as if she's about to ask the impossible. Simply the inconvenient. "Could I have a word?"

"Why don't I like the sound of that?" He removes his reading glasses and squints from behind his desk at the far end of the rectangle.

She'll have to go to him; walk the long walk. "I hoped I was a better actress than that."

"Ursula, I was *bluffing*." Aldo pushes himself to his feet and holds his arms wide. "If it's about the script, I'm gonna tell you, you were right."

"I was?" Can this be the same man who had demanded take after take (just how many, Ursula lost count), insisting there was nothing wrong with the words? *"No, it's your delivery. Go again."* The same man who refused her a five-minute break? *"No one leaves the set. It will destroy any rhythm we have going!"* "I know, I know, I shouldn't have been so dismissive. It's the accountants. They have me in handcuffs. But I did *listen!*"

It is difficult to share in his delight. Her bladder full to bursting point, Ursula had broken down, tears of sheer frustration washing away years of professionalism. Now, when she is nearing the end of her contract. It was behaviour the crew would have expected from the film's young starlet. And after everything she said to Dora!

"As I watched the rushes, the line you suggested was right there in my mind. I hated it when you came out with the line as it was scripted. Hated it." Aldo shakes his head and scrunches up his mouth. "What I'm saying is I was wrong. So," he claps his hands, palms on opposing diagonals, and clasps them together, shaking them. "We reshoot. Tomorrow!"

Crestfallen, Ursula finds herself wetting her lips, struggling to take this in.

Aldo freewheels his arms, incredulous. "That's what you wanted, isn't it? Don't tell me you've changed your mind!"

At any other time, the novelty of hearing Aldo's frank admission would feel like notching up points, proof Ursula still has some sway. Now, it means only one thing. A set-back. Only a day, but a day she can't afford. "No," she says, but her 'no' lacks conviction.

"Come on." Aldo beckons with his free hand. "Out with it."

"I wish it *was* the script I came to talk to you about."

"Has that little bitch been playing up again? There's always one cast member who's intent on sabotaging the entire production, and this time round it's Dora de goddamn Whitt. In the business *five minutes* and thinks she knows better than me. I heard about what you said to her, by the way."

A noise comes from the back of Ursula's throat. It is not the noise of someone taking credit. Nor is it denial. No good deed goes unpunished in this business.

"What if *I* don't want to work with *her* again? Does anyone stop to think about that?"

Another small sound, this time empathy. "But you will. She has something."

"Well, it's not grace, it's not discipline, and it's certainly not craft!"

"I think it might be her legs." Ursula allows herself this and smirks as she does so, detecting Patrice's influence.

He sneers begrudging agreement. "It's not just me I'm thinking of. Tantrums like hers bring down the energy. But today, miracle of miracles, Dora de Whitt didn't threaten to walk off set. Your little chat must have done some good."

There will be no better moment to make her case. "Aldo, the thing I wanted to discuss, it's a family matter. I was wondering –"

He looks away and pushes at the air, as if to keep whatever troubles she has brought to his door at bay. "Oh, no, Ursula.

Three weeks. Three weeks until the end of the shoot, and then you can go back to England for good."

Three weeks might as well be a year to a five-year-old. And it's a long time for an angry ex-husband to be left brooding. "I only have two more scenes." Correction: three, including tomorrow's re-shoot. "I wouldn't ask unless I had to, but is there any way you could –?"

"Re-schedule the whole shoot around you? Inconvenience everyone else? That's what you're going to ask, isn't it?"

There is no point suggesting otherwise. Any change, however small, will impact on budget. Ursula lowers her eyes.

"It was *you* who decided to make England your base. *You* who said that you could honour your commitments from there." Ursula senses rather than sees how Aldo jabs at the air with his hand. This is not the time to remind him about the European projects he said would come her way.

"This thing. It isn't something that will impact on the studio, is it? I could do without having to clear up after another fiasco."

Ursula doesn't appeal to Aldo as the father of three sons he rarely sees. He, too, makes sacrifices. There is no medical emergency. No one has died. She is well aware that any explanation she might offer will make the matter sound trivial. *I can cope with turning on the radio to hear someone who's never met me say what a terrible person I am, but I cannot have another child of mine hate me.* "I guarantee you it has nothing to do with the studio, or the film."

He turns, one eyebrow raised in a way that unnerves Ursula. "That's not what I asked."

She breathes; considers the question from a different angle. Is Aldo trying to give her a way in? "It's damage limitation." Yes, that's what it is. "I want to prevent something from becoming news. Someone has told my son something that should have come from me, something he isn't old enough to hear." Her eyes pool.

"Spare me." The look Aldo throws Ursula is a combination of discomfort and suspicion. Why wouldn't an actress turn on the taps in an attempt to gain sympathy? "I don't have the appetite or the inclination for domestic dramas. If I can manage this – and I *do* mean if – I'll expect you to do press conferences at the airport, here and at home. Work with publicity on your angle. A scandal so appetising no one can look away, or a mission of mercy, I don't care which." Aldo punctuates sentences by pointing his index finger. "Just turn this into a positive."

Already Ursula can see the headlines. She'll be under fire for posing as a gracious and loving mother. Painted as someone who never knows where to draw the line. Well, it won't be the first time. She holds up her chin. "Anything you say."

"Oh, and make sure you're photographed with that goddamn pooch of yours. Coming down the steps of the plane. I can't credit it, but audiences love that dog."

"Dogs don't have bad sides." Perhaps Ursula can get away with throwing the journalists a few harmless scraps. When asked if Marcus likes having an actress for a mother, she said, 'He's got it into his head that I'm an international spy. I don't have the heart to break it to him.' But Aldo slumps into the chair behind his desk. His mind has moved on to the next problem that needs solving, which may or may not be re-scheduling the shoot. She can't leave their conversation here. Ursula must have something definite to tell the children when she calls them. "When will you be able to let me know?"

He looks up and growls. "You really are pushing your luck."

Her hands are behind her back, fingers knotted together. "I know."

"I respect you for not trying to sell me a story, that much I will say."

"You'd see straight through me. You always do."

He throws her an accusatory look, as if to say, *If this is an attempt at flattery, it's beneath you.* "I haven't said yes. I've said if. *If.* Now get out of here."

It is not a no.

Not a no.

CHAPTER FORTY-FOUR

PATRICE

"I'm Doctor Vaughan." A doctor then. "I've examined your husband."

"Charles? Has he been taken ill?"

"I'm afraid," the doctor clears his throat, seems hesitant, "I've had to call for an ambulance. His condition is critical."

The man – the doctor – is looking at Patrice. She feels as if she is expected to react, and react in a very specific way. Instinct tells her that 'critical' is a shade worse than 'serious', that her reply should convey her understanding of this. "Is he conscious?" she asks.

"Dipping in and out." Dr Vaughan's wince seems to indicate that, as far as Charles is concerned, unconscious would be infinitely preferable. He turns his head briefly in the direction of the upturned chair.

The brawl? Patrice blinks. All she can see is a pair of shoes, but it is the only evidence she needs. They are the hand-stitched brogues Charles likes to order from Jermyn Street. One of those things he is particular about. Another man is bending over him now. "Do you have any idea what happened?" Patrice looks from the chair to the doctor.

"My initial thoughts, such as they are…" Why is he unable

to meet her gaze? She nods in encouragement. "I think, before we do anything else, we should sit down and have a discussion."

Sit down? Surely urgency is called for. If manners were not central to her make-up, Patrice would point: *'That's my husband over there!'* But stronger than any such urge is the sense of her mother's disapproval. *We mustn't make a scene. Be a brave girl.* "Before we have a chat, shouldn't I go and see Charles?" Glances are exchanged between the men – the doctor, Berthram and Vincent – glances that exclude her. Exactly how her chauffeur and the newsman have become part of the equation Patrice is not sure, but here, in the smoky atmosphere, she can feel it: apprehension. People waiting for something to play out. She senses that a charade is taking place; that they are giving her time to ready herself.

"Doctor Vaughan!"

They – she, the doctor, Berthram and Vincent – turn as one. The man who was leaning over Charles is now upright. He gives a solemn shake of his head.

Dr Vaughan gently squeezes Patrice's arm, just above the elbow. "Excuse me one moment, ma'am." Unhurried, he crosses the room, bends his head towards the other man, confers and then, with his back to her, goes down on one knee and leans over the upturned chair.

What little doubt there was is ebbing. Patrice can feel her own pulse, hear it in her ears. Above the drumbeat of her blood is a high-pitched singing. A single tone that neutralises all other sound. Berthram's mouth is opening and closing but she cannot grasp what he is saying. He indicates a nearby card table topped with green baize. Emerald green, like the dress she wore to her coming-out party, while other girls paraded in white, a cross between first communicants and brides. No one blinks at the fact that a chauffeur has not only included himself in the doctor's invitation to sit down, but takes the lead. They must assume that, as a household employee, Berthram will be party to whatever arrangements come next. At her right side, Vincent also seems to think Patrice needs shepherding. "You too?" she asks, but does not argue when he pulls back a chair for her. Perhaps she does need help. The moment the seat makes contact with the backs of her knees, Patrice's legs buckle.

"Ma'am, this is the chairman."

She looks up, trying to attach the word to the man towering over her. Late middle age. Overfed. Morose.

"Your grace." Words he might use to defer to her, so why does Patrice feel as if she's being dismissed?

Patrice selects appropriate options from a well-worn phrase book. "Do please sit." There is no real way to prepare for the moment when the truth must be confronted. She indicates the chair closest to hers "I'd like to thank you for admitting me today. I'm well aware that it breaks with protocol."

With a slight pinch of his trouser-legs, the man sits. He seems at a loss. His eyes fix on the upturned chair. Patrice agrees. Charles shouldn't be left lying there like that. It's undignified. But Dr Vaughan cannot be interrupted. He holds his chin and is nodding. She catches snatched syllables, a low murmur of agreement.

The doctor's head is dipped, his pace slow, as he walks back towards them, stopping at Patrice's side of the table to address her: "I'm terribly sorry, ma'am. Restricted blood flow to the brain can cause all manner of complications. There was nothing we could do."

Charles!

Patrice finds herself blinking at the doctor, glad now that she was persuaded to sit, that the chair has arms she can grip. "So quick," she hears herself say. "I suppose that's something to be grateful for. And the fact that he was here, among friends." Odd, how one feels compelled to comfort others. That's where the old training kicks in.

It is too early to give a name to her feelings. She is now one person, no longer part of a couple. Later she might say that she felt as she did when she lost the second of her parents. Then, Patrice called it being 'orphaned', but 'orphan' hardly seems appropriate for a woman in her late fifties.

To her right, an exodus is beginning. Silently, several dozen men in dress suits file past in slow procession towards the double doors, intent, blinkered, as if below in St James's Square, the Pied Piper is playing. When a single pair of eyes flicker darkly in her direction, Patrice nods. A grimace of acknowledgement, almost as if she has caught the man out, before his gaze returns to the backs of those in front.

"Before you go, gentlemen. If we could agree that nothing that has transpired here today leaves this room."

A strange turn of phrase, but then White's has always had its own rituals and protocols. Most probably, they have never had a duke die on the premises before. Perhaps, like Terrence, they are keen not to find the place crawling with press.

"Agreed."

"Agreed."

"Well." Dr Vaughan resumes once more. "I will issue the medical certificate, stating that the cause of death was a stroke. There's absolutely no doubt in my mind that that was the case."

A stroke. Patrice contemplates this, telling herself that death might be a better outcome than the alternative. Charles would have hated being an invalid.

"Can I ask, ma'am, when the duke last saw his own physician?"

Jolted back into the conversation, Patrice is unprepared. "I don't know exactly, at least not in a professional capacity. You see, Dr Fisher is a regular guest." She frowns. Why doesn't someone right Charles's chair? "A moment ago. You mentioned something about blood pressure?"

Again, that exchange of glances. "I did."

"Charles's blood pressure was a bone of contention. Dr Fisher – did I mention his name?"

"You did, ma'am. I know of him. By reputation."

"He would take my husband's pulse and Charles would thank him, ignore his advice and carry on as he always did." It would be disloyal to say that Charles drank too much, but anyone at White's must know his habits. "Should I telephone?" Patrice asks. "He would be able to give me the date."

"Provided he saw the duke within the last fortnight, there's no need."

"Oh, it would have been within the last fortnight, most definitely."

"In that case, I see no need to involve the coroner, but of course I can only speak for myself. Can I –" The doctor brings his fist to his mouth as if reconsidering. "Can I perhaps check that we all understand what happened here today?"

They all look to Patrice, these men who have been avoiding her gaze. She looks to Berthram, who nods at her in the way that she herself might nod to someone in need of encouragement. She, in turn, looks to the doctor and raises her eyebrows.

"Before I informed you of your husband's condition, what's the last thing you remember?"

Patrice opens her mouth to speak, but is met by a blank. Her brows come closer together. Perhaps if he could be more specific. "What, in particular?"

"Do you remember arriving here, for example?"

"I –" The portraits on the staircase. The founder members. But that can't be what Dr Vaughan wants from her.

"Go back a little further, perhaps," he prompts.

This, she does know. "I was at my club, as I usually am. I, uh…" Patrice blinks. This must be what shock is like, she supposes. Only natural under the circumstances. "I assume someone must have telephoned to say that Charles had been taken ill and asked me to come straight away. Is that right?" It must be right. That's how these things are done.

Next to Patrice, the chairman clears his throat of gravel. "That's right, ma'am. I made the call."

She exhales her gratitude. Now that he's confirmed it, she does seem to remember Elise telling her that there was a call from her husband's club, directing her to the telephone booth. "It will be more private than the bar, ma'am." The coldness of the receiver against the side of her face. How grateful she was for the chairman's businesslike manner. "So that was *you*."

At this, Vincent shuffles in his chair. Patrice cannot help it, the shuffling irritates her. He's a grown man, not a bored schoolboy. Unless, *unless* he's trying to draw her attention. "And Vincent, am I right in thinking you were there when the call came through?"

"That's right, ma'am. We'd been talking. At the bar."

The gaps are closing. Now his presence at White's makes sense. She can hear Vincent saying, "You shouldn't go alone," and despite Patrice's protests that she wouldn't be alone, that Berthram would be with her, he'd insisted on coming. "Then Berthram, my chauffeur, brought us straight here." The doctor was right. It *is* good to nail down the order of things. Now she can turn her thoughts to Charles. Poor Charles! To have suffered a fatal stroke when he was so close to completing his life's work. But he's sown the seeds for the abolition of capital punishment, that's what matters. *Eyes bulging, bloodshot, veins pronounced.* Perhaps it's because the memory of Valerie's face is so raw that an image of her husband comes easily to Patrice. Perhaps the reason they've left Charles in such an undignified position is to spare her the sight of him. If that's the case, she is grateful.

The doctor appears to address Berthram. "My feeling is that we can contain this."

Is it the issue of the coroner that concerns the doctor? No one else seems to find it necessary to ask. It must be.

Dr Vaughan takes his time, looking each member of their small circle in the eye, pausing when it comes to Vincent. "How about you?"

Vincent is sitting very still, one thumb vertical and pressed into his lips. He shakes his head, though barely, as if engaged in an argument with himself.

"I'd be more comfortable to hear you say it."

Patrice sits tall, finding she also wants his answer. She does not like the idea that a knife might be used, that organs will be examined, to verify what is already known.

"Nothing will come from me."

"Do we have your word?" the chairman asks, a moment of unsettling intensity.

"I've already said, *nothing* will come from me." The journalist is shaking. It wouldn't have occurred to Patrice that Vincent might be upset by Charles's death.

When it comes to Patrice's turn, the doctor says, "Ma'am, is there anything you'd like to add?"

It's so hard to think when all of the small duties she'll be required to perform seem to be forming a lengthy queue. "I wonder, doctor, if you might answer a question for me."

"Gladly." Still, Patrice has the sense that Dr Vaughan is looking at her as if she's a curiosity in a sideshow.

"Regarding the arrangements. My husband and I, we never discussed what would happen. Charles's family plot was in the chapel at Staghurst, but of course the house is no longer in his family. I wonder if I might have him taken down to my family's mausoleum at Whitlocke?"

CHAPTER FORTY-FIVE

VINCENT

Vincent sinks down into himself, elbows on knees, hands on head, his fingers overlapping but not quite intertwined. *Is this my fault?* In his periphery he sees the chairman's polished shoes, their punched holes and rigid lines of stitching; one of Dr Vaughan's hands, a wedding ring, ash collecting at the end of his cigarette. Grinding his teeth, Vincent feels a violent need to apportion blame. He sits up and lashes out: "You have a man and a woman who've proven that they're completely incompatible, with no children to take into account. Why couldn't they just divorce?"

"A gentleman *never* tells tales on his wife." The chairman acts as if repulsed. "Were any member of White's to do such a thing, I'd make a very strong recommendation for his expulsion."

Honestly, these people think they have the monopoly on decorum! Why should 'telling tales' come into it? But perhaps, *perhaps* the chairman and the doctor know something he doesn't. It's possible, he supposes, that the duke asked Patrice to divorce *him* and she declined. And if accusations were to be aimed at a wife, if a judge were to condemn her character or use his platform to voice opinions on sexual morals (as has happened in several divorce cases Vincent has covered), that would be another matter entirely.

"And imagine if the wife were a duchess," the doctor says.

The character of a duchess must remain untarnished, Vincent can see that. "Still. There has to be a better way out than this." He doesn't go as far as to look over his right shoulder, to the place where, until a few minutes ago, the duke lay sprawled. "He must have known she'd find out eventually, if not from me then from someone else."

"I gather you have something to tell us," the doctor prompts.

Vincent hears himself sigh. He sits up and faces the two men. *Could I have stopped Patrice, or am I overestimating my influence?*

The chairman sits forward. "What was it that you told the duchess?"

Under no other circumstances would Vincent trust these chinless wonders. They represent everything that's wrong with Britain, everything that needs to change. But of one thing he's certain: they'll do everything in their power to protect White's and its reputation, which can only be to Patrice's advantage. Although he's hesitant, thinking about it, within White's inner sanctum, much of what Vincent has to say may well be common knowledge. "You're aware that, a few years ago, one of the duke's business ventures turned sour?"

Shallow, rapid nods from the chairman; distaste for a subject best forgotten. An indication, perhaps, that there's been talk, and that such talk is frowned upon.

"To do what he thought was the honourable thing, the duke had to sell all of his personal assets. Some of the duchess's too." Again, chairman and doctor exchange glances. It strikes Vincent that they too may have found themselves among Hawtree-Davenport's victims. If so, are they surprised to learn what their settlements cost the couple? "He may have kept up the appearance of being flush, but the reality was that the duchess kept him on a tight rein – or so she thought." He rolls his eyes at the hopelessness of it all. "Recently, it came to my attention that the duke has been siphoning off her belongings. Small things at first, to raise a little extra 'pin money', but it wasn't enough. Not for his tastes." Patrice had dismissed Vincent before he could mention all that he'd discovered. "Then came the theft on the day of the coronation. The police received an anonymous report that a man had been spotted on the roof of their London home. There was no evidence of a break-in, just an open window and a ransacked room."

"Jewellery, wasn't it?" Dr Vaughan flicks ash from his cigarette.

"That's right. The day before the coronation, pieces normally locked in a bank vault had been delivered to the duchess, so she could see how they'd look with her outfit. The original plan was to keep everything at the house overnight, but the duchess must have got nervous and returned everything she decided not to wear. From the timing, it seems likely that the thieves expected a greater haul."

"Quite," says the chairman.

"Everything pointed to an inside job – the duke and duchess safely out of the way, staff given a day's holiday, et cetera. The insurance company put a man on the case, but he didn't uncover any firm evidence."

The doctor breathes out a stream of smoke. "You'd need nerves of steel to point the finger at a duke."

"The same conclusion the insurers reached. They paid up."

"And that's what you told the duchess?" The chairman looks confused, as if, to him, such a thing would be excusable in the course of a lengthy marriage.

Vincent runs one hand over the short ends of his hair at the nape of his neck. "Not about the theft, no. She didn't give me the opportunity."

"Then what *did* you tell her?"

Oh, what the hell. They can't protect the duchess unless they know what they're protecting her *from*. Besides, even if they keep a lid on the rest, details of the duke's finances may be made public in the aftermath of his death. "For some time, it seems, the duke has been forging the duchess's signature on various documents."

The doctor flinches slightly, as if this were unexpected. "What kind of documents?"

"All sorts, but the most critical is a mortgage. Raised against the duchess's estate."

"Whitlocke?" Veins stand out on the chairman's forehead. He looks appalled.

So this is what matters to you. Not insurance fraud, not a breach of trust, but mention land and that's another matter.

"And you told her this when?" Dr Vaughan asks.

"A couple of hours ago."

"How did she react?"

"Disbelief, as I'd known she would." Vincent nods at the chairman. "That's why I went armed with evidence."

"And then?"

"Then?" He shrugs. "She dismissed me."

"With no hint of what she intended to do next?"

"Not that she shared with me."

The chairman frowns. "But you came here."

"I came here," Vincent says slowly. "You can't drop a bombshell like that and assume there won't be repercussions. I thought the duchess might go to see her solicitor to verify what I'd told her and *then* confront the duke. And so I waited outside. Close enough to hear the instruction she gave her driver." The second moment when Vincent might have stepped in, and all he'd done was flag down a taxi cab. He clasps and unclasps his hands. It all comes out in one miserable rush. "I never imagined, I mean to say that in all the time

I've known the duchess, she has never lost control. And then she acted as if she didn't remember."

Dr Vaughan clears his throat. "I don't think what we've just witnessed was an act."

"How is it possible that someone can do something," Vincent gestures, skirting around the words *like that*, "and have no memory of it?" All he has to go on is his own experience. Miserable mornings when he's woken with a word on the tip of his furred tongue, the rest a fog which gradually lifts, unveiling shades of shame or embarrassment.

"Studies have been carried out on patients who have committed crimes, violent crimes in particular. Having only partial recall is relatively common, having no memory at all less so – but it's certainly possible. However much in control the duchess appeared to be, we can safely assume she was highly emotional. That in itself can trigger a temporary dissociative state."

"So she really *wasn't* herself." Vincent's next thought twitches. "And if she really wasn't herself, then there's an argument it wasn't murder."

The doctor purses his lips. "There would be considerable risks in assuming a jury would reach the same conclusion."

"Considerable!" agrees the chairman.

It's difficult to escape the irony. The wife of a prominent abolitionist convicted of his murder. Even if the Queen were to exercise her prerogative of mercy – which isn't a given – the disgrace would remain. "In your opinion, doctor, what is the possibility of the duchess recovering her memory?"

"If she'd been drinking, for example, any amnesia might be temporary."

"The duchess doesn't drink. I offered her a shot of whisky, thinking she might need it for shock, but she handed it back untouched."

"So we must consider the alternative. Memories can only

be recovered if they were formed in the first place. If stress levels were particularly high, the system responsible for coding and consolidating memory may have been disrupted. In which case..."

You cannot recall what is not there to recall.

And the way Patrice looked at him, with such astonishment.

After checking his meaning is clear, the doctor continues. "You saw for yourselves how receptive the duchess was to the idea that she'd been summoned because Charles had fallen ill. The more she repeats the story, or the more that version of events is repeated to her, the less likely it is that she'll be able to distinguish it from real memory."

To trust that this is what happened – what *will* happen – seems to Vincent to be a huge risk. What if they cover this thing up only to find that Patrice has handed herself in at the nearest police station? What then? "And if she has a sense of *something?*"

"There *is* no in between," the doctor is adamant, "which is not to say she won't experience some guilt. We've already heard you ask yourself if you were responsible." Vincent finds himself staring at his shoes. He wasn't aware he had spoken out loud. "The duchess may well feel the same. If she'd arrived a few minutes earlier, could she have prevented her husband's death? Even people who are completely innocent can be persuaded of their guilt."

Vincent's mind turns to Timothy Evans, persuaded to confess to the murder of his wife and daughter. It is possible to be guilty of something, not the thing you're charged with, but for that guilt to haunt you so much, you'd confess to something else. *And God knows, we're all guilty of something.*

But there is a nagging something. "What if she had a direct reminder?"

The chairman looks irritated. "What are you talking about, man?"

"She has photographs – the evidence I took to show her."

"Not even that," the doctor says. "But to set your mind at rest, I'll pay her a visit. I've given her man sedatives for her to take tonight, so I'll leave it until the morning. First thing."

"Say you come away satisfied that the duchess has no memory of this afternoon's events," Vincent turns to the chairman, "can you vouch that your members will keep this under wraps?"

"Absolutely."

The answer is too forthright to be convincing. "It would only take one person to act on their conscience. After today, we'd all be accessories."

"I *rely* on our members doing *exactly* as their consciences dictate."

Vincent almost finds himself laughing. *White's and the Freemasons! Honestly!* His cynicism doesn't go unnoticed.

"What's the alternative? To see a duchess tried for murder? How could that possibly be in anyone's interests?"

The trial would be a circus, an exposé of the upper class, of how they feel that they're beyond the law, beyond convention, beyond morals. Of their respect for the institution of marriage rather than its vows; how their concern is the continuation of England's great families and their traditions and estates. In other words, a gift for any journalist. But despite her sharp tongue, despite the fact that Vincent has occasionally found himself at the receiving end of it, he has always reserved a soft spot for Patrice. Almost inexplicably, he finds himself in agreement with the chairman. "It wouldn't," he admits.

"Then you have no choice. You'll have to take my word for it."

CHAPTER FORTY-SIX

A word in the right ear. The Amalgamated Engineering Union and the Electrical Trades Union give five days' notice of their intention to strike. Management protests that fourteen days is the norm. Deaf to any suggestion that the strike's been a long time coming, newspaper bosses point out that, not so long ago, the Minister of Labour described their industry as a model to all others in labour relations.

Warnings that the strike will be labelled 'unofficial' do no good. Five days later, Fleet Street's great printing presses grind to a halt. Seven hundred workers down tools and leave by the doors of various buildings, hands in pockets, cigarettes in grim-set mouths. If they're fired, they will have no legal recourse. They dare not head off for a pint. Chances are they won't even get strike pay.

Lights still burn in Fleet Street offices. The journalists, photographers and secretaries haven't walked out. Typewriter keys strike regular rhythms, punctuated by the melodic rings of carriage returns. Hopeful of a quick resolution, editors oversee the production of daily layouts. One such editor checks a draft obituary for Charles Hawtree, duke of some ghastly backwater or other. *Distinctly lacklustre.* He grinds his cigarette stub into the ashtray. Yes, there's a promising paragraph about his campaign against capital punishment, but the piece goes nowhere. The name, Hawtree? He isn't related to the king of world speed-records, is he? More's the pity. Of course, what the piece really needs is a skeleton in a closet.

"No go today, gov."

"Well, that's one less thing to worry about." He sets the article aside.

Outside newspaper offices, vans remain idle. Vendors occupy their usual doorways and street corners, lest they lose them. Instead of bawling out headlines, their eyes are downturned, hands clasped. One almost looks as if he's praying. *The London Cry* speculates that London may be without its papers for a month. A whole month? Impossible!

Sensing opportunity, the BBC lengthens its news coverage, reporting that a guerrilla organisation known by the initials EOKA has begun a campaign against British rule in Cyprus; that planes have taken to the skies above West Germany once more after the post-war ban is finally lifted. Londoners without televisions (the majority) and who crave their daily news fix, queue outside the offices of the *Manchester Guardian*. Those who arrive too late to snap up a copy crane their necks to read from pages posted in the windows.

Saturday arrives. Betting men are left high and dry without their normal source of tips. When money is lost on the horses, offending slips are balled in fists. It seems very clear who's to blame. But not even the bookies are happy. Takings are down by ninety-five per cent.

If you're a socialite in the know, you can get your information direct from source. On the same day that eighteen-year-old Duncan Edwards, the Manchester United left-half, becomes the youngest player ever to be selected for the England squad, Nancy Mitford turns to a fresh page in her diary and writes about how she got stuck with Mr Atlee at a party. Even he couldn't say whether or not Winston is going. It makes everyone so very fidgety.

Certain though he is that Winston is going, Vincent Stewart is no less fidgety. True, the strike threatens his livelihood, but other matters are preying on his mind. Dr Vaughan sought a second expert opinion from a neurologist, who is satisfied that Patrice Hawtree has no memory of what happened at White's. Dr Vaughan quizzed the duchess's personal maid, and reports that nothing Mrs Crossland said about the duchess's behaviour gives him cause for alarm. A couple of migraines, but she's always suffered with her head. What the doctor cannot say is if Patrice will remember anything of what Vincent told her. And if Vincent tells her again (it should, he feels, come from him), whether she'll experience a second blind rage. Whether she'll say it's just as well that the duke is dead.

Two weeks into the strike, lay-offs begin. Secretaries go first because there is never a shortage of efficient secretaries. Post boys are next to receive their marching orders, and with them go their dreams of climbing the corporate ladder.

Spared the full onslaught of press speculation and commentary, the prime minister resigns. The cabinet is called to the boardroom at number 10 to meet one last time. Churchill emerges from the famous front door to cheers, cigar and walking stick in hand, a top hat replacing his usual homburg. He gives the crowd what they have come to see: the famous V-salute. No one could accuse him of looking ill. He hides it well.

On the top decks of buses, readers open the April edition of *Lilliput*, which features an illustrated article about a racing-car called the Emperor, and how its driver, David Blakely, has built 'a 130 mile per hour special'. On the fifth of the month the Emperor is written off in practice, metal crumpling like tin foil. Miraculously, its driver escapes unscathed.

Handwritten signs appear in the windows of fish and chips shops: *Bring your own newspaper!*

'Spy Scandal Reaches Boiling Point'. Pressure mounts for the government to declare a public enquiry and come clean about the 1951 defection of Burgess and Maclean.

A meeting takes place at Shoreditch Town Hall, raising hopes that the end of the strike is in sight. The drawn and haggard faces of management, union officials and engineers as they leave the building swiftly crushes any such optimism.

The Conquest of Space is playing at the Plaza cinema in Piccadilly. Young Andre Neilson (known as Andy) goes to see it with his mother, a Mrs Ruth Ellis, and her friend, Mr Desmond Cussen. Mrs Ellis's landlady notices that she, Andre's mother, has removed all of the photographs of the man she introduced as 'Mr Ellis', and has replaced them with photographs of herself. It is something of a shock to learn that her tenant used to be a glamour model.

The funeral of a little-known duke takes place at Whitlocke, his wife the duchess's family seat. His death was unexpected, and the service is a discreet but dignified affair. Those who attend hoping for a glimpse of royalty must satisfy themselves with sightings of notorious star of stage and screen, Ursula Delancy, rumoured to be a close personal friend of the duchess. The pallbearers are in household livery, the coffin draped with the flag featuring the red lion and the three escallops. Mourners queue patiently in line to offer condolences to the duchess, who remains veiled – the usual armour against unwanted social interaction. They restrict themselves to saying that it was a fitting send-off, but among themselves many wonder if the chairman of White's was really the right man to deliver the eulogy.

A woman who once worked as a glamour model, the mother of two young children (ten-year-old Andre and three-year-old Georgina, who lives with the woman's ex-husband), waits outside a Hampstead pub, where up-and-coming racing driver, David Blakely – the man she hoped would become her second husband, a man who did not at first tell her that he was already engaged, who has continuously cheated on her, extracted large sums of money from her, has been violent towards her and whose violent behaviour led to her being sacked from her well-paid job as manageress of a drinking club, whose child she miscarried only ten days ago after he punched her in the stomach, who one day insists he cannot live without her and the next does everything in his power to avoid her – is drinking with a male friend. The woman likes this friend. That's to say, she doesn't object to him as much as she does the Findlaters. The woman is petite, wearing horn-rimmed spectacles and a light-coloured suit. She does not look like a threat. In her past life, she has perhaps been a threat to wives, though she would argue otherwise. In the growing dusk the woman bides her time, concealed in a doorway. She has been drinking Pernod and crying. Streetlights come on. Nine o'clock. In her handbag, she has concealed a Smith and Wesson that she will later tell police was given to her by an American serviceman at the club she managed. Security for a debt. The door of the pub opens and, finally, the man she has been waiting for emerges. As David Blakely goes to get in his motor-car, she takes the gun from her handbag, calls his name, points and shoots. She counts three shots, but is later told there were six. The woman immediately asks a bystander to call the police. Learning that the bystander is an off-duty policeman, she then asks him to arrest her, declaring, "I am guilty," and then, "I'm a little confused."

On Easter Monday, those who forfeit their lie-ins to queue for a copy of the *Manchester Guardian* can be forgiven for missing the headline towards the foot of the front page: *Man Shot Outside Public House*. The report provides little detail. The public house was in South Hill Park, Hampstead. Dead on arrival at hospital. Woman helping police with their enquiries. That is the sum of it.

With his ear to the ground, Vincent Stewart makes connections that don't occur to ordinary readers. Duncan Webb of the *Sunday People* and Duggie Howell of the *Daily Mirror* are already hot on the case, having wasted no time in bidding for 'The Ruth Ellis Story'. Already, Howell has charmed his way into Ruth's Egerton Gardens flat. Once the strike is over, *this* will be the only story people want to read. It's newspaper gold. Forget any facts that are inconvenient. An ex-model divorcee, who shot her racing-boy lover will be presented in court as a jealous woman, scorned. A woman whose husband filed for divorce on the grounds of mental cruelty after she abused and nagged him, and falsely accused him of having improper relations with other women when she, herself, worked as a hostess at a private members' club. The public will lap up every sordid detail; the will-she-won't-she of it. Does Vincent want in on it? How could he not? He enters an empty telephone booth, dials his contact at the union and utters four words. "Back to work, boys."

At last, following a lengthy meeting at Holborn Hall, the unions agree to the wage-deal that has been on the table from day one. The loss to the newspapers is totted up at between three and four million pounds, depending which set of figures you prefer. What with all those people out of work, ordinary people ask, 'Was it worth it?' Cogs whirr back to life. Black ink stains fingertips once more. Blazoned across the first front pages to be spewed from the presses is a photograph of a platinum blonde in her late twenties. A cold-blooded killer. Vans leave depots. *The Daily Sketch. The Evening News.* 'Your *Star* again.' They pull over at kerbs outside shops and railway stations, back doors open even before handbrakes are cranked. String-tied bundles are stacked high on hand-held trolleys. Before the day is at an end, no one will care that they missed the full details of Sir Winston's resignation, the forthcoming general election, the death of Einstein, let alone how a little-known duke suffered a fatal stroke. Instead, in every pub and Lyon's Corner House, around every dinner table, on front doorsteps and over garden fences, talk will be of one subject and one subject only. All of England will know the name Ruth Ellis.

CHAPTER FORTY-SEVEN

PATRICE

"Thank you for coming all this way, Mr Kenyon."

"It's no trouble. No trouble at all. We could hardly expect you to make the journey to London at a time like this. If I could begin by offering my condolences."

"Thank you," Patrice says, and takes a moment. "You remember my estate manager, Mr Woodham?"

Solicitor and estate manager exchange nods. There is never any ceremony with Woodham. As usual, he is dressed for the outdoors. Land management takes up the greater portion of his time, which is how he likes it; it's where his expertise lies. The solicitor seems unnerved by his presence.

"Do please take a seat." She indicates the chair on the opposite side of the desk. "What about you, Mr Woodham, will you sit?"

"If you don't mind, ma'am, I'll stand."

"I've brought the duke's will," the solicitor begins to rummage, "as you asked." He produces the ribboned scroll and offers it to Patrice.

"Would you?" she asks Mr Woodham, who steps forward and takes it. "Actually, that's not the reason I asked you here," she continues.

"Ma'am?"

"A set of photographs has come into my possession." Patrice places them on the desk, a neat stack, not dissimilar to a deck of cards, which she shunts sideways so that he can see the extent of them. Patrice does not say that she has no idea who could have planted them in her handbag. A member of White's, obviously, but no one knew in advance that she would be at her husband's club that day. Which begs the question: did someone at White's intend to blackmail Charles? "They show that someone has been forging my signature."

Mr Kenyon leans forward, moves his reading glasses onto the bridge of his nose, and studies the photographs closest to him. "May I?"

"Do, please. Ignore the sales chits from auction houses for the time being." Patrice has Mrs Hargreaves working on an inventory of furnishings and art. Already there is little doubt in her mind. "The ones that I'm particularly concerned about are these." She points to a group of four. "They appear to suggest that a substantial mortgage has been taken out on Whitlocke."

Patrice watches the solicitor's face cloud. "That's right, ma'am," he says, his voice dragging a little.

"You agree that they appear to relate to a mortgage?"

Kenyon has a coiled look about him, as if he would like to get up and run. *You* knew *about the mortgage?* "Ma'am, the letter of instruction, the duke assured us –"

"What letter?"

"I don't have it with me. I'm afraid I didn't come prepared..."

"Have I got this right? You're telling me that the duke brought you a letter of instruction, supposedly from me, asking you to negotiate a mortgage on my behalf?" *My God, Charles, what have you done?*

"Ma'am."

"And, with everything you knew, you didn't think to check? Was picking up the phone too much trouble?" They didn't like to challenge a duke. That is what it boils down to.

"We verified your signature. And all subsequent signatures."

Patrice raises her eyebrows. "Just how many were there?"

"There were several forms. The duke took them away for you to sign."

"The signatures are good, I grant you," Patrice admits. "But as you can see, the duke seems to have had rather a lot of practice in recent years."

"I-I can't comment on the other documents."

"Forget them for now. Let's concentrate on the mortgage. Where do I stand?"

Mr Woodham clears his throat. "Ma'am, would you like me to leave the room?"

"Stay," she says without taking her eyes off Kenyon. "I'd like you to interrupt if I stop thinking straight." Patrice slows her speech. "Well, Mr Kenyon?"

"The bank acted in good faith…"

"So the mortgage stands?"

"Is there no trace of the advance?" It comes from Kenyon as a plea.

"Let us assume the duke used it to settle a debt. If I can prove I wasn't party to the agreement, can I get the money back?"

"*If* we can trace where it went, with a sum this size, the matter would most likely end up in court. Then, if we were successful in reclaiming the money, the creditor – or creditors – would have the right to claim their losses from the duke's estate."

"There isn't enough money in the duke's estate to cover it, we already know that." Patrice's blood fizzes unpleasantly, the sensation like a sugar rush. "I take it I won't inherit his debt?"

"No, ma'am, you won't."

"That's something." This sounds like a police matter, but how will it look if she involves the police?

Woodham interjects. "Ma'am, if I may?"

"Please." Patrice finds herself batting the air.

"If there's no hope of persuading the bank to write the mortgage off, what about the repayments?"

Woodham is right. Who has been paying the mortgage, assuming it has been paid? She looks at Kenyon who seems to be suffering his own personal agony.

"Our instructions were to take the money from your trust fund."

"My –?" Patrice allows herself a moment. There is little option when she can barely speak. "It's as if I've been robbed twice!" Anger melds with grief, and while the grief at Charles's passing had moved inwards and lodged there, Patrice's anger demands an outlet. Charles was no better than Davenport and, like Davenport, Charles is not here to answer for his actions. There is only Kenyon. "Mr Kenyon, as of now you are no longer my solicitor. I will have Mr Woodham prepare a list of the documents you hold for Whitlocke. If you will kindly package them up, along with my personal papers, I will send Berthram to collect them."

There is nothing more to be said. Little in the way of eye contact. Kenyon scrapes back his chair and stands.

"And Mr Kenyon."

"Ma'am." He is not the same man who walked into the room.

She follows him into the hall. "Kindly inform your partners that you will be hearing from me."

From the hall Patrice goes to her room and reaches behind her neck for the clasp of her black dress. When the zip resists, she tears it apart with both hands *He got away with it. Charles got away with it – by dying* yanking and clawing until there is just enough give so that she can force the garment over her hips. Then, when it is about her feet, she stamps out of it and goes to perch on the edge of the bed. The dress lies there like something slain, one arm reaching out to Patrice, a desperate appeal for mercy. *How could you? How could you do this to me?*

"Ma'am," Crossland says, entering the room, taking one look at the disarray and doing what she is paid to do: seeing things for what they are, without comment or judgement. "What would you have me do with it?"

There is no option but to put up a fight. It will all have to come out, all of it. Oh, there will be sympathy, no doubt. But behind her back they'll be saying, What a fool! "Have Woodham burn it," says Patrice.

"Where to, ma'am?" Berthram holds the car door open.

"The telephone box in the village."

"Very good, ma'am."

There is no queue, thankfully, and Patrice already has the receiver in her hand before she realises she doesn't have the right money. She opens the door of the telephone box. "Berthram, I don't suppose you have any coins you could lend me."

"Try pressing button B, ma'am."

She does as he suggests and hits the jackpot.

"Ah, Elise, is Vincent Stewart there this afternoon?"

"Just a minute, I'll fetch him. That is you, ma'am, isn't it?"

"It is, yes." Patrice is fidgety as she waits for the unhurried hello. "Vincent, do you remember some time ago that you made me a tentative offer about your services?"

There is a pause. "I do, ma'am. Before the strike."

"Were you serious?"

"I was."

"The thing is, I've come into possession of a set of photographs that appear to show some rather incriminating evidence. I can only think that they must have been planted in my handbag while we were at White's that day."

Again, the hesitation. "You don't remember?"

"What should I remember?"

"I gave you the photographs. Just before we were called to White's."

She raises her hand to cover the mouthpiece for a moment. "I don't know what was in the pills the doctor gave me, but I seem to have lost a whole day."

"You've had a terrible shock, ma'am."

"I suppose I have. I was going to ask you to validate the photographs for me, but if you already know..."

"I took most of them myself."

"Then you saw the original documents?"

"The ones from the auction houses, yes."

"How?"

"Chance. I was at Sotheby's, following up another story, when a lot from Whitlocke went under the hammer. I had a word and was told they had sold various items over the past few years. It didn't sound right to me."

"I won't even ask how you got hold of the photographs of the mortgage documents."

"Best not."

"I'm – It's hardly surprising that Charles had a stroke. The secrets he was keeping must have sent his blood pressure through the roof!"

"I dare say."

"I'm reluctant to involve the police. It's probably foolish of me, but I don't feel ready. Not yet, at least."

"That's understandable."

"I don't suppose, Vincent, that you or any of your contacts have any experience in tracing money?"

Patrice, who is on her way to the library, hesitates. For the life of her, she can't remember what seemed so urgent. It was there and now it has gone. She fails to mentally re-trace her steps. Everything is unravelling, and so quickly. "You stupid old fool!" she utters out loud. Perhaps Charles was right!

No. She must stop thinking that way. Take charge.

From her left comes a small metallic clank. The suit of armour stands as it has stood since her childhood. The armour is no family heirloom, but something her grandfather decided no country house should be without. He carefully wove it into their history (bravery and heroism being so very important), but the truth is that someone else's relative may or may not have died in battle wearing this suit. Patrice faces it as she would a friend one has grown distant from – which is to say that she looks to see how he is weathering in comparison to her. She used to come up to the 'metal man's' thigh. Eye to eye (or, more accurately, eye to visor), it surprises her to discover she has caught him up. The pointed feet have always troubled Patrice and continue to do so. They could trip a man up. And as for getting on a horse.

Her heart skips. Just behind the pointed metal foot there is another foot; small, brown-shoed. Judging by its size, no one to be afraid of. It is some time since Patrice has spoken to a child. She has never been very sure how to approach children, but she remembers very clearly how she hated being talked down to. She herself felt very sensible, especially when compared to the adults, people with peculiarly narrow concerns and priorities.

"How d'you do," she ventures softly.

"How d'you do," comes the reply, a young boy's impression of the man who may or may not have died in battle.

Patrice lifts the slotted visor and clanks it shut again. "How very odd. No one there."

A hiss. "It's me. Marcus. I'm hiding."

Patrice would hide from the world if she could. "May I join you?" she whispers back.

"There isn't enough room for two."

She puts her hands on her knees and strains her neck. She can see that there are already two, although one of them is Ursula's lapdog, Percy. "Too bad. It's my house," Patrice says.

"Is it?" A section of the boy's head comes into view between the knight's knees.

Is this boast true? Can Patrice still call Whitlocke hers when the bank owns the lion's share? What she will have to give up to keep it has been very much on her mind, but the sense of belonging, the strength of feeling she has for the old place means that she will make as many sacrifices as are required. She will not see it turned into a hotel, so the townhouse must go. And she may have to open the house to paying guests. For now, she rallies. "We've met before." A handful of occasions over the past two years.

"They said I should keep out of your way."

"They did, did they?" It was well-meant, she supposes. There should be rules, of course there should, but not the ridiculous rules of her childhood, when she was constantly made to feel as if she were a nuisance. If she's going to live here (and that seems to be her decision), and if Ursula continues to live here (and her contribution to the household expenditure is not unwelcome) they must learn to rub along. "In fairness, you have made a jolly good job of it."

"Oh, I'm not hiding from you."

"No?"

"No. I'm hiding from my mother."

Patrice decides not to pry. Even a five-year-old should be allowed a little privacy. "Well, I can understand that. I often feel like hiding. Especially at the moment." Her voice thickens. She has the answer for why her parents found grief so difficult. It is not something you can put a sticking plaster on and say, 'There, there. Run along like a good girl.' Particularly not after discovering what she has discovered. That her marriage was a sham.

"Is that because –?" The boy stifles his question with a gasp, and the gasp with both hands. The dog gives a yelp, shoots out between the pointed feet of her metal friend, claws scrabbling for purchase on the marble floor. "Percy!" Marcus yells, but his grasping hands admit defeat. He has shocked himself, another clue to the nature of things he has been told he must not do. It is possible that, like hers, the list has grown too long to remember. A protracted game of Grandmother Went Shopping.

"Don't worry," Patrice says. "He'll be back."

"I guess."

"You may have heard that my husband the duke died recently. Is that what you were going to say?"

His reply is a timid, "Yes."

"Well, you mustn't be afraid to speak of it. Or to ask any questions you have."

On all fours, the boy is looking up at Patrice as if he knows he's been cornered and is waiting for her to make her move so he can attempt to scarper.

"He's buried here in the grounds." She crouches down to the boy's level. "Did you know that?"

"I did. I was there."

"Then I should thank you for coming. Your first funeral, was it?"

"Yes." Marcus sits back on his heels.

"What did you make of it all?"

"I liked it very much. The horses especially."

"The horses were particularly good, weren't they?" Patrice feels inexplicably satisfied by this observation. If she had to pick a positive from the day, she too would mention the horses. "I wish I'd had the chance to get a closer look, but I was rather tied up."

"One of the men with the top hats showed me. There were four, all black, with feathers." Her narrow view allows her to see how the boy conjures a plume with one hand then brings a hand down to each side of his face at eye level. "And things to stop them seeing."

"Blinkers. They're to stop the horses from getting spooked."

"By the ghost?"

Patrice finds herself blinking, although the choice of words was hers. "By the living, mainly."

"You're not allowed to stroke them."

"Not while they're working, at any rate."

"I wasn't allowed." Marcus's voice is a shrug.

"No." She remembers. With an absolute clarity, Patrice remembers being an only child in this house, and what a marvellous and terrible and strange thing it was. Everything else fades into insignificance. "You know, that isn't the best hiding place, not by a long shot. If you aren't too busy, I could show you."

"You're not going to take me to the place where they put the bodies, are you?"

The question takes Patrice aback, then a certain wickedness takes over. "Would you like me to?"

"No."

"Then no. That wasn't what I had in mind. I thought I might show you the stables, actually. When I was a young girl, we used to keep horses."

"What happened to them?"

"Horses need to be exercised and there was no one who was interested in riding them. I must say, I rather miss them."

"Perhaps you could get some more." Two hands appear followed by the boy, crawling on his hands and knees.

"Wait!"

"Why?" He startles.

"Your mother. I'd better make sure the coast is clear." Patrice moves forwards until she has a clear view of the corridor and then checks the staircase. "Quickly." She beckons with all the urgency of childhood. "Follow me."

CHAPTER FORTY-EIGHT
CAROLINE

Her breath hitches. Goosebumps surface. So *this* is Ruth Ellis, ex-manageress of the Little Club, the job that could have been Caroline's. The woman whose boyfriend Caroline unknowingly singled out, then knowingly continued to see because it didn't seem to matter. Valerie – who'd been more alive than anyone she'd ever known – was dead. How could anything ever matter again?

And now the boyfriend (Caroline never thought of David Blakely as hers) is dead too.

Dead.

At twenty-five, with little to separate him from the public schoolboy he was.

Caroline is confronted by her past self, a ghost she thought she'd left behind. It's hard, so far removed, to admit what she wanted from their encounters. Not just oblivion, but something more. She remembers – how clearly she remembers – thinking that it would have been easier *not* to feel. Easier for it to stop. She blinks back moments. Being carried from the club down to his car. A bare shoulder. Feeling her power, then the realisation that she was powerless. "You should watch your mouth." Doubled over from a fist in the stomach before she even felt the spread of pain.

There is that same shock now, shock that someone whose skin was next to hers, whose heartbeat pounded through Caroline's frame, whose sweat she'd been drenched in, whose salt she'd tasted, who could flatter and humiliate, inflicting pain enough to cancel out any pleasure, is gone. Not from trying to push the needle on the speedometer higher and higher, something that might easily have happened to anyone who thrived on adrenalin. But from gunshots, fired by a woman who says she knew what she was about.

"It is obvious when I shot him I intended to kill him."

These blinked-back moments stop, start, stop, reanimate. Like the stick men Caroline draws for Marcus, each on a fresh page, so that when you thumb through the notebook, they play in an unbroken sequence. Caroline isn't on every page, but she's on some of the pages. She is part of David's story – and yes, she admits that she continued to follow his progress. All the way from Whitlocke.

If the Emperor hadn't been written off in practice on the fifth of April, he would have raced at Castle Combe on the ninth.

There had been talk of him driving for the Bristol Aeroplane Company at Le Mans on the tenth. He shouldn't even have been in Hampstead that day.

Caroline studies the photograph of the unsmiling platinum blonde and thinks, *She has a hard look about her.* Hard she may be, but she's no Haigh or Christie. The streets aren't safer with Ruth Ellis locked up.

She looks at the woman, reclining on pillows and thinks, *This choice of photograph was deliberate.* Some people will say that's a come-to-bed look. Perhaps it was. But those aren't come-to-bed clothes.

The woman's weight rests on her left arm, that arm a prop. She's unsteady. Look again at that hard expression and you can see it's glazed. Light is absent from those eyes. A long shift working at a club will do that. So will time spent with a man so unpredictable that you can't guess what's going to come your way next. And to see David portrayed like some hapless fellow, lured to his fate by a femme fatale.

Did you fight back? she asks the photograph: Ruth Ellis pictured in her open-necked blouse. *Or did you want the pain? Did you provoke him?*

Caroline looks at the striped scarf knotted around her pale and narrow neck. From the scarf back up to the face, which seems suddenly and inexplicably fearful, and thinks, without any element of doubt, *They're going to hang her.*

The newspaper is a baton in Caroline's hand, the concealed photograph still speaking to her, so her grip produces a nagging feeling that prods old bruises buried deep under the surface of her skin. *You say you weren't yourself, but what if you were? What if that was the real you and this is the fake?* In need of an anchor, Caroline looks in on Marcus. Light enough seeps in from the corridor. He's sprawled diagonally, covers thrown off. *This is my life now. This is who I am.* Convincing herself was never going to be easy. Caroline the nanny, with her own room at Whitlocke, with money enough to satisfy even her mother's demands, to keep Betty safe, had thought herself a distant cousin of the person she used to be. Her head thrown back in laughter that doesn't quite ring true. A glass raised to her lips. Knowing eye contact. It would be so easy to fall apart again. Now that she's been there once, she has no need for a trail of breadcrumbs. Part of Caroline will always be drawn there.

She has a sense that the order she has built into her new life is unravelling as easily as one of Norma's knitted creations. Unless she does something, Caroline will think herself into a corner. There is only one person she can go to, one of the few to know of her connection with David, the only person to translate her recklessness as a cry for help. But Patrice has issues of her own. Discreet as they are, Caroline has overheard the housemaids. Talk about the mess the duke made of Whitlocke's finances. It seemed to Caroline when she first came here that the place was run for the benefit of the staff. Now there are nervous whispers about tightening of belts.

She closes her eyes. She needs advice. Badly.

David and Ruth were cheating on each other, not just with one other person apiece, but with multiple people. David never said a flattering word about Ruth, in fact he said he'd been trying to shake her off. On several occasions, he told Caroline that he'd made this absolutely clear to Ruth, and Caroline believed him, given the way he boasted about his 'other women' so that she might understand exactly where she stood. And – wasn't it pathetic? – this had actually made Caroline feel *special*. When David chose her, he was choosing her above the woman he was living with and several other women who might have happily made themselves available. Ruth was not the only woman to have been taken in by David Blakely, but it was left to her to avenge them all.

Caroline shakes her head in despair. Could she have stopped this terrible thing from happening? If, at the time she wore his bruises, she'd gone to the police and said, 'If he's doing this to me, don't you think he's doing it to the others?' But she knows exactly what their reaction would have been. They'd have looked down their noses at her and said, 'What others?' As if women 'like them' don't deserve dignity and respect.

This, when Patrice took a lie to the police, a lie that could easily have been investigated if anyone had a mind to, and was believed. That's the difference between them. The duchess may have further to fall, but she'll never fall to the same depths as the likes of Caroline or Ruth.

She knocks on the drawing room door, listens for the

muted response and enters. The duchess isn't alone. Ursula is keeping her company, lapdog in possession of her lap. "Oh, I'm sorry," Caroline stammers, thinking it best to retreat.

"No need to be sorry." Patrice's smile is no disguise. She looks pale. Always slim, she is now gaunt. But Caroline is glad to see her out of her widow's weeds. Black wasn't the duchess's colour. "Join us."

It's impossible to refuse the invitation. Caroline enters the room, sits. It isn't often that she censors herself in front of Ursula, but she doesn't want her employer to know everything she left behind. And yet when Patrice asks, "You read the article?" Caroline can hardly deny it. Not when she's carrying the rolled newspaper.

"I did." Her mouth is dry.

Patrice turns to Ursula, who sits in the pair to her own armchair, and says, "The murder in London, the one I told you about."

Ursula frowns. "Terrible, isn't it? I expected gun crime in the States, but here?"

"There's something I didn't mention. Caroline and I both knew the young man."

Ursula's eyes widen. "You knew him?" Caroline finds herself in the glare of the spotlight. "How?"

Again, Patrice comes to her rescue. "He visited the club a few times with his racing friends, and I bumped into him occasionally at weekend parties. Given *who* Blakely was, I don't see too many people jumping to Mrs Ellis's defence." So Patrice believes it too: Ruth Ellis will be sentenced to hang. "But the state doesn't like to be seen to execute women. If convicted, there's still nine chances out of ten that her sentence will be commuted." Good betting terms, then. "I learned rather a lot from Charles about capital punishment over the years. People expect me to carry on his work and it's something I feel I'm capable of. When the time comes," she looks to Caroline, "I wonder if you can think of anything that might help Mrs Ellis." She turns to Ursula with an aside. "Blakely wasn't a very pleasant individual."

She mouths an 'O'.

"He could be cruel," Caroline says, without prior knowledge that she was going to speak. Blood rushes to her cheeks.

"Caroline, I remember you telling me that you saw something you'd prefer not to have seen." Again, to Ursula. "His treatment of a young lady."

Caroline nods. "What would I do with that information?"

"Present yourself at Hampstead police station." Patrice touches Ursula's forearm. "If you can spare Caroline, of course. Berthram could drive her so she needn't be away for long."

Please. Please say that I'm needed here. Ask if it wouldn't be better if I wrote.

"Of course you must go. Norma and I will both be here. I'm afraid I still have a lot of making up to do before Marcus brings himself to trust me again."

"When the time comes," Patrice repeats.

CHAPTER FORTY-NINE

URSULA

"It's a disgrace." Patrice is fuming and Ursula is glad to see her fume when she has been so subdued of late. "The defence only cross-examined two witnesses. Two! Apparently, nothing the others could have said would have proved useful."

"Why?" Marcus asks, keen to latch onto a distraction because he doesn't like scrambled egg the way it's served in the dining room (though he knows it's a tremendous privilege to be invited to breakfast downstairs.) He likes Norma's scrambled egg, straight out of the pan, with toast soldiers that have had their crusts cut off.

"Marcus," Ursula says tentatively, "Don't interrupt Mrs Hawtree while she's reading her newspaper." Patrice takes several dailies ("An overview," she calls it), the last of which she brings to the breakfast table.

"It's perfectly alright," Patrice answers, turns her full attention to Marcus and smiles. "'Why?' is always an excellent question."

Marcus shoots Ursula a look. She tried putting him in his place, but he was right and she was wrong. Seated on two cushions, Marcus is only chest height to the dark wood table, but it is clear that this newly-scored point makes him feel taller.

"Let me see." Patrice takes a deep breath and sets aside her reading glasses, as if she's in for the long haul.

Ursula looks at her son across the cruets, the tumbler of milk, the half-eaten plate of scrambled egg. She tells him with her eyes that she isn't someone who needs to be right all of the time. She's wronged him, she knows that, and she hopes he'll find a way to forgive her.

"First thing's first. Before we get to cross-examination, Marcus, do you know what a witness is?" Patrice insists she isn't good with children, but that's not true. She's proving herself capable of extreme patience with someone who, like her, is effectively an only child.

"No." Far from being deflated by this admission, Marcus is keen to learn. His question has been taken seriously. *He* has been taken seriously.

"It's usually a person who has seen something happen," Patrice tells him. "But in court cases, there's a second type of witness. They weren't actually there at the time when the thing the person stands accused of was supposed to have happened."

When Ursula looks at her son, she imagines Patrice in his place, a watchful child with a shrewd expression, exposed to conversation that parents and grandparents assumed would go over her head, while she was bursting with stifled questions.

"Although you see something happening, you don't necessarily understand what's going on. And so the second kind of witness is someone who can help explain it to you. An expert witness. In the case I'm reading about, a man was shot, and so they asked someone who knew all about guns."

"A cowboy?"

Ursula brings her napkin to her mouth to disguise her smile. Marcus's current obsession is *The Lone Ranger.*

"On this occasion," Patrice remains straight-faced, "he was ex-military, but no doubt a cowboy would have been equally knowledgeable. In a criminal court, there are two sides: the side who are there to prove that someone is guilty and the side who are usually there to argue that person's innocence."

Marcus's frown deepens. In his world there are two sides, the goodies and the baddies. Whatever the cost, the baddies must be got rid of.

"I say 'usually'. In the case I've been reading about, the woman accused of the crime made a full confession, without realising there were things she might have said in her own defence."

"Is that the lady?" Marcus points at the photograph on the front page of the newspaper, another picture of the peroxide blonde. (It is surprising just how many photographs exist of someone who isn't a film star or royalty.)

"Yes." Patrice turns the newspaper around so that he can see.

What is her son thinking as he looks at the photograph of the woman with the blonde hair, pencilled eyebrows and dark lips? Ursula's mind tunes to Phyllis Dietrichson's admission in *Double Indemnity:* 'I've always been bad.' Does Marcus judge whether people are goodies or baddies by how pretty they are, how old they are or how they dress?

"Both sides can call witnesses," Patrice goes on. "First of all, the side that has called the witness asks the questions that they think will draw out information to support their case. After that, the other side is allowed to question the witness. That's the part that's called cross-examination."

"They try to catch the person out?"

"That's part of the idea. If one side can show that the witness has lied or exaggerated, or just isn't as sure of their facts as they should be, then the jury might decide they can't trust the witness, and ignore everything he – or she – has said."

Ursula watches her son absorb this, as if it's confirmation of something he already knew. He trusted her, his own mother, but she kept something – something he had a right to know – from him. She let him go on believing that he didn't have a father, when apparently *everyone* has a father. Marcus had to hear it from someone he'd never even met, never mind that he was related to that someone.

"What's the other part?" he asks.

"What?"

Ursula still finds Patrice's 'whats?' abrupt. Her mother always corrected her, insisting that 'pardon?' was the proper thing to say. Apparently, her mother was wrong.

Her son is unfazed. He's a big fan of 'what?' "You said catching them out was only part of the idea."

Patrice plants her elbows on the table and leans forwards. "Clearly we have a barrister in the making. I do believe you're cross-examining me, young man!"

He laughs, delighted. First the 'what' and now an adult with elbows on the table. "Yes!"

"Well, the thing is, witnesses can only answer the questions that are put to them. They might have a really important piece of information, but if no one asks for it, they must keep it to themselves."

"That's not fair," Marcus protests, his grip on his cutlery tightening. "The witnesses should be allowed to say everything they know. They shouldn't have to wait for the right question."

Ursula smarts, but keeps her silence. She will not attempt to untangle herself from this mess. You cannot tell a child that you expect complete honesty no matter what, then say that you withheld something because you were trying to protect them. Life is simpler in the movies. It's rare that a goodie becomes a baddie or that a baddie becomes a goodie. In the movies, baddies always get their comeuppance. That, Marcus would consider fair.

"Mommy?" Marcus says, his voice strong and determined.

She wants so much for him to come to her so that she can pull him into her lap, kiss the top of his head and hold him. Ursula ached for him while she was away and now that she's home, he's keeping his distance. And she is jealous. Jealous of Caroline and Noo-noo. She's even jealous of Patrice.

"Mommy, please can I get down from the table?" Marcus is asking for her permission only because she's taught him that he should.

"I think you should ask Mrs Hawtree. She invited you to sit at her table and she's been very kind to answer all of your questions."

"Mrs Hawtree, please may I get down from the table?"

"You may."

"Good boy." Ursula nods. "Run along and find Caroline."

Patrice watches him trot towards the door. Percy, who has been sitting under his chair, scrambles after him. Then she says, "I'm sorry how that panned out. I got a bit carried away."

"Not at all. These things need to be talked about. It doesn't help if I keep tiptoeing around the subject."

"A lot of people steer away, don't they?" Patrice is, of course, talking about Charles. "I get terribly angry about it, but then I think, really, I'm being unfair. If someone asked me right now how I am, would I know?"

Ursula smiles, trying to set all other thoughts aside. "How are you?"

Patrice sips from her teacup and ponders the question. "For the first time in my adult life, I feel completely alone – no offence meant."

"None taken."

"And I have questions, so many questions!" She gives a short, derisive laugh, but seems to crumple.

"What is it, Patrice?"

She shakes her head. "A hellish mess is what it is!"

A sudden bereavement is not so different, Ursula imagines, from her break-up with Mack. When he made himself completely inaccessible to her, it felt as if something had been wrenched from her soul. "Try me."

"Where to start?" Patrice closes her eyes, breathes out, obviously trying to compose herself. "It turns out that Charles had got himself into financial difficulties – and not for the first time. It's a pattern that goes back years, but this time I knew nothing."

Ursula reaches across the table for Patrice's hand.

"To do what he did next, he must have been desperate. Selling one or two pieces – art, furniture, heirlooms that had been in my family for years."

"He sold *your* things?"

"If only that were all. He took out a mortgage against Whitlocke. In *my* name."

"How is that possible?"

"He did what men always do," Patrice snaps. "Claimed to be acting as his wife's representative."

"That can't be right."

"It's not over, not by a long shot, but each argument brings a fresh objection. So, to borrow a phrase from your son, it's not fair. And if I don't seem like your typical widow in mourning, it's because I'm not." She pushes herself up from the table. "I'm seething." She is shaking. Ursula can see it. "How could he have been such a cad in private while working for such a noble cause?"

"Patrice," Ursula stalls. She can hardly ask a woman in her own home where she's going. "What will you do?"

"One thing at a time. Right now, I think," flat-palmed, Patrice taps the newspaper, "is time to do something for Mrs Ellis. I will employ my letter-writing skills."

Alone at the table, Ursula turns the newspaper around so that she is staring into the face of Ruth Ellis. She's followed the story so closely it almost feels as if she's been pursuing it. To say she's driven by compassion would be convenient, but that isn't the half of it. At first, what piqued Ursula's interest was the connection between Patrice, Caroline and David Blakely; the fact that he'd been to a club she herself had visited. Then she saw Ruth's photograph. A killer who is both female and attractive. A woman who'd dared to leave a violent husband, but instead of hiding away (as all battered women should), she picked herself up, dusted herself down and said, 'Here I am.' She had the strength to find a new lease of life, a well-paid job. Add a sexual frisson to the recipe (nothing as simple as a *ménage a trois*), throw in allegations of social aspiration, tease readers with intimate details from court appearances – how Ruth was granted permission to have a peroxide rinse before the trial, with Shack's of Shaftesbury Avenue supplying everything that was necessary. How 'he only hit me with his hands and fists'. The wardrobe she chose for her court appearance. 'An off-white tweed outfit with black velvet piping' (add the designer's name, change the location, and the column could have been about Ursula). Photographs the newspapers unearth expose parts of her life previously hidden from her family. The details barely need embellishment, but journalists embellish because the public's appetite – and here Ursula must include her own – is insatiable. Centre stage in court number one, Ruth Ellis is a *cause célèbre*. It shames Ursula that she can't get enough of this personal tragedy regurgitated as entertainment. Of all people, she should know better.

Ursula has tried telling herself that her interest is professional, exploring Ruth's motives as she would when studying a character. In *Far Begotten* – her Oscar-winning role – Ursula played downtrodden Elizabeth Miles, but when lifelong victim turned murderer, she was treated as a perversion of nature. Like Ruth – well, not quite like Ruth, whose arrival in court was met by cries of 'common tart' – Elizabeth aroused little sympathy because she didn't look the way a victim was supposed to look. Now Ursula finds herself interrogating her interpretation of Elizabeth's character, as if there is something she might have overlooked, something more she could have given. And it's this behaviour of her own she finds so shocking. Ruth Ellis isn't some film character, for goodness' sake! She's a woman; a complicated one no doubt (how can all that complexity be captured in a newspaper column?) who has led a blighted, messy life. The mother of two young children. (What have they been told? And how much of it will her three-year-old understand?) Ruth has parents of her own, sisters and brothers.

And she has been condemned to hang.

An eye for an eye. A life for a life.

Model Smiles at Murder Verdict. Even as she reads the headline, Ursula imagines the heart-clenching moment when the judge asks the foreman of the jury if they have reached a verdict and the response, "We have, my Lord." The tension in the public gallery (where seats have been paid for, at thirty pounds apiece) for those excruciating stretched-out seconds when the jury members know something no one else knows: Ruth Ellis's fate. "We find her guilty, my Lord." Ursula feels the pull at the corner of her mouth as she tries to recreate the smile a woman might give the judge when she feels she deserves to die.

She knows what comes next.

Everybody in the courtroom knows.

The judge must pronounce the death sentence, because that is what a guilty verdict demands of him.

Ursula doesn't share Patrice's confidence that, because she is a woman, the odds are stacked in Ruth's favour. Instinct – hard-won experience too – warns her that Ruth Ellis will be made an example of.

When women kill, more often than not they kill their own children. Desperate acts stemming from what is referred to – generally by people who haven't suffered from it – as 'baby blues', or the stigma of having a child out of wedlock. Others that might be described as acts of mercy. Occasionally, women might act against a father or husband in self-defence. What they do not do is take a gun and shoot an unarmed man.

What's more, when Ruth Ellis stood up in court it almost seemed that she deliberately sabotaged herself. Admitting that she lived with Blakely while still married to another man; that she was not really in love with him; that after she became pregnant by him and he offered to break off his engagement and marry her, she had an abortion. She gave the jury nothing to like. It was a cold picture she painted of herself.

But will the world really be a safer place when Ruth is no longer in it? Only once in court did she crack. When shown the photograph Blakely had given her of himself, the photo that was signed, 'To Ruth, with all my love, David', did she break down and cry. But by then the jury thought they had the measure of her. When the judge invited her to sit, Ruth pulled herself together and refused his sympathy. And when the questions continued, when she had given her account of what happened that Easter Sunday, Ruth admitted – she actually said this – that she'd had a peculiar idea that she wanted to kill Blakely. She used those words. Thanks to the quick thinking of her counsel, she was given the opportunity to add that she was unable to control her compulsion, but the medical expert wrote this lack of control off as female hysteria. Still, to Ursula, this thing we call justice feels so wrong. There can be no winners. If Marcus asks 'Why?' she must find a way to explain that in some cases killing is right.

How can that be?

She must do something. There must be a platform she can

use. Ursula begins to dig into today's envelopes. A request to open a car showroom, to introduce a fellow actor at a film premiere. Here's one: to compere a gala charity performance in aid of the St John Ambulance at the Royal Festival Hall. 'The egg in the box', as it's become known. Two thousand nine hundred seats. Can she do better? The National Brass Band Championship of Great Britain's Grand Festival Concert at the Royal Albert Hall. They've been let down at the last moment. Less prestigious, but double the audience. And it's only a week away.

On the morning of the brass band championship, Ursula opens a newspaper and reads an article about herself. Nothing new, nothing noteworthy, just a reminder that, no matter how respectable her body of work, no matter what she does for charity or the arts, she is not forgiven. After all these years it shouldn't matter, yet it does. Ursula's eyes glaze. She has prepared her speech, committed her lines to memory but later, as she zips up the dress she will travel in, as she clips on her earrings, she thinks, *If the public won't change their opinion of me, no matter what I do, surely it's time to stop trying to please them.* Consulting no one, she allows herself a brief telephone call.

"Vincent, it's Ursula. Ursula Delancy."

"Miss Delancy, is it Patrice? How is she?"

The urgency of the journalist's question takes her aback. Unsure what he knows, Ursula keeps it short. "Coping, I think."

"And healthwise?" There's a hesitation in Vincent's voice, a holding back. She imagines that he isn't alone and has to be guarded about what he says. "Does she seem well?"

"As well as can be expected for someone who's had a terrible shock."

He scoffs. "One on top of another! Miss Delancy," his voice is low, "I know."

Ursula winds the plaited telephone cord around her index finger. "You know?"

"And, if I have anything to do with it, no one will read about it in the papers."

"Well, that's something. Actually," Ursula is keen to get away from the subject, "it was something else I wanted to talk to you about."

"Oh?"

"What are you doing this evening?"

"That depends on whether there's a story in it for me."

"I'm hoping to make a few waves."

"In that case, I'm entirely at your disposal."

The Royal Albert Hall has always put Ursula in mind of a Roman amphitheatre. To the sound of applause (not something she trusts entirely), Ursula steps into the fray, the pipes of the grand organ towering high above and to her left. Earlier today, on arriving, she paused to hear someone putting it through its paces. Mahler's Symphony No. 8. Now the stage is filled with rows of empty chairs, a music stand in front of each. The auditorium, a series of circles (circle upon circle), glows red. Ursula was last here for the Chelsea Arts Ball at New Year, five thousand merry-makers in fancy dress, some wearing far less than she would ever dare to. Tonight's audience is sedate by comparison. Ursula looks out upon the sea of seated people, Union Jacks and homemade banners declaring various allegiances. Munn and Felton's Works, Horden Colliery, Crossley's Carpets. She looks at as many of them as possible, acknowledging the faces that are focused on her face.

"Ladies and gentlemen," Ursula begins, silencing the applause. She grips the lectern, keen to avoid having her hands hanging loose at her sides. "You might want to wait and hear what I have to say." Laughter. "I know you're all here for an evening of music. I, too, am very much looking forward to hearing the finalists in the National Brass Band Competition of Great Britain." She breaks off to nod while enthusiastic cheers die away. "I don't know what you've read, but I myself do not play." Ursula's expression is heavy with mock regret. "Not even the triangle. Which is rather a pity because I'm partial to silverware." She extends one arm to draw attention to the Challenge Trophy, displayed on its dais. For what she will say next, she must mute the jovial tone that has crept into her voice.

"But first, ladies and gentlemen, I'm going to ask for your patience, because I *cannot* come to London and speak to an audience" – not celebrities, but ordinary people, giving their Sunday best an airing, showing support for friends and relatives – "without mentioning something that's very close to my heart. The condemnation of a young woman for a crime committed under extreme provocation."

The atmosphere shifts, something almost tangible. A whisper of, "Is she really going to…?" then a stunned hush. She imagines Vincent's eyes raking the auditorium, his furious pencil scratching away.

No one has any doubt who she's talking about. There is no need to mention a name. But she will. "Why do I feel an affinity with Ruth Ellis? It's not as if our paths have ever crossed. Let me explain. I *know* how a set of facts can be presented in such a way that there appears to be no way to stand up for yourself, certainly not without hurting the people you love." Ursula pauses here, bows her head momentarily. "I also like to think that I know a good manuscript when I see one." A cough. Shuffling in seats. "Oh, you don't think court cases are scripted? Think again!" She silences the murmurs. "I've read the Old Bailey transcripts. They're very good. When the jury was told not to concern themselves with adultery or sexual misconduct; when they were told that Ruth Ellis was not being tried for immorality but for murder – now that really is an *exceptional* line – when they were instructed not to allow their judgement to be swayed or their minds prejudiced in the least degree because, by her own admission, Mrs Ellis was a married woman when she committed adultery, or because she was having affairs with two different lovers." Glances are exchanged. *She is. She's saying this – at a family event.* "When they were told these things repeatedly and were then instructed to dismiss them from their minds, what do *you* think happened?" Ursula's knuckles whiten as she picks out a face in the front row, a face that remains transfixed while others lower their eyes.

"When they looked at the accused, the jury didn't see a victim driven to despair. They saw the peroxide blonde the newspapers have been in such a frenzy about." She finds another face, a woman this time. Middle-aged, most likely a housewife and mother, a deliberate choice. "I've actually heard it said," Ursula ambushes the woman by laughing, allowing her incredulity to ring out, "that some people object to Mrs Ellis's immorality far more than they do the fact that she killed a man. If that is the case – *if that is the case* – then those people who *think* they know who *I* am because they've read fragments of my story might decide *I'm* as guilty as Ruth Ellis." She nods now, at the shufflers in their seats, at the dry-coughers, as if to say, *Good, you should be uncomfortable.* "Believe me when I tell you, you do *not* know Ruth Ellis. All you know are the facts the newspapers thought would sell – and let's face it, they have four million pounds to recoup. All you know is what the prosecutor wanted the jury to know, the information that the defence was *allowed* to present, in other words a final edited, filtered version.

"I too have been called an unfit and undeserving mother, a foul harpy, a trollop, an immoral and shameless woman, an example of evil womanhood." With every description, Ursula seeks out a new face; sees if she can detect any shame. "Someone who puts the public in harm's way because the very sight of me on screen might corrupt them. And I have absolutely no doubt that after tonight, I'll be accused of taking advantage of someone else's misfortune to drum up publicity for whatever film or play I happen to be promoting at the moment. In the past, I've allowed fear to stop me from speaking out, but there comes a moment when it is no longer possible to remain silent. For me, that moment is now." Ursula looks up now, up to the gods, the uplit arches. "I ask you this. Does the fact that so many lost their lives in the war mean that we should fight any less for one life? Do you think we should have any less regard for the life of a young woman who has convinced herself of her guilt than for one who is convinced of her innocence?

"I don't believe that we have become so hardened, so lacking in compassion. Tragedies cannot and should not be ranked, and the ranking of them should not be used to justify the execution of a young mother.

"We know that Ruth Ellis lost a child only ten days before she held a gun in her hand. Any woman who's suffered the loss of a child will know how devastating that can be. We've read that Desmond Cussen saw how terribly bruised Ruth Ellis was. These brief snapshots should suggest to us that there was much more that we haven't been allowed to see. And yet Mr Justice Havers directed the jury to approach the case without any sympathy.

"Without any sympathy.

"We have a judicial system that *demands* jurors decide the fate of a young woman – a woman driven to do this terrible thing – without sympathy. Is it any wonder that the jury took just twenty minutes to arrive at their verdict? Truly I ask you, is that justice?"

CHAPTER FIFTY

RUTH

Sisters share. It's what they do. They're told to share nicely, but even when it's only an apple passed between the pair of them as they sit swinging their legs, they are watchful. "Oi, it's my go," Ruth would say, six years Muriel's junior, making sure her sister didn't try to cheat her out of what was rightfully hers.

Ruth was eleven when the unspeakable thing began. Eleven. By then, Muriel had already given birth to Robert. 'Never talk about it, do you hear? If anyone asks about the baby's father, you must say he's in the army.' Perhaps it was because Muriel had Robert that their father turned his attention to her. And though it wasn't something either of them had asked for, or wanted, or could bear to speak about, the shame and the secret of it was something they shared.

Ruth thinks about it. That night during the Blitz when Father was on fire-watch duty, and she'd stayed out with him to see the sky lit up with a display to rival any Guy Fawkes' night. A piece of charred timber felled Father, masonry buried him. Ruth could have walked away: no one would have been any the wiser. But it was she who dragged him from the debris. And for the life of her, for the life of her… She lets her head drop and grips the thin mattress.

It is not the only thing Ruth struggles with. Why, when her father left the family behind to look for work in London, did she follow, track him down to Southwark, and move in with him. (Didn't she always run towards trouble?) It was Edna Turvey who convinced her. Edna, the woman her brother Julian returned with from North America. Walked like the queen and always wore black. Flattered by a mature woman's friendship, Ruth didn't warn Edna what they'd be letting themselves in for. When Muttar turned up unannounced, she found Father in bed with Edna. And Ruth could hardly say, 'Would you prefer it was me?'

Besides, by then Ruth had Joe, a young apprentice from the firm Father worked for. Ruth knows Muriel saw Joe with his arms wrapped around her. Knows *she knew what Joe was to her. When her sister first arrived in London and had yet to make friends of her own, Joe said, "Why don't we invite Muriel to the pictures?" Ruth thought herself lucky. A boyfriend who was willing to make an effort with her sister – who was not just any sister, but the mother of an illegitimate child. But they sat in the dark, Joe with one sister on either side, and Ruth, realising he was holding Muriel's hand, humiliated. What a fool they must have taken her for! And when, avoiding her gaze, Joe admitted that he'd fallen for Muriel, when he had the nerve to ask if she minded, Ruth said, "Of course not." What else was she supposed to say? He should have known the answer.*

But with Muriel accounted for, perhaps Ruth had the chance for something of her own. Someone she wouldn't need to share. She met Clare Andrea McCallum at a nightclub. To be honest, it was a dive in an air-raid shelter. Ruth had never heard of a man being called Clare before, but he was Canadian, and Ruth had never known a Canadian before either. He'd got down on one knee when she admitted that she was pregnant with his child. A man who'd lived with her and, when he was away on active service, wrote twice a day. Even when Muttar dispatched Ruth to a home for unmarried mothers, Ruth knew she wasn't like the other girls because she had her French-Canadian serviceman waiting for her. He'd bought her a posh white pram in France, complete with a lace canopy, she boasted. It was only when he kept putting her off that she learned he had a wife and three children back at home. Even now Ruth doubts he would have had the courage to tell her. She had to find out from her own mother, who'd taken it upon herself to write to Clare's commanding officer. And Ruth swore – swore on her son Andre's life – never to make the same mistake again.

But she did. With men, Ruth always made mistakes.

Club work brought her into contact with men from all walks of life but there, she called the shots. They would have nothing from her – not even conversation – unless they paid for it. And make no mistake about it, Ruth made them pay.

Until she met George Ellis, that is. Ruth was twenty-four with an eight-year-old son, and not everyone would have been prepared to take him on. George was forty-one, divorced, but a dentist with a respectable practice. It's not as if Ruth walked into the relationship blindfold. Knowing George had a drink problem, she named her terms: he should seek professional help. But only days after the wedding, he was back to his old ways, and the fights – oh, the fights they had! She'd gone running back to her mother, covered in bruises, once with a bald patch because he'd pulled out a fistful of her hair. All this when Ruth was expecting again. Before Georgina was born, she'd had to admit to herself that her marriage was over. Still, it came as a shock that George was the one to file for divorce, who claimed she'd falsely accused him *of cheating, a man who thought nothing of flirting in front of her; George who wanted custody of their daughter – his namesake – and now has forced Ruth into agreeing to put her up for adoption.*

After George came David. David, who was unavailable

because he was engaged to a nice young lady from the Home Counties. David, who spent his weekends in Penn, where everyone knew he was having an affair with a married woman. David, who a fortnight after Ruth miscarried his child was already carrying on with the Findlaters' nineteen-year-old nanny.

Ruth told the police that she was confused. After all, she's not the first woman to have been beaten, not the first woman to have been cheated on, nor the first to have been made to feel as if these things were her fault. But other women don't go out and shoot the man responsible. Now, only now, does it begin to make a peculiar kind of sense. They tell her she didn't just fire the three bullets she recalled. Before Easter Sunday, Ruth had never fired a gun. She has an idea that once she started shooting, she couldn't stop herself. The actual number was six: one for her father, one for Joe, one for Clare, one for George, and one for David. The last, as Ruth realised even as she stood over David's body, she intended for herself.

When asked by her solicitors if she intended to plead guilty or not guilty, Ruth had been determined to plead guilty. She should never have allowed them to convince her to try and save her own life. But the fact that she was found guilty doesn't mean they were innocent.

CHAPTER FIFTY-ONE

CAROLINE

"Miss, I don't know what you've read in the tabloids, but Mrs Ellis handed herself in. There was never any reason for us to look for anyone else."

What Caroline has read is this: *Ruth Ellis does not matter any more than her two most recent female predecessors to the hangman's noose – Mrs Merrifield and Mrs Christofi. But what we do to her – you and I – matters very much.* Those words, written by William Connor, struck her deeply. A reminder that what happens to Ruth Ellis *is* her responsibility. More so than the millions who will be drawn into the story, because she knows. She *knows.*

Safe within the confines of her pockets, Caroline's hands are fists. There has to be a way to make this thing stop. "Ruth Ellis pleaded not guilty," she says.

The police officer seems nonplussed. "Tactical, most likely. I hate to say it, Miss, but if you thought that you had vital evidence, you should have come forward earlier."

"I assumed other witnesses would be called at the trial!"

"That was a matter for her defence." The police officer resumes writing in a ledger. "As far as I know, Mrs Ellis hasn't appealed against her judgement. If you can prove she lied, or if you know anything about where the gun came from, then that *would* be interesting."

Caroline's wasting his time and he wants her to know it. "What if I were to tell you that there were others like me?"

"Then you have to ask yourself, with what you've just told me, are you doing Mrs Ellis any favours?"

However painful it might have been, however much she was quaking, Caroline had intended to tell the police everything she knew. Everything that had happened to her and everything David had boasted of. The affair with his best friend's wife, the married woman in Penn, the cinema usherette, the other conquests he casually tossed into the conversation, as if Caroline's feelings were of so little consequence. How he took pleasure in watching for her reaction. If she gave none, he would press her: "What do you think of that?"

She remembers shrugging. "I don't think anything about it. It has nothing to do with me."

"Exactly! And that's what I can't make Ruth understand. Who I choose to see really has nothing to do with her."

It was Ruth this and Ruth that, while Caroline was just a someone. "In that case, perhaps it would be best not to mention it at all," she told him.

A moment's clarity. That may have been the first time he hit her. Yes. Yes, she thinks it was. How can anyone who hasn't suffered violence at a partner's hands understand? But Caroline tells the police officer none of this. None. Because he looks up from his paperwork to shoot her a look of pure disdain. A man is said to have a 'loose zipper', as if he has very little control over it, but a woman... a woman... And here she is, masquerading as a respectable young nanny to the son of a well-known actress, when, by her own admission, she's a little slut. "Does your employer know you're here?" His tone is vaguely threatening.

"She suggested I come." It is not quite a lie.

The laugh he gives is short, derisive. "Now, why doesn't that surprise me?"

"You know nothing about Miss Delancy. Nothing." Caroline turns on her heel and doesn't stop until she is on the pavement, unfocused, nostrils flaring. *Stupid, stupid!* Rage turns to humiliation, to shaking, but this cannot be defeat.

Berthram is there, opening the car door, gently saying, "No joy, Miss?"

"There must be something else I can try. I don't suppose you've heard of a solicitor called John Bickford?"

"I'm afraid not."

"Never mind," she says and asks him to take her to the club. One of the journalists will know the name of the firm.

Yvette does a double-take as she walks out of the cloakroom and sees Caroline. "Well, well, look who it isn't," she says drily, and leans on the bannister to shout down the stairs, "George, you're not doing a very good job of keeping the ruffians out!" But then she smiles and goes to hug Caroline. "Come here!"

Cigar smoke and hairspray. *The blind bend, the high hedgerow, the headlights.* Caroline feels as if she's returned to the scene of a crime. "How are you?" she says.

"Fine, as long as I don't stop to think for too long. But look at you, so serious!"

"Is Terry here?"

"No." Yvette swings her hips as she leads the way into the bar, looking back over her shoulder. "*I'm* in charge."

"You've been promoted!"

"So he tells me. I'm not sure I can spot the difference. What about you? Are you here to ask for your job back?"

"No, just an errand in town."

"Pity." Yvette lifts the hatch, goes behind the bar and reaches for a glass. "Have one on the house. It's still gin, is it?"

"I barely drink these days."

"But you'll have one with me."

It isn't a question. Yvette is already pressing a glass to the optic of one of the backlit bottles. And Caroline feels as if she could do with a drink.

"To absent friends."

"Absent friends."

They clink glasses. Caroline's eyes wander to the duchess's corner: empty. Over to the table by the bay window where she first sat with Sandy. Valerie is nowhere and everywhere. She shudders.

"Strange to be back?" Yvette asks.

"Too many ghosts."

"You heard about your racing driver?"

"I could hardly avoid it."

Yvette shakes her head, which has less to do with disbelief and more to do with a situation narrowly avoided. "The Steering Wheel set must feel as if they're jinxed."

Caroline blankly shakes her head. "What now?"

"Le Mans? Eighty-four dead?"

She feels the breath leave her. "How?"

"A car catapulted into the crowd. It was carnage. Nobody's fault, so they say. But Mike Hawthorn, who you've met, he blames himself. Elise, another drink for Raymond when you have a moment! And here's Mr Stewart! I'll get you your pint."

"Hello, Vincent." Caroline smiles, embarrassed without knowing why she should feel that way.

"See who it is?" Yvette raises her glass, gesturing towards Caroline.

"Well, well." He removes his hat and sits it on the bar.

"Actually, Vincent, could I have a quiet word? Perhaps we could use the duchess's corner. You don't mind do you, Yvette?"

"Mind? We haven't so much as heard from her. Though I suppose that's hardly surprising."

Caroline wanders deeper into the chatter, into the bragging, into the laughter; she is spun around by a regular who puts his mouth close to her ear and murmurs something suggestive, not recognising that she's a different person now.

The moment they are seated, Vincent asks, "Is there news?"

Her brow twitches. "News?"

"Never mind. False alarm." Caroline can see him, closing part of himself off.

"Patrice didn't send me. It's advice I'm after. I hoped you'd be able to help."

"Fire away."

"I have some information about the Ruth Ellis case. The police aren't interested. I thought of taking it to her solicitors, but all I have is the name Bickford."

"Cardew-Smith and Ross," Vincent says without hesitation. "Ely Place. What's the information?"

"I knew David Blakely." Her eyes dip.

The noise he makes in the back of his throat suggests this comes as no surprise. "Bickford's working on a reprieve, but he's doing it without Mrs Ellis's co-operation." He takes a long drink.

So much effort going into saving the life of someone who doesn't want to be saved. Who is now selling her life-story, all that she has left, because it's the only way she can pay her legal fees and ensure her children are taken care of. "It may be nothing they don't already know." Caroline bows her head, degrading images imprinted on her retinas. "I'd like to avoid having my name brought into this."

"Family?" Vincent asks, not unkindly, and she nods. "Tricky. Go to Bickford and your statement will be on the record. And further proof that Blakely was a *lamentable species of humanity* won't make a blind bit of difference. They've already said that doesn't come into it."

"You don't think Ruth Ellis will get her reprieve."

"Not unless the Queen intervenes, no. But I *do* think this case has the potential to change everything. If there's anything that adds to the argument against capital punishment, I could use it."

Caroline thinks of Haigh and her relief at the news that he was dead. How he still made her feel as if he had cheated the families of his victims. And, despite poor Timothy Evans, those feelings have not quite gone away. She is almost embarrassed to ask: "Are you in favour of a complete ban?"

"Actually, I'm with the duchess."

"Oh?"

"A system that recognises which people are likely to pose a danger to society and which are not. We lag a long way behind our European neighbours on this."

Caroline lets this sink in. "Could you say 'An anonymous source, also worked as a hostess', but make no mention of this club?"

"Got it. This is a case where anonymity might add to the allure."

CHAPTER FIFTY-TWO

Last Bid to Save Ruth Ellis. The Home Secretary returns from a trip to Wales. The official position is that he has been staying with his sister. Unofficially he wanted time to reflect before meeting with a committee to review the fors and againsts. Despite petitions imploring that he exercise clemency, many others have urged him to let the law take its course, to guard against the widespread use of firearms, to act in support of Christian family values. Allow Ruth Ellis to live and it will open the floodgates, resulting in a spate of women killing boyfriends, wives murdering husbands, prostitutes murdering clients. The darkness that lies just below the surface of the everyday will be exposed and allowed to flourish. No longer will we have to guess how many lives have been pushed too close to the edge. There will be a body count.

The Home Secretary has considered the latest newspaper reports, which suggest that Mrs Ellis had an accomplice (something that has yet to be confirmed); evidence from Bickford about her alcoholism, her fragile mental state, the fact that she was running a fever following her recent miscarriage. He himself has sympathy for the argument that there are various degrees of murder, but the law as it stands makes no distinction between them.

For the three women at Whitlocke, the silence – the lack

of news – is agonising. The townhouse has been shut up since Charles's funeral, but has yet to be sold. Now that her husband is no longer here to object to how Patrice chooses to handle the matter, she welcomes the opportunity to do what will appear, outwardly, as assuming the duke's role in the abolition movement. There may be something of use in his London study, some research, even a persuasive phrase. A decision is made. They leave a tearful Marcus in Norma's care.

"It's not a film, Mommy." For the first time that Patrice has seen since Ursula's return, the boy clings to his mother's legs. "It's not even work."

Ursula crouches down to his level, the gravel crunching under her feet. "Some things are more important than work. I'll only be gone for a few days, I promise." It is heart-breaking to see her heart breaking.

He struggles from her clutches and runs to Patrice's side. "I want to go with Mrs Hawtree!" he insists, fists tight, knuckles white. He is upright, a little soldier.

Clearly, Ursula is hurt. Even Norma looks put out. Nothing Patrice can say will right this (she finds herself in the strange position of not being sure she wants to), so she addresses the boy. "I need you here to keep an eye on the place while I'm gone. Can you do that?" She says this loud enough for Mrs Hargreaves to hear.

Marcus looks up, still uncertain; considering the importance of her request, weighing up whether it is something worthy of him.

Patrice happens to know that she has a key in her handbag. It is an old thing, found in the grounds by one of the gardeners, the sort that looks as if it might be important, but no one has been able to work out what the devil it's for. It is entirely possible that the key has nothing to do with the house but was dropped by a visitor who was playing croquet on the lawn, and found its way into a flowerbed. She fishes for it;

gives it to Marcus. "Here we are. Have Norma put this on a string so you can wear it around your neck."

The boy stands a little taller, and she turns from him and gets into the car. Patrice dare not look at him again. What a strange thing it is, to have made such an impression on a child. After doing so little.

They are pursued down country lanes and across Tower Bridge by forks of lightning. Crossland, who insisted on going ahead to give the townhouse an airing, greets Patrice with uncharacteristic tears. The duke, the suddenness, this intolerable heat, and then the worry of how they would fare in the flooding – did they hear about the lightning strike at Paddington Station? And now the news. There will be no reprieve.

They are too late. Despite everything, Caroline cannot accept it. Cannot believe that Ruth Ellis is to hang. Vincent didn't mince his words; he told her straight. And sitting opposite him in the club, she believed him. But everyone she spoke to since her return to Whitlocke – the women – insisted there was hope. Hope is all we ever have, even if the odds seem stacked against us. Once everyone stops hoping, the fight is lost. There seemed to be sense in that viewpoint.

Ursula, who has never in Caroline's presence suggested any inclination towards religion, is crossing herself. "There but for the grace of God," she murmurs.

Caroline shudders all the way from the nape of her neck to her feet. It's impossible to say how close she might have come, had Patrice not given her a way to remove herself from the situation. Like the good Sunday School girl she once was, it seems natural to say, "Amen."

But Patrice seems adamant that this is not it. Cannot be it. "We fight until the very last. Come on." She thrusts out a hand. Caroline finds herself staring at a square-cut diamond. Fingers beckon impatiently. "Up you get." Until Patrice uses those words, Caroline hadn't realised. She looks down and sees that she is sitting on a plush red carpet on the bottom step of a house she has never set foot in before. It embarrasses her to discover she is so weak.

She gazes up at Patrice. *Where does your fight come from?* She takes the hand, hauls herself to her feet, smooths the back of her skirt against her thighs. Caroline wants to believe Patrice possesses intelligence not intended for public consumption. She doesn't need to be told what that information is. What Caroline needs is something to put her faith in.

In that moment, an egg timer is turned; sand begins to trickle away. Ursula remembers watching the sand as a child, how the trickle seemed to speed up after the halfway point; how the last of it entered the funnel and spilled, pyramiding below. Back then, she was in control, with the power to make a decision: watch until the final grain fell, or at the last possible moment turn the egg timer, continuously upending and upending so that there was never a final grain. Her powers were limited; something always called her away – dinner, homework or bath time. All she ever did was delay the inevitable. And in the case of Ruth Ellis, wouldn't a delay be the cruellest thing of all?

"There but for the grace of God." From the telltale trace of her own fingers on her forehead, Ursula realises that she's made the sign of the cross. Ursula as Gladys Aylward would often do that. Ursula as Ursula almost never. But sometimes prayer is all that's left.

Will Ruth have been told that she only has two days to live? She assumes so. What final preparations will she make? In her own mind, Ursula would spend the hours making plans for Silvia and Marcus, hoping to protect them from the brunt of what's to come. She'd write letters so that they might understand that what the newspapers choose to print isn't the whole truth, just a story that editors thought would sell the most copies. Lord knows, Ursula's penned plenty of letters along those lines, but never under such terrible circumstances. How could you manage it? The answer is that you'd force yourself. You would sit at whatever desk was available, dressed in your regulation-issue clothes, with your regulation-issue pen, and find a way to write the things that must make up for absence, for loss, to explain why you couldn't say goodbye in person, what you'd have given to hug them one last time. The boy, Andre; the little girl, Georgina. Perhaps, in Ruth's place, she'd include something about what the children should say when other people tell them she's not in heaven; that heaven isn't for people like her. Ursula's vision blurs. But she'd tell them that she believes there's a place somewhere, a place where they'll all meet again.

"Ursula?"

It is Patrice, holding a door open for her.

"Yes," she says, swiping at the corners of her eyes, mentally signing *Mummy*. Adding kisses. "Yes."

Drama of Ascot Bid to Save Ruth Ellis. A tannoy announcement at the Royal Enclosure makes public knowledge of what was supposed to be a private last-minute bid to save Ruth Ellis. The expression on Patrice's face as the three women listen to the news suggests that everything is as she would expect it to be. Reprieves come at the very last minute. Just like they do in the movies.

Ruth Ellis has done something extraordinary. At the eleventh hour, she has sacked her solicitor and appointed Victor Mishcon in his place. She is co-operating.

"What does it mean?" asks Ursula.

"Mean? It means that she's changed her mind," says Patrice. "She wants to live."

"This is unbearable." Ursula pushes herself out of the

armchair. "Even if Mishcon can prove who gave Ruth the gun, what difference will it make?"

"It would raise all manner of questions." Patrice seems to be growing in confidence. "For example, did that person give it to her for a specific purpose? Did he know what she intended to do with it?"

Ursula's bloodstream feels fidgety. She paces back and forth in front of the fireplace because it's impossible to be still. "Do you think she'll have been told what's happening?"

"No." Patrice, from her armchair, sounds very sure. "Not until there's certainty."

How can Patrice appear so composed, as she sits there among her husband's boxes filled with research materials and notebooks? "I think I need to step outside," Ursula says.

"You must do whatever you need to do."

"Perhaps I'm not thinking straight," Ursula says after bursting free from the study and immediately encountering Caroline in the hall. "Just suppose they track this person down. Suppose he admits to giving her the gun knowing what she intended to do with it. Surely that only adds to the argument that the shooting was premeditated?"

Caroline closes her eyes, shakes her head. "The thinking seems to be that the sentence will be carried out tomorrow or not at all. If they can find this man, and he confirms Ruth Ellis's side of the story, it would be wrong for her to be punished before him."

"But why would a man who's happily stood by while Ruth Ellis took the blame admit he was part of it?"

"Because he doesn't think they'll hang a woman."

He too thinks there will be a last-minute reprieve.

There is no news. Caroline feigns exhaustion, but it's an excuse. The truth is, she can no longer be in a room where the silence is so laden with thoughts. There's no comfort in company, not when she's begun to feel that she may never forgive herself for being so cowardly. She allowed Vincent to persuade her because she wanted to be persuaded. She wanted to believe that going to see Mr Bickford would be the wrong thing to do.

Imagine, Caroline thinks as she undresses, imagine getting ready for bed knowing it's the last time you'll ever do so. The hour has passed when everything has begun to be the last. Already, Ruth Ellis will have eaten her last evening meal. Caroline pushes up the sash window. A mugginess hangs in the air. There's no breeze to be had. She thinks of Marcus, lying in bed with his covers thrown off. At Whitlocke, the dark is absolute, the stillness so strange after London, noises sudden and startling. At night, the shriek of a mating fox always translates into terror and pain. A country girl, Caroline should know these things. Here, the rumble of taxi cabs and cars and buses may be muted, but they are a constant. Almost like the sea. A tangled mass of barbed wire forces its way to the front of Caroline's mind, the concrete cubes designed to stop tanks landing on the beach. She and her family thought they'd escaped the worst. Until they found out that gun and torpedo boats were stationed nearby. Then Felixstowe became a target. She smokes a cigarette, then another, right down until she feels the burn. Caroline won't sleep tonight. *Stay here and keep watch with me.* This will be her vigil, her Garden of Gethsemane.

Later – how much later Caroline cannot say – somewhere below, the telephone rings. It is silenced sharply, answered, she presumes.

The itch to creep out to the landing is too much for her. She peers down over the bannisters. It is like being up in the gods at the theatre. The cheap seats.

"Thank you for letting me know," the duchess says, and taps the bridge of the telephone. She is slow to lower her arm and replace the receiver, as if it's a great weight, and then she seems reluctant to let it go. She raises her hand, covers her mouth and lets her head drop forwards. Caroline cannot bear to look at her neck. She moves her focus to the face of the grandfather clock in the hall below. It is a little after 2 a.m. Ruth Ellis has less than seven hours to live.

CHAPTER FIFTY-THREE

Patrice has spent the night in Charles's armchair. Her body is reluctant to straighten, but she forces herself to stand. She will not go to Holloway. Remember what Charles said about those people who blocked his way? *Are you here to protest, to make sure justice is done, or are you just here on a jolly?* She has no desire to be part of the jostling, the pushing and the shoving, the protests and the wailing and praying. The others may go. She understands their need; she understands that Mrs Van der Elst will be there campaigning, even as a woman dies (a woman who only eight days ago wrote, *No doubt you have heard, I do not want to live*).

The timing of their departure is the only point discussed over a solemn and simple breakfast prepared by Crossland. Not so early that they risk being hemmed in at the front of the crowd.

"If it all gets too much, we want to have the option of walking away."

Ursula and Caroline are dressed almost identically: raincoats, headscarves, sunglasses. They will be too hot, but two women in sunglasses are less likely to attract attention than one. Berthram is holding the door of the Bentley open. Patrice nods. She has already said her good morning.

On the top step of the porch, Ursula turns and takes her arm. "You'll be alright. On your own."

"I shan't be on my own," Patrice says. "I have Crossland."

"Of course you do."

Patrice shields her eyes with one hand as she watches the car drive away. If ever there was a day when rain would seem appropriate, but it is a fine day, as fine as it was on the day of Charles's funeral.

The traffic is a slow crawl.

"The world and his wife have taken a detour today," Berthram says by way of an apology.

Caroline has no idea what to expect, but when they finally arrive what she sees first (and what will be her lasting impression) is Holloway's turreted entrance. She dips her head for a better view out of the rear window of the car. The crenellated walls look fortress-thick. Impenetrable. (That's the whole idea, she supposes.) Mounted policemen must be able to see over the cappings of the wall that surrounds the prison, but for men, women and children who stand on tiptoes, their only view will be the back of the person in front. Not that seeing is the point, not in any visual sense. It's seeing this through. Caroline swallows and feels the movement in her throat.

"Berthram, can you drive past?" Ursula asks.

It makes sense not to be dropped off where there is a waiting wall of journalists and photographers, who can only make so much of the atmosphere, even the handful of louts and rubbernecks who are here to derive some kind of sick pleasure.

The handbrake is on, Berthram is at the car door, but Ursula seems disinclined to get out. The longer she stays put, the more likely she is to draw attention to herself. Caroline takes her hand and squeezes. There are no rules for today. Both have read about hangings in the newspaper, but never before have they felt so personal. A silent agreement is reached. They walk back along the opposite pavement, only the clicking of heels passing between them. The day tastes of pollen and traffic fumes. They pass cloth caps, headscarves, raincoats, cigarettes. This is where, without speaking, they decide to remain. By no means empty but far less crowded. Women with prams, small well-behaved dogs on slack leads. So many have been drawn here, their bond a sense of helplessness. Knowing that something terrible is about to happen and they are powerless to prevent it.

No one shows the slightest interest in Ursula. (So this is what it takes.) There is no eye contact. It is not a time for humanity to seek comfort in each other. All around, faces are taut, drawn, shell-shocked. People fold arms across chests, as if to guard feelings they have no names for, or stand with hands clasped as if they might pray. There is a sense that they have all done this, all bear some responsibility for what is about to happen. On the opposite pavement, photographers hold cameras high above their heads, too late for the prisoner's friends and family. There will be no more flowers, no more petition papers. Cameras are raised, higher, higher. There's only one thing they can hope to capture now. The announcement. And with this realisation, Caroline tucks one hand inside Ursula's elbow. It is a terrible thing, the waiting. Caroline allows herself to absorb the full weight of it, because while Ruth's suffering might soon be over, the suffering of her family – those poor children of hers – is too great even to contemplate.

As the hour approaches, people check their watches more frequently. Around her, men take off hats. Around her, women with rosary beads. A small portable radio is tuned to the BBC. *Warming up the wireless.* She remembers the drill. Scrambling for a place on the sofa as Caroline now scrambles for a foothold in the world. Her legs feel weak, but she will hold herself upright. The radio breaks the silence. Whatever the owner's motive – whether it is to hear the second the deed is done or to respectfully mark the moment – Caroline welcomes it, if only because it gives her focus. The whole of her being is concentrated in her intake of breath.

Patrice had been so sure, but she did all she could, and it wasn't enough. Others will say it was not her fault, there was nothing more she could have done. *All* of the speeches and petitions, the impassioned appeals, reminders conveyed by transatlantic telephone calls that the civilised world was watching, all fell on deaf ears. But that is not her concern. Patrice has failed. It's as simple as that. Somehow one must find a way to accept it, but acceptance will not make it any more tolerable. This is where she will stay, quietly, in her husband's study among his things; a husband she is less sure of in death than she was in life. Patrice goes to the tray on the table besides Charles's armchair. She pours a generous measure of whisky for him, a whisky soda for herself. If ever there were a day to break with habit, it is today. She turns on the wireless, then returns to her armchair, lights a cigarette that will remain unsmoked, and waits in world-weary silence for the first of the nine o'clock pips.

NOTES

This story was inspired by the discovery that the subjects of three biographies I read on the trot had connections with Ruth Ellis, the last woman to be hanged in Great Britain. I then turned to my bookshelves for a yellowed paperback that has been in my possession for over thirty years. *Ruth Ellis: A Case of Diminished Responsibility?* The book begins with a foreword in which co-authors Laurence Marks and Tony Van Den Bergh reveal how, during their research, they both discovered that they had various connections to players in the case of Ruth Ellis, if not Ellis herself. One of David Blakely's other lovers. The partner of a psychiatrist who had treated Ruth Ellis. The brother of the manageress of the Steering Wheel club who had thrown Blakely and Ellis out for having a drunken fight on the premises just days before the shooting. The Catholic priest who, while serving as a prison chaplain, had sat on the Home Office committee tasked with deciding if Ellis was fit to hang. Not mentioned in the foreword is that according to Muriel Jakubait's book *Ruth Ellis: My Sister's Secret Life,* Tony Van Den Bergh was himself a member of the Little Club at the time when it was managed by Ellis. Also featured on the 1953/4 membership list were royalty including King Hussein of Jordan, King Farouk of Egypt, King Feisal of Iraq, socialites such as the Duchess of Argyll and Lady Docker, film stars such as Douglas Fairbanks Jr, Victor Mature, Burt Lancaster and Diana Dors, stars of the racing fraternity such as Donald Campbell, Stirling Moss and Mike Hawthorn, photographers Anthony Armstrong Jones (who later married Princess Margaret) and Anthony Beauchamp (who was married to Sarah Churchill), and Stephen Ward (who, ten years later, was a central player in the Profumo Affair), as well as notorious London landlord, Peter Rachman, and 'Dandy' Kim Caborn-Waterfield, described by Jakubait as a 'better class of criminal'.

It rapidly became apparent that post-war London's afternoon drinking clubs were key to 1950's culture. Few other places offered the opportunity for ex-servicemen and bored businessmen to rub shoulders with a roll-call of police, royalty, politicians, intellectuals, journalists, celebrities and gangsters.

But even those who had never met Ellis had an opinion about her, and all were affected by her demise.

Within two years of Ellis's execution, The Homicide Act 1957 became law, limiting the death penalty by restricting it to certain types of murder. It was followed in 1965 by the Murder (Abolition of Death Penalty) Act. Changes of this magnitude aren't brought about by one case alone, but reading about the many tragedies that befell Ruth Ellis's children and family members served as a stark reminder that the prevailing penal system punished (some might say condemned) not just those found guilty, but those they knew and loved.

In 2003, the Court of Appeal heard the case to have Ruth Ellis's murder verdict overturned. The judges ruled that she had been tried in accordance with the law as it stood at the time.

The story of Gladys Aylward's life was not turned into a film by Paramount Pictures. Alan Burgess published a biography of Gladys in 1958 called *The Small Woman* and 20th Century

Fox bought the rights for a film version they called *The Inn of Sixth Happiness.* Gladys Aylward was initially consulted about the making of the film, and the plan was to film on location in Formosa, but the Nationalist Chinese Government objected to any suggestion that poverty and deprivation existed before the arrival of the Communists. Instead, filming took place in Snowdonia and in various Chinese laundries and restaurants in London, Liverpool and Cardiff.

Decca Radar was originally Barnett Samuel & Sons, who were renamed The Decca Gramophone Company Limited after they invented the portable gramophone player. Like many companies, it diversified into war work, launching its first marine radar, the 159, in August 1949. I have it on good authority that it took its name from the number of the London bus that passed the Brixton laboratory where the radar was manufactured.

ACKNOWLEDGMENTS

I drew inspiration and collated information from a number of sources, including *Ruth Ellis: A Case of Diminished Responsibility* by Laurence Marks and Tony Van Den Bergh, *A Fine Day for a Hanging* by Carol Anne Lee, *Ruth Ellis: My Sister's Secret Life* by Muriel Jakubait with Monica Weller, *Forget Not* by Margaret, Duchess of Argyll, *The Duchess Who Dared* by Charles Castle, *Ingrid Bergman* by Grace Carter and *My Story* by Ingrid Bergman. Any misinterpretations are my own.

Heartfelt thanks to The Sanctuary, the best online writers' group a writer could ever hope to belong to. To Clare Flynn for her cover quote and to Carol Cooper, Jean Gill, JJ Marsh, Lorna Fergusson, Alison Morton, Karen Inglis, Liza Perrat, Jane Dixon-Smith and Roz Morris for input into the cover blurb, help with technicalities and so much more.

A mountain of praise to my roll-call of beta readers, especially Carol Cooper, who voluntarily subjected herself to an early draft, Beth Allen, Karen Begg, Sheila de Borde, Anne Clinton, Kath Crowley, Mary Fuller, the lovely Dawn Gill (jewellery designer to the stars), Bronwyn Kotze, Lynn Pearce, Sarah Marshall (who also provided a potted history of Decca), Matthew Martin (OK, he hasn't read it yet, but he's going to – very soon – as long as Stephen King doesn't publish anything new this year), Delia Porter, Will Poole,

Julia Powley, Julie Spearritt, Liz Carr, Sheila Christie, Sue Darnell, Sarah Hurley (so good they named a town after her), Liz Lewis, Amanda Osborne, Sally Salmon and Peter Snell, patron saint of indie authors and bookseller extraordinaire (allegedly retired).

Extra special thanks to my editor, John Hudspith (http://www.johnhudspith.co.uk) and Andrew Candy of Tentacle Design for his fabulous cover design.

And not forgetting proof-reader Perry Iles (contact him at chamberproof@yahoo.co.uk), JD Smith Design for typesetting, and, last but by no means least, all of the team at Clays.

ABOUT THE AUTHOR

Hailed by *The Bookseller* as 'One to Watch', Jane Davis is the author of nine novels.

Jane spent her twenties and the first part of her thirties chasing promotions at work, but when she achieved what she'd set out to do, she discovered that it wasn't what she wanted after all. It was then that she turned to writing.

Her debut, *Half-truths & White Lies*, won the Daily Mail First Novel Award 2008. Of her subsequent three novels, Compulsion Reads wrote, 'Davis is a phenomenal writer, whose ability to create well-rounded characters that are easy to relate to feels effortless'. Her 2015 novel, *An Unknown Woman*, was Writing Magazine's Self-published Book of the Year 2016 and has been shortlisted for two further awards. *Smash all the Windows* won The Selfies (Best Independent Fiction Author) 2019.

Jane lives in Carshalton, Surrey with her Formula 1 obsessed, star-gazing, beer-brewing partner, surrounded by growing piles of paperbacks, CDs and general chaos. When she isn't writing, you may spot her disappearing up a mountain with a camera in hand. Her favourite description of fiction is 'made-up truth'.

A personal request from Jane: "Your opinion really matters to authors and to readers who are wondering which book to pick next. If you love a book, please tell your friends and post a review on the site you made your purchase from."

OTHER TITLES BY THE AUTHOR

Half Truths and White Lies

I Stopped Time

These Fragile Things

A Funeral for an Owl

An Unchoreographed Life

An Unknown Woman

My Counterfeit Self

Smash all the Windows

For further information, visit https://jane-davis.co.uk. Sign up today at https://jane-davis.co.uk/newsletter to be the first to hear about future projects, pre-launch specials, discounts and competitions. You'll also receive a free eBook of reader favourite *I Stopped Time*.